On The Eve
Of Morning

First paperback edition May 2024

Cover design by Brandon S. Johnson

ISBN 979-8-218-41536-5 (paperback)
LCCN 2024909252

Website: www.kassandragrace.com
Tik Tok: @kassandra.grace.writes
Instagram: @kassandra.graceeee

To My Guide,

*He who opened my eyes & led me to
see the world with renewed light.*

This is all for You.

Prologue

I never used to believe in fate, that idea crafted lazily by humanity that we are all destined to something so greatly beyond our control. That was back when I had believed I was in control of my own life. But fate is unavoidable in the ever-present flow of time. I once, long ago, heard a quote by a philosopher, a Roman man that I hadn't thought much of except for what my education forced me to think of him. Not until his words became the very advice I had chosen to neglect.

"Accept the things to which fate binds you." And I am bound. It is one of the only things that I am sure of.

Fate is what got me here, though I'd spent each day desperately trying to ignore its presence. Fate is what formed this ineradicable sense of hopelessness. Fate is what told me that hopelessness is all this is worth.

I write this sitting on a Neo-Italian boating dock—formerly known as Turkey—approximately 2,700 kilometers from home, void of any form of hope aside from an inaudible voice telling me that I should have some. I haven't seen my family since last night, and I fear I'll never see them again. I fear either the sun above me or the waves beneath me will consume me before I have time to redeem myself.

Ultimately we pick our own pain, but pain itself is not ours to pick. If one picks the beauty of snowboarding, they are picking the pain of the crash. If one picks the beauty of medicine, they are picking the pain of its failure. If one picks the beauty of risking it all, they are picking the pain of the moment when it, inevitably, is all lost.

I once thought that when that moment came—when it all was soon lost—such a moment would be gone quickly. But I'm afraid it never actually leaves.

I'll give the short version of how it all began, for it is not worth more contemplation than what I have already given it. March 13th, 2146. My brother had a basketball tryout for a league in Belgium. My father was preparing to take Viridian when we got the news on a television broadcast.

"'*There has appeared a relatively large primordial black hole in our solar system, inevitably sucking the earth in the sun's direction. Scientists are investigating what can be done about it, given its various unknown qualities, but it seems very likely that this could be the cause of complete and utter societal, environmental, and global collapse. I'm here with Doctor Ethan Brunii to discuss the options at hand. Doctor Brunii?*'

'*Yeah, Jennifer, it is incredibly unlikely that there is much we can do to change the trajectory of where this is all headed.*'

'*So there's no way we can, I don't know how to say this but, get rid of the black hole?*'

'*Not without creating a gravitational pull larger than that of the black hole which is . . . I hate to say impossible, but . . .*'

'*What about evacuating from the planet? Is that an option?*'

'*Well, it is important to note the black hole arrived through an already present worm hole beside our sun, operating as a means for interstellar travel which is potentially worth utilizing. We also certainly have extensive knowledge of our surrounding solar systems. All this to say, it could be an option, yes. However, it's more a matter of time in regards to how extensive construction on such a vessel would take.*'

'*And how much time do we have?*'

'*It's hard to say. It could be years, two max. More likely it will be months, but for many, depending on tolerability to the impending heat, it could be even weeks.*'"

There was much swearing after that and I had retreated to my room, locking the door and staring at a poster on my wall for many hours. I hardly left the house after that day. I had no reason to. No reason to deal with the ever-growing heat or to watch my city be destroyed by the spiraling minds of humanity, for the main result of panic is, and always is, disorder.

But I never forgot what was said about an evacuation vessel: a spaceship. It seems foolish now that I was putting my hope in science fiction films that always ended in half of the heroes dying. But when my younger brother told me about the Qadim, a form of foolishness took over me. I believed I had a reason to think I could board it, that I could orbit a distant star, that then, life would be capable of being lived. A part of me wonders now if that is why Sitka had told me of it in the first place. If he believed it would cast some stubborn, optimistic idea into my mind, knowing it to be in my nature.

It seems it did. But it wasn't until weeks later that I acted upon it.

I had found my older brother in the backyard. He sat in a lawn chair with a can of soda in his hand. His blond curls had grown to become more mangled as weeks passed us by. The night had been dark and stars had ever so subtly coated the weary sky and I had been awake, for I feared the sound of silence.

"It's not safe out here," I had stood behind Viridian when I said it. His free hand flew out beside him as though to swat away my remark. "It's not nice out here either. Why would you want to be out here?"

I sat down on the chair beside him as his brown fingers played with the can as though there had been condensation upon it. There hadn't been. I heard a boom in the distance. My body jolted the slightest bit. He didn't move at all.

"Why are you up?" I don't believe he truly cared for an answer, but I spoke anyway.

"Some nights there's no point in trying to sleep. Not when . . ." I couldn't find the words to finish but he nodded anyway. And so my eyes lifted towards the stars. They seemed muted beneath the smoke in the air. The moon had been absent but I searched for it anyway as heat began to coat my face.

"There's a fire that's been growing on that hill for the past week," Viridian extended his arm outward when he spoke. My eyes lowered from the sky down to where his hand sat upon the dancing of red in the distance. I hadn't noticed it before.

I shrugged. "They'll put it out."

He snickered at me. "Only for a bigger one to start."

"Maybe."

There had been a long pause. Condensation grew upon my arms. Terror grew inside my mind but I wouldn't let him see it for fear of him using it against me.

"We need to get out of here, Eve," he spoke quietly as though his words were a sin. Our eyes met so suddenly. "Not even just Cordellia. We need to leave the planet."

I continued to watch him. My fingers traced one another. "And what if it's a hoax?"

"Does it feel like a hoax to you?" A drop of sweat rolled down my forehead as he said it.

I shrugged. "Could be."

"You're in denial."

"No I'm not."

He snickered, only for his face to turn so incredibly stern a moment later. He took a sip of his soda. "Then I'll leave." He looked away. "I'll go to the Qadim and I'll leave you here to watch that fire consume our house." He pointed back up at the hill. "Then I'll let you write me a letter, telling me again that it's a hoax and you can hope that it will get to me. Because you can't call me, you can't text me. The radiation made sure of that. We're alone here, Eve. We're hopeless." Our eyes met once more and somehow, without using words, we were able to come to an accord. To an understanding of what we both had to do.

We planned it all that night. How we would tell our parents our idea, how we would convince them to go to the Qadim if they insisted on remaining. Breakfast that next morning had been one shade away from a disaster. We ate wheat bread and strawberry jam and I stared uncomfortably at my mother as she fumbled around the kitchen, in a crazed, obsessive attempt to find the water jug she had picked up just that day.

"It was at the food stand this morning when I went," she had said so soothingly when I asked her where she had found such a delicacy as strawberry jam. "There were only a few jars left so I thought I would get one as a treat." A forced smile had spread across her cheeks as though to comfort me but it did just the opposite.

"Why did you only get one?" My father asked from across from me.

"They were limiting the amounts."

"*They*?" Viridian perked up beside me. "Who is 'they'? I thought we didn't have any government in Cordellia to limit us."

My mother rubbed her forehead. "We don't. But someone has to take some authority during a time of chaos."

"That is . . . actually the exact *opposite* of what the Bill of Rights says. Article 10 states that if anyone tries to gain power they should be banished by the people to refuges or sent out of the country completely!"

"So there is a government then." I mumbled. I regretted it immediately.

"I don't know!" My mother slammed a rag upon the counter. "I don't know, okay? I don't have all the answers anymore. I really wish I did, but I don't." She stood still for a moment, and the rest of the room echoed her idleness, her eyes fixed upon a point on a far wall. Something stirred in my mind. It moved down my spine and to my lips and soon I was speaking, for it seemed only then was the opportune time.

"Merû?" I began to say in Cordellian. She looked up at me. "V and I wanted to talk to you about something."

"What is it?"

"I don't know how else to say this." Something like a prison began to form across my lips. My words were trapped inside for a single moment before they all came spilling out.

"We're ready to leave."

She stared at me, "What?" Her eyes remained fixed as she sat herself down beside my father. "What do you mean 'leave'?"

"Cordellia, Merû." Viridian intervened. "We can't be here anymore with everything that's going on. It's . . . shall I say, *challenging*?"

"And leave the only home we've ever known?"

"This isn't home anymore."

"Sure it is. You have your sister and your brother and—"

"—and the psychopaths destroying the city—"

"—and me and your father—"

"—and the burning sun so that we're stuck indoors—"

"—and we're *happy*, Viridian."

My brother's eyes shot over towards my mother in a pulsing anger. Bright green lasers emerged from his pupils, slicing any sign of plasticity from upon her cheeks. "Don't you *dare* try to tell me that we're happy."

She stared at him. Tried to hide the pain behind her jade eyes. Then, she shook her head.

"We cannot leave our home. Why would you ever even *suggest* that?"

"Because I can't live like this anymore!" I screeched with my hands slamming upon the table and my bread landing face down. I had gone on a rant after that—an explanation of the pain I was suffering. A moment of vulnerability. A moment I regret.

I don't recall what I said, nor a single one of the million thoughts that I had thought. But I remember my younger brother's response, "I agree."

My father glanced over at him. His glazed over gaze seemed nearly hopeful for once in a lifetime. "Where would we go?"

Viridian quickly answered. "Israel. Sitka said they have a ship taking them off the planet—"

"The Qadim, yes. I've heard of it." My mother replied.

Viridian paused. Stared. Nodded, "Right, so we can go to it—"

"We can't *go* to it."

"Why not?"

"They're only allowing Israeli citizens onto the ship."

"So we get false documents."

My mother chuckled, shaking her head, "Are you *kidding*, Viridian?"

"What?"

"We don't look Israeli," Sitka mumbled. His head had been hung low and he fidgeted with something in his hands. "You and Merû especially. You're the epitome of Cordellian, blonde hair, green eyes, dark skin." Viridian had stared at me, his tongue rotating in circles around his mouth.

"We can dye our hair then."

"Where would you get hair dye?" My mother asked.

"Even then, where would we get false documents?" My father continued.

"I know a guy." We all froze, staring at Sitka.

My mother gaped, "You . . . what? How?"

"It's this guy in Munich who used to be famous for forgery. Remember that field trip I took in grade nine? I saw him there. "

"And you think just because you saw him once in grade nine that you'll be able to waltz into his house and ask him for documents? Sitka, we have no money. Cordellia doesn't have a currency! And I am not willing to do what everyone else in the world is doing and steal from one another."

The next words I spoke I fear I will recall forever.

"Merû," I began. My voice shook ever so slightly. "I'd rather die knowing I tried to survive than die without doing anything at all."

Oh, those foolish words. Perhaps if I had been wiser I would have left them unspoken.

It was that morning I believed all was going to change. That we would leave the next day, retreating to a land that did not want us. But weeks seemed to go by and nothing soon transpired and I was left spiraling in my thoughts, afraid of the unknown but even more so of the comfortable.

And then it all slowed. May 17th, 2146, deep into the night or rather on the eve of morning. It all slowed the moment I sketched those words onto that page. Words I still wish I could have found more of a purpose for.

That is where I leave you for now.

"In the hopes of a fully free people, this establishment eliminates the actuality of a common known government and shall be established instead as a land under the rule of the people. The existence of anarchy under this establishment shall be defined as the absence of government in hopes of the freedom of the people. It is created in hopes to debilitate the overpowering control that France once had, creating a land of complete individuality and expression, absent from social and political hierarchies, aimed at recognition for all citizens."

Cordellia Bill of Rights, Article II. Signed, February 21st, 2026, Apgar Cordell

Part I
"The Fall"

[1]

Silence

Dear Darbii,

I've come to realize that I prefer the shouts over the silence. At least the shouts are consistent when they come. Silence is staggered and staged. It hopes to grant me peace long enough for the chaos to startle me once more.

I haven't told you about it all yet. I wish I had sooner. I wish I had been able to have more time with you before it came to this. But it seems as though time is only a deception. Crafted by humanity, destroyed by nature.

All this to say, it has come. The chance to leave this insanity behind and journey on into a new definition of it. I hate to say that I'm afraid of what awaits. Even more so, I hate that I was the one with this reckless idea in the first place. It's not like me.

Perhaps I'm giving myself too much credit. I only thought of the idea on my own time, Viridian brought it into existence for us all. He was the one who suggested it to someone other than himself. Maybe we're more similar in our desires than I've had the ability to realize.

I don't know when we're leaving, but I hope it will be soon. My merû told us to begin packing about two weeks ago. The gruesome task has driven me into the late hours of the night, writing letters like these to people I'm afraid I will never look upon again, rotting in a silent room as my thoughts drive me wild. But at least now are the days in which I have the hope of being able to leave it all behind soon enough.

I'm tired of watching the world slowly burn and knowing there's nothing I can do to put out the flames. I no longer leave the house and I don't recall the last time I have, both because of the heat and the desire not to give that black hole more attention than it's due. It will get its full reward when it kills us all. I hate that my fate has to be determined by something other than my own actions. I never planned for it to be this way.

So we're going to give it a shot. We're going to try and run from the inevitable, as humanity always seems to do. That's what led to the building of the Qadim in the first place, I imagine. I fear our chances of survival through it are slim, though I cannot allow myself to think of such things for too long. If we are able to find a way to get onto it with false identification, then maybe we'll again have a shot at life. Sitka said he knows of someone who can help with that. It all seems impractical, but it's all we have.

I'm looking at a picture of us now. It's from grade seven when we had a ballet competition together and you came in first and I second. I remember trying to be proud of you rather than upset, but even now I can still see the bits of anger accented red across my brown cheeks. I'm pretty sure I had just finished crying in the bathroom too and that's why my eyes seem more red then they do brown. It was back when I had begun to grow out my hair again because I couldn't handle how much my curls poofed out. We were so young. It's hard to believe I'll be eighteen soon.

I hope I see you again, Darbii. I believe I will, whether it be on the Qadim or the other side. I hope you follow me to either. I don't know how I'll make it without you. Perhaps I will not, but I can atleast hope that I will. I don't see what harm that could do me now.

I love you, my friend,

Eve.

Only people that believed they were dying wrote letters. I knew it from the beginning of all of this, when I had spent every evening addressing them to people I believed I would never see again. There was a large envelope addressed to Darbii, sitting at the top of my black duffle bag beneath my desk. I slipped a new letter inside every night.

For I had become nocturnal in those days, hiding beneath the canopy of twilight. I had learned to despise the sun, with my blinds always trapping me inside of that coffin.

But at the time, I had believed there was still hope. I see now—as I write this all from Neo-Italy, in a notebook whose pages have been torn and damaged—that it was foolish, the trust I had placed so recklessly in the Qadim. That thing which had allowed me to begin to open my blinds inch by inch out of some narcissist faith I had. So that I could see a glimpse of the sun's glimmer only to desire to remember the joy it once brought me.

The moon shone through that inch of open curtain the night I wrote that letter to Darbii. It casted its cool glow upon my open duffle bag, highlighting the layers of clothes piled upon each other, layers of life I had hoped to take with me once we left. Years that had seen me and retreated as I chased after them. Chased after the years of friendship printed across paper. After the stories collected inside my kindle.

Chased after the years of ballet, stained brown upon the insides of my pointe shoes, sitting still on top of everything else. I felt a tear sitting in the corner of my left eye. It stung more than the pain of running from it all. I wiped it away.

I wonder now, as I write this, what I would have done instead, had I known I would never see those shoes again.

Boredom found me. Angst swept itself inside my bones and I reached for the candle that sat upon my desk. Soon, I was turning away from the past, watching those memories slip away as I made my way to that steel door between my coffin and the hallway. I stumbled down the stairs, down towards our living space, a light emerging from the kitchen. Viridian sat at the peninsula. His emerald eyes flickered beneath the tasing of the low candle light.

I stared at my older brother for a few seconds. "Why do we always meet like this?" His eyes widened in the way of panic, raising an eyebrow to extinguish his surprise in seeing me.

"Because we can't sleep."

A beat. I sighed. "It's been two weeks."

"I know."

"It's ironic isn't it."

He stared at me plainly. "What?"

"Meeting like this again. Two weeks later. When we were supposed to be gone. "

"Why are you trying to make this poetic?"

Anger bit my tongue and I bit it into place. I sat down across from him. He raised something to his lips, taking a bite out of it and my eyes narrowed.

"What are you eating?"

A pause. "Food." His cheeks were red in the way they become when one has been caught.

"Viridian, we have limited portions, Merû said–"

"I know what Merû said." He lowered his palm, placing his slice of bread on the counter before him. His eyes were somber yet ridden with pride. I felt fire burn my cheeks.

"Then why don't you listen to her?"

His eyes were focused past my body, and soon, he shrugged. "Don't want to."

"V—"

"Hey, I'm an adult, remember?" he pointed towards himself, "Nineteen," then he pointed towards me, "Seventeen. Your birthday is coming soon and then you can decide things for yourself."

I stared at him. Stared at his eyes that no longer focused on this paralyzing room but instead looked down upon the fire of the kitchen candle. His finger wiggled back and forth through the flame as I searched my words more carefully than he ever would.

"Viridian, it frustrates me that you don't seem to care about the requests of everyone else."

"*Requests*? Demands, maybe . . ."

"What?"

He rolled his eyes, still not looking up, "I do care, Eve, okay? But I'm not willing to forfeit living just to make everyone else happy."

"What's that supposed to mean?"

Back and forth, his finger moved, "If I'm going to die, I'm going to live a little bit before that happens."

"You're not going to die."

He raised an eyebrow at me like he always did. "Eve."

"What?" A pulse of annoyance stretched through my body. My breath lept forth from my lips and rolled through the fire, extinguishing it in a second. Both of his eyebrows were lifted now. Our eyes met so intensely that flames seemed to melt the air around us. He reached into his pocket, retrieving a lighter and bringing the blaze back to life. I rolled my eyes and yet, in that moment, I knew what he was thinking. I knew he never truly thought that we would make it through this. He had always made that clear.

Looking back on it now, the worst part was, a deep part of me had always agreed with him.

But I shook my head anyway. "If we make it onto the Qadim and get off this burning planet–"

"That's unlikely. You realize that, yeah?"

"V."

"I'm not trying to scare you. I just don't want you getting your hopes up if we're probably just going to all burn up and die anyway."

"V, this whole thing was your idea in the first place–"

"I know–"

"You don't have hope in your *own* idea? That's moderately hypocritical."

The corners of his mouth lifted towards his eyes. His crystal teeth patronized me. "Look at you with your big words tonight!"

"Viridian." I watched my question float through his brain, tossed one way or another, a star thrown through galaxies until it entered his own. His grin fell just the slightest bit.

"I have about as much hope as what's reasonable." I shook my head at his words. Flames burned my cheeks and pressed smoke into my pupils.

"You're such a pessimist."

"Realist." He watched me. Watched the all consuming water orbited the corners of my eyes. It felt as though for the first time I was again realizing why we had never been close. Because my brother always cared too much about being correct that he'd not once worried about whether it was helpful. And worried even less if it destroyed me.

So I reached for my candle. I stood and I turned from him, until I was in the laundry area across the room, grabbing a sweatshirt out of a pile of clean clothes. "University of Performing Arts, Greece," it read across the green fabric.

A tear landed upon the writing.

Viridian sighed behind me. "I don't want you to be hopeful if your hope is false, Eve. Do you not understand that?"

I spun back around towards him. "Why? Why do you care?"

All he did was grin. So I ignored him, for fire pulsed through my veins and I wouldn't let it erupt onto him. Because if he couldn't control anything, at least he might have been able to control me.

And soon I was turning away, finding the stairs behind me, ignoring his lips when a groan inevitably limped off of them. "Go to bed."

"I am."

Then I was staggering down the hall, slamming my bedroom door behind me. The metal reverberated through the house. Rang like a gong. Pounding. Pulsing. Encircling every pessimistic thought in my mind that I tried to ignore, for at that moment, I had wished he wasn't right. I had told myself that he wasn't.

But I knew he was. I see now, looking back on it all, that I had always known he was. I knew I had no chance of surviving any of this. I knew my hope would fail. Who was I to think that I could escape the doom outside of my window? And even if I could, how could I believe that I would survive my mind's madness as I spent my days staring out a spacecraft window, the sun slowly fading into darkness? How could I escape the insanity that would form?

And so I slammed my curtains shut. The moon's glow ceased in a second, and I was blowing out my candle, my room pitch black when I tossed myself upon my bed. Tears fought to find my cheeks and I forced an ever so stubborn resistance upon their push. I wouldn't let them win. Not this time. For I believed that I was stronger than them. Stronger than that weakness they tried so deliberately to force upon me. Stronger than to give into those hopeless ideas of a stolen freedom.

Stronger than the silence that haunted me.

[2]

The Lone Star

My room was warm the next morning. Warm, but not quite hot, a tease of the outside world, I suppose. My eyes were dreary and scarred by tears as they never failed to be, for they fought the same war every night.

But those wars have ceased by now, as I write these words.

Yet, I arose in hope. That feeling had touched me in a never ending anticipation that maybe that day might finally have been the one. The day that my mother raised her finger and we all would follow it out of the country. Because we didn't know how much time was left.

I could hear her humming in the kitchen down the hall.

So I pushed myself up out of bed. Pushed my muscles that didn't want to move and pushed my bones that were slowly rotting but I pretended that they were not. And my gaze grazed the tarnished glow of the Cordellian flag on the wall beside my door. It was sapphire stained in the same way the sky out my window once had been, yet blotchy and sagging with age. In the center rested an alabaster star, molded from a thick, bulging fabric, bright, as though it were shining. As though that single star had understood its solidarity. It's exclusivity as the only anarchist country on the continent.

I turned from the flag as I had every morning for as long as life had been upon me. I turned, fearing its light would not follow me when I left its presence entirely; when I went on to Israel.

My mother's hums became a low whistle. I approached her down the hall. She sang one of her favorite songs from when she was a child, one she

24

had introduced me to a few years back. We would scream in the car together and I would get caught up in laughter every time. For that is how life had once been together.

I found her standing in the kitchen, hunched over her coffee mug, a dark liquid dripping ever so slowly into it. Her brown index finger and thumb had played with the handle as though such a motion would expedite the process. She wore her doctor's scrubs, her blonde coils pulled into a bun, collapsing over her head. Her green eyes watched her hands as she took the mug into her palms. It was one my father had carved for her as an anniversary gift a few years back, speckled white with her favorite cherry colored flowers and her name printed across it in pink: Yemasii.

Her cheeks had lifted when her gaze met mine.

"Hey baby," She began to shuffle around the kitchen, slamming cabinets as I stood still. "How are you? Did you sleep well?"

"I—"

"I picked up some things from the food stand this morning." She opened the fridge in which no longer trapped in the cold and she stared at the nearly empty shelves. There was a moment of hesitancy in her tone. "I couldn't find any fresh fruits but there were a few dried bags, so if you could let Viridian and Sitka know when they get up—"

"You're going to work?"

She stopped, turning away from the fridge and moving towards the door, watching me as if the question I had asked was void of meaning. "It's Wednesday."

"I know but I . . . it's been two weeks now, Merû. When are we—" She quickly shook her hands, motioning to silence me. I stared. Blinked. A strict cautiousness had been flushed red up her cheeks.

"What . . . " I mumbled. "You think someone is listen—"

"You can't be too careful." Her expression quickly lifted to a smile, one I could read right through to the fear that rested behind its hollow door.

I felt my father's light footsteps behind me. My mother grinned at him.

"Ävon." She approached him now, pulling him tightly into an embrace. He placed a kiss upon her forehead. "I'm headed to work. There's a few things for you all in the fridge. Please be frugal." I could hear the attempt to hide the anxiousness in her tone.

I sighed. "Merû." She pulled away. Looked up at me.

"What?" All I could do was stare at her until the hardness in her gaze fell into a patronizing sympathy. "We'll talk about it later, alright?"

"Will we?"

"I am already running about seven minutes behind. I'll be back this evening. I love you both." She took a step backwards out the door and I mumbled a small, "I love you too."

The door shut.

My gaze found my father. His brown hands held an old pencil he once would use to measure out wood for carving and he spun it around in his fingers. He smiled upon me gently as he always did, though I could see from the messiness of his black curls that he was distressed.

"What are you doing up so early?" His face remained coated in a light red layer, brightening the brown in his eyes.

I tried to smile back. "I wanted to say goodbye to Merû." That was a lie. I couldn't sleep, "And I . . . " Anything near to a coherent thought dissolved from my mind until all I felt was hollowness. My father watched me. He held the pencil still for a moment before placing it down. His hands grasped the counter as though to press clay into a sculpture. Then his cheeks lowered in the same way they always did to ask me what was wrong.

"If she won't tell me, maybe you will." I looked up at him. "When are we leaving Perû?"

"Soon enough."

"Soon enough?" My eyebrows caved in upon themselves, and my head threw itself away from him. I inhaled. Held it there. "I hardly slept last night. Do you know why?" My eyes lifted to his level. He simply stared at me. "I hardly slept because I am so used to hearing explosions in the distance. People screaming. Seeing fires across town. And last night it was silent, which was somehow worse than the noise. That is not how it should be. That is not how we should be living our lives."

Viridian appeared at the bottom of the stairs. His green gaze stared in upon me and I stared back. I watched him walk to the pantry, pulling out an old box of stale cereal.

"Please don't over eat, Viridian." My father said. Viridian walked back into the kitchen, grabbing a bowl from the cabinet and pouring the cereal inside.

"There isn't a lot for me to eat, so we won't have a problem there." He sounded irritated as he spoke and I watched him sit down in the same location I had found him the night before. Watched as he reached towards the counter as though a spoon would appear beside his bowl but none was to be found. He looked at his bare hand for a long moment and so I moved towards a drawer, opening it and tossing the rounded utensil his way.

I glanced back up at my father. "So then why are we still here?" I was able to say. "We're giving these people more time to harm us. How do we know we won't get preyed upon next?"

My father looked back over at me. His eyes were soft but stern. "We don't."

"So . . . we're just gonna sit here and live in fear until we die?"

"We are still *leaving*, Aetheria." Only my father called me by my full name.

"When? We have no way of knowing when the Qadim is leaving and you and Merû haven't changed a thing about your lives. Every day we're still . . ." I groaned. My eyes left my father, finding Viridian behind me, watching us both, his spoon held halfway up in the air. "Can you help me out? Why are you so quiet right now?"

He shrugged. "I'm just . . . listening."

"You never 'just listen.'"

"It's my new thing I'm trying out."

"Oh my—" My forehead slammed into my palms, gauging a headache into my skull.

I found the gaze of my father once more. "Is it that you and Merû are afraid of something or—"

"No. No, no, no…"

"Because we haven't even talked about it since breakfast that morning. I don't . . . understand . . ."

"Change is never timely, Aetheria." My gaze was so firmly at that, I could hardly believe it was me doing it. Perhaps it had been the narrowing of my eyebrows or the twitching of my lip that had made me say it.

"Well we can make it be."

He shook his head ever so patiently. "No we can't." And for the first time in this spiraling of thoughts, I felt weak. A sudden softness met my tone.

"Are you worried someone's going to find out about us leaving, yes? Did I crack the Da Vinci Code?" He watched me. "Everything we're planning is legal anyway, right? That's what the formation documents say."

"I know."

"Do you know something that I don't? I can handle any information you have, Perû." I paused. "In fact I feel like I deserve to know about anything that you know." My father lowered his head into his hands, shaking them all left to right in slow motion.

"I don't have any information." He paused. My breath was held firm in my chest. "I'm just being careful. There's so much uncertainty right now . . . so much that could go wrong. The truth is, people can no longer be trusted." I stared. Thought about it. And soon I was shaking my own head, staring back up at my father.

"Perû, people *deserve* to be trusted. With everything going on right now, it's the least we can do to respect each other." I watched as he opened his mouth to say something, paused and closed it again.

"Then trust me," He began to say with such sternness I hardly believed it was from his lips, "When I tell you that we have not deviated from the plan, Aetheria. That it is my dying desire to keep you all alive and safe. We are still going on because it is the only way that I can fulfill this desire. Do you understand?"

I don't know when his hands ended up upon my shoulders. When the stone of my body began to crack beneath the weight of his grip. As I nodded in response, something shattered inside of me. Adrenaline turned to longing. Anger turned to despair. Then I sunk into his arms and he held me close. Tears found their home upon my cheeks. And from my lips emerged the only words I knew to say for emotions I couldn't quite comprehend.

"I'm sorry."

If Not Now, Then When?

I haven't been able to figure out why I thought it would make a difference. Why leaving or staying would change anything for my fate. For I walked back up towards my room after that, believing so honestly that my life would be worth something, had I left.

But now I have left, as I write all of this. I can declare truthfully that there is no difference.

Sitka's room was the door before mine. Music reverberated off of his walls as it always did. The melodies would often stumble into my dreams and I would watch scenes of my hands laced with those of death, waltzing through a ballroom. I was never afraid.

I stopped before his door that day on the way to my room. I stopped and listened to the harmonies and wondered what went on behind closed doors to warrant such sounds. My head felt the slightest bit light. My heart felt the faintest echo of longing and so my hand met the metal before me and pounded on it. The substance was cold against my fist but the silence that replied in my brother's place was colder. I pounded once more. His voice arose from the other side. "Who is it?"

"Your sister."

"What's up?" He said it more as a statement than a question. I fought the urge to be annoyed.

"I haven't seen you in . . . " I thought it through for a moment, "A day or two."

The door opened. He poked his head out. A smile formed across his cheeks in the most unconvincing of manners. His black curls fell into his eyes and I reached to brush them away.

Then, his smile sagged just the slightest bit. "Hi."

I simply stared at him. "No fifteen year old should be alone for days on end. Not even an introvert." He smiled brightly once more. No words arrived from his tongue. "Are you doing okay?"

"Yeah, I'm fine."

His eyes fell to his hands and mine followed. I watched his brown fingertips play with a round piece of metal. My head tilted the slightest bit to the right. "What is that?"

He looked up at me. "It's just for a . . . project."

"Where did you get it?"

"Corbyn." His best friend. I wondered how long they had gone without speaking, just as I and Darbii.

I nodded. My head lifted to see his face. "Do you need anything?" I saw the look in his eyes. The longing. The breaking. The burning of his thoughts into embers without rest. His hands slid into the pockets of his hoodie so that only his body was holding the door open and I watched his gaze fall to the floor. A river ran through my mind and thought to enter my eyes. I refused to let them do so. Not in front of him.

"We're leaving soon enough, okay? I'm . . . " I shook my head, glancing down for just a moment, "I'm trying my best."

His gaze lifted towards me. "It's been . . . " I watched him sort through a timeline that emerged easily from my lips.

"Two weeks."

He stared at me. A hardness came over his gaze as words ran off his tongue. "We don't know when the Qadim is leaving."

"I know."

"If not now, then when?"

Something screamed across the house.

Rang.

Blared. Boomed. Banged.

My eyes narrowed quickly. "Is that you?"

"No." And then he stepped out of his room, the door slamming behind him and we were shuffling down the hall, down the stairs, down to where my father and Viridian stood in the kitchen. The dissonance was daring. Draining. Confusing.

My hands slapped my ears. My mind boiled inside the burning sound.

"What the hell is that?" Viridian screamed over the noise. Sitka appeared in the hallway. My heart pounded to the staggering rhythm.

We shuffled around the kitchen. My father's hands had been fists. We opened drawers. Cabinets slammed. Platters clashed. Glasses clattered. They added to the dissonance. Then, the sound silenced itself. A lifeless voice replaced it.

"*Attention all citizens of Cordellia: It is mandatory that no one leaves the country at this time under any circumstances in order to protect yourself and others. Unless for authorized business endeavors, all travel to outside countries is prohibited. This is for your own protection. Thank you for your understanding and cooperation. Hail Cordell.*"

In a flash of a moment, I had seen my class standing before the Cordellian flag, passionately proclaiming, "*Helii Cordell*" in our native Cordellian tongue. We stood with thankfulness for our ancestor.

For the establishment of our governmentless land.

"What the . . . " Viridian stood paralyzed beside the front door, mirroring my own stance. "We don't *have* a government. Who the hell is giving us orders?!"

"This isn't right." I mumbled. My eyebrows were pulled into a straight line across my face. Then my gaze was grazing the back of my younger brother, kneeling into a lower cabinet of platters.

"What are you doing?" I inched closer to him. He pulled his head out, pointing at a spot in the back of the cabinet.

"There's a speaker back here."

My heart stopped. "Built into the cabinet?"

"Yes."

My father stared over at my younger brother. "Sitka *what*?" Sitka simply shook his head.

"This doesn't make sense." Viridian mumbled.

"No." Sitka looked up at our older brother. "No, what doesn't make sense is the fact that we're even getting a transmission. Remember solar flares before all of this? That's pretty much what's going on. It's why we're having black outs, it's why—"

Viridian rolled his eyes. "How about the fact that there is a literal speaker in our kitchen cabinet, Sitka?"

"But how are they *using* the speaker under these conditions?"

And soon my gaze met my father's across the kitchen. I stared into his panicked eyes and I knew I hadn't needed to speak for him to comprehend my thoughts, but I did anyway.

"What do we do now?"

He stared into my hollow gaze. Stared into the fear boiling inside of it until he was nodding ever so slowly.

"Now, we rebel."

[4]

A Pacifistic Fear

"The idea of Pacifism shall be taught at a young age to all citizens in hopes of absolute peace among Cordellians. In the absence of law enforcement, peace shall be regulated and kept in accountability by the people. In the case of an aggressor, the people shall have full authority to banish or send the individual to a designated location of refuge."

Cordellia Bill of Rights, Article XI. Signed, January 21st, 2026, Apgar Cordell.

I had been in my room when my mother got home. My door was open by an inch so I could listen to my father explain to her what had happened.

"There's a speaker right there, Yemasii." I could hear his voice echo from inside the cabinet.

"I don't believe you."

"It's right there!"

"Why did I never know about this, Ävon?!"

"You think I did?!"

I simply sat on my bed and listened. I stared at my phone that sat before me on my sheets, that thing I hadn't used in weeks, and yet, I was enthralled by its irony. Of how it was charged by the sun, of how it could not die for such reasons. And yet, the very flares it relied on for survival had become so strong, so overpowering, so to make it void of purpose. For now it had become simply a shell of something useful. I'm not quite sure why I still kept it so close to me.

Since his trip to the hospital a year or so ago, Sitka had found a strange interest in jazz music. I had thought it to be ironic, how the quietest member of the Elko family had the noisiest habits.

His music had been even louder that evening.

Once I found the strength to move, I tried once more to pack, as it seemed I was forever doing. For I had faith the announcement meant we would leave sooner and fear that it meant we wouldn't leave at all.

I kept my pointe shoes at the top of my bag. A foolish attempt to keep me hopeful.

My door opened behind me. My head leapt up from where it had been fixed upon my bag. Sitka stood on the other side.

"Knock, Sitka." His eyes jumped anxiously around my room, pushing his black curls out of his face.

"Sorry." A pause. "Where's Viridian?"

"Probably in his room . . . ?" I replied, noticing the enamored expression set upon his face. "Why?"

"Can you grab him for me . . . please?"

I squinted and stared. "Why can't you do it?"

"He listens to you better than me."

"I doubt that." He stared at me. I stared back. A sigh limped its way off my lips and then I was grabbing my candle and following him out my door and down the hall to my older brother's room. I pounded on the door. Nothing happened. It was locked when I tugged on it.

I pounded on it once more. "V, Sit wants you." The reverberations grew louder the longer he took to answer. Then, the door flew open. I almost fell through to where he stood.

His body leaned towards me as his hands held the doorway. His eyes were blazing and hair crazed and I found the slightest scent of smoke hiding behind him.

"Gosh Eve, could you do that any louder?"

I smirked. "I can try if you want me to."

His eyes fumbled in a circle around his head. "What does he want?"

"I don't know."

Viridian groaned. We followed Sitka down the hall and he was escorting us into his room as though we were under arrest. The door closed behind us. Locked. Items had been scattered across his floor, the concrete nearly imperceivable. Mechanical metal pieces and stacks of clothing and boxes with sophisticated locks. The blinds across the room had been shut tightly, a candle upon his desk acting as the sole source of light. The air smelled of a harsh odor and another softly dizzying scent I couldn't quite identify. The navy sheets of his bed had been thrown and thrashed and tipping off the mattress. A textbook sat open upon his desk to an image of a heavily petaled maroon flower, zoomed in on an image of a thorn. I noticed his Cordellian flag sitting in a crumpled ball on the floor beside his desk. And soon he was turning towards his record table beside his desk, that old thing that he converted into a crank player for the current times. And then he was increasing the volume of his music. We all stood still for a moment.

"What is this about, Sit?" Viridian asked. Sitka was on the other side of his bed, kneeling down on the floor, removing a black box from beneath it. He placed it on his comforter, opening it away from us to conceal the contents. Then, he looked up.

"This is going to startle you." He had looked us each in the eye for a moment too long. Then he was removing two items from the box and moving towards us. "But I need you to have these."

It had taken me a moment to realize what he had placed in my palm. How the cold coal-colored metal rested in my hand so heavily. It had been dense and dreary, shaped as a boomerang, attempting to slip out of my grasp back towards where it had rested prior. Or perhaps that had just been my reaction once I realized what it was.

It was a gun.

"Oh my gosh . . . " Viridian's voice seemed to trail off in the distance as my eyes stayed focused on the weapon. A drum pounded inside my ears.

"Where did you *get* this?" I demanded. My eyes darted from the gun up to my younger brother, who had stood so still in the presence of such malice rested in my palm. "You can't even get these things in this country how did you . . . "

"There's a lot I haven't told you." Sitka said, his light eyes suddenly seeming a shade darker.

"Well you better start explaining!" Viridian yelled. My eyes had found him. His tilted torso and furrowed eyebrows and the rose skin around his mouth was pulled in tight. He looked terrified.

Sitka swallowed. "I will."

"You will?"

"Later."

"Sitka, there might not be a 'later!'" I practically screamed.

"Just trust me."

"You're handing me a . . . a *gun* and telling me to trust you?" The word felt like taboo as it escaped my lips.

"Yes."

"Sitka I . . . "

"Just make sure our parents don't find it."

Viridian rolled his eyes. "Because we'd be disowned if they did."

"It's an understatement." My eyes darted back down to the weapon in my palms. They seemed to shake beneath its weight and yet I couldn't seem to find the strength to release it.

To this day I wish I had been stronger at that moment.

But instead I was stuck gripping that weapon as though it was the life of me when it was really just the death of others.

Sitka removed two more items from the box, extending them to us.

"Here." He said. I feared to take it. "It's a holster. You wrap it around your hips under your pants to keep the gun inside . . . so no one can see it." He made a motion around the rim of his black jeans.

"I cannot believe this . . . " I heard Viridian mumble beside me. He was shaking his head, staring at the two items in his hands. And then, reluctantly, he began to tie the holster upon his body.

"What else were you guys expecting?" Sitka's eyes squinted inward as he spoke. "Did you really think we would be able to make it across the entire continent without having to defend ourselves?"

"I was hoping so, yes." But even as I said it, I recognized the naivete of the thought. For Paris had already erupted into flames and it was part of the only country in the world without weapons. Had I honestly expected the rest of society to have sustained sanity?

"That isn't how the world works, Eve. Cordellia is nothing like everywhere else." Sitka's words had read my mind and for a long moment, I had stayed staring at him, trying to pick through my words to find which ones would change his mind, but perhaps my mind would be more easily changed than his. So I tied the holster upon my hip. It felt suffocating.

Viridian turned to leave the room a moment later. I reached for my candle and followed him, laying my electrified eyes on Sitka one last time before closing the door behind me. We stood still in the hall, our eyes meeting and colliding into each other.

"Viridian, I . . . " I didn't know what words to pick. "How did he get them?"

"I don't know."

"If Merû and Perû found out they would—"

"Kill us. I know." I watched my brother pull in a breath of air and hold it hostage. I didn't see him release it.

"We could leave them here." I immediately regretted my words.

"For the psychopaths to find? No way. You've seen what they can do with matches, just imagine what they could do with a gun." I nodded. "Just . . . hold onto it."

"I don't even know how to fire it—"

"Pull the trigger?" He chuckled. "You've seen movies." His white teeth were crystal balls that only I could see through to the fear that lay beyond. "Just . . . make sure Merû and Perû don't find it on you." I wanted to leave it at that.

"But what if . . ." I swallowed. "What if I end up needing to use it?"

"You won't."

A pause. "Right." And as Viridian turned, making his way towards his room and placing his gun into the right side of his jeans, I knew that even he didn't believe his own words. Even he was fearful of the day that he might have to use his weapon, or his weapon might be used against him.

[5]

Daisy

The gun stared at me.

It sat on my bed, sinking into the fabric, sinking into a lake, yet never missing my gaze. It was as though I had neglected an item of value. A relic, perhaps. The adornments of a pharaoh. That it had slipped into my grasp against my solemn will and so I had drowned it. Abandoned it. Left it to sink beneath waters and decay against the winds of time. But it was cursed.

Maybe I was cursed. Looking back on it now, as I write all of this, I think that I might have truly been. Cursed by such power to destroy. By such fear of doing so that, through my ever impending fears, it might then be done. Doomed by deeds that no human should have the power to deal.

And so the desire to leave that cynical thing behind ate at me. Devoured me until only my beating heart remained, reverberating through the impending walls of that room. But the fear of neglecting it, the fear of someone worse finding it, pressed its foot down upon my heart. I would be foolish to leave it here in my home in Paris.

Even more so, for some reason, I feared I needed it.

The shouting in the kitchen had settled down a while before then. No longer could I hear the words that were shared. Perhaps none were. Not until I heard her voice emerge from thin air.

"Would you all come down here please?" My mother's shout traveled up the staircase, reaching my ears. Spinning in a circle around them and back out as though I had never heard it in the first place. I didn't move, just for a

40

moment. Just as I tried to grapple with the fear of what fate she had decided for us all.

I was afraid that her fear of the unknown would tear apart my future.

"Sitka, Eve, Viridian." She called again.

Go.

I found the strength to pick up the gun. To shove it into a drawer inside my desk for the time being. And then I was grabbing an already lit candle and shuffling out of my room, hardly paying regards to my steps that moved faster than my mind. Soon enough I was in the kitchen, staring at my mother and father at the other side of the counter. She had her hand placed firmly on a piece of paper in front of her, tension built up in her green eyes.

"Sitka and Viridian!" She called again. "Gosh, this is like herding cats!" I swallowed. A few more moments went by before Sitka was beside me. Then Viridian. No one spoke.

My gaze fell again to the paper resting underneath her fingertips. One only used paper if they wished for no one to hear their words. I felt my stomach begin to ache.

And soon she was removing her hand, revealing writing beneath. Scribbles that startled me so greatly that they seemed as though they were in another tongue:

Your father told me about what happened. I want to still give you all a chance at life, even if it puts us in potential danger. I feel it is better than doing nothing at all. However, I will not make you do anything if even one of you does not feel comfortable with the idea. I need an answer quickly.

Silence remained. Dwelling in unease. But only for a moment.

"Yes." It was Sitka. His voice had been laced with a confidence that I, to this day, cannot quite comprehend.

I hadn't moved at the sound of his tongue. My eyes wouldn't let me. They stayed fixed at my mother's handwriting, stained like coagulated blood across the paper.

This had been all I had wanted. All I had hoped for since breakfast all those days ago. A chance at life beyond the confines of mere survival. A chance to take even just a glimpse into a life I had always desired. For it to even be an option once more. And yet, I remained so hesitant to reply.

I see now, writing this all from Neo-Italy, that terror is merely insight. That the risk one takes always results in an inescapable pain. And the fear of the pain is only a preparation for its coming.

"Yes." It was Viridian that time. I could see him nodding in my peripheral vision, his gaze fixed anxiously on my mother. Then, all eyes were on me.

Me, who would determine life or death for everyone.

Me, who couldn't understand how I held such power.

But I did. And I held on to it until I could find the ability inside of my bones to let a single word roll off my tongue.

A word I have now, reflecting back, come to wish I had never gained the strength to speak.

"Yes." I lifted my eyes from the table. Lifted them to my mother's gaze. Watched her carefully as she nodded. Smiled. And soon she was turning the paper over, revealing a single line of writing:

Go get your things.

Then, everyone was shuffling back to their rooms as I stood stuck in the realization of what such a phrase meant.

We were leaving right now.

Darkness consumed me. My candle danced around before me as the sole source of light and I looked up to see my father across the counter from me. Our eyes met and stared into one another and a single name blew past my mind.

"Darbii." My mouth lied open just the slightest bit. "I need to tell Darbii." His gaze softened in the way it does to ask me what I mean. "I wish I could just text her, but I can't. Do you give me permission to take the car to her house? I need to get there somehow. I'll walk if that's what it takes." He only watched me. Pondered. "Do I have permission to take the car?"

"No." My heart dropped until I watched him move towards the front door. "I'm taking you." He grabbed the keys off of the counter. "If you get jumped, I'm getting jumped with you."

A grin stumbled across my cheeks as I stumbled across the room to where his hand rested upon the open door. I looked upon the way his fingers wavered so slightly against the steel, though his body remained perfectly still.

I stepped out into the open.

The air bit my cheeks and smoke churred inside my nose. My eyes began to water and my head began to spin and I was looking up upon the sky where it slowly began to dim. The piercing sun met my hollow gaze. Its razor eyes shaved the skin off of my bones, calicing what remained. It stared at me in its undying anger. In a gruesome, destructive wrath with lack of cause. For what had I done to make it hunt me so selfishly? To follow me about my days, watching me drown deeper into despair, awaiting the day it should deliver me to my death.

Its accomplice rested in roguery at its side. Its glare had been darker than the sun's. Hidden, yet remaining as the topic of my attention. Staring with such condemnation, with such patronization. I saw him as a man—a judge at court—clothed in a sable suit, his eyes matching the seams around his cuffs. They were that of obsidian, so dark I couldn't seem to see through them. Ridden of all humanity, the silencer of any sympathy the sun once had. Staring, stripped of emotion as he sentenced me to death.

The sun and the black hole.

I had never thought a day would come when I would find it necessary to juxtapose those two phrases.

But there they reigned above me, their polar opposition casted in destructive symmetry across the red sky. The sun was bright, too bright.

It still is, to this day, too bright.

But beside it had rested darkness. A darkness that could not and still cannot accurately be depicted into words. I had often found it strange how so often in history, humanity had condemned themselves for causing the destruction of nature. But now, nature had destroyed itself.

So I stared at the dirt beneath me. Stared at an earth clenched so tightly by despair and yet, at the time, I still believed I would find hope upon the Qadim. I had believed my foolish ambition more than I believed the confines of reality.

But things change. Naivete adapts into despair and soon one no longer sees the power they possess in holding a gun but rather the way it smokes.

"It's warmer." I looked over at my father as he climbed into the driver's seat. "When did it get this warm?"

He watched me. "When was the last time you went outside?" I couldn't remember. Perhaps it was those two weeks ago when my brother and I had decided to leave.

So I approached the car. I looked out across the flowers that once grew around the entryway, now covered in ash and I looked at our grass now dusted brown. But a single daisy grew up from beneath the burned ground. A single sign of life beyond what my mind knew to comprehend and beyond what I, at the time of writing this, allow myself to believe in. I stared at it for a long moment in such utter wonder. Stared at it as though I would never see such beauty again and I suppose I never would.

Then I took it into my hands and carried it into the car.

[6]

Insanity

"In place of this absence of government, an emphasis on personal choice shall be established. Citizens should, but are not required to, enroll in schooling until age eighteen, obtain a job in order to access free services, including food, supplies and housing. Citizens are given the ability to choose which services they would like without the use of currency. The absence of law enforcement shall be replaced with the accountability of citizens with one another."

Cordellia Bill of Rights, Article IV. Signed, February 21st, 2026, Apgar Cordell

What sends a person into insanity? What must occur to lead someone down such a severe path of becoming ruled by their actions rather than their good judgment? When the mad voices evolve and one's own conscience dissolves, who is responsible for such an exchange?

For, back then, I simply judged those people of my town. Those that destroyed things without remorse. Those that lived on the streets and in abandoned buildings and waited around until their lives eventually evaporated into thin air. But now, it seems I am one of them, at the time I write all of this.

I stared at one as we drove the road in silence. I stared at a woman sitting along the sidewalk, her gaze wide and hair frail along the edges. She held a can of something, her hands limp across the tin. Her eyes had that hollow taint of insanity that humanity had grown to possess and for a moment, I feared her seeing us.

My father must have seen her too, for he began to drive the slightest bit faster.

"If we just get there and back as quickly as possible, we're less likely to get attacked, right? We'll be safe. It won't happen."

My father nodded slowly at my words. "Just get in and out when you get there."

My head turned out the window. "When was the last time we've even driven anywhere? Without . . . the fear of getting attacked?" A genuine fear. For those that had lost their minds were known to assault moving vehicles.

My father sighed. "A very long time."

I saw an olive tree up ahead. Its bark had been burnt and its branches had bowed. Its discolored leaves laid limp upon the brown. I could only imagine what had caused such a burn. What pain nature or humanity had entrusted to it.

Each tree I saw past mimicked its mourning. They drooped just the same, browned just the same. It had seemed as though the sun had stolen their idiosyncrasy from their hands.

I wondered when the world had become so melancholy. When the very land around me had decided to reflect the disdain within me. When had life lost its color to total darkness and a burning light? When did memories become both menacing and mournful? For a while I wondered once more, could I even escape this? Was it even worth it to try? I feared again that I was destined for death.

Looking back on all of this again as I write, I realize that I wasn't as oblivious as I thought myself to be. I had lived in avoidance, truly, but I wasn't oblivious, not nearly. I understood reality completely. Understood the toils of death as though it was the friend back then that it is to me now in Neo-Italy. But I shared then the same fatal flaw that I do now: my unwavering ability to drown in my stubbornness.

Tents were lined up along the road the deeper we entered into Paris. People wailed beneath them. Open fires danced around the cobblestone and clothless people danced around the flames. A woman laid directly in the dirt, staring up at the sky. A man sat on the curb without a shirt, playing with his beard and taking sips of an unidentifiable liquid. A young girl held a match, spinning it in his fingers. My father sped by.

"There has to be something someone can do about this." I mumbled. "This is just . . . awful."

"Yes it is."

A boom sounded in the distance. I leapt from my seat. My father accelerated once more.

We pulled into one of many Parisian town centers. A bronze statue sat atop a grass field of two men linking arms. Apgar Cordell, the founder of this country, now gone to ruin. The man who freed Morocco from France's oppressive rule, those 120 years ago. The man who established Cordellia, void of government, void of dictatorship. Who took the eastern half of France as retribution, no matter what other histories said.

He stood with his teeth turned to a grin, with his right arm locked with another man. With the figure of the revolution, of the joining of Morocco and France into their own world, a truly free world: Karl Marx himself. For Cordell had been the only man to ever truly understand what Marx had hoped for in the proletarian revolution. The only man to carry it out effectively.

It had been disheartening, to see such former success stretched in ruin.

"What would they think," I mumbled, "If they saw the way this country has become?"

My eyes lifted to my father. I watched him nod slowly. "They would want us to fight for our dignity. No matter what that entails." And to us, that had entailed leaving.

Darbii's house was a few streets over. It sat between two smaller homes, its evening shadow cast upon the cobblestone street. The deep green siding wrapped around towards painted white railing meeting at the front door and forming a quaint porch. The grass had grown an underlying shade of brown, parched beneath the rim of the house. Darbii's bedroom was just above it. Her window had been cracked open as it always was.

I got out of the car at the corner. Faced the heat and found her window and pushed it up further, peering in through the ivory curtains into her room. My gaze jumped between ruffled sheets on her bed beneath the window, to the piles of clothes on the floor, to the empty beer cans crumpled into bits on her desk. The whole house was silent. They must had taken a trip to the food stand.

And as I stared into her room, my mind was flooded with the sacred nostalgia of endless prank calls, the spilling of secrets, the echoes of laughter I feared I would never hear again. I watched it all as though I anticipated she would pop out and surprise me. That her green eyes would be filled with wonder. That her brown waves would spring from the top of her head in a mad grasp for enthusiasm. And I would throw my arms around her one last time. Smiling. Tears stained across my reddened cheeks.

But the room remained still.

I simply stared. Stared at the blissful days that had grown to become hollow memories. Stared at her face in my mind's eye, slowly fading out of focus until she was gone.

I opened the window a crack more. My body slid inside and landed atop her bed and my feet found the floor. I felt the weight of the room. The hollowness of such unease. My hands found her sheets and adjusted them to where they were meant to rest. My body moved to her desk where cans were thrown about and I felt my throat go dry. So I reached for them, gathered them together and tossed them into the garbage can beneath her desk and in their absence, I saw a notepad sitting upon the wood. My fingers fumbled for the pen beside it and I began to scribble down a note:

Darbii,

We're leaving for Israel confidentially. Tonight. It is bittersweet to think we'll never make it back. I love you and miss you more than words can say.

- Eve

Tears filled the dimples on my cheeks. Rain roamed in desert lands. A long second lingered as I stared upon my words, and then I left them to be. Then, I was on the other side of the window once more, sealing it shut. It separated me from her, creating the boundary between nightmare and reality. Or perhaps, even then, the line no longer existed.

Then, I let it all go.

The lights were off in the car when I arrived back. I sat down and felt the weight of silence rest upon my bones. Felt the heat settle into my cheeks in heaping loads of honey. I reached for the flower in my pocket and held the stem in my hands.

"Was she there?" My father's voice had been somber. I shook my head. I don't know if he saw me.

"I left her a note." My voice cracked on the last word. He nodded in reply. Then my hand extended out towards him. He stared down at the arched petals inside, beginning to shrivel into nothing. I smiled. Forced it across my cheeks, for it was all I could do.

He met my smile. Then he took the flower and placed it in his lap.

[7]

On Last Letter

My mother was in the kitchen when we arrived home.

Her head was buried inside a cabinet we never used. Her hands fumbled through items I couldn't make out, items I had never seen before. She mumbled something under her breath until her eyes shot up towards us, standing at the door.

"Goodness gracious, where did you two go?" her green gaze was wide, and her blonde hair was mangled. My father simply looked at me. He had warned me in the car that he would not lie to my mother. I had nodded and said nothing in reply.

So I stared at her now. "We haven't used the car in weeks so we thought we'd just take it around the block. Warm up the engine."

She simply watched us for a long moment. Her eyes were held in the way they always were when she was clearly unconvinced. With that slight tilt of the inside edges in opposition to the wideness on the outside. A rush of wind rolled through my bones when she finally spoke. "Everything worked okay?"

I stared at her for a long while after that. So long that it must have become plainly obvious that I was lying. Then, I replied. "Yeah everything was . . . normal."

"Okay then." Her head leaned sideways, motioning towards the stairs. "Hurry up."

A beat. A single moment of idleness. A single wave of tension passing through my body until I was turning. Until my eyes were blurring and I

50

fought to find the stairs. I don't remember my mind telling my feet to travel back up to my room. To zip up my black duffle bag, to stare at it sternly with tears staining my cheeks.

But there I was, and it was happening.

My eyes fell upon the stack of paper, those I had used all of those many days for letters I would never send. They sat with the misplaced reverence of an idol upon my desk. I could feel their eyes watch me. Their laser gaze targeting my soul, gripping my mind, spinning it all in circles. Finding my stomach, tossing a rock inside.

There's time for one more letter.

So I sifted through my desk drawers. My fingers flew across fragments of a life short of being lived in search of a pen to make meaningless markings upon paper. They moved past a postcard from Varna, Bulgaria, a small beachside town I had always wished to visit. Past erasers snapped in half from when I had revoked my thoughts too earnestly. Past notes with quotes scribbled across them, dried silly putty Darbii gave me in second grade, photographs of my last nutcracker. I thought I could still hear the music.

And then I saw the gun. It had been carelessly tossed to the side of the drawer. Its hellish nature seemed to have burned the wood inside my desk, or at least that had been how my mind had portrayed it to be. Our gazes met once more. I fought with my conscience whether to leave it behind or make it mine.

Soon, I slipped the weapon on my side.

And so I sketched my words upon white paper, tears colliding, falling down on my hand. Tears of mourning, tears of hope. Tears of anticipation for dreams that could come to pass once again. A tsunami grew upon the page that I couldn't seem to escape. That I couldn't seem to see through to the messy words I had made:

Dear Darbii,

This is it. May 18th, 2146. This is the last letter I'll write to you before I'm gone. Before I see you on a distant star. Until our gazes collide again and arms with them and I feel you in my embrace and maybe begin to believe that we're okay.

I'm trying to have hope in this moment. Trying to believe that day will come. That we will see each other once more in a day when our hope is easy to obtain and not forced. It's the least I can do to keep myself alive.

Eve.

There were a million more things I wanted to say, but only time would determine if I might one day find a way to say them. But for the moment, the most it seemed I could do was leave the letter upon that empty desk. To leave it in an act of hope, as though it had the ability of being sent her way, but it did not. Perhaps it was enough to dream of such things.

I blew out my candle.

Then, I reached for my duffle bag, throwing it over my shoulder. My phone still sat on my bed and I stared at it. Wondered if it was even worth taking but something inside of me reached for it anyway.

I stopped in front of the mirror before I left my room.

I stared at the stickers around the top of the glass, from past trips and concerts and phrases that had made me laugh. I took note of the way my black curls reached towards the bottom of my chest. Untouched. Unharmed. A sheltered child, an unseen smile, a baby bird not yet grown enough to dream of leaving its nest. I saw how tightly my skin had been pulled across my cheeks, accented by dark freckles and a light smile across my lips. I hadn't realized I could still carry a smile so bright. I looked at my brown eyes, resting upon my cheeks, reaching down to where my bones collided, forming a mirthful masterpiece.

My gaze fell to my tshirt below. A deep black, fresh out of the wash, pressed perfectly around my skin. It swayed over my sable jeans, long and stiff and dark to match the fabric above. And in their pockets sat my hands. Those hands that carried life, that brought words to existence upon a page, that expressed my feelings so deliberately. Then, my eyes finally found the black boots I wore upon my feet. My favorite accessory.

I stared at myself for a long time.

I saw the strength I carried.

I will be okay.

And so I left my room with the door open. Perhaps it had been an act of rebellion against the coffin that my life had grown inside. My footsteps followed my younger brother down the hall into the kitchen. The rest of my family already stood there, on their faces holding looks of fear or anticipation or a word that meant both; a word I could not find. They each carried a bag of their own.

My mother looked at me. Her eyes pierced a piece of the anxiety in my stance and soon words rolled off her tongue. Her gaze didn't leave me as she said it.

"This house served us well." There had been a pause. It felt like a million moments and one all at once as I stood still, viewing everything from outside of my body. I saw the kitchen window out to the yard of summer days spent in the splendor of sprinklers. I saw green apples, my favorite fruit, eaten in the heat of July. I saw tiny fingerprints on plastic cups and mouths consuming lemonade. I saw winter nights with fireplaces. Wednesday mornings with backpacks. Tuesday afternoons with homework. My name etched into every crevice and corner and gray painted area upon plain walls. And when I couldn't seem to see anything more, I saw the reality of everyone beginning to shuffle towards the door. Slowly. Meticulously.

I was the last to move.

The last to stay standing beside my kitchen island, staring at what surrounded me. The last to shed a tear before my mother blew out the lights. The last to remain in the dark as if something held me to the ground, pinning me in place. The last to feel my throat burn and dry up and then . . .

Go.

I couldn't.

You have to.

I know.

And against all the will inside my bones, I moved towards the front door, the very searing air that escaped from the outside seeming to push me back in. But I resisted it all. Resisted every urge that told me to turn and run. To escape to my room and just spend a little while longer there. To stare upon the posters on my walls, the piles of clothes scattered across my floor. The years of life I had lived, the ones I would never know again.

But I couldn't run. I couldn't turn around.

Because I knew that then I would never leave.

This was my future now.

Then, I was outside. Bursting through into the darkness. The heat seemed to dry the tears on my cheeks in an instant. To remove the evidence of the battle I had chosen not to fight. Not this time.

I found myself staring at the moon. I watched its light reach the furthest corners of the sky as I made my way to the car. I stared at its spotlight stuck down upon me as I opened the door, placing myself down in the middle row beside Sitka. I watched it through the window as my father started the vehicle. Stared as we inched forward, away from the only home I had ever known. On to an unpromised salvation.

And I felt my heart break.

I felt the weight of the sky crush it.

But the moon.

It saw me.

[8]

The Elko's Exciting Adventure

I think that's something that I've learned from all of this, looking back as I write about it all. That some things which are unknown are meant to remain just that: unknown. Some lands are meant to remain undiscovered, some questions unanswered. I do deeply wish I had realized it sooner. But I hadn't.

And so I sat in that silent car, questioning how in that instance it seemed that silence had become our companion. For never before had it been.

It stretched the circumference of the vehicle, watching our very bones slowly turn to dust. Watching, but doing nothing. Letting us decompose for it only knows that is where we would always end up, one day or another. And maybe then, it would dig our graves, carve our names into stone that no one would look upon. For by the time we were gone, so everyone else in this cruel world would be, and only silence would remain.

I stared out the window as we ventured through lands I had once known, now covered in darkness. The local supply stands, the community pool, the lake at which I spent my 16th birthday. Buildings were swept under the rule of ruin. Cracks stretched up the sides of cobblestone walls as veins without the presence of blood, covering doorways, inching into the crevices of windows. Humanity remained absent among the rotting of nature. And in the distance, on some far-stretched mountain, my peripheral vision caught the faint glow of fire.

My eyes jumped between the sky and the terrain, incapable of deciding where they wished to remain. Soon, they met the moon again. Then, my mother chose to speak.

"How are we all doing? It's quiet back there," her voice rang from the passenger seat. My head turned slowly in her direction, seemingly against my will. I had made eye contact with her in the rearview mirror for a moment. Then, I looked away. There had been a momentary lull as she waited for one of us to obtain the desire to reply. No one did. She nodded slowly.

"Okay, looks like I'm on talking duty." She looked back out the windshield. "Well then, on that note, may I present to you a very well-written and thoroughly thought-out presentation by Yemasii Elko, also known as 'The Elko's Exciting Adventure.'"

Viridian piped up at that. "Adventure? That's what we're calling this?"

"Viridian." She looked at him in the rearview. "Not right now." I stared out the window as I listened to her fingers shuffle through papers. I held my breath by accident.

"Whether or not you all believe me, I've been preparing for this since breakfast that one morning." My gaze shot over at her. She had a paper map stretched out across her lap, staring at the intricate markings across the yellowed material.

"Where did you get the map?" Viridian mumbled.

"Had it in a file from a while ago. I was trying to plan a road trip." Her head hadn't moved in the slightest as she spoke. "There's a large suitcase of food in the trunk that I've been collecting from supply stands each day. I've been going to various different ones in order to not raise suspicion. I know we don't have . . . any money." A tenuous pause. She reluctantly released a sigh. I held my own in. "But, based on the length of the journey, the amount of supplies I have saved up should cover us as long as we limit our portions." For once, I wondered if that had been the entire reason why we had waited so long to leave. If my mother had recognized she would have needed the time to prepare us to do so. And yet, I couldn't help but feel a tinge of anger towards her failure in saying something sooner.

"We'll keep our eyes out for locations of refuge for the night. Of course, we'll check hotels too. I've heard reports of them being flexible in terms of payment, you know, with the absence of work and so forth." There was another moment of silence. "The car's solar energy should function even better with the extreme radiation. I have a fanny pack of medical supplies in case of emergencies—" she patted her pack on her stomach. "So, overall, everything is looking good. Once we get the identification in Germany, it should be a clear shot to Israel and on to the Qadim." A longer pause. "Is anyone even paying attention to me right now?"

Me and my brothers murmured a yes.

"Okay, because I'm getting no response right now—"

"Yemasii." My eyes raised to meet my father when he spoke. His pale-turned hands clenched the wheel tightly, sending shots of blue through his knuckles. His eyes had been fixed upon my mother in a cool stare as though to say, "Don't push it."

"How long until we're out of the country?" It was then I found an opportune moment amid the silence to ask. There was a lull as my mother assessed her map.

"It's about a three-hour drive."

Viridian huffed from the row behind me.

"Five, actually," Sitka's brown eyes were focused on his phone when he chimed in. His hair climbed into his eyes and bounced a bit beneath the rocking of the car. The screen illuminated his pores and I wondered for only a second how his device was working, for mine hadn't in too long to count. I stared down upon the object in his hand the moment before he shut it off. I couldn't recognize the program it was open to.

"What? Why?"

"Right now we're headed towards the Belgium border—" he began again, quickly slipping his phone into his pocket and looking around his seat at my mother "—which is fine for now, but we'll need to head towards Germany soon."

"Why do we have to go to Germany right now? We can head that way tomorrow when we get identification—"

"No we can't." I stared at my brother for a moment. His gaze had been fixed hard upon my mother. His eyes were wide and pupils shrunk in stature until all life seemed to dissolve from his being. Until there was only anger. Merely frustration embedded into the whites of his knuckles, gripping the seat before him.

The thought had become concrete without warning.

My brother was lying to me about something.

"We need to go to the German border," he began again. "I am promising you that the security into Belgium will be impossible to get through. There's a specific spot that will be the easiest to cross and it's on the way to a town called Verborgen just east along the border. It's a longer route, but it's the only way that we will be able to get out." My mother stared at her map for a moment, then back up at him in the mirror.

"Sitka, how do you know this?"

"I did research."

"Research about leaving Cordellia . . ."

"You just have to trust me on this," he finally said, his voice firm. A pause. My mother slowly nodded.

No one spoke as our vehicle hovered into a small town, the lights in every window off, the red and yellow brick walls speckled graciously with holes. I remember so clearly that the land had been silent. The lack of sound was like that of an uneasy push and pull of a tide, of waters that wouldn't quite form into waves. Yet, the uneasiness was familiar. Rows of homes remained as tombstones for those who had once belonged to them. They were as weapons left behind on a battlefield. Objects that had kept their master sheltered until they had been used for his demise. No newcomer to ever look upon those weapons would truly know what they had done. They could create assumptions, stories—legends that dissolved into myths—but no one would ever know the truth.

"What happened here . . ." Viridian mumbled. His voice shattered the uneasiness that had clouded each of our minds.

I shook my head. "Humanity rebelled against itself."

"Poetic, Eve." My eyes rolled at his ridicule.

We were out of the town quicker than we had come, and my father pulled onto a freeway aimed in the direction of Germany. Sitka smiled beside me. And as I watched the road ahead, anticipating the future days to dawn, I began to feel my mind grow dry, my emotions fading into the moon above. So my eyes closed in hopes of rest. In a desperate desire to gaze upon darkness.

Instead, I saw images of fire. Images of water that couldn't quench the flames. My eyes shot back open. And for a moment, I feared I would never truly rest again.

Hėlii Cordell

"This establishment shall have the ability to be fully self-sufficient, though trade should still be orchestrated with other countries in order to remain at peace. Such countries include Italy, France, Germany, Spain, Belgium, and more under NATO. All trade correspondence shall be done by those with additional education from out of country universities, and in operation of supply sources, and, later on, transferred over to artificial intelligence beings, once their existence is made helpful and prominent. Those in charge of supply sources are responsible for the transfer of power to these beings once the time has come."

Cordellia Bill of Rights, Article X. Signed, February 21st, 2026, Apgar Cordell

I sat awake. Sat with my eyes fixed out the window and upon the moon for a time longer than I could count. Not a thought struck my mind, but rather an ever-growing sensation of dread that sat encapsulated into a single dark object in my skull. And even more so, an impending reality of what I had done, of the life I had abandoned, of that deep, demented feeling that I couldn't seem to escape.

That I was destined to die.

I shook it off.

For the first time since we started out, the car jerked. My gaze shifted to the front window, my attention stolen by a large wall a few meters ahead, formed from twisted, black wire as hands held in unity out of fears of being destroyed. It reached desperately towards a bleak sky in hopes of mirroring its darkness. Yet, every few seconds a flash of light would appear from inside the wires, electricity pulsing through as Christmas lights during Halloween. The tainted twinkling showed down upon the artificial intelligence beings standing below, their figures as statues, strangely still against the blaze. It was a mystery to me, why such a place had electricity.

My father slowed up as he approached the wall. His eyes were on Sitka in the rearview mirror.

"What do I do?" Sitka watched him too. Watched as his gaze shifted to a panic, concealed lightly by the shadow of the night. Soon, an answer was given.

"Let me drive."

"What?"

"I know what to say to get us through." My father stared. I watched wheels turn in his brain. Watched them process the request as some kind of cryptic message. The moments of consideration then ceased as he began to shift his position, climbing over the middle console and retrieving the place of Sitka beside me. He stared intently at my brother, who eagerly gripped the wheel. The car rocked forward.

"What are you going to say?" my mother asked.

"Just trust me." A pause. "And don't act suspicious."

We pulled in front of the first AI. Its feet moved forward with a careful precision, its movements like that of silk, its iron fingers twitching as snakes upon a rock. Its build was perfectly proportional, as though a true human rather than something so clearly artificial. Its limbs were duel toned, crafted from paneling of dense crimson and stone-shaded metal. Its eyes were like olive pits, dark and demanding, lifeless and void.

The one that stood beside our vehicle took the appearance of a woman in its mid-thirties, the plates of metal upon its head giving the illusion of red hair with strips of gray. It stared into our car, its eyes as sable lasers, scanning each one of us. Sitka's window dissolved with the touch of a button. The AI being smiled through its copper teeth.

"*Héla swor, guhurt xu jé?*" it said in Cordellian. *Hello, how are you?* The words felt robotic, yet somehow still alive.

"*Guhurt, mhert,*" Sitka replied.

"*Yelii xu, pûrt?*" It asked. *How may I assist you?*

"We are authorized personnel headed to Germany for a business transaction." My brother removed his phone from his pocket, revealing a screen to the AI. Its cybernetic eyes narrowed down upon the white glow, zooming in and out in a disjointed manner. Then, it pulled away.

"Under what jurisdiction?" *Jurisdiction.* It took me a long moment to process what that word meant.

Especially in the context of a country void of government.

I felt my cheeks go warm in an instant. Rivers began to drip from my palms down upon my jeans. Thoughts I couldn't quite place hopped in circles around my brain. My gaze zoned out and in and back out again, and I was soon searching to find the face of Sitka. And then, he was there. His hands rested so solemnly upon his legs, his curls idle across his skull. He sat with such ease in the throws of confounding phrases. I caught his eye in the rearview mirror. Recognized an expression of understanding inscribed across the lines on his cheeks. And then, a smirk.

"*Hélii Cordell.*" The world seemed to freeze at Sitka's words. An uneasy stillness stretched into the vehicle, wavering and yet somehow still stagnant. I felt my fingers fall to fists. I watched my mother's do the same. And with a final moment of tension, a nod struck the neck of the AI, its body removing itself from beside our vehicle.

The gate into Germany dissolved before us.

We passed under the wall. I watched it overhead. The shocks of electricity ceased, pure darkness stretched in its place. My eyes narrowed and stared even more closely as we met the other side, unharmed. Astounded. Terrified. Maybe there was a word for both.

Sitka stopped on the side of the road. He stepped out of the car, my father taking his place. The wall reappeared behind us, and Sitka reappeared beside me. My father merged onto an empty highway in the direction of Verborgen. My gaze wouldn't turn from Sitka, and his wouldn't meet mine. But I watched as he sat with such tension. With his hands cupped together in his lap. With his eyes ablaze and shoulders reaching towards his hair that toppled upon his face. On his cheeks rested the smallest of smiles.

Silence stretched only seconds more before I spoke.

"Sitka, what did you say to her?"

He didn't bother to look over at me. "You know what I said."

"But why did it work?" His eyes stayed fixed before him. Moments passed before he spoke.

"It's a glitch in their programming," he soon said. "But only at this part of the border, which is why we needed to leave this way."

". . . right." I looked upon him longer. Watched the smugness in his smile and then watched as it fell back into its normal relaxed placement.

My mother began to speak. Only then did my eyes falter to something outside my window.

I was tuning out her words at the sight of it all. As I took a glimpse into this small town. Each building was carved and shaped separately from the one before. The red and cream brick rolled up and down the cobblestone block, dancing to the shifting candlelight around and amid. I spotted a woman inside a building, her body rocking back and forth to a muffled rhythm. A man shouted something in an unknown tongue. Someone was stopped in the center of the sidewalk, simply tying their shoe lace. In the abundance of trees, parts of branches remained green. A few cars hovered down the rounding roads and past bustling restaurants, the echoes of Laughter meeting my ear.

Laughter, my once good friend, now merely a memory. A face I thought I wouldn't again see. But now you have stared upon me, your gaze as strong, as peaceful, and as stunning as a symphony. Perhaps you hadn't yet forgotten about me.

Viridian stirred behind me. "Where are we?"

I felt a grin begin to sneak up the side of my cheeks. The words that rolled off my lips had been a medicine to my mind.

"Germany."

[10]

European Curency

I wondered how Germans seemed to remain in satisfaction rather than distress. How they weren't held hostage to their homes, mourning what they knew was soon to come. I wondered about the way they seemed to overlook the heat, to live in laughter amid such a thing. Maybe it was as simple as they learned to linger in the appreciation of the hazy weeks they had left. Or perhaps they chose to ignore the inevitability of death in hopes of continuing life before it struck.

But more than anything, I wondered why those of my country had been unable to operate in the same manner. Why insanity had stolen the best of us.

At first, I thought the buzzing was merely my mind's interpretation of the scene around me. Of the lights burning so bright. Of the world spinning faster than I knew it still could, in the presence of joy rather than disaster. Perhaps it was the feeling of my head spinning, speeding desireof it all. That was all it had to be.

That was until everything clicked into place. Until my nerve endings came to realize that the feeling was from outside of my body, not nearly a fabrication of my mind. It took me looking away from the window to identify the origin; my phone, sitting still in my back pocket.

I hadn't received a text message in months. Not since the chaos erupted.

Sitka had used his science terms to explain it to me. That the sun's increased radiation had thrown off the majority of transmissions, leaving smaller devices nonfunctional. And even larger devices were only capable of receiving shorter range transmissons.

There was no reason I should have received a text. Not at that point.

I reached down towards the back pocket of my jeans, the small device of clear glass glowing at the sight of my face. There upon my lock screen, a single message sat still:

> ➤ From "Unknown," 24:16
>
> "It won't be safe where you're going."

I read it once. Twice.

Then, my heart stopped.

No one knows we left. But it seemed as though someone did. *They can't. There's no way.*

The note.

So then it was Darbii. Simply one of her pranks. A wicked, downright dishonorable prank. One that she would laugh at, and I would stare upon in terror, and we would both get in trouble for.

But she wouldn't do that to me. Not in this way, after months void of communication. It was unlike her.

So then it was my brothers. One of them. It had to be. Either the one dozing off once more behind me or the other beside me, staring intently again at his phone screen. There was no one else who would pull such a prank. But even them, in all of their cleverness, wouldn't do such a thing to harm me in the midst of our shared anxieties.

So what if it's not a prank?

It had to be.

My father found a hotel along a quieter street where the voices had calmed, and candlelight had lowered to a light creme rather than a piercing white. People lingered around houses and sat upon benches. Men with smiles too big and women with brown-toned bottles in their boney hands, laughing a tone too loud. I wondered how they could stand to so willingly dwell among the heat. For even as we left the car and strayed into the shadows, I could feel the residue of the sun piercing every known area of my body. My lungs lifted and dropped with the weight of chains. My hands melted into my side. Soon we were beneath a large brick building, a sign plastered upon it reading, "*Komfortgasthaus Vos Verborgen.*"

Three figures sat at the door, all dressed in black.

Their mouths were covered by bandanas, their stares so cold that they pierced the heat of the evening. A girl sat on the bottom step, her long blonde hair thrown recklessly over her shoulders. Another girl sat behind her, her black hair crumpled into a long, messy braid, her head pressed back against the cobblestone wall, forcing it to crumble. A man sat behind them, his build as that of a wall, his hazel hair cut short upon his skull, and black eyes as the soul of a ravenous beast.

I swallowed. Sweat seeped into my palms, and as I looked down to my legs to wipe them, I couldn't help but notice how my own dark outfit mirrored theirs.

My father approached them.

"*Excusez-nous.*" They looked up. Each eye stared at my father with gazes as bare as a stone carving. He stared back. "*On doit passer à travers.*" The French language met my ear with such ease. For once, I became so incredibly aware of the necessity of knowing the prominent tongue of all of Europe. Thankful that I did.

The blonde girl on the first step looked behind her at the black-haired girl. Their gazes had met. Smiles had risen.

"*Die Franzosen.*" She said. The other grinned.

The blonde girl's chin raised ever so slightly towards my father. "*Das Hotel?*"

"The hotel, yes. We need to get through."

"Why?" He looked startled.

His head tilted ever so softly to the side. "Excuse me?"

"Who gave you permission to be here?"

"...I—"

"Was it one of us? Because I don't believe I recall doing so." His mouth sat slightly open as though the right words would land upon his tongue. Then, it closed. They all grinned.

"Are you the owners?" My mother placed her hands in her pockets as though to grow in confidence or rather stature.

The black-haired girl grinned. "We are now."

My mother stared at them. Nodded slowly. "Well, um . . . if you know of any other hotels in town that we could go to for the night, I—"

"You're wanting a place to stay for the night?" It was the blonde girl again. She had pulled down her bandana at that point so that it rested lightly upon her neck. I noticed the softness of her face, the shallowness of her lips, the roundness of her chin. The structure of her jaw looked the slightest bit like Darbii. She would have been beautiful if not anchored by pride.

My mother sat with her mouth slightly open. Swallowed.

"Yes, but we can go somewhere else, it isn't a problem." The girl looked back at her partners in crime.

The black-haired girl smiled. Raised an eyebrow. "Die Franzosen." They snickered again.

"What do you think, friends, should we let the French invade us for a change?" The blonde girl spoke louder than necessary, warranting Viridian's reply.

"Funny thing is, we're Cordellian."

She grinned. "*Ah, die Cordellianer. Ist das schlimmer?*"

"*Vielleicht.*" The man spoke for the first time.

"*Wahrscheinlich.*" The black-haired girl gave her own reply. The blonde girl's head was turning back towards us. A demented smile slid up the side of her cheek.

"Where's your payment, Cordellians?" Silence spread. The black-haired girl touched an object on her hip. It reminded me of what rested on my own. My fingers began to slide back and forth between each other. My mother stepped slightly backward. My father's statue went tense.

"I'm sorry, um . . ." He swallowed. "Payment?"

"You know, money—" A thump echoed upon the pavement. My eyes flew to Sitka tossing a bundle of orange dollar bills onto the floor in front of the blonde girl.

European currency.

He stepped backward immediately, returning to his typical slouched stance. Every eye stared at him for just a moment. Just until she picked up the stack, getting one last good glimpse of my brother, beginning to count up the amount.

I had only ever seen European currency used by my grandparents in France. Never by anyone of Cordellia.

And most certainly never in the form of paper.

The blonde girl finished counting and looked back up at us with a grin. "Enjoy your stay, Cordellians." They all stood and moved to the sides of the door. My father said something in reply, and then we were stepping through the large wooden door, and my eyes could not stray away from my shaking hands.

European currency.

How did he . . .

"If anyone asks," my father began to say once the door had closed behind us. He stopped to look at Viridian. "We are from France." A pause. A pause that was just a beat too long. "Because I don't know what the consequences are if the wrong person discovers otherwise."

Sitka's Secrets

There was an AI being standing in the entryway. I hadn't noticed it until we were turning down the hall. It was behind the counter once used for reservations, standing so still it seemed as though it no longer was of function. It took the form of a man in its mid-fifties. Its body was plated in black lines, its arms stiff at its side, its proportions seemingly faulty. And in its dark eyes had the softest blue glow. My breath had caught in my throat.

The entryway was pitch black, aside from a small candle on the floor in the corner, close to being burnt out. The hall had smelt of mildew and nearly of rot. As though the art of living had died inside its walls, and the residue was left for us to suffer through.

I sought a glimpse into my parents' conversation as we walked down the hall. They spoke so softly that the tight walls of the area couldn't even taste the tone of their words. Yet, a few lines, I was able to gather, just before we stopped in front of a metal door.

"Are we safe here?" My mother's voice wavered.

"It's just for the night."

"Anything could happen in a night."

My father took a long pause, "We'll lock the door."

The room we chose was separated into two areas. In one rested two large beds covered by white satin sheets, wrinkled along the seams. A chiffonier was cradled against the far wall beneath a window, the curtains waving lightly in the pull of some unidentifiable draft. The ground was coated in concrete, creeping towards the second room. A single bed rested in the center beside a mini kitchen and a wooden door leading to a restroom.

It had been a matter of minutes before everyone was in bed. Viridian and Sitka shared a mattress in the first room, and I rested alone in the one beside them, my eyes fixed on the ceiling. Thoughts madly circled my mind. The message I had received earlier found me in fear once more. The words stained red a white tapestry; "It won't be safe where you're going."

I looked at the bed beside me. Viridian slept quietly. Sitka rested juxtaposed to me, his eyes open wide, his breaths short and staggered and scattered against the popcorn ceiling. It unsettled me then, that my oblivion to his long-hidden secrets had become clearer the further we retreated from Paris.

Curiosity entangled itself around my tongue. A small mumble soon escaped it.

"How were you able to get us across the border? *Really.*" My eyes were on the ceiling again. I was listening for Sitka's response. A long moment passed before it came.

"I told you. It was a glitch in the AI programming."

"How did you know about the glitch?"

"Research." I shook my head lightly. Thoughts burned as embers blossomed into flames.

"And how did you even get the money?" I spoke with more intonation that time.

"That's irrelevant."

"No it isn't, Sitka. You know it isn't." To that, he didn't respond. I turned my head around on my pillow again towards him, resting my hands on my stomach and breathing through my fingertips. His eyes were closed, the wheels in his brain powering down.

I felt fire burn my cheeks. "I wish you would stop lying to me." A beat of silence.

His eyes slowly wiggled open. "I'm not lying to you."

"You're obviously keeping secrets."

"That's not the same thing as lying."

"Well it's pretty similar!" I didn't know how else to say it. I could have spoken in metaphors and he would have known what I was asking. But metaphorical questions only resulted in theoretical answers, and right then, all I sought was the truth, plain and simple.

"Corbyn gave it to me. The money." Centuries passed before he said it.

"Corbyn?" I mumbled, more to myself than to him. "He's fifteen. How did . . ." Sitka stayed silent. *Corbyn Azul. Sitka's best friend. It's nonsense.* "Where did he get it?" Silence. "Where did he get it, Sitka?"

"His perû, okay?"

"Why couldn't you just say that?"

"Because I'm done answering questions." I watched him turn towards Viridian in my peripheral vision as if cutting the thread that kept the hem of our conversation together.

"Sitka what—"

"No, I'm done talking, Eve. I'm going to sleep." His words were abrupt but direct. "You should do the same." I stared at him as he wrestled in the sheets, pulling them over his shoulder and up to his ear, only the top of his black coils sticking up from the rest of his body. And I felt the weight of his words, for a moment. I felt it rest into my chest but more so, I felt the weight of what was left unspoken. For that could have the ability to crush me, and I would have no idea.

[12]

Herr Krüger

"This establishment shall be involved in the growth of scientific advancements under the categories of medical, artificial intelligence, and more, and shall engage in the exchanging of ideas with outside sources. Additional schooling outside of the country must be acquired to engage in these research oriented jobs. All research and experimentation must be done under CordellReasearchCo. The advancement of weapons for warfare shall not be explored in the case of eradicating peace."

Cordellia Bill of Rights, Article VII. Signed, February 21st, 2026, Apgar Cordell

I had a dream that night. An AI being stood in the shadows, its blue eyes glowing in the darkness of night. A single light shone down upon an object in its hand: a gun. A gun pointed at me.

My mind was awake before the sun the next morning. I was unaware at that time, but many of my coming days would be spent in that similar fashion. Of rest always presenting itself as an object of terror. Of my thoughts consuming my every waking hour, of my emotions filling in the gaps they left. For that is all my life is to me now in Neo–Italy, as I scribble these words down upon paper.

But I wasn't at that point just yet. For in that moment, not a thought crossed my mind. I only looked upon the sun outside my window as it rose and I seemed to feel so closely the pain of its presence.

I changed into a pair of brown patched jeans that rested just above my waist. They were overlapped by a white T-shirt, matching the style of the black one from the day before. I stared upon the holster I had placed in my duffle bag the night before, upon the gun beside it. And for a moment, I considered leaving it behind. But I recalled those dressed in black and I feared their intentions with such a thing in their possession.

It was a four-hour drive from Verborgen to Munich. My mother insisted on driving that stretch of the journey. No one argued.

I tried to look upon the land, and yet I feared to. For this world could never be what I had always dreamed to see it as. It seemed ignorance was truly my bliss.

But I caught sight of it all in a certain land of which's name I did not know. In a town less like Verborgen, for feeble laughter did not reverberate off the yellow brick walls but rather that all consuming sound of silence. The residue of flames forged patterns into the terrain. Lampshades lay in the streets. Blood dyed the grass red. Blackened vehicles, charred teddy bears, and the faint smell of smoke.

I almost believed I could see the source of the destruction as I stared upon a home on a street corner. The front window had been smashed, shards of glass scattered across cracked pavement. In my mind, I had seen an image of humanity turning on itself. Mothers on daughters, fathers on sons, brothers on sisters. Even for a moment, I truly believed I could see a woman sitting on the pavement, her legs pulled in towards her chest. Her white locks were tossed across her face, moisture pasted like paint across her cheeks. I thought I could see a man standing over her. They shared the same alabaster skin, the same rises and falls of their forehead. And soon, objects were being ejected from his palms, colliding into the scarred skin of the woman. Cries escaped her lips.

Was humanity doomed?

It couldn't be.

I don't believe I retain the same opinion now, while writing this. Not after I have seen all that we can do to each other.

I didn't look out the window anymore after that. Not until we made it to Munich. It had been unlike any other town I had seen. Its buildings were larger, vaster, decorated with heritage yet plated by the future. Amber brick arches brimming with metal features looming over silenced citizens below. It felt more alive as Verborgen had been, but not because death's inevitability had been ignored, but because it had been accepted.

I saw such a reality in the faces of strangers. Crowds were present but no one was together. Each eye was covered in the presence of unavoidable loneliness. That deep blue tint around the pupils had become simply lakes that no one would travel to see. Men dressed in clothing that retained their dignity while their crooked posture retained their mourning. I watched a stray dog run down the road, barking, whining, crying. No one seemed to see it. The weight of such hollowness fell upon me. For there was nothing I could do to comfort such a world.

My mother drove us down a busy street into the main square. Sitka directed her down a road just east to where Herr Krüger was planted—the forger he knew of. He had spoken to her with such unfathomable confidence as though he had been to that very place before. The crowds became scarce in those parts, the abundance drowned beneath the looming shadows of the buildings. Sitka stopped us beside one. A place with a creme brick cutout and a golden-rimmed roof falling towards a sign with the number 22598 printed across it.

The door below the number was propped open. I couldn't help but notice Sitka's smile at its sight, and soon my gaze quickly found my mother. She was staring at the opening with her eyes narrowed in the way of suspicion.

"This feels too easy." She mumbled. Her eyes met my younger brother. "You've been here before?"

Sitka nodded. "Yes."

"Why?"

"Because . . . my field trip."

"That isn't a good enough explanation, Sitka." My brother didn't reply and my mother continued to stare. "You met this man?"

"Yes."

"Does he remember you?"

"I don't know." He swallowed. "And I won't know until we go down there."

My father kept the keys clutched tightly in his palm as we followed Sitka into the shadows of the overhang. Then we were stumbling down flights of stairs, and soon an archway was before us, paved with thick steel and ivory cracked stone accents.

He didn't look up when we stepped into his workshop. The walls were plastered with metal, the floor constructed of cracked concrete, scattered with tools and built up with mounds of junk. A drab brown coat was thrown across the floor in the corner, and I saw movement beside it, perhaps a mouse. A clock ticked in the center of the wall. The sound echoed through the space. Krüger sat hunched at a high table in the center of the room, a dangling chandelier lit with a single candle hanging above him. It illuminated his wrinkled hands, pressing metals together deliberately, dangerously.

"*Bonjour*? Herr Krüger?" He remained stationary at the sound of my mother's exclamation. I stared at his hunched stance, at his spotted gray hair, tossed like a rag across his head, meeting the rim of his back. He hadn't looked up when he replied.

"No one uses that name unless they want something from me." His vowels were harsh. His tone pierced the pensive air as a cutting wind.

"My name is Yemasii Elko, and we're requesting your help."

"We?" At that, his head was lifting. Turning. His gaze had been riddled with pique, his blue eyes sunken like drops of rain into his sandpaper skin. And soon, his gaze was dashing between each of us, his eyebrows sunken low into his face as his jaw lowered. "By gosh, there's a whole damn family in here! How the hell did you get in?"

"Just . . . through the doors . . ."

"They were unlocked again? Those bastards . . ." His eyes were on a spot just below the ceiling, as if to pin away a fit of rage that fought to approach. Soon, his gaze began to shift, to fall, to tumble down a mountain and stop at the base, right where my younger brother stood.

An eyebrow raised. "I've seen you before." Sitka's gaze grew ever so slightly. "I never forget a face."

Sitka swallowed. "Yes, sir." Krüger's tongue twisted in knots inside his mouth, the levels of his face growing and shaking and obliterating in a moment but still not shifting to a smile.

He spoke pensively. "What do you want from me?"

"Herr, we need your help." His gaze remained on Sitka as my mother spoke. "My son said you would be able to forge us documents into Israel."

"Ah, you're wanting to save yourselves, aren't you." He took one last look at my brother before he began to grin. Then he stood, slapping the wood of the table beside him and inching his way towards us, his teeth yellowed and bottom lip twitching beneath his breath. His approach slowed at the sight of my mother and Viridian, his gaze stopping upon their blonde hair.

His grin dropped. "Are you bastards from Cordellia?"

"France."

"Yeah you definitely look French . . ." His head lifted and lowered in an intricate repetition. A chuckle pushed off of his lips. His tongue had been twisting tightly inside his mouth again as my heart rattled in my chest. A pause. Something about his tone shifted. "I *can* help you. But I need to be paid."

"I have money." Sitka's duffel bag was on his desk in an instant, his hand buried beneath its black interior, his gaze shuffling around faster than his fingers. Krüger had appeared beside him, watching his uneasy eyes instead of his hands.

"You knew the Dirksens, didn't you?" His face was close to my brother's. Too close. Sitka's shuffling slowed.

"No sir," His voice cracked on the second word. He removed his hands from his bag, placing down three stacks of orange-colored bills. A threatening silence sat between the two of them.

"Hm." Krüger picked up the first stack, removing the rubber band and placing it between his teeth, beginning to shuffle through the money. He mumbled something under his breath. I couldn't hear what.

"You're um . . . you're a forger, yes?" My mother's right hand itched her opposite elbow as she spoke.

Krüger didn't look up. "Uh huh."

"You're from Germany?"

That time, he did. "What does it look like?"

"I'm sorry. I just—"

"You want to make sure I'm safe?" The air went sour. The room grew silent. He set the money down and leaned forward against his work space. "I've been doing this work for thirty years. I know the ins and outs of law, social security, all that bureaucratic nonsense. You're safer doing this with me than a government official whose boss trained them how to do these things two weeks ago." His hands reached back down towards the money. "Now. As for payment, this should be enough for chips for you all, assuming I still have five left." He grinned. "Because you are not the first people to ask this of me, believe it or not."

There was silence for a moment. My mother squinted. "Chip?"

"Yeah, you know, arm implant?" He chuckled.

"Oh no no, we're just wanting documents. Not . . . a chip." Krüger stared. Stared at my mother. Stared at the tension beginning to boil over across her cheeks. And soon, he began to smile. To grin. Then laughter erupted from within him, and my face was growing warm.

"Don't tell me that you really thought Israel was still using paper identification." His eyes were narrowing now. "Those bastards are too advanced for that sort of peasant shit. They put chips in their citizens' arms to identify them."

My heart stopped.

[13]

NOW.

"I am *not* letting some random man put a chip in my arm."

"There isn't a choice, Viridian." I stared at him as I spoke. His green gaze had been pressed with such pure annoyance. The shadow of Krüger's building loomed over us, the golden-rimmed roof blinding my vision as I tried to find sense in his maddened glare. His eyes stayed strayed from mine when his head shook.

"I don't know what the hell is in that thing, Eve. It could be . . . I don't know, *poisoned* . . . or something."

I stared at him. My lips rolled in on each other, and soon, I sighed. "Okay. Fine. I'll give it to you. The whole thing is . . ." I rolled my eyes reluctantly. "It's weird. But—"

"But? You have a but? Did you even hear what you just said?" I didn't say anything. "This man didn't want us here from the start. Why the hell is he helping us now?"

"We're giving him money?" I tried to smile.

"Well he could very easily kill us and take the rest of our money. No one would ever know!" I stared. Squinted. Blinked.

"Are you being serious right now?"

"Yes, I'm being serious."

"Viridian, that's psychotic."

"Yeah? Well that's kinda what this world has come to and whether you want to believe it or not, Germany is no exception." My eyes were glued to him, trying to dissect the words he'd thrown before me as though there had been more to read between the lines. But I knew there was not.

"You know what?" I finally said. My arms crossed tightly across my chest. "I don't want to do it either. The thought of it makes me sick. But we will *die* on this planet if we do not have that chip." I shook my head for a moment. "I'm not willing to fear something that could be harmless, especially if it's the only shot I have at staying alive." For once, I feared the very words that escaped my mouth. I feared my plagued ability to forfeit comfort in the name of survival, my morality. Perhaps that had been the very reason that Viridian feared the chip. Not only what it would do to him physically but what it would do to his consciousness. Perhaps there was something wrong with our actions far beyond what we could understand.

Then, the thought ceased.

"And what if it doesn't make a difference?" I hardly could hear the words that had slipped off of his lips. My eyes found him in an instant. His green gaze was set so solemnly upon me that for a moment, I hardly believed that gaze belonged to him. I watched him tuck his arms into eachother across his chest in the way of discomfort. My face felt pale.

Then, I took a breath. "Do you really believe that?" He hesitated for a second too long to deliver me any true form of comfort.

"No." His words were meek. "I don't . . . at least I hope I don't."

"We have to make this sacrifice, V. We have to choose to trust him," I said the words more for my sake, out of remembrance of what I had said to my father only the day before. When I had told him that people deserved to be trusted. An idea I still seemed to stand by.

"I know." Viridian finally said. A breath limped off of his lips and he was turning back down the stairs to Herr Krüger's basement.

The chips were stored in a three-lock safe beneath a portion of the concrete flooring. I watched Krüger remove the case from its hiding place, noticing the lack of dust across the top of it.

He had made sure the doors were locked before retrieving the case. It was then that I deeply became aware of the illegality of our actions. Those to which we had all consented. Again, I feared my morality was fumbling from my fingers.

Looking back on it now, as I write this all, that might have been the moment in which it first had.

My mother clinged by my fathers side as it all began. I watched him whisper things into her ear as though to resolve the conflict that had clearly come to be in her mind. I'm not sure his words did much of anything, for the intensity of her stance did not falter.

The chips were the size of a grain of rice, rectangular and crafted from a dark metal, wrapped in blinking red and blue wires. I felt as though they had eyes, watching me, smiling upon me. Their grins were juxtaposed with deception.

I tried to trust them anyway.

My father volunteered to go first. Krüger shuffled to a computer on the far side of the room. He asked my father a few questions that I couldn't seem to hear through my heavy breaths. He handed him a paper. Slipped the first chip into a large syringe.

Everything moved too quickly.

My mother watched the procedure with even more anxiety than me. Her hands were clamped around each other in front of her torso. Her jaw was tight, her eyes barren from emotion.

I barely saw the syringe as it entered my father's skin.

Sitka was next. I didn't watch.

"Do you have a name preference?" Krüger was staring at me then. I watched him through the blurriness of my eyes. Through the dizziness of my mind.

"Excuse me?"

"Have you not been paying attention?" He watched me. Chills reverberated through my bones. "Fine, I'll pick one for you." And soon, his fingers were flying across a keyboard, and I was shaking as though the earth was erupting and I was falling into it. Perhaps it was.

He looked at me. "Birthday?"

"June 25th."

"Year?"

"2128." Something printed beside him.

"Your name is now Sarai Elkolai," He slid a paper across his desk in the center of the room. Lines of writing were printed like a label across its faded white background. "Make sure to memorize that information."

He approached me moments later. The chip had already been in the syringe. I seemed to have forgotten how to stand still. Then the plastic was against my skin, and it was cold, yet it burned.

"Does it hurt?" My throat was dry when I spoke. Herr Krüger answered only with a pause and a grin. And without any warning, he was pressing the back of the syringe towards me. A sharp, piercing pain shot through my shoulder in an instant.

He moved away from me.

It was finished quicker than it had begun.

The cold plastic left a circle on my arm, a red liquid wandering down towards my elbow. Herr Krüger reaches for a wipe, removing the dripping blood from my shoulder and placing a bandage made of a light steel over it. It immediately began to remove the pain.

I felt a buzz in my pocket.

Krüger moved onto my mother as I reached for my phone:

➤ From "Unknown," 13:30

"You need to leave Munich."

I was frozen in time.

"The bandage is made of nanoparticles that are designed to take the pain and quickly heal the wound, probably in the next week." My eyes were unable to find Krüger. "Don't be surprised if your arm is sore for a while though."

"Yes, we use this technology a lot where I work." Relief resounded in my mother's tone.

"Are you a doctor?"

"I am."

I watched him approach her. Watched the syringe meet her arm in the same manner that it met mine. Watched her stand still as I shook. Her eyes squeezed together and quickly unfolded as it entered. I couldn't help but look away.

My phone buzzed again.

➤ From "Unknown," 13:31

"Quickly."

My face flushed. I looked up at my family, their stares all focused on Herr Krüger. My bones rattled beneath my skin.

"I worked in the medical field for a little while," I hardly heard Krüger offer up information about himself. "Until. . ."

"Until the chaos?" My mother piped in. I was shaking . . .

He shook his head. "No, no no. Much before that." A pause. My ears were muffled. "Those damn socialists. Tried to make me do research on what they wanted me to. Stupid stuff too. I got bored."

My mother hid her discomfort well with her smile. "Yes, that's a bit like where I work. You have to be a part of the main organization or your research is deemed invalid." Krüger was at Viridian's arm now. His gaze slowly lifted at my mother's remark. My eyes were too blurred to see exactly where they focused.

"Oh yeah? Strange. That's more of a Cordellian way of thinking. France is fairly capitalistic."

➤ From "Unknown," 13:33

"NOW."

It took too long for everything to finally click into place in my mind. But then it did.

We needed to leave. Now.

"Guys . . ." I began. The syringe shot through Viridian's arm.

A crash erupted from above ground.

Muffled screams followed.

I turned and sprinted up the staircase. My eyes were blurred. My mind was messy. I approached the sun above me and the black hole beside it and the two were blending together before my eyes. My legs were dragging me towards the muffled screams evening out into a crisp slap through my ear drums. Dragging me towards the main square in search of the cause of the commotion. My eyes found a helicopter. It was crashed, encircled by dancing flames.

Oh no.

Oh my gosh.

I stumbled backward. Humanity pushed me forward. Flames erupted and spattered and reflected across blackened metal plating. My mind sought to wander from the destruction, but my eyes scurried away from its will. And then, I was searching for signs of human life amid this mess, but none could be found; it had to have been flown by AI. Perhaps a system malfunction. Affected by radiation and flawed human minds. That was all. But the closer I looked, the more I recognized the helicopter's familiarity.

I shifted my stance. Stared at the side door, dented almost to a 90-degree angle. Flames broke through it, dancing to a silent song. And then I saw it. For a moment, I didn't believe it. But it had been real, right before me. A large, white star in the center of the door.

It was a Cordellian helicopter.

[14]

The Building Of Lies

I looked away from the scene—the image of what I had seen flashed before my eyes. I closed them—the screams still echoed. I folded my hands together—the fire erupted in my palms.

And the worst part was, I knew why this had happened, why they were here.

At least, I thought I did.

It would seem like that would be enough for me to turn away from this foolish dream of salvation. But it wasn't. Instead, I was so ridden with distress that my mind couldn't even look that far into the future.

Instead, I stumbled into the shadows. Shied away from where my family had crowded into the commotion, staring at the helicopter right along with me. My gaze ran from the sun to the cobblestone beneath me, and my hands were burning beside me, reaching backward into a building. My skull pressed against the burning stone wall, my eyes closed, my head filling with a pounding ache. Its beat had been staggered. It danced from one side of my mind to another, a child with feet pounding into the ground without caution, without cause. Enchanted by movements that seemed innocent, yet haunted with a grin projecting otherwise.

I needed to escape this pain, these emotions, this fear. I had to find my hope again, my peace. It was right there . . .

"You look distressed." My eyes opened to my mother. Her arms rested at her side, her green gaze small with perplexity. I stole a breath, resting my head back against the wall behind me.

"Of course I'm distressed. I just watched a helicopter burn up."

"There was no one inside. It was controlled by AI." She hesitated. "I'm sorry, I thought you knew that."

"I do."

"And as far as I'm aware, no one on the ground was harmed."

"I know that." I swallowed flames that fought to burn my throat.

My mother was then reaching for me. She wrapped her arms around me, holding me close. I tried to let it push the child out of my mind. My eyes shut.

"I love you, you know that right?" I nodded. My chin was pressing into her shoulder.

"Yes." Fear continued to conquer me. And in a single moment, the thought struck me. Slicing the remaining breath out of my lungs. My eyes shot open, and I was staring at a disjointed marketplace across the road. As I stared into the waning gazes of mankind, I realized again that we were all destined to die.

I was destined to die.

No.

"The helicopter was Cordellian," I said it out of impulse. So, so quietly I almost wondered if she had heard me. Then, she pulled away.

"I saw. I wasn't going to say anything."

I fumbled through a single breath. "So then . . . you've thought it too."

"Thought what?" I hadn't fully admitted it to myself. I didn't want to. I feared it would make me selfish or scattered so strongly that it would cause me to stumble.

"What if . . ." I tried to force the words off my lips. "What if we're being hunted?" She froze. Ice consumed her stance, sending her skin white. She stared me deep in the eyes for a moment as though reading blurred letters inside my pupils. Her bottom lip shook slightly.

"What? Eve, why would you say that?"

"We left Cordellia after being told not to leave, and now a Cordellian helicopter appears in Germany of all places, right in the town we're in. Merû, what if someone is tracking us?"

"How would they be doing that?" She rushed her words.

"I don't know. But—" My head attempted to shake the words out. "Things are . . . very clearly being kept from us. I mean . . . Sitka, for example."

"What about him?" I stared at her for a moment. She couldn't be serious.

"He's hiding things, Merû. The money, passing over the border. The questions that Krüger was asking him. Do you not see it?" Her eyes were on the pavement. I tried to watch the wheels turn in her brain.

"I do." She said, "But it's not worth doing anything about right now. Whatever his secrets are, they're keeping us alive."

My jaw dropped. "You have to be joking."

"I'm not."

"What if it has something to do with us being followed? Wouldn't you want to know?"

"I know your brother. If he thought it was something we needed to know, he would tell us." She took a step away from me. My mind couldn't seem to wrap itself around her words. And then her gaze was back on the helicopter. I watched it graze the rim of the dimming flames. People were gathered around it now, throwing water upon its roots.

"Don't say anything to your brothers. Please?" She was looking back at me again. My gaze shot over to her. Breath withheld itself from me for a moment.

My eyes soon widened. "Are you going to tell Perû?"

"I don't know."

"You have to tell him. You can't just keep secrets—"

"Your father, Eve, is a very strong man," she said. Her gaze remained astray from me. "But he also carries things heavily. If I choose to tell him, I'm choosing to cause him severe distress multitudes stronger than what he is already facing."

Though I understood her caution, she still failed to see what she was giving me. Handing me willingly as though it had been an early birthday gift that I would open and celebrate with passion. Because I knew her well enough to know that if she recognized it, she would take it back in an instant:

Lies.

Lies for me to keep. Lies for me to build on top of the ones I had already created myself. My hand found my phone in my back right pocket, flooded with messages from an unknown number. My other found the gun on my left hip. Two things I was hiding from her.

Lies.

Two things I desperately desired to disclose to her. Two things that seemed to be driving me mad. I had once told my mother everything, but now it seemed as though I was doing to her just as Sitka had done to me.

Except I knew that Sitka was keeping secrets, and she had no idea that I was.

We said goodbye to Herr Krüger before we left. He seemed glad to see us go. My mother told him we were off to Salzburg next, perhaps to have the comfort of believing someone else was looking out for us.

I sat in the far back row of the car that time. The seats were more worn there, cracked and chipped beneath the force of the sun. I gazed out across the city around me, resting for just a moment in a perplexity, in a consuming comprehension of the life I was so recklessly leaving behind. It may have been the first moment I truly realized this, that all I have ever known of this world would soon be gone. The first moment my heart ached for it all.

Sitka sat in front of me. He stared at his phone as he always did. My mother leaned back to look at him as my father started up the car.

"Whatcha looking at?" Sitka's eyes jumped at her. His breathing seemed to pause for a second too long.

"Just seeing if any games still work."

We were on the road. Munich drowned into pillars of untold stories behind me.

I used to wonder sometimes what it would be like to say goodbye to a friend for the last time—without knowing it to be the finale of it all. Would a part of you understand? Would your body feel something, perhaps an anxious stiffness that your mind couldn't fully comprehend?

Or maybe you would understand it completely. Maybe your tears would drown your hopes of the possibility of future memories. Maybe death was less mischievous in his workings than I had always imagined him to be.

Or maybe it was none of that at all.

"Alright, my friends. We are off to a great start." My father shattered our collective silence from the driver's seat. "We have the chips, we're almost out of Germany. So far, things are looking good." No one replied. No one looked at him. I feared what would happen if I internalized his words, and so I avoided the temptation to do so.

But I did anyway.

And in the midst of a soft moment, I realized how right he was.

The vast unknown lay ahead. Lands I had yet to see, that I would know for a moment and never again see. Lands of lingering confusion and secrets and lies and questions forever void of answers. In my fears of the future, it seemed that already in the past, so much had gone wrong.

And yet, there was so much right.

So many fears I had already seemed to face. So much success that didn't seem to make sense.

So I stared out my window. Stared at the cobblestone streets turning to cement. At the fresh evening glow of the ambidextrous sky, painting one side pink and the other periwinkle. And at that moment, I seemed to forget about the helicopter. For merely a second, I seemed to remove the memories of the conversation with my mother from my mind. I seemed to forget the distrust I had in Herr Krüger because, for maybe just a moment, things seemed to be okay.

Hope seemed to be alive.

There was a buzz in my back pocket.

➤ From "Unknown," 18:25

"Keep your eyes open in Salzburg."

My heart dropped again.

And there I went on, holding onto more secrets. Secrets I wished I could ignore, but they couldn't seem to ignore me.

[15]

Stronger

"The development of the Cordellian language has been created and established in an act to create a new and completely individual land from the surrounding, pre-established countries. Both the French and Cordellian language shall be instructed in schools in order to provide the ability of effective communication with other countries. See Cordellain Language Manual for more information on language."

Cordellia Bill of Rights, Article VIII. Signed, February 21st, 2026, Apgar Cordell

Hohensalzburg Fortress. The crown jewel of Salzburg. Where royalty had once made their home, becoming merely a hotel for those who had lost everything. My father insisted we fit into that category. I disagreed.

The fortress was refined, the rolling fields on the southern side of the castle rising and falling where they pleased. Crawling up the sides of mountains, viridescent spikes became one with the black hills of rock, going back for miles until they disintegrated. Consumed by the hazy sky, the layers of plush clouds, the sun peaking through them and slowly stumbling back behind the mountains. Back into its coffin, where it hid itself from the sky.

The wind was hot and quiet when we entered the main square beneath an alabaster stone archway. People laid out as herds across the concrete pavement as far as what was visible. Baskets of wilted red flowers sat on window-sills below carvings in foreign languages. I watched a young girl reach for them, her tiny hands swollen, her tenacity almost leading one to wonder if the withered stems would bring life. Austrian patrols stood around the people, staring out of the corners of their eyes. Children screamed, others slept in silence. The contrast was unnerving.

I watched the way my father stared at the setting. He clutched his suitcase firmly. "This place is strange," he said.

A patroller approached us. He held a notepad in one hand, and his other rested on a holster upon his person. He barely looked at my father before he spoke.

"*Combien?*" He removed his hand from his holster, revealing a pen in his large palm.

"*Il y en a cinq de nous. Est-ce vous avez de la place pour nous rester?*" He looked up at my father, then at my mother. Stared at her for a moment.

"That is our job, is it not? To give you a place to sleep?" He escorted us across the square towards a stairwell. I stared at my father's hands clenched upon his suitcase in front of me. My mother stood stiffly beside me.

"Did you tell him about the helicopter?" I mumbled.

"No." I watched our feet step in sync.

"Do you think he knows?"

"He hasn't said anything to me about it yet." We stopped in front of an iron gate. My father stood a bit too close to the patroller, his arms crossed carefully across his chest, his bag then upon the ground. His eyes were ever so narrowed down on his cheeks.

I stared. "Do you think that he's acting a bit . . ."

She looked over at me. Read my mind, "A little bit, yes."

"I'm going to put you in a room inside as there are so many of you," the man said. He began to unlock the iron gate.

"So many of us? Do you not typically get parties of five?" The patroller stopped. Turned towards my mother. He stared at her for a long moment before he spoke.

"Not particularly." And soon, we were led up a staircase to a large room coated with blanket-covered floors and sealed by an ancient wooden door. The man was gone in an instant. We stood in a silent circle.

"I don't like this place," my father finally said. He set his suitcase down. Looked around the room with a ghastly undertone to his gaze. "I don't want anyone changing their clothes tonight. In case we need to leave quickly." The trusting side of me wanted to believe him to be ridiculous. But I could not think of anything other than the text.

Keep your eyes open in Salzburg.

There was a reason I was always so fond of the moon. I supposed I always had been since back in the days when Viridian and I used to sneak up on our roof at night and stare at it for hours, fumbling into the throws of sleep beneath the stars. But then, as I looked upon it, after fearful days that had passed me by, I began to believe that the sun's pain had been counterfeit. That it had all been a tormenting dream, daring to distract me. That my aptitude of emotion was ominous, surreal, perhaps even a hoax.

Foolish, that's what it was, I see it so clearly now from Neo–Italy. My questioning had always been so foolish. The fact that, for even a moment, I could have believed this all to be a farce was an act of pure naïveté. I had spent too long fooling myself for the sake of my comfort. And the way it all had to end . . . Well, we'll get there soon enough.

So, I stared at the moon that night, sitting so still out the barred castle window. It rested softly over the village, their gray roofs nestled beneath its glow. It stared at me, and I at it. I watched it closely. Watched its rises and falls, imagining what lay amid the dark side. I tried to replace the images of helicopters with its invisible eyes fixed on me.

A rush of fear paced through me once I recognized how stagnant those images were—those visions of the crash. How restricting they were evolving to become. How it seemed as though it had done this to nobody but me. For everyone else slept so restfully.

I am stronger than this.

That was when my mind remembered the messages from an unknown number. The only messages I had received in three months; from one who seemed to have foreseen the helicopter's arrival. One who seemed to have wanted to protect me from it.

I remembered how I had thought about blocking that number on the car ride here. How something inside of myself wouldn't let me.

So I stared at the moon, a consistent form of comfort. I stared until I began to notice my mind drifting,

my eyes, waning,

my ears, muffling.

Rest, yes,

please . . .

Bam.

No, it was more of a boom.

I couldn't tell what it sounded like, but I had seen it.

Fire.

It danced in a circle where the door should have been.

I reacted before I had time to process. My feet pounded across the castle floor and carried me to the balcony on the other side of the room.

My mother. My eyes searched the interior of the room for her. She was following me.

My brothers. They were in front of me.

"Is everyone okay?" The sound of my father's voice had been found as a relief.

Viridian was squished tightly into me. "What the hell just happened?" His voice was silenced by the sound of others.

"*Telt ba'khér él û'prii, juh?*" *Did we get them?* It was a woman. Her words were creaky and unsteady. I saw her shadow cast upon the wall through the dancing of the flames. It had been long, stretching up upon the bricks, stained as splattered blood. It took me a long moment to recognize what I found so familiar about her voice. Perhaps the sharp sound of a vowel or the raising of the soft palate. It was not until a man spoke that I realized.

"*N'û'sav.*" *Not sure.* They were speaking Cordellian. My mind nearly went black.

"*Ko espii zut ha telt ėl û'kess.*" *I damn hope we did.* A third voice, another woman.

"*Û'ciir salii,*" it was the first woman again.

Search the room . . . They were looking for us.

Hunting us.

We need to leave.

My moment of paralysis ceased. My eyes darted around the balcony. They raced each other as competitors rather than friends. They raced down to the long drop below; death guaranteed. They traveled to the top of the castle, maybe only ten feet high. *Climb.*

"Those damn Cordellian bastards." It was the man's voice again. "Must have left already."

"Krüger said they weren't all that bright," The second woman. *Krüger . . . I know that name . . .* "Guess he lied." *Krüger . . . he ratted us out?*

"*Ba'khėr û'pat'a û'sfėl, a?*" *Where could they have gone?*

"*Sou û'cön û'riit.*" *Just keep looking.*

We need to go.

My eyes dashed to Sitka. His were already on me. I watched him watch the wall, spotted and speckled with stone pressed in and sticking out, eroded with age. His gaze found me again. I nodded.

We pushed past our family, moving towards the foot-wide railing. My forearms were upon it in an instant, and I was pushing myself up and pulling my feet underneath me. I stood. The deep drop below reached up its ominous hand. I tried not to look back.

My father called my name. His whispers scattered in the wind. My eyes scanned the bricks up and down the castle, searching for slots to secure my palms. I placed them upon an alabaster stone a bit above my head and another at my shoulder level. My feet found two grooves just above the railing.

"Eve, what about our stuff?" Viridian said it a bit too loud. My eyes rolled.

"Are you kidding? Leave it! We don't have time!"

The brick stung my almond skin, stabbing as a thousand dreadful suns. I moved my body up the building, gripping each stone tighter than the last. My breath slowly staggered.

Don't look down.

My hands found the ridge of the roof, resetting my forearms on the rounded edge. I pushed myself up, holding in the screeches of pain inside of me. The castle walls were beneath me, and I knelt there for a moment, keeping one hand on the edge for stability and staring at the palm of the other covered in the likes of speckled red pen marks.

Sitka followed behind me. He moved quicker than I had, grabbing my free hand as he reached the top, and rolled onto his side. My mother was next, then Viridian and my father.

My father.

My father, who I couldn't get to go on any festival rides with me back home. My father, who had always refused to travel by aircraft. My father, who closed his eyes as he climbed. My bones rattled beneath me.

"Put your left hand there." I pointed to a brick my palm had rested upon before. He opened his eyes for just a moment, closing them again once his grip was secure.

"Good, you're doing good," my light words rolled heavily off my tongue. "Now put your left foot there." I pointed again. He moved. I felt heat move from my cheeks to my ears.

"You're so close, Perû," I said—I said at the moment he tried to move his right hand. The moment it slipped.

A cry escaped him.

I held back the one inside of me.

Me and my mother reached for his wrists, dragging him towards the roof. He rolled over the ledge, slight tears speckling the bottom of his cheeks. His favorite shirt was torn at the bottom—a shirt he had bought a few years ago when he had taken me and my brothers on a camping trip.

His eyes found me. "You're grounded."

I laughed. Maybe too loud, for the voices in the room below grew quiet.

Santa Claus Is Coming To Town

Viridian and I used to play a game around our house when we were young. One of us would be the dragon and the other the knight. The dragon would chase the knight around the backyard, and the knight would find a way to kill the dragon. Sometimes, we would sneak atop the roof. One of those times, I slipped. Viridian caught me.

I felt as though I was slipping. Slipping into a nightmare. As though a dragon was hunting me and there was nothing I could do to escape; yet I ran as though I could.

Perhaps that was the eternal curse of humanity, one I hadn't realized at the time, but I see so clearly now in Neo-Italy, since time has passed. That we all hoard a restless desire to run when there is nothing worth running to.

The roof was a long line of large triangles. Pyramids with secrets within their walls that I could only hope to slip across unnoticed. The shouts were again behind us, growing as a rising tide.

They were coming.

"Perû, where are we going?" Viridian's voice reverberated off of the roof in front of me. He ran side by side with my father.

"Somewhere safe."

"Okay, so, do you have any idea where that might be?" His sarcasm was loud. My father pulled himself atop the second pyramid in the row, sitting down upon its ridge and looking out across the roof. The rows seemed to go on for miles, drowning beneath a dark haze until they met the edge, colliding with the courtyard below where refugees slept uncovered. Walls spread around the courtyard and round to the hills beyond, alternating between flat and A-frame roofs until they drowned in the distance. Until the haze became so heavy that even white lies feared it.

I watched my father's eyes move to the left and then the right. They landed upon a chimney in between two pyramids, the residue of smoke charred across the rim.

"The chimney," he finally said.

Viridian's eyes narrowed in confusion rather than sarcasm. "What?"

My father pointed towards it. Then he slid down the other side of the pyramid, landing with his knees bent and immediately stumbling through the gap towards the pillar in the distance. We followed. Our breath became drenched in sweat. Footsteps sounded a ways behind us. Shouts followed almost comically. The path of my father began to sway in the way of an ever-receding tide. Then, he was standing in the ravine below the chimney. His hands gripped the sides of the building, closing his eyes as he climbed. My breath found a home in my throat. Soon enough, he was beside the chimney, reaching his hands down to our own. His eyes were only half open when his palm found mine. I wrapped my fingers into his. Sweat passed between them. The heat of the night was catching up to me.

Then I was beside the chimney, looking out across the roof. And I was seeing them, three figures a few paces from the rest of my family. They moved hurriedly across the roof as if they had done this before, as if they had been trained to do just this. Their prejudiced shouts from earlier rang again in my mind. Shouts in my own language, against my race. A strange paradox wrapped a thread around my finger and squeezed it ever so tightly as I stared at the figures' movements. Tried to find some form of familiarity in their dark eyes.

My father pulled my mother and brothers up to where we stood. The predators remained not far behind. My eyes found my father again as he stared a tad too cautiously at the chimney. I saw his hands shake.

"Perû, you have to go." He looked back at me. Swallowed harshly. I felt the enemy behind—a phantom hand touched my heel. "Perû!"

He threw himself towards the top of the chimney and shook viciously as he pulled himself up, fidgeting around the ridges for his feet. His shoulders stretched beneath his shirt. Breath ran from his lips in a fit of smoke. And soon, his torso was atop the ledge, his feet dangling inward.

"Looks like I really am Santa Claus now." His smile had been counterfeit as he stared inside the black hole below. Stared as though a second set of eyes stared back at him. The silence was unprecedented. And then he dropped himself down, crashing so strongly that the whole castle beneath us seemed to shake. A puff of smoke slapped me across the face.

"Are you okay?" My mother leaned past me. Silence.

He coughed. "Yeah just uh . . . well, I can't see." I smiled.

"What . . ." I turned to Sitka. His eyes were fixed wide. "What is he talking about?"

"You know because the soot—"

"No, I mean when . . . the thing about Santa. He's not . . ." I stared at him for a moment. His face had gone white beneath the waning moonlight. Then, I realized.

"Oh my gosh." I couldn't help but let a smile spread across my face. "You still believe in Santa."

"Let's go!" The voice came from below. I hadn't even noticed my mother jump. I turned towards the chimney, a grin still stained maroon across my cheeks.

"Shut up," Viridian dragged out the "uh" sound as though it would em-phasize his pleasure taken in his teasing. "Sitka, you're *joking*." I stared at the chimney's height. It towered over me, casting a shadow of the night across my pebbled cheeks.

My hands gripped the brick in an instant, callusing the stains of red upon my palms. I cringed as I climbed. Night seemed to grow darker beneath the pressure of my eyelids. Heat swam to my lungs. I grabbed the ridge of the chimney and dug my elbows into the surface. My bare skin was scratched heavily. I hovered over the stone rim, dangling my legs down the chute and staring into the ominous abyss below.

It was dark. Too dark for my mind to fabricate any form of comfort. The harsh smell of smoke poisoned my nose, spinning with the already present heat in my lungs. A cough escaped my lips. Light echoes traveled up through the chimney, the voice of my mother whose words I couldn't bring myself to hear. I panted through my chest.

And then I saw the moon. Its warm glow had been enough for me to force myself down the narrow chute.

A heavy thud followed me there. Wind escaped my lungs in an instant.

I couldn't see. Smoke and soot and whatever else remained to haunt a chimney stung at the cuffs of my eyes, clawing my pupils apart. I couldn't breathe. A hand gripped my right wrist. Another wrapped around my back, dragging me forward to my feet. The feeling of my mother's touch was familiar.

"Are you alright?" she asked. I coughed. My eyes opened slowly, and I wiped them harshly with the heels of my hands.

"Yes." A second thud sounded behind me with a hysterical laugh at its side. Viridian.

"They should put one of those in at Khan Carnival." Khan Carnival, the carnival that came to Paris every September when life had been normal.

Viridian stood, aggressively exterminating the soot from his eyes. I stared at his blond hair, now dyed black with soot. A laugh found its way off my lips.

He looked up at me. "What?"

"Your hair." He staggered over to a large mirror on the wall, staring at himself for a moment. Silence. Then, he burst into a fit of laughter.

"I look sexy." We stood in a large hallway, one end wrapping and curving and disappearing behind a stained stone wall. At the other was a large staircase, the steps of slightly rotted wood circling down into an abyss. Behind me laid a lounge room with couches and cushions and paintings from ancient days. No one was inside.

One last thud echoed through the hall, followed by a chorus of coughs.

"I'm never doing that again," Sitka mumbled.

Footsteps sounded on the roof.

We hurried for the stairs, Viridian helping Sitka to his feet and patting him on the back.

"Did Santa get you what you wanted for Christmas this year, little buddy?"

"Shut up." The footsteps grew louder. The two of them scrambled to the staircase, Viridian still laughing.

"So you're telling me that you're smart enough to sneak us out of the country without getting caught but stupid enough to still believe in Santa?"

"Well *clearly* I managed to get us caught!"

We took two steps at a time down the staircase, meeting a hallway at the bottom, then a steel door to the courtyard. The haunting followed, that crass sound of footsteps remained above. I feared they would follow us forever.

[17]

Too

It felt too easy getting through that courtyard. Too easy, climbing down the mountain to the town below and onto the Kapitelplatz where our car had been parked. From what I could tell, no one was following us. Not anymore.

Aside from them. The inaudible voice.

> ➤ From "Unknown," 3:03
> "You need to leave Salzburg now. There's nowhere for you to hide here."

I stared at the message. My father yelled at me to hurry into the car. I didn't know where we had planned to go at three in the morning, but the words of the message stung my sleep-ridden eyes.

For only a moment, I hoped I wouldn't give into its words, but I did.

We can't stay in Salzburg.

I was in the passenger seat that time. I didn't know how I ended up here, nor did I wish to be there. My mother was in the far back. I'd like to think that I didn't know why.

But I did.

It was clear by the way she stared out the back window. By the intensity in her posture. By the way her eyes darted around the windows into the crevices of the streets and drowned into the dead ends. She was watching for the hunters.

The engine started up silently. My father sped down an alleyway. The city had been short of street lights, the crescent moon blazing as the only luminance in sight. My father dimmed his headlights. We passed by silent houses, silent streets, silent windows with nearly perceivable candles lit inside, their flames dancing ever so slowly in some unidentifiable breeze. I sat cross-legged. My arms wrapped tightly around my knees as I stared into the abyss before me with eyes of burning fire.

"Why is no one following us?" Viridian's voice vibrated the seat behind me. No one replied.

My father pulled onto a one-way road, running beside a roaring river. Its appearance was absent in the dimmed headlights, the sound of waves the only indicator of its existence. Even the stars seemed to hide under a dark sheet as though they feared our presence. Trees loom overhead, shadows cast as phantom hunters in the night.

That's when I noticed the lights behind us. Another vehicle.

It followed behind us for a little while. I couldn't see faces through the brightness of their headlights. The world grew in brilliance, the streets soon evolving into a dark gray rather than a blanketing blackness. I stared out the front window. The reflection of light shown in the rearview. I ignored it.

It was nothing. No one.

Anyone could have been awake.

The car remained coated in silence. I glanced up at the rearview. They remained at a consistent speed behind us, and so I looked back out the windshield. The road began to curve around a bend, wrapping itself around the ever-roaring river. My hands gripped my legs tighter, sweat rolling into the seams, my eyes blurred in the subtlety of our headlights.

The brilliance behind us seemed to grow brighter, a trick to the mind I first deduced. I stared at the lines on the road, passing by in a constant rhythm with my father's speed. The light behind us still seemed to grow brighter. I looked up at the rearview mirror. They were closer to us than before. Much closer. Driving faster.

Too fast.

"Perû . . ."

"Ävon, speed up," My mother's words shattered the silence that had fallen over the car.

And then, in an instant, my bones jolted backward inside my skin, a rumbling erupting from the hood of the car. My father drove fast. Too fast. I kept my eyes focused out the front window, the echo of the light growing like a bacteria behind me.

It was too bright.

Chaos came with it, the shouts of my family, their words a foreign language pressing into the crazed confines of my mind. I made sense of nothing. Not the pounding of my head or the rattling of my heartbeat against my eardrums. Nor the buzz from my pocket.

➤ From "Unknown," 3:08

"Stay to the right of the road."

Confusion laced with an unprecedented anger stirred my mind. They mended themselves together into a manic mess, and I stared through the seams at the single word that rang clearly: no.

Perhaps it had been my stubbornness or rather my carelessness that made me say it.

"Stay to the left." My father stayed staring at the road. His eyes darted to me for only a moment.

"What?"

"Stay to the left of the road."

"Why?"

I looked at him, then back out towards the road. "It's a gut feeling." I could feel his eyes on me, dashing between the road and the rearview and my hazardous gaze. My hands cramped in my lap. His turned blue upon the steering wheel. And then, for a reason I couldn't understand, he listened. The car rocked to the left, and I willingly leaned with it, and the lane once beside us then ran beneath us.

"Why are you moving closer to the river!?" Viridian screeched from the backseat. My father's fingers were shaking. His voice shook with them.

"Aetheria told me to!"

"Why the hell would you listen to her!?" Something caught in my throat. I turned to face the rows behind me. My mother hadn't shifted from her polarized stare out the back window, and Sitka sat in the row in front of her, his body balled up tightly and brown eyes launched out the window beside him. But Viridian had been directly behind me, leaning forward to meet my eyes. His brown cheeks boiled red with pride and anger, or a word that meant both that I couldn't seem to discover. And in the raising of his eyebrow, I felt the heat upon my own cheeks rise, mirroring his pride.

"What's that supposed to mean?" I said. He squinted his verdant eyes, a single blond curl falling across his forehead. His lips sealed so tightly that I was almost surprised when they opened again.

"Oh shut up, Eve."

"No, I want to know what you meant by that."

"Why the hell do you care?"

"Guys. Not the time." My mother groaned from the backseat. I ignored her.

"Because you're my brother, idiot."

My father's eyes shoot me in the head. "Aetheria!"

Viridian kept staring. So long I expected him to smirk or at least raise an eyebrow. But his gaze remained the same, coated in some deep underlying desire to see me wounded by him. I didn't seem to think before I spoke again.

"Do you think I'm stupid or something?" He rotated his tongue around his mouth, the pupils in the depth of his gaze seeming to shrink until they were barely perceivable. His next words came without a single moment's notice.

"You're not stupid, you're weak. You always give in to your emotions and never even try to pay attention to the bigger situation. You're selfish as hell."

And for a moment, the blinding lights behind me didn't seem to matter, nor the potential shadow of death they cast us beneath. Nothing but the words of my brother carried weight upon my mind. And if I was to die at this moment, at least I would die knowing what he really thought of me.

"Ävon, they're gaining on us!" My mother screamed from the backseat. My phone buzzed again.

> ➤ From "Unknown," 3:11
>
> "What are you doing??"

The road curved around a deeply darkened building, the river escaping to the other side of it and departing from us. But only for a moment. We were beside it again. The reckless water roared louder, the wall of its separation resting nearer to us. Too near.

"Keep to the right, Perû!"

"They're beside us, Sitka, I can't!" My eyes fell to the window next to me. I found a woman in the driver's seat, a small smile spread across her pale face, her eyes piercing the windshield before her. Her shoulder-length curls jumped up and down at the movements of the vehicle, ever so solemnly yet oh so recklessly. A large man was squished into the seat beside her, his face showing no sign of emotion.

The car inched closer, progressively forcing us to the left. We remained mere inches away from the barrier between us and the river. I could nearly hear the cobblestone scrape my father's door. The gun dug into my side. I thought about using it for a single moment. My legs tensed, my fingers dug into the palms of my hands. It burned. I didn't remove them.

"Get them off of us!" My mother screamed.

"I'm doing my best!"

I felt my phone buzz again. I didn't try to look at it that time. My jaw was tight. Too tight. My arms were made of sticks that rested stiffly to my sides. My eyes dashed around the car and to the window to the left, where the river roared. Enemies were on either side, and the only thing keeping us from them was that brick barrier.

But then, it was gone.

And then, my father lost control of the wheel.

At first, I thought it was the other car colliding with us that created that crashing sound. But that had been before I noticed the water crawling up the side of my window.

Flirting With Death

My feet were cold.

I couldn't remember the last time they had been. Heat was the only foe I knew. Perhaps I even had begun to think the cold to be an ally.

But death was cold. I was convinced of it by then. Maybe the only thing truly keeping me alive had been the heat, though I had sought desperately to escape it. Maybe death was always what I had really wanted.

No it's not.

Fire burned through my veins. My arms both shook in freezing calamity yet burned with desire. My eyes bounced out from their enclosure inside my head, and I stared at the water rising slowly up my feet. Shouts rang across the car. Shattered my eardrums. Muffled them to the point of a well known uncomfortable silence.

And in one paralyzed moment, I was stranded in a sea of paranoia. Waves of recollection and warning flooded all around me, and none of my senses seemed to operate as they once had been designed to. For in a single moment, I recognized the enormity of our situation.

The paralysis broke. I wrapped my hand around the door handle, prying it outward, expecting water to explode through the vehicle in an instant. It remained still. A gravestone. My gravestone. I pushed again. Harder. My forearm met the metal with such intensity.

"It won't open, I already tried!" my father shouted. We are stuck. No, we couldn't be. I couldn't let this happen to them.

What do I do?

The thought met me for just a second: I am destined to die.

No.

I didn't know what instinct came over me that caused my hand to slip into my back pocket. To remove my phone from within the seams and stare at that message that had been sent moments before this mess.

> From "Unknown," 3:15
>
> "Prepare to swim."

My fingers flew across the keyboard.

> To "Unknown," 3:16
>
> "What do I do?"

Not even a minute went by before they replied.

> From "Unknown," 3:16
>
> "Break the windows. Wait for the car to fill. Take a deep breath and get ready to swim up and out. Be prepared for a current."

I can't do this.

Yet, my left elbow still collided with the window beside me. A crack began to form at its center. Water moved quicker up my leg, tickling the hairs around my ankle.

"What are you doing?" My father yelled. He lurched towards me and grabbed my wrist so tightly I feared my very bones would snap beneath his weight. *No, let go.*

"Perû, let go of me," I said it a tone too calm.

"What?"

"Let go of my wrist, I need to break the window." He let go. I tried to look him in the eye through the darkness, but my gaze could only find the door behind his head. "Break the window." He stared at me.

"What?" It was Viridian. "Are you *serious* right now?" My father still looked at me. He seemed to be assessing me, addressing me, waiting for something in my gaze to shift to make him realize that I was worthy of his trust. Then, he nodded.

"First you get us into this river, and now you're telling us to break the window. Are you stupid?" I didn't look back at my brother. Instead, I turned back towards the glass beside me, staring out at the water rising around me, feeling it growing upon my ankles. In a manner more calm than what seemed possible, I responded to my brother.

"No, Viridian, I am not." I swung again at the window. The crack grew larger, stretching to the tops of the heavens and into the pits of hell. My arm filled with a stinging pain. *The gun.* Something rattled through my bones at the thought. *But they'll see it.* I swung again barehanded. The sound of pounding echoed across the car.

Shattering glass echoed from Viridian's seat behind me. It had been so loud that I didn't at first recognize the shattering of my own. Not until the current threw me back towards my father and shards of glass sliced my arms. And then, I was screaming and gasping and choking all at the same time as water ran into my lungs. I coughed. Hard. Harder. So much that my eyes began to bleed with tears, and my vision was blurred by more than just the night.

I couldn't stop coughing.

The water was at my knees at that point. The car slipped forward as it filled. I couldn't see anything. My eyes were sealed shut, shielded from the gushing that pressed me up upon the center divider. My phone buzzed in my back pocket. The gun dug into my hip.

"Swim, Eve!" My father had called from behind me.

"The car has to fill up first!" More water entered my mouth. I was choking again. Harder. It turned to lava in my lungs, and I was burning from the inside out.

It was at my waist. Stinging nearly as profusely as the cuts on my arm. Had it sprayed onto them too, or were those drops of blood?

The car tilted more.

The water was up to my stomach. It whipped my arms thirty-nine times, and I feared the death that would come at forty. The stinging evolved into a sharp throbbing, and I couldn't seem to breathe through it all. Pain was everywhere.

"What are we doing?" My mother screamed.

"Waiting!" My father. I think that's who it was. The water muffled his voice.

The current met my neck, suffocated me, and pulled me closer to the inevitability of death.

I forced my eyes open. They began to shake and flutter and create some tormenting tension behind my pupils. But even in my persistence, it was too dark.

I can't see.

I pulled my hands to my eyes. My arms vibrated beneath splitting pain. The car filled even faster, water warping and rushing and wrapping around my chin, and still the black of night consumed my sight.

I let the water pull me to the top of the vehicle, holding my face as high as I could. Darkness was an enemy that my eyes were learning ever so slowly to defeat. Soon, I spotted the window a few meters away. My only key to survival when the water covered me in,

Three . . .

Two . . .

One.

Breath escaped me. I was under in an instant. My ears blurred. All sounds scattered from around me. My eyes locked themselves away to see solely the darkness within me.

No. Open.

They shot open. My arms were flailing in all ways beside me as though dull knives hoping to slice the water around me. But I only remained still.

My gaze grazed the window. A firm fist pushed me forward, and common sense sensed my presence once again, and I was swimming towards the window, breaking through to the other side.

Into the rapid river.

The current grabbed me. Dragged me. Pushed me as I tried to move my way towards the top.

Air.

It was the only word that seemed to hold any value.

My head grew dizzy. My eyelids pressured me to grant them company. I met the top of the waves in a moment. Air retreated back to my lungs until they were attacked again, and I found myself beneath the waves.

And then it all became a circus. Oxygen swung from the rafters to the floor, and once I caught sight of it, it sprung away again. Water was a great beast before me, and I feared that if it saw my fear, it would seize me. It was all a brutal game of tag. Air, ran and laughed at me as I suffered this pain.

The current pulled me on further. It kept me along the right side of the river. Stone walls stood stoically beside me, too high for me to grasp, too low to have kept me out of this storm. *Air. Shore.* The two words became companions in my mind.

My gaze grazed the land for a place gracious enough to grant me restoration. But all looked the same. And I was beneath them.

Except there.

That one green cut-out, paved by the slender spikes of grass and tree roots growing and poking and prodding out from beneath them.

There, my hope was found.

It approached quickly. I steadied my arms before me. Tried to keep my head above the waves. Its distance quickly grew to be a memory.

And then I was fighting to find the strength to throw myself towards it. I reached for the tree's roots, shaking and decaying and crying. The pressure in my hands grew in agony. My legs remained caught in the current. My hands were wet and slippery, and I was finding myself gripping tighter than what seemed probable. Every single ounce of strength was being drained from my muscles, and my mind couldn't seem to chase it down.

I screamed. My legs rested in the waves. My hands began to slip, so I removed my left one, wrapping my forearm around the root and then my right one after. The bark pierced my cuts, and I was screaming, and no one could hear me.

Then, my legs were free, and they were dripping water across the burnt grass below me. I was coughing again, and this time, I didn't try to stop it. For my coughs proved that I was alive.

[19]

Bloodied Tears

My eyes were bleeding.

Their moisture met my cheeks, creating puddles upon the base of them, and I wondered how many of them had drowned in the river beside me.

Grass dug into me. It pricked the slashes across my arms. My arms that dripped with bloodied tears. I was paralyzed. Stuck still upon this ground that I didn't want to be on. Lost in these thoughts, I didn't want to think. Drowning in this fear rather than the river.

The fear that I would never see my family again.

The sudden realization, once adrenaline subsided, that it was all my fault.

The gun still dug into my side. Its presence was a curse.

You would think that would be enough. Enough for me to recognize that this emphatic belief in a destiny of death was true. You would think that I would give up on this whole thing in hopes of a comfortable death. But it seemed I believed myself to be more resilient than I was, stronger than I truly was. It seemed that I believed that the world could slowly cave in on me as it already was, yet never come to the point of erupting upon me. But I had been ignorant, I see so clearly now.

I fumbled for my phone in my back pocket, my arms seeming to scream louder in terror. It was still in one piece, modern technology unharmed by water damage. A message from many minutes earlier sat upon the screen.

➤ From "Unknown," 3:20

"They won't be gone for long."

At first, I thought it meant the hunters. But then realization swept over me in a wave of both terror and peace as though the two weren't mutually exclusive, and I thought so solemnly of my family. And then I was staring at the trees through which the river rested, and I couldn't help but wonder if they rested at the bottom of it. Because how could an inaudible voice know more of my circumstances than I?

And yet, something inside of me believed the message. Because the last time I had ignored its contents, I had regretted it. I suppose I made a decision, then. A decision to listen to those words from that time forward.

I released a staggered breath. I swiped to the flashlight on my phone, shining it down on my arms. Blood had been stained brightly across them. Specks like those that had been upon my palms, yet viewed through a telescope. Reflections of the red sun seemed to grow larger upon my dirtied skin the longer I stared. Water began to form again against the corners of my eyes. *Merû would know what to do.*

Coughing brought me out of my concentration. The sound pierced my ears, and blood pushed itself so rapidly through my veins, and I was pressing myself up into a sitting position. Water and blood dripped onto the grass beneath me, and I was peering through the trees to where the river rested so rashly. Brown hands were latched around tree roots where mine had once been. I stared. My muscles tensed. And in the split second between moments, I was hurrying over in their direction, and my gaze fell upon Sitka. My jaw fell towards the floor.

"Oh my gosh," I mumbled. His clothing was torn, his hands were maroon and splintered, and my eyes were searching his reddened gaze for some idea of what to do. His mouth rested slightly open, and his skin sagged beneath paralyzing thoughts, and his eyes were stained with such terror that my own became present again before me. I grabbed his forearms, and my own were screaming as I yanked him towards the grass beside me. I cried out. My voice was lost in the river. He gripped my arms, and I tried to ignore his fingers digging into my wounds.

And then his legs were out of the current, and I was pulling him on top of me, and tears were draining down my cheeks in the direction of my clothing, soaked again in the water washed upon him. I held him so tightly, so close to my body in fear of ever losing him again.

"You're alive." His breath was buried in my arm.

"So are you." A small smile stretched my cheeks, and these tears seemed to be of joy for merely a moment. Sitka rolled to the right of me, and I was left to hope in the buzzing echoing from beside me. To hope in the inaudible voice that had then proven itself to hold truth in its words.

➤ From "Unknown," 3:25

"Stay here for the night. You will be safe."

There had been no hesitation in the sigh that I allowed to limp off of my lips. My back was pressed back into the grass. Sitka's panting grew to a murmur beside me. We lay surrounded by a cathedral of trees, hidden from threats of the surrounding world.

"Let's stay here for the night," I whispered just over the sound of the river. Sitka stirred. "What about everyone else?"

"We can search for them tomorrow. It's too dark right now. We'll just get lost." A slight burning breeze blew my hair across my cheeks. "It will be safe here." His stirring ceased, and I was left staring at the stars through the waving leaves of the trees above. Watching the moon as it waned away. As it spread sleep across my hollowed eyes, placing wonder into my withered dreams.

A river rolled by us. Its glass touch trampled rocks and riveted through narrow valleys and lingering hills. On one side of it sat a long row of buildings, each sprayed with its own curated color, crafted by the clouds. They rolled up and down cobblestone streets and wrapped around humanity living along its lands. There had been a bridge across the river, casting a shadow upon a shallow section, segregating that area from the rest. Children danced in the shade, words spinning off their tongues and bouncing back by echo. One ran towards where we lay. He stopped beside the tree next to us, staring at the peeling bark, like petals plummeting towards the earth. The boy reached for the trunk, snatching a piece of bark, staring at the shaded lines for just a moment. Then, he was running back to his friends and they were on the sand, nestled beneath the bridge as they got to work.

They were building a boat. A boat I knew wouldn't float. Not with the type of wood the boy had chosen to use.

My mother lay beside me. Her body rested upon the speckled sand, her hands tucked behind her head. Her hair was pulled up into a bun, falling down upon her forehead. She stared at the little town across the river, her green gaze gleaming in the glowing light of the sun. A smile was set upon her cheeks. It had been glued there the moment we arrived in Colmar.

"Me and my friends used to come here on weekends," she began. She hadn't spoken since we had found that spot on the sand. "We would sneak out of our homes, and my friend Delanii would drive us here. She always managed to have some booze in the back, and we would camp out on this beach and drink until we got caught."

"You?" Her head turned towards me, and I was almost surprised to see her smiling.

"I was more like Viridian than I was like you." She paused. Her eyes were back on the river now. "But even in his wildness, I just continue to be amazed by him. I see much of my own youth in him. The good and the bad. But he has more goals than I ever did."

"More goals than you?" She nodded. "But you're a doctor now."

"I changed. Became more realistic. I realized that I couldn't spend all my days running around Cordellia with my friends and drinking and partying. Not if I want to survive here."

"So you were like Darbii?" She paused. Hesitated. Nodded.

"I was like Darbii."

The Other Voices

Darbii.

My eyes shot open, and my body seemed to convulse forward. My mind was scattered. My arms were aching.

The first thing I heard was the rushing sound of water. Loud, distinct, crisp.

Like the sound of a helicopter colliding with the earth.

Shouts rang through my ears, strained, harsh, terrified.

I stared through the trees. My body obliterated and came back together in a million blood-colored pieces, and I thought I saw the face of Darbii through the branches. Her green eyes blended with the verdant leaves, and her cheeks were torn and bloodied. And soon, the leaf that held her visage was tumbling down towards the river and my jaw fell with it.

What have I done.

Then the words of my mother were there. They seemed so real.

"Eve!" My head spun. My stare fell towards her, her bright green eyes gazing upon me, her crazed blonde coils pulled up into a bun.

Not merely a ghost of my imagination.

"Merû," I mumbled. She was stumbling towards me and throwing her arms around me, and I let out a small gasp as her fingers met the cuts across my arms. She pulled back.

"Oh, dear." She took my forearms into her palms. Stared at them.

"From the car window." She nodded. A pause.

"The water should have cleaned them enough," she began. "They should be wrapped up." She was opening the fanny pack around her waist as my eyes traveled across the green cathedral, stopping upon my father and Viridian, both consumed by sleep.

"When did you find us?" I asked.

"Last night. We found you and your brother asleep and decided not to wake you."

"How did you find each other?"

"We were all in similar areas. Went looking for one another. I found your father on the sidewalk and Viridian sitting on a bench a little bit away from him." I looked down at the grass below me, feeling my mother's gaze on me. "Are you doing okay?"

I shrugged. "I haven't been awake long enough to know." She chuckled. But then my mind traveled back through last night's events, through the confusion of it all, the fear. And somehow, it found its way to a hidden and dark cave, the walls carved with words. Ideas I had crafted, seemingly without even realizing. Then, they were marking my mind so blatantly.

All of this was my fault.

I would've liked to believe that it wasn't, but lying to oneself was like choosing to take poison. For it had been my stubbornness that had found us in that river on the outskirts of death. My secrets that had left my family unprepared for what was to come. For my mother and I had seen that Cordellian star on that helicopter. We had known something greater was going on, and yet we chose to stay silent.

Silence wasn't golden; it never had been. Instead, it was black, hidden, and frightening. A wicked scheme remaining underground, buried in the minds of people who refused to let their thoughts be known to mankind. Evil people. Those were the ones who remained silent, whether or not they recognized their enormity. Most did not.

But these thoughts, these ideas, they are all more concrete now as I look back on all that has happened. Perhaps I am communicating it all better than what was accurate for the time. For then, it had only been a faint impression. A distant idea that I was at fault. That I was wholly to blame, because I was. That my silence was a weapon used against myself, but my voice was just as equally harmful.

And so words escaped my mouth quickly in fear that they would never be said if they were ignored then. "Should we have said something?" I whispered it, meeting my mother's gaze. She raised an eyebrow.

"About what?"

"When we saw the helicopter. And the Cordellian star on it. And we knew that someone was after us and didn't say anything about it." My gaze shifted to my father and Viridian. "They would have been more prepared if we did. This all would have been easier, or maybe it wouldn't have even happened. We should have just said something—"

"No." My mother's harsh tone startled me. She stared at me, her eyes narrowed inward upon themselves, her head shaking ever so slowly. "Don't you even try to speak of what you 'should have done.' We do not have time for that, Eve. I cannot have you regretting things when there's no guarantee of even the next hour. You are only guaranteed right now. This single moment with me. That is it. So you make mistakes, *I* make mistakes, but we get over them, and then we move on. Dwelling on them will do nothing for any of us. Today we're going to get up and we're going to keep walking and we're going to forget about all of the things that we 'should have done.' Okay?" A smile stretched the length of my face. I nodded. She shook her head.

"No, I want to hear you say it."

"Okay."

"Good." She patted me on the back. "Now let's wrap up your arms, alright?" She dug through her fanny pack again, my gaze falling upon Viridian. His eyes had been opened that time. I stayed focused on him. And then I looked away.

"I'm hungry as hell right now." Viridian declared. We sat in a circle on the seared spikes beneath us. My mother had found gauze in her fanny pack and had gently wrapped my chiseled wrists, my arms turning to snake skins, crawling towards my shoulders. They burned even stronger beneath the sun's cursed glow.

I sat on the outside of the circle formed by my family, the slaughtering sounds of the river running through my ears, drowning my thoughts, hurling them against careless currents. I tried to focus on a single spot on the ground.

"Can you stop swearing, Viridian?" My mother was soon saying back to my brother. "Please? You could say you're really hungry and it would have the same effect."

"It absolutely would not," Viridian spoke with more gusto than what I had the soundness of mind to deal with. "My stomach could explode all over Eve right now with the lack of food in it."

I shook my head. "Don't . . . even say that. Please. That doesn't even make sense . . . " We dwelled for a moment in silence. Everyone stared at their own points on the ground, and suddenly someone was shouting.

"What are we sitting here waiting for?" Sitka's sudden exclamation was startling. "Are we going to keep going or—"

"We did almost just die," Viridian snickered. "You know, kinda trying to decompress from that."

My mother rolled her eyes. "We did not almost die. You're being dramatic."

My father shrugged. "We kinda did."

Viridian grinned. "Thank you. I appreciate your support."

"You probably wouldn't have even noticed if I died . . ." Sitka mumbled, glaring at the grass beneath him. Then, his eyes lifted ever so slightly in the direction of my other brother. Viridian watched him. Blinked.

"What the hell is that supposed to mean? Why is everyone mad at me right now?"

"Are we not going to talk about it?" Everyone's gaze shifted to me. For the first time in many minutes, I looked up, inspecting them each individually. My father's red-stained hands gripped the grass beneath him. Sitka's eyes were glazed graciously with paranoia, locked into a state of nightmare meeting reality, the two not quite mixing. My mother's shoulders were tense, raised just a bit too close to her ears but at such an awkward distance from her chest that I could hardly understand how she rested comfortably. And then there was Viridian whose green gaze pierced me so purposefully and yet so obliviously that I could hardly stand to look upon him for even a moment. My father finally spoke.

"What?"

"You all heard what I heard last night . . . when we were on the balcony?" No one said a word. My eyebrows were narrowing in. "Herr Krüger *told* them where we were." Everyone's eye contact with me had broken in the way that bones shattered beneath a hurricane, and they were all staring at their own spots on the ground again. I shook my head. A quiet current swept us all up into its pull until Viridian began to mumble.

"I knew we shouldn't have trusted him."

I looked at him. "Well we had no reason to think that at the time."

"We absolutely did."

"Would you just shut up for *once*, Viridian?"

"Eve!" My mother glared at me. Then I watched her eyes search through the archives of her mind, meeting my father's gaze in the process. "I mean, how can we know for sure?"

"They said his name." I began. "Repeatedly. Before and after saying prejudiced things about Cordellians. Not to mention, he was the only other person who knew we were headed to Salzburg next. Is there any other evidence you need? Because I probably have it."

She looked over at me. At first her eyes were angry, soon softening as her gaze settled upon my fingers. I picked at my nails, creating jagged edges where they were meant to be smooth. The cuticle around my right pointer finger was bleeding. Silence spread again between us, and I could feel my stomach ache and my mind go blurry. We should have just stayed home . . .

You should have told the truth.

There seemed to be another voice in my head.

"So what's in my arm right now?" My father's gaze found my mother. "You inspected it." She shook her head.

Sighed. "It looked just like what he had claimed it to be."

"It's probably a tracking device."

I glared at Viridian, "Shut up."

"Could be . . . I sure hope it isn't." My mother spoke with such calmness I hardly realized we were discussing the same topic. My father watched her.

"How can we tell?"

"We can't."

"Not even if we . . ." He motioned towards his arm where the chip was planted, moving his hand back and forth in a slicing motion. I gagged.

"No. We'd need a device to read what's been placed inside the chip and we don't have access to those."

"Why wouldn't we just get rid of them?" Viridian asked quietly. "If we're not sure what they actually are, why wouldn't we just . . . ?"

"Because what if they are what Krüger claimed them to be?" my mother said. "They could be our ticket to freedom." And then I was shaking my head, and my eyes were moving towards the river beside me, watching through the trees at the water that flowed so viciously. For only a moment, I had wished it had consumed me. But that moment passed quickly, and then words were rolling off my lips so deliberately, so meticulously.

"Who are these people? And why does it seem like they want us dead?"

[21]

An Unsteady Strength

We left a while later, moving on to the next town over for food. We believed it to be safer than remaining in Salzburg, fearing who there would continue to hunt us. So instead, we allowed the heat to do so, trudging through the burning streets, and for a moment I wished I was beneath the river once more.

I walked with nothing. No bag on my arm.

Everything burnt inside the castle walls.

All my memories I had been gripping tightly, slipping like sand through my fingertips.

My mind tried to process it all as we took the two-hour trek to the next town over. It tried to understand how this had all happened. How I had managed to lose the last of my memories inside burning walls.

Perhaps that was really the pain death pushed upon people, a pain I hadn't previously known to be possible. It drained everything out of you, erased bits and pieces of you. Your memories, your dreams, your identity. It pulled piece after piece out of you until you were simply just skin and bone and cloth covering your hollowed places. Until there was nothing left of you.

Then, it took you.

I remembered the letters I wrote once we made it to a coffee shop. The letters I had spent days leaving fingerprints of my fearful thoughts inside. The ones that my optimistic side hoped one day to deliver to Darbii personally. But that day would never come to pass.

And a part of me said it was my fault.

Another said it was inevitable.

And when the two met, they furiously fought, and I couldn't seem to make out which was which in the dance of their fury.

I remembered my pointe shoes when we sat down at the table. The years I had spent working to achieve their possession. The endless days of building strength. The cycle of sun turning to moon—of swollen ankles and sticky sweat, all in a persistent, endless grasp at strength.

I feared my weakness was what had stolen them from me.

"This is so good." I was staring out a window when Viridian spoke. There was a brick wall in view, white, lightly speckled with dirt around the edges. Nothing else. I saw my mother nod out of my peripheral vision, taking her own sip of coffee. Her map was laid out across the table as she stared at a highlighted path. It was wrinkled around the edges where it hadn't quite dried out all the way from its home inside her jean pocket.

"So good." She replied. "Have you tried the bread yet?" I glanced at Viridian through the sides of my eyes. A warm loaf rested before him, steam rising towards his nose and scratching the surface of his cheeks. Then, he ripped a piece off the side facing him, placing it upon his tongue.

He smiled. "This is going to be gone in about one minute."

Everyone stayed in silence, indulging in their delights. I stayed staring out the window. A stray cat inched into the alleyway. I watched it stand still for a moment before plopping itself down upon the concrete. It laid on its side as though it were dead. A thought appeared to me but I forgot it immediately as it seemed I was prone to do. The smell of the warm bread made my head grow light. Something warm began to grow in my throat.

"Are you going to eat?" My mother was staring at me. I glanced down at my own loaf before me. My eyes stared back out the window.

"Eventually."

"Does anyone know how long the walk is to . . ." My father hadn't finished his sentence. I already knew that he spoke of Israel. The Qadim. *The savior that owes nothing to me.* The savior that owed it all to us.

Viridian sat a bit straighter now. "I'm sorry, walk?"

"About a month," Sitka spoke nonchalantly.

"Why are we walking?"

I was rolling my eyes at Viridian. "Cause we drowned the car, idiot."

"Eve," my mother snapped at me.

Sitka continued. "Well . . . I guess it would be longer than that since we're going to have to sleep."

"Unless we get anti-sleep pills." Viridian shrugged, and I sighed.

"Oh yes. Because we'll definitely have access to those."

"There's a train station in the next town over." My gaze faltered from the window, meeting the shopkeeper behind me. He stood against the counter, drying his red and blistered hands with a towel. A smile was set upon his thinned cheeks. He looked about thirty years old. His eyes were soft, but previously poisoned by rain and around his neck sat a golden chain with a locket. I wondered whose picture lay inside. "Sorry, I couldn't help but overhear you." My parents' gazes met, and my father raised an eyebrow ever so slightly.

"Trains are still running?"

My mother looked up at the man. "Thank you." He nodded.

"Where are you all headed?"

"Romania to visit family before the . . ." I waited for her to finish her sentence. She didn't.

"And you're coming from France, I assume."

"Yes."

"I thought trains were running in France." There was a pause. I swallowed. My eyes found my mother as she stared at the man for a moment, sparks flying in her mind perhaps, but her face remained stagnant.

"Into France, but not out of it." She was lying. I wondered if he could tell.

I took the bread to go.

It sat in a brown paper bag in my hand as we walked. The streets were bare, and we arrived there in forty-five minutes, buying tickets as though we were on vacation.

The train we boarded was crafted from a slick white metal, lines of silver plated along it. Long winding windows made their way around the sides, tinted deeply to resemble the night. Solar panels were placed on the roof, trapping the sun for power. The interior was decorated with plush, dark blue couches and chairs, and metal tables were staggered in between them. I found a couch in the corner, away from the rest of my family, my gaze fixed out the window on the Austrian Alps, still somehow coated with a thick layer of snow. My head spun. It seemed to worsen by the minute.

I should have eaten something.

Trains traveled at the speed of an old-fashioned airplane, making the 569 kilometers to Budapest only an hour and a half in length. Long enough for me to recollect my thoughts, to find that hidden hope again, for I knew it still lived somewhere. Long enough to stare at the casts on my arms, seeming to drown the skin beneath them. Long enough to try to ignore their burning. The spinning of my head. The breaking of everything inside of me, and yet everything around me was still.

Until the vehicle launched forward. That was when I remembered the messages I had received. When I recalled the good they had served me. When I wonder if I was capable of seeking out the strength to respond.

And then, somehow, I did.

> ➤ To "Unknown," 12:03
> "Who are you?"

I stared at the letters on my screen, but it seemed impossible that I had truly sent them. My fingers began to shake beneath my phone as I watched the message. Watched it as though it would change. My stomach turned. Ached.

A message appeared beneath mine.

➤ From "Unknown," 12:04

"Elijah."

I stared at it. Stared as my heart beat the drums in my ears. Blinked. Then, I shook my head.

Never had I met someone with such a name.

➤ To "Unknown," 12:05

"I don't know an Elijah."

➤ From "Unknown," 12:05

"Not yet."

Not yet.

The words sat like coagulated blood on my screen.

➤ To "Unknown," 12:06

"What do you want with me, Elijah?"

➤ From "Unknown," 12:06

"I want to help you."

➤ To "Unknown," 12:06

"And what is it you think I need help with?"

➤ From "Unknown," 12:06

"Well, from my understanding, you believe that you are destined to die."

I reread the message. Once. Twice. A third time. And soon, my heart was beating even faster than I perceived to be possible, and my mind was spinning in circles, and the train seemed to be moving backward instead of forwards.

He said it. He admitted what I could not.

I shoved my phone back into my pocket. My eyes fixed on the ceiling, and my lungs seemed to have retired.

Why should I trust him?

He was not Herr Krüger.

It felt as though everything began to fall apart around me, and my mind was a rattlesnake shaking its tail, and I was hardly noticing Viridian sitting down in front of me with his blond curls purposely covered with a hood. A hood to hide his hair because we were being hunted.

Hunted everywhere.

His eyes stayed focused on mine. I felt them from where I was staring at the ceiling. They were squinting slightly, and I was trying to ignore them. It barely lasted.

I frowned. "What."

"Are you mad at me?" I looked down at him. His gaze looked sorrowful and ridiculing, as though the two were the same thing. Perhaps to him they were. For a moment I stared, feeling my breath loosen a bit and looking back out the window.

"What do you think?"

"Well clearly I think you are if I'm asking you."

I nodded. "Good guess." I could feel his gaze still on me as I stared at the Alps. They were nothing more than an abstract painting blurred together.

"Is it because of what I said about you in the car last night?"

"Good for you, Viridian, you're not oblivious." I looked over at him that time. Watched as he shook his head. Chuckled. My hands tightened into fists.

"Gosh, Eve . . ."

"What?"

"It really isn't that big of a deal."

"Who do you think you are to tell me what is and isn't a big deal?"

"It was just a joke."

"Ah, a joke while we were in the midst of almost *dying*. Touché." I rolled my eyes and rubbed my cheeks in an attempt to extinguish the fire growing upon them. "And you *definitely* sounded like you were joking, might I add." My eyes didn't recede from him, even when he turned to look out the window. His hood slipped slightly backward on his head, and as he stared down at his feet. I wondered if I could see a tinge of guilt in his gaze.

"I'm sorry, Eve. Honestly." Perhaps I had. I shook my head, my hands slipping beneath my legs, my eyes falling to the floor.

"Okay."

"I don't really think that about you. I really don't. I . . ." His voice was a fishing line, pulling my eyes back upon him. I watched closely as he pulled his hood back over his head, his gaze refusing to meet mine. "You don't . . . um . . . you don't need me saying things like that to you . . . especially with everything right now." He paused. Swallowed. I watched him closely. "I'm just kinda under a lot of stress . . . um, clearly, so . . . I say things I don't mean, you know?" I did. For I felt as though I had already done just the same. Maybe we were more similar than we realized.

[22]

Gyönyörű Budapest

I awoke to someone shaking my arm. Viridian stood over me. His hood was still pulled over his blond curls. My head pounded, and my eyes were blurry as they stumbled up towards him.

"We're here." It took me a moment to recall where I was. The white train walls surrounded me. A navy cushion beneath me with the unnatural ability to lull me into sleep. A dreamless sleep. I had hoped for an absence of dreams.

My eyes were opened just a bit wider, and I could feel the residue of rest just beside my lips.

"Where?" I mumbled.

"Budapest." *Budapest* . . . I tried to make the word make sense. *Hungary*. "Hurry up, we need to go." Then he pulled me to my feet, ignoring the pressure he placed into my slashed arms, and soon I was beginning to remember my pain.

I grabbed the bag of bread beside me. My nails dug into the brown fibers, nearly meeting my palm on the other side. My wobbling feet were following my brother out of the train and onto the platform below. Cream arches surrounded me, hugging doorways and windows tinted by stained glass. They were decorated with golden embellishments, portions hidden by transparent screens. Stairs floated down alleyways to the concrete platforms below and people stood with bags in their hands going up and down, eyes focused on the ground. I saw a woman curled up on a bench, tears stained red upon her cheeks. She held a picture frame in her hands. Children ran through the station, laughter on their tongue and torn garments on their body. Majesty reigned in the slight scent of half-baked bread in the air and the phantom taste of salt upon my lips. Gum and coke and other colors I did not know stained the blotched milky ground beneath me. And I looked out at the beauty and the despair alike, suddenly wishing I could stay there for just a little while.

Maybe that was the first time I truly realized that I would never be back on earth again.

My mother stood to the left of me, her paper map sitting open in her hands. She slid her right finger across it, outlining a path that I had seen her draw on the train.

"We need to be heading to Serbia next," she said. I tried to nod. My head didn't seem to move. Her eyes lifted to look around at the screens and the phrases of an unknown language pressed upon them. I could see the panic beginning to grow in her eyes just as I saw confusion birthed in those around us. Various gazes met us and stared at our desperate state in the way of either perplexity or ridicule, I could not decide. My hands grew into fists at my side. My breath grew heavy.

And then a woman stood beside us. A red, white, and green patched uniform fit tightly upon her small body. I looked at her looking us up and down, following the lines of skin peeking out from beneath our clothing. And once she had gotten a good taste of our appearance, her eyes lifted to a grin.

"*Segíthetek?*" The woman stared at us, her face crinkling and rounding around the cream edges. She stared as my eyes jumped up to my mother. Confusion set in upon her cheeks that she tried to hide with a counterfeit smirk. Then, the woman was nodding, her smile softening around the corners of her cheeks. "*Français?*"

My mother smiled back. "*Oui, nous recherchons le train pour aller à Serbia.*" The woman looked away for a moment, placing her finger against her forehead as though to press a thought down towards her lips.

"Serbia, huh." She thought a bit longer. Looked back at my mother. "I believe the next train is leaving out of a different terminal in just a little while. The station is a bit confusing, so I will take you there." Before we had a response to give, she was walking away, her feet moving faster than her small body seemed able. My family's gazes all jumped between one another, and soon we were hurrying after her, maneuvering through the crowds of people that surrounded us.

"I love to take visitors to the other side of the station," she began to announce to us, a sort of peppiness in her tone. One I couldn't quite understand. I stared at the back of her neck, noticing red sores rising up from her skin. I frowned. "It makes me feel like a tour guide, since we go through the city to get there. And I get to show them *gyönyörű Budapest.*" We emerged through a large doorway as she said that last part, the sunlight hitting us on the other side.

"Beautiful Budapest," she translated. My jaw lowered. We stood upon a hill overlooking the city, rounded and squared rooftops like pyramids staggering down the mountain. They shone amid the sun's harsh glow, meeting a long bridge across below. Underneath the gold embellished arch sat a creek, once a river, the brown water trickling through cracked stone. Tall buildings with gray and white spires stretched towards the sun, crowded by structures of alabaster stone, carved so carefully and complexly.

The streets were empty. Occasional figures passed by, wearing clothes of azure and ash, accented by their amber eyes and angular jawlines. They walked quietly, holographic screens floating in front of their faces, old shows and movies they had managed to save, playing as they walked. There was not a smile in sight.

As we continued on, my eyes fell upon small clusters of crowds, leaned up against walls, wrapped up in silk cloth, loud cries erupting from within them. They shivered in the heat, tears stained across their rugged faces, uttering things in a language I couldn't understand.

"Who are they?" The woman's gaze followed mine as I watched them. She sighed, nodded.

"Ah yes. They are the *akik nem látnak*. They who do not see." She looked back at me as if that was enough of an explanation.

"They have a psychological condition," she continued on. "They're convinced that they don't see the black hole or . . . feel any heat." I stared at them. Stared at their distress. The puddles of tears they drowned in, the layers of cloth that consumed them. I shook my head, feeling a slice of my heart shatter.

"Does anyone know anything about it? The cause?" my mother's voice echoed ahead. The woman practically laughed.

"All science is focused on getting off the planet right now. No one is worried about a few crazy people." I wanted to leave it at that, but I couldn't help but stare at them. To watch those people that had nothing. No help, no one desiring to discover what pained them.

There was a girl beside me. No more than ten. She had been wrapped in blue linens, her long black hair tucked beneath them, her knees pulled to her chest. She looked up at me, her eyes piercing the peace in my soul. Everything seemed to freeze, and I was stuck staring at this girl, watching the universe erupt in her eyes.

"*Je* . . ." I tried to say something. I knew she couldn't understand. A tear grew in my left eye, and my gaze was falling to the brown paper bag in my hand, the bread from this morning. I placed it beside her, and she was staring at it, blinking quickly. "*C'est pour vous.*" She opened the bag, removing the loaf of bread from inside, staring at it. Her small fingers pressed into the dough, and a smile lifted upon her cheeks.

"*Te egy vagy közülünk?*" She looked up at me. I shook my head.

"*Je ne comprends pas. Je suis désolé.*" She stared at me. Blinked.

Shouting erupted behind us. My eyes shot over to a woman a block back that had been in tears a moment earlier. She stood on her feet, her voice cracking as she screamed in a language I couldn't understand. I swallowed harshly. Two men grabbed her, pulling her away from the road into which she had thrusted herself. They tugged her down an alleyway. Her shouts echoed behind me.

"Let's get you guys out of here," I heard our tour guide from a few paces ahead. My eyes caught one last glimpse of the girl before I turned, running ahead to meet my family. We entered the other side of the train station, rows upon rows of slick white vehicles coming into view.

The woman approached a sign on a far wall. She stared at it, mumbling something under her breath, inspecting the foreign words plastered upon it. Slowly, she nodded, a smile spreading across her cheeks.

"*Oké!*" she exclaimed. "Your train is at the last row over there." She pointed somewhere across the building. "It leaves in forty-three minutes. You can pay here." She motioned towards the screen. Sitka stared for a moment, slowly stretching his arms towards his pocket and removing the stack of money remaining from this morning. The woman stared at him. Her smile faltered.

"You don't have digital currency?" He shook his head. She groaned, moving to the counter to the left, returning with a holographic screen. She pressed a few buttons, exchanging the money with my younger brother. There was a brief moment of quiet as the tickets printed. She handed them to my mother.

"Alright, you guys." She smiled at us each individually. "Have a nice ride. Enjoy Belgrade." And with that, we were walking away, my father leading the way to the train. In the staggering of my steps, my mind couldn't help but think of the people we had seen. Of the distress set upon their fragile faces, unlike anything I had before known. My mother was beside me, lingering behind the rest of our family. I could tell our thoughts dwelled together.

"Those poor people," I mumbled. She nodded.

"Yeah."

[23]

Phantom Eyes

Phantom eyes followed us aboard the train to Serbia. I saw the stares of hunters in the faces of strangers. I saw the piercing eyes of the woman from Salzburg driving her vehicle alongside us. She lingered everywhere. In the crisp, cold eyes of the conductor. In the naïve faces of children. There was not a single unfamiliar face I could see that didn't seem to reflect her intentions.

And so I stared at the floor.

But that was where my mind greeted me. Where my thoughts met me and departed in an instant, sending the residue of shockwaves through the front of my skull. Where bombs were dropped, flares and explosions sent through every muscle in my body, and I couldn't run away.

And then there were the moments that, to this day, I might never overcome. Those in which I thought I saw water rising up the side of the train window. Those when such a paralyzing terror struck me that not a single thought could roll through my mind. And I tried to breathe as though it would do anything. But that, too, was demolished.

So all three and a half hours I spent on that black leather couch in the back of the train, I found no rest. My stomach turned in hunger. My eyes stared in terror. The gun dug into my side as though it sought to impale me. The image of the Hungarian girl dazed my brain, and I was stuck wondering if there was more I could have done.

But there was nothing. For what could one helpless person do for another?

It was 21:35 by the time we arrived in Belgrade. The air seemed to be even warmer there, as though such a thing was possible. The train station walls were wrapped with large metal signs and scattered faces, and a population smaller than that of Hungary. Perhaps people were giving up on hope.

Perhaps I should've too. While I still had time. But I, in my foolishness, did not.

"Alright, let's see what's next." My mother unraveled her map from its creases. We stood on a platform between two trains, clustered together in a circle as though it would protect us from something, I'm not quite sure what. My mother tried to hide the franticness in her tone with a counterfeit smile.

"Bulgaria's the next country over," my father replied.

Sitka stared at my father. "Are we not stopping to sleep for the night?"

"You can sleep on the train. We need to keep moving."

My mother looked up at him. Something seemed to shift in the setting of her eyebrows. "Ävon, maybe we should stop . . ." She stared at him for a moment. Her eyes squinted inward in the same way that Viridian's often did. My father stole a breath, not releasing it as he leaned in closer to her. His eye seemed to twitch.

"We need to start moving faster, Yemasii. I don't know how long until the Qadim takes off . . . we could be running out of time." He said that last part quieter than the rest.

Then we were shuffling through the train station, moving through arched doorways and past small clusters of people who didn't acknowledge our passing. A franticness was placed on each step and it seemed to strengthen the further we traveled. Soon, we stood before a large screen beneath a doorway, locations listed off in Serbian and French side by side.

"Bulgaria . . . what town would we go to?" My mother scanned the board above us. Her gaze was caught in such an extreme concentration. "It's a fairly large country, so there has to be a few options." She glanced over at my father this time. His cheeks grew to a crimson shade, and he almost seemed to be breathing heavier. I watched the way his hands sat restlessly in his pockets.

"Right?" He sighed. His lips were pulled in a straight line across his face. Still no response. "Ävon, what is it?" His hands left his pockets. His arms were crossing, his gaze pinned to the screen like paper pinned to a wall. My eyes followed the path of his gaze, searching to find sense in his distressed stare. My tongue traveled the length of my bottom lip. Then, I noticed what my father saw.

"There's only trains going west," I mumbled. Hesitation dragged in my mother's response.

"What?"

"We need to go east to Bulgaria, but there are only trains headed west," my father intervened. A pause.

My mother tilted her head slightly to the side. "Why?"

"I don't know." Sour silence formed between us all. Sitka took a taste of it.

"It looks like we can go north or south."

"Right," my father confirmed.

"So we could go in from one of those countries."

My jaw sat slightly open. "How do we know that *they'll* let us into Bulgaria?"

My father shook his head. "We don't."

"So is it a Serbian or a Bulgarian rule that won't let us in?"

"I don't know."

"Wait, so you're saying we can't get into Bulgaria?" My gaze shifted to Viridian. He held the expression of a confused dog.

I blinked. "How did you miss that part of the conversation?"

Viridian's eyes grew wide. "So we have to *walk*?"

"Probably," my father and I said in unison.

"There is no way."

My eyes rolled. "You're telling me that you are nearly a *professional* basketball player and you can't go for a little stroll?"

"Across the entire continent? No."

"You die if you don't."

"Well I'll die walking too!"

"Would you two be quiet for two seconds, *please*." My mother glared at us. Her arms were crossed, her jaw clenched, and her eyes quickly corrected their focus towards my father. "So what do we do?"

He shrugged. "Let's just . . . ask someone about it, for starters." The help desk was to the right of the sign. My mother led the way. She rested her forearms on the counter and rung the bell, the reverberations stinging my ears. A woman appeared a moment later. She was in her late 20s, her black waves rested just past her shoulders. Her gaze seemed as though she had been preoccupied.

"*Zdravo, kako mogu da vam pomognem?*"

"*Français?*" The woman forced a smile, turning towards the corner of the counter, removing two earpieces from a small metal basket and slipping one to my mother. They both placed them inside their right ear, the woman repeating her words, my mother responding in French.

"We're trying to get to Bulgaria but there seems to be no trains headed east," my mother said. There was a pause as the muffled mumblings of the woman commenced.

"Really? Why not?" The woman spoke again. Her tone seemed to be harsh.

"Oh really." A response. My mother shifted uncomfortably. Her arms rested as wooden planks at her side.

"It's alright. Thank you." She slipped the translator back onto the counter. Paused in preparation. And then, she slowly stepped back towards us, a look of desperation set upon her face, growing like flames dancing up the sides of her cheeks. I could feel my heart drop. My stomach turn, groan. I felt dizzy once more.

"What'd she say?" my father asked.

"She . . ." My mother's eyes peeled over. "She said that Bulgaria isn't accepting any outside travel at the moment and that Serbia isn't allowing any trains to travel east."

"That doesn't make any sense."

"It doesn't?" She stared at my father. He seemed to tilt his head.

"Does it?"

"I think it does. I think they're not wanting people to get to Israel." His mouth opened slightly.

"What, so they just want their people to die?" A sharp exhale escaped my mother's lips. I zoned out of the conversation after that as though a tide was pulling me away while I longed to stay on shore. My fingers dug into the sand, but no grip was found. I was stumbling, falling into it, and it was consuming me. Grains licked the top of my head and ate at my skin. And I was staring up at the moon, wondering how it didn't hold the power over humanity. How we had decided that we could rule over each other. Decide life and death for each other. Deciding it to be our right.

"Let's stay here for the night then. We'll start walking tomorrow," my father's words pulled me out of the tide. I stared at his face over the waters. A buzz echoed from my pocket.

➤ From "Unknown," 21:43

"There's an abandoned hotel on the outskirts of the city. I'll send you the address. Stay there for the night. It will be safe."

There was a single candle alive in the hotel when we arrived. It shone through a half-opened window on the second story, beaming light upon the crème-colored bricks and up to the stories above. The windows were shattered, shards of glass collecting like dust on the dirt road in which we stood.

But the window of the candle was in one piece. A single small crack rested on its interior, rolling up softly from a bottom corner, meeting the second larger crack in the middle.

Then, the candle went out.

Then, my heart stopped.

We stared at the window in silence. It seemed to crack more the longer our eyes pierced it. My hand betrayed my mind as it wrapped slightly around the gun I had been given.

"Who's there?" It was a man's voice. It came scathingly from the same window. I could hear him shuffling around, looking for something. My hand tightened. Then, a bright blue-toned flashlight was shining down upon us, and my eyes seemed to be bleached against my will.

"We mean no harm," my father began. He tried to make himself appear larger. "We're just looking for a place to stay for the night."

"Who *are* you?" There was a pause. "Why do you speak French so well?"

"Eve?" My hand's grip loosened around the weapon and I was staring at the window even more intensely now. I recognized that voice. The flashlight turned off. The sky above was lighter than what lay behind the window. Silence became a well-known anthem. And then there was movement.

Someone whispered. Someone else shuffled around the room. I couldn't make out a motion. I tried to release my grip on the gun. My hand seemed to have gained full independence from my mind. My bones rattled from more than just hunger. My head was aching. It strengthened by the second.

Stillness returned. My father shouted something. No response came.

Then, the red door at the base of the building began to open. Shaking. Creaking. My bones seemed to have turned to stone. It flung fully wide, a girl standing on the other side. She was short, her legs like stakes as they burrowed into the ground. Jeans wrapped around her skin, and a short tank top rested across her olive neck. Her arms were bony and slightly bruised, and her green eyes seemed to pierce the breath from my lungs. Her long, brown waves rolled like ribbons in the wind, stretching across her cheeks to where a permanent smile sat.

And then it clicked. It was Darbii.

[24]

Everything Is Okay

This isn't real.

But it seemed as though it was. As though my imagination had met reality and the two had shared a kiss.

That isn't her.

But her eyes told me otherwise. Growing and gleaming between shades of green beneath the blooming moonlight.

I had no control over the way my feet thrust me forward. The way I toppled and tripped over uneven ground and sent shards of glass flying into each other. It didn't matter. Nothing mattered but her eyes, staring at mine, smiling, laughing, crying. Because it was her. My best friend. Her—who I had believed I abandoned—her, who I wasn't meant to ever again see, standing before me. Her, whose smile had once been my delight and her laugh my poison. Her, who found me when I couldn't find myself. Who picked me up when I fell. Who held back the waves of the storm so I might be able to walk through them.

Her, who never once let me down.

And then, my arms were colliding with hers, and I was holding onto her so tightly, and her laughs were like the soft falling of petals. They were a disease, contagious, and I was sick alongside her. Sick inside some sacred joy that didn't seem practical—but what was living if one lived trapped inside practicalities?

Her embrace was as warm as a summer day before they turned wicked.

143

Her grip around me remained like the tight clench of a jaw that had become common upon my cheeks.

"I thought I would never see you again." Her voice was pure. Innocence drowned in franticness. A voice I never thought I would hear again. The voice that narrated my memories.

"I thought I would never see you."

And for a moment, I seemed to believe that maybe all of my pessimism had been faulty. Maybe that thought telling me I was destined to die had only been created to make me stumble. A spell I had cast upon myself, a poison I had taken thinking it to be a fine wine. Perhaps everything I had believed to be wrong with this world had been a lie.

Maybe everything was okay.

Her father stood beside her in a moment. His hands were held like a secret behind his back, his brister hair combed sideways on his head. He stood a bit too tall. Darbii pulled away from me. I watched how she moved slightly away from him as he passed us by, approaching my family.

"So I guess you followed us." Darbii giggled.

"Did you see the note I left you?" I asked. She shook her head in reply. "When did you leave?"

"May 19th . . ." Darbii said. Paused. Thought. "There's no way that was just yesterday."

"We left on the 18th." I said. She stared at me.

Her green eyes grew in confusion. "Where did you leave it?"

"On the notepad on your desk."

"I didn't see it there." She said. I stared at her. "What was it?"

I shook my head slowly. "Just to . . . tell you we were leaving." My head spun. A universe erupted into being in my mind. If she hadn't found it, that meant someone else had.

Not necessarily.

But then it was all hitting me like a baseball bat smacking a ball, and everything was coming back to me in a whirlwind. The helicopter in Germany.

The hunters in Austria. The pain and pressure and panic that we had all been put through.

All because of the note.

That can't be true.

"Whatever. It's not that big of a deal, I guess, since I found you anyway." Darbii shrugged and smiled. Then she turned back towards the door and the long staircase hidden behind it. "Come on, I have something I want to show you." She was running back up the stairs, and I was trying to follow, but my legs were planted in place, and I was staring at the brick building as though it would come crashing down on top of me.

Maybe I deserve it.

Of course I didn't.

And then I followed her.

She led me to the roof of the hotel, where red and yellow cushions were spread out across the floor, and candles with the smell of almond and vanilla danced in the burning breeze. Burnt-out string lights reached like branches from poles across the night sky, swinging with the wind. Heat blistered my boiling body, and somehow, I found the strength to ignore it. I plopped down upon one of the cushions, my gaze meeting the sea above, the moon an anchor, grabbing hold of my soul. Consuming the angst built up inside of me and drowning it among the waves and water.

"You want a bottle?" I had almost forgotten Darbii was standing before me. A yellowed glass bottle sat in her palm, pressed as a potion against it.

My hands buried themselves into my lap. "What is it?"

"Rakija. It's a Serbian brandy. Very strong, but very good."

I raised an eyebrow. "Where'd you get it?"

"I stole it from a deserted liquor store."

"You stole it . . ."

"Hey, no lectures right now. I might die soon . . . which would typically be a shit excuse, but I think it works these days." I watched her. Watched the memories that passed by my mind. The images of crumpled beer cans across her room. The promises of "the last time." The promises she never kept.

"Do you want one or not?" she asked again. My breath became heavy.

"I haven't eaten all day, so that's probably not the best idea."

Her eyes grew a bit. "Why haven't you eaten?" I shrugged. "Well you need to eat something, girl." She moved back across the balcony, shuffling through a backpack, returning with an apple and a sandwich, slipping them into my open hands. I stared at them. My jaw dropped without my command.

"Where did you get these? I haven't seen food like this since . . ." I couldn't remember when.

"My perû." She moved back across the balcony. "I guess he kept a stash of emergency food or something. I don't know. I don't ask." She returned with a water bottle in one hand. "Here, you're probably dehydrated too." I took it from her, immediately taking a long drink of it. A rakija bottle sat in her other hand. She extended her arm out to me. I looked her dead in the eye. She stared back. Shrugged.

"No pressure, but . . ." She hesitated. Smiled foolishly. "You might never see me again." Her voice was too innocent for the words that emerged from it. Too innocent to recognize the weight of her tongue upon my conscience.

"Right, no pressure," I smirked as I said it. She pulled her lips into a straight line across her face.

"I mean it."

"I know you do." I smiled again. My eyes moved down to stare at the bottle in her hand. It stared back. I swallowed, and then I sighed. "What do I have to lose at this point . . ." So I took it from her, and she smiled, and it seemed to place itself next to me while the apple found its way into my hand. The rouge object stared at me harder than the bottle had. Its radiant gaze shattered the glass inside my eyes, and the shards fell down upon my bare skin. Upon my shredded arms. They seemed to burn again. My body tensed beneath the pain. Then it shook. Darbii said something that I couldn't hear.

I took a bite. Quickly. The flavor of the fruit made my throat throb. My head spun, and in an instant, I was wondering if I would pass out to the ground. If I would explode. Implode. Erupt. Erode. I ignored the fear. Mindlessly chewed through the sour taste. Forced another bite then grabbed the rakija bottle beside me. I couldn't tell the color through the yellowed glass. The logical side of me said it was dumb to pop the lid off and connect the rim to my lips, but the careless side did it anyway. The liquid hit my tongue, stinging brutally as I swallowed, coughing.

"Oh *gosh* that's strong."

Darbii laughed, gesturing outwards with her arms. "Hey, it's good though, yeah?"

"If you say so." I was rolling my eyes and forcing myself to take another bite of the apple. Darbii plopped down to the right of me, sipping from her bottle as if it hadn't just burned the skin right out of my throat.

She chuckled a bit. "You know what would be crazy?" My eyebrow raised in her direction. "If we both found boyfriends on the Qadim." She giggled. I stared at her.

"*Both*?"

"Yeah."

"Darbii, do you not remember anything about me? Has it really been that long?" She looked over at me. Her tongue rolled in circles around her mouth, forcing laughter off her tongue. Then she was standing again, moving back across the balcony.

"No, I know. You have that whole thing about not dating until eighteen."

"Because it's stupid—"

"No, you're right."

"There is absolutely no point—"

"*But*. You are almost eighteen." I went quiet as my gaze found her. She sat across from me on a cushion, her feet pulled beneath her and hands tied together in her lap. She stared plainly at me for a moment. Then, a smile began to lift upon her rose-tinted cheeks.

My eyes narrowed. "What?" She shook her head. "What? You're plotting something."

"I am not."

"I know that look, Darbii." She grinned. And then her arm was reaching behind her.

"I wanted to get you something more for your birthday but . . . of course, with everything . . ." She shook her head. "Anyway, I got this for you back in January because it reminded me of you because it's green and pretty and . . ."

Her arm extended out towards me. A notebook rested in her palm. It was a deep, delirious green, velvety upon my touch. I looked down at it as I took it from her hands. A smile grew across my cheeks. It morphed into a grin.

"You brought it all this way?"

She shrugged. "I had hope I'd see you. In case you were . . . headed the same way as me, I guess." I looked up at her. She was smiling so softly.

"Thank you." She nodded once.

"You have to write me a poem now."

I smiled. "A poem?"

"Yeah, isn't that what you write?"

I shrugged. "Used to."

"What do you write now?"

"Just . . . thoughts." I thought for just a moment about the letters I had written to her. Gone. Burnt. Locked away inside castle walls. My eyes were no longer upon her. They stared down upon the forest inside my palms. I smiled a bit more. "Thank you, Darbii. Truly." I took one last look at it. Dreamed of a day in which the words inside would reflect the whimsical nature of its outside. Perhaps I would use it on the Qadim, to anchor my every thought down into something. And then I placed it to the left of me beside the apple. Then, my mind was stumbling back through the conversation, on to where she had first mentioned the Qadim. My eyebrows grew closer to each other.

"Wait, you said us *both*. What happened with you and Faraj?" Her gaze fell to her hands. She nodded.

"Damn. I forgot that you don't know."

" . . . what?" She stared at the crevices upon her fingers. She stood again, moving back beside me. Her words seemed to come out the moment she hit the cushion.

"He dumped me." Something inside of me settled and rose up at the same time, and I tried to find the words to make up for her emotions.

"Oh, Darbii . . . when? And *why*?"

"About a month ago . . .? He . . ." She paused, staring at her hands. They were shaking. "He told me that he wanted space before we all . . . well, *die*." She forced a laugh. "But then I heard from Bethanii that he was just . . . sick of me. And wanted someone better." She was laughing again. Her teeth had been white lies.

"That jerk. You know that isn't true, right? He never deserved you." Darbii stared at the floor. Her gaze was contemplative, the bottle sitting as a silencer upon her lips. She shrugged. "Darbii."

"No, yeah, you're right. I know."

"I really am so sorry."

"It's alright. I didn't . . . I don't need him." There was a pause, a restless silence settling into the stillness of the burning night. I could see the pain stained across my best friend's face, hidden beneath a smirk, plastered like a poster for a play with an unexpectedly upsetting ending. I could see Faraj's face in my mind's eye, his dark skin and dark eyes, and the deception in his grin. I could feel again the anger I once felt when I looked upon him.

The silence between us grew to be unbearable. My lips began to move.

"I almost died the other night." Darbii's gaze was still on her hands as it slowly found me. Then, my words seemed to process in her head.

"You . . . *what*? How?"

"My perû drove our truck into a river . . ." I hesitated. "Well technically it was my fault."

"Your perû . . . wait what?"

"The room we were staying in got blown up, and we were running away from people that were chasing us—"

"People were chasing you?"

"Oh. Yes. Did you know people are after us because we're Cordellian?" I laughed through my anger.

"Holy *shit*, Eve!" She was sitting up at that point, staring at me as she processed it all. Somehow, I was smiling. "I don't understand. How was it your fault?"

"I . . ." I paused. Thought of Elijah. Something rose in my throat. "I haven't told anyone about this yet." That got her attention. Her legs were crossed as she watched each of my minute movements. Then, I was staring at the moon, waiting for its guidance. For it to tell me that it was okay to tell Darbii. That I could let the secret just a little loose. Because I couldn't carry the full weight of it any longer.

It felt as though I was forcing the words out of my mouth.

"There's been an unknown number messaging me and helping us out of near-death situations. Someone named Elijah." She looked at me. Her expression stayed stagnant.

"Do you even know an Elijah?"

"No."

"But . . . texts aren't going through. How is he messaging you?" I shrugged. The same thought had struck me the first time he messaged me in what felt like so long ago. "How does this have anything to do with your car?"

I let out a breath of air. "When we were running from the people that were chasing us, he sent me a message to stay to the right of the road. And me, being . . . stubborn, told my perû to stay to the left of the road . . . then we ended up in the river." I felt my eyes grow wet and weary. My tongue slid across my bottom lip.

"So . . . your perû's bad at driving," she said. I looked at her. Shook my head.

"No, I directed him wrong."

"And *he* made the car end up in a river. You weren't the one driving."

"It was pitch black out. He couldn't see where the road ended and the river began!"

"And you could?"

"No . . ."

"Right, so it's not your fault." I didn't reply to that. "You need to stop being so hard on yourself. Stress less, cause you're the best." I chuckled. A tear escaped onto my left cheek.

"I don't think that's how that phrase goes . . ."

"Doesn't matter." She smiled, reaching into her right pocket, searching for something. I watched her pull out a cigarette and a lighter, pressing the objects together, a flame formed on one end of the cigarette.

I shook my head. "Where did you get that?"

"I brought it." I released an exhale and somehow managed to laugh through my disappointment.

"Okay, you need to learn how to deal with your problems better."

"What? It calms me down."

"Temporarily."

"Right. For the duration of time I need it to." She extended the cigarette out to me, a small spreading across her face.

My eyes widen. "Absolutely not."

"Yeah, I know." She looked away. "Thought it was at least worth a shot."

"Is that supposed to be reverse psychology or something? Because it's not working."

"I didn't expect it to work."

"But you thought you'd try anyway. Just for kicks and giggles."

"It was *not* a reverse psychology attempt." I raised an eyebrow. Her gaze met mine out of the corner of her eye. "And even if it was, admitting to it would defeat the purpose."

I grinned. "I got you."

"You did not."

"I totally did."

She rolled her eyes, smiling. Took a puff of her cigarette. "You're allowed to perceive the situation however you please." Then, she reached for her phone in her side pocket. "Now, this is why I always had music downloaded."

I smirked. "What, you knew the world was going to end?"

"Something like that." An upbeat tune began to play from her cell phone, and soon I was throwing my head backwards.

"Oh my gosh . . ." I said. It was a song we always used to listen to back when life was normal. We used to drive around town and blast it out the windows and laugh at people walking by whose glares stayed glued to us.

"It was a miracle what happened late last Sunday night
I looked too deeply into all the truths I've tried to hide
The moon stood right there to watch me
It gets so exhausting.

"Seeing photographs of a life that wasn't lived
Searching graveyards for a homely place to lay my head
I watched the mountains but they crumbled
The seas but they took me down."

She was standing at that point, dancing across the floor in front of me, rakija resting in her palm and cigarette between her lips. Her smile was glued across her cheeks, and laughter on her tongue. Her movements were silky and strained, and soon, I was laughing like a child again. Then the chorus came and we were singing together.

"I got bored of my tears
Sinking too near to my lips where a smile had fled
Tired of my fears
Trembling beneath my eyes ignoring this dread
It was a match made in heaven
My fingers laced with the rays of the sun."

And soon, joy became the ally that I had forgotten I once knew.
Maybe everything was okay.

[25]

Headache

I dreamed of the Hungarian girl.

Her broken blue rags were turned into robes of royalty. She stood in a dark room. Light seemed to radiate off of her smile and in her eyes seemed to lie a hopeful hunger.

I looked away.

My head was the first thing I noticed the next morning. It seemed to have morphed into a door, and someone was pounding upon it, their fist creating indents on my forehead.

I remembered the rakija.

My eyes opened.

The sky was red and radiant and unassuming as its gaze grazed the bandages on my skin. Darbii sat on the other side of the roof. Her palms clasped a yellow bottle, her gaze sat vacant on the floor. Her eyes soon found me.

"You okay?" Her words were riddled with discomfort, and I was watching her through that burning headache. Through that burning skin. My eyes were blurred.

"Yes I'm fine."

"Sleep well?"

I shrugged. "As well as I can while the world is ending." Darbii smiled.

"In an unknown country, at that."

"Right, I forgot about that part." I sighed. Placed my forearms beneath me and pushed myself forward. A storm met me above, crushing into my skull. Furious winds wrapped around my head, shook it, and obliterated it. My palm tried to fight by pressing against my forehead.

"Gosh, my head hurts." There was a lull of silence.

"I'm sorry." I stared at Darbii's eyes. They seemed to have turned a darker shade of green since I last saw her. It was the first time I noticed how much her pain had truly poisoned her. How much those three months had stolen from her.

"I wish I would have visited you, Darbii." Her eyes lifted a bit higher towards me. Head tilted. "When it all began. I wish I would have just dealt with the heat and went to see you."

She shrugged. "You did what we all did."

"I would have driven but—"

"The psychos would have found you and tried to steal your car. I know." She watched me. Smiled. "It's okay, Eve. You didn't do anything and I didn't either. It's on both of us." I looked down at my hands clasped in my lap. The skin was parched and peeling. I moved them towards my eyes, wiping the haziness from within. My body felt as though it was going to melt, but it seemed as though I was used to it.

My head ached more.

What have you done.

"My merû still worked," I said. Darbii stared.

Shrugged. "Well she's a doctor."

"She walked to work. Everyday." Wheels clicked into motion in her mind. Her eyes widened. "All the way to CordellMed?"

"Yes."

"That's like . . ."

"An hour and a half on a good day."

Her jaw dropped. "Holy shit." She laughed. "Well then yeah, I guess we could have done better." She continued to giggle. I smiled with her. But the smile seemed forced at the knowing of what I should have done. How I should have done more to protect her from herself. How everything I had done—the notes I had written her—was merely symbolic of a day I might see her again.

Of a day that was never promised to me.

But those three months had been.

"I wrote you letters. About everything I did every day." My gaze couldn't seem to find her. "I guess it was my way of trying to still feel connected to you. I left one in my room symbolically and the rest . . . they all were left in the room we were chased out of that night. Burnt up, probably." She didn't look at me either. I felt as though I had dragged us both to the river from that same night to drown in our guilt as though it had absolute power over us.

"I wish I did something like that," Darbii mumbled. "But I wouldn't even know where to start."

"You're an incredible writer, Darbii." She shrugged.

"Maybe at some point I was." She pondered it. And soon, she was laughing. For once, I couldn't tell whether or not her laughter was genuine. "Me, on the other hand, I just drank . . . a lot."

I sighed, "Darbii . . ."

"I know." Her smile was a shifting shadow. "I wish I could quit."

"Why don't you?" She stared at the bottle in her hands. Its yellow tint looked like glue across her blistered fingers. Then, she was shaking her head ever so slightly.

"I don't know. It's . . . it's kinda the best outlet I have right now, you know? Just to process . . . everything. And . . . to be honest, I'm worried I won't ever find anything better." I watched her hands. I watched her mind try to control them. I watched it scream at her to put the bottle down, to toss it away, to throw it off the balcony, and hear it shatter on the street below.

But I saw the way her hands grasped it as though it had become more similar to muscle memory. And the more her bones remembered her grip around it, the less her mind remembered how it had gotten there in the first place.

"Sometimes I wonder if there's a reason the Israelis get a chance at life again and we don't," she said. "If they're like . . . I don't know, more worthy or something."

"More worthy?"

"Probably not the best word."

"No it fits . . . I think." The thought had never occurred to me before. But I knew it wasn't true. "I think it's more just a matter of fate. Israel has the most advanced technology of our time, so their fate is survival." There was a pause. Not a single bone in Darbii's body shifted as she spoke.

"My mother always used to say that fate is for those too weak to determine their own destiny." She looked back up at me. "I like to hope sometimes that I'm not truly weak."

I never heard Darbii mention her mother. Not since she passed. The last time I could remember was a month after the memorial, while she was getting ready for a party; her first real party. I was in her room, sitting on her bed, making it no secret that I believed it to be a bad idea. Before she left, I heard her mumble to herself, "Merû would never approve of this."

To this day, I still don't know if she knows I heard her.

That was four years ago now.

Soon after she began to complain that her father had always yelled at her. She never knew why. I remember the first time I saw her with bruises. I convinced myself it was a marker.

"Darbii!" There was a shout from down the staircase. It came minutes after what we had morphed into playful conversation. "We need to be leaving soon."

"I'm coming, Perû," she replied. She was tense. Too tense.

"Will you be fine? You know, with your perû? I know he . . ."

"Yeah I'll be good," she cut me off before I could find the words to finish. Standing, she capped her bottle and placed it into her duffle bag, tossing it over her shoulder. My eyebrows raised.

"That was a fake smile." It seemed to grow and fade at the same time.

"Yeah, well, sometimes you have to fake a smile for the sanity of others."

My face fell. It tumbled down from the sky as a damaged rocket.

"You can come with us, you know. My family would be more than happy to have you."

She shook her head. "I know. Thank you." I stared at the mess in her severed gaze. I didn't know what else I had expected from her. I knew she was attached to her father like a thin thread, so ready to snap. But she gripped it so tightly that even if it did snap, she would tie it back together.

I followed her downstairs and out the big red door. My family stood facing Darbii's father.

"Where are you headed next?" I heard him ask my mother.

"I believe Bulgaria."

Bulgaria. The word penetrated something inside my mind until memories were crawling back to me. Images of a postcard lodged into my desk. Of that project in Grade 9 that had made me obsessed with such a place for so long..

"Can we go to Varna?" Everyone's gaze fell on me. "It's in Bulgaria, and it's on my bucket list . . . and I don't think we'll ever be back here." My mother slowly nodded.

"We'll talk about it." I found my way beside my family and Darbii beside her father. Her feet seemed to plant stiff into the ground. Her hands wrapped around her torso in an obscured stance that she undermined with a smile.

"Hey, don't die without me." I forced a smile across my lips at the sound of her voice.

"*You* don't die without *me*. Seems more like something you would do."

She laughed. "I already have planned what I'm going to say at your funeral, you know?"

"Oh yeah?"

"Good friend, good dancer, bad partier."

I raised an eyebrow. "You've thought about this?"

"You haven't?"

"No, I don't typically think about my best friend dying." She laughed.

And soon, she was pulling me into one of her sweet embraces, and I was left hoping this wouldn't be the last time I felt one.

"See you around," she said. I tried to force a smile across my cheeks, but tears seemed to come instead.

"Yeah," I nodded and pulled away, staring at the rain that created puddles at the edges of her cheeks. I wished I could wipe them away.

My gaze faltered for a moment. It found its way to Darbii's father, standing beside her. It reached towards his hands tied like a knot behind his back, a piece of paper poking out of the back pocket of his jeans. I stared at its sporadic crumples like bullets being fired into the night. There was writing across it, rushed and scribbled. The black pen markings were smeared across the damaged paper. The longer I stared at the words, the more familiarity I found in them. And suddenly, I was recognizing the writing as my own. I scanned the letters again. Twice. Three times. Soon, they were forming words, and I was making out the phrase, "leaving for Israel."

Then it hit me; it was the note I had left for Darbii on her desk.

The one she hadn't seen.

Her father turned towards me a moment later. There was a grimace disguised as a grin set across his pasty cheeks. His hair fell like a flood across his forehead, and he was extending his hand out for me to shake, and my eyes were staring in unease at his palm.

"It was good to see you, Eve." His words were crisp and clear, and mine came back to him as the inverse.

"Thanks," I said. I ignored his hand and turned towards my family, the text ringing over again in my mind. *Leaving for Israel, leaving for Israel, leaving for Israel . . .*

Why didn't he tell Darbii?

I glanced up at Darbii one last time as we began to walk away. She was staring at me, her cheeks raised into a smile that seemed to falter into confusion around her eyes. And then I looked away. Looked at my feet as they moved without my mind telling them to. I should've turned back. Grabbed

Darbii. Taken her with us. She had never been safe with her father; I knew that already. But what if there was more to his crudeness than I had once thought? What if my instincts not to trust him had been more than correct?

Who is Mister Soddom, really?

"You're supposed to say 'you too,'" my mother mumbled. I ignored her. Politeness didn't amount to anything in the face of evil.

I looked over at my father as we continued down the road. My heart was still racing. His eyes found me, his blank stare changing when he noticed the look of worry upon my face. He gestured to me to follow him as he pulled away from the rest of the family.

"Mr. Soddom has the note," I whispered once I was beside him. His hands were pulled behind his back, and he was staring at his feet.

"What note?"

"The one I wrote to Darbii telling her that we were leaving. Remember?" He pulled his lips tightly towards his mouth, glancing down at me, clearly not understanding my point. "I asked Darbii if she had seen it, and she said no, and then I saw it in Mr. Soddom's pocket when we were leaving. I guess he just . . . took it without showing it to her . . .?" He nodded slowly for a moment, staring at the ground as he walked. He crossed his arms.

"So what do you want to do about it?" he asked.

I shrugged. "I don't know, what can we do?"

"You think Mr. Soddom is crooked. Don't you," he said it more as a statement than a question. I forced myself to shake my head. It burned my headache.

"I mean . . . I don't know—"

"Because I would agree with you." My eyes shot up at him.

"Where is Viridian?" My mother's exclamation brought me back to the present. I was looking around us. She was right. He wasn't there.

"Did we leave without him? I could have sworn he was beside me just a moment ago," my father called.

"He was! Oh, that *kid*!" A hover car pulled around a corner a few blocks ahead of us. Its red coat was glaring at us beneath the harsh cast of the sun. It seemed to be moving towards us. I stared at it for a moment.

It *was* coming towards us.

Quickly.

It didn't slow the closer it got. I began to wonder if it saw us. If it would stop. I seemed to stand a bit taller as its light hums grew louder and brighter and breathier. And then it was in front of us, stopping seconds away from hitting my mother. It rested a foot above the ground, the tinted black window suddenly disintegrating before my eyes. A boy sat in the driver's seat, his dark skin accented by blond curls and vibrant green eyes.

My jaw dropped.

"Get in," Viridian said.

"You stole a car?!" my mother practically screamed.

"I'll explain later, just get in." She shook her head.

"You are *so* grounded."

[26]

Desperate Times Call For Desperate Measures

"You know, I've always wanted to drive one of these." It was the first thing Viridian said once we were all in the vehicle. My father, Sitka, and I all sat squished into the backseat, I in the middle. My mother sat in the passenger seat beside Viridian. Her arms were crossed, and her eyes were stuck like glue out the front window. There was such an extreme tension in her green gaze I feared it would burn through the windshield. Viridian glanced over at her for a moment. He looked her up and down before continuing. "Come on, you know it's pretty cool."

"You *stole* it!" She yelled, throwing her arms out to the side. Viridian was unfazed.

"Desperate times call for desperate measures."

"We are *not* desperate."

"Really?" His words were so impaired by sarcasm to the point of even him chuckling once they left his mouth. The car went silent. My head pounded. The sunlight out the window seemed brighter than usual.

What have you done . . .

My mother's map had already found its way back onto her lap, shaking ever so slightly at the speed of the car's travels.

"Drive slower, please," she broke the silence. Viridian hesitated to reply.

"Well I'm kinda . . ."

"Kinda what? Kinda running away from the person you stole it from?"

"Well I wouldn't word it like that but—"

My jaw dropped. "Oh my *gosh*, Viridian!" I slapped my legs as I said it, which somehow caused him to drive even faster. My father's forehead was in his palms while my mother screamed at my brother. I couldn't make out a single word of what she was saying. Sitka laughed silently.

"We're going to have to have a serious talk with you at some point," my father was exclaiming, and Viridian was glaring through the rearview mirror.

"I am an adult, ladies and gentlemen!"

"Right, and you're going to end up in an adult prison one of these days." I was trying to hold back my laughter through the headache. Sitka snorted beside me. And then we were both laughing, and I could no longer seem to find breath in my lungs. Viridian shook his head at us.

I heard tires skid behind us.

My laughs slowly dissolved as my whole body turned around, staring out the window behind me. There drove a large black truck, and through the front window was a man, an angered expression engraved into his eyes. I clenched my jaw, then my fists. Swallowed.

"Viridian, you're an idiot." He looked back at me in the rearview mirror again.

"What?" Then he saw what I saw. "Shit!" And suddenly he was punching the gas even harder, and I was being thrown backward in my seat. The world around me felt as though it was spinning, and I couldn't tell if it was from the vehicle or intoxication.

But then it all came back to me. Then, I remembered where I had seen this before.

Salzburg. By the river.

My heart raced,

    ran in circles,

        round and round.

Then, the car was spinning, and Viridian was pulling hastily onto a crowded highway, and I couldn't seem to find my breath where my lungs had betrayed it.

"You are a *terrible* driver!" I screamed through my staggered breaths.

"I know that!" He was dodging cars at that point, racing in between other hover vehicles and those that cruised across the ground. He pulled a lever, the vehicle rose a bit higher, passing ground vehicles overhead and moving perpendicular to them.

My head spun. Turned as flying saucers.

I saw our car crashing into the river.

I saw the water rising up my ankles.

I saw the panic in my father's eyes.

And suddenly, I was shaking violently, and my hands were vibrating, and I needed to leave the car. I needed to go somewhere. Do something. Anything.

Nothing.

I need to get out of this car.

Viridian swerved. I was thrown into my father, squashing him against the window. He groaned. *I'm so sorry.* I thought I said it out loud. A loud scream erupted from the front seat.

"Why are you screaming?!" my mother yelled at Viridian.

"I'm not screaming!"

"You're squealing like a child, Viridian!" I hardly heard Sitka's laughter in reply. For all I could see then was the river beside me, below the bridge we rolled across.

No. Oh my gosh.

No, no, no.

I stared at the water, dried to a drizzle, as the river in Budapest had been beyond the train station. If we fell down there, there would be no escape from death. Not that time. We would fall and break and cry out in agony, and no one would hear.

No one would care.

I tried to cry through the fear. My eyes remained a desert.

But then we were on the other side of the bridge, and Viridian was passing over cars again, moving towards an off-ramp.

"Where are you going?!" my mother's words seemed muffled. Viridian looked over his shoulder behind him.

"They were right behind me!"

"Bulgaria is that way!" She pointed down at her map and then up towards the sign on the freeway above, bright blue, the name of our next destination printed clearly across it in French. Viridian's gaze moved towards her hand, noticing the sign in his rearview mirror.

"Ugh!"

"Just let me drive."

"I am in the middle of a car chase and you think I'm going to give the vehicle over to you?"

"I think you lost them, Viridian." It was Sitka that time. Viridian looked around himself without slowing down. The streets were empty. He blinked. Twice.

"Yeah, I think you're right." I tried to slow my breathing as he pulled back onto the freeway. Tried to focus on a single point on the ground to clarify my blurry vision. I remained shaking in shambles.

What is wrong with you?

My mother insisted on driving.

She wanted to be the one in control when we crossed into Bulgaria. The one to lie to the AI being at the border, telling them we were from there. Returning home after visiting family. The one who explained that we lost our license plate going over a bump on a rural road when really my father had removed it and left it in a garbage pile in an alleyway. The one who seemingly remained without anxiety when they threatened to take us to further questioning. And then, the one to pass over the border, for no human employees could be found to perform such a task.

We stopped outside of a rundown restaurant. It was run by a single elderly man who hardly understood French. He got my order wrong, but I was incapable of eating it anyway. And so we sat inside the car, parked in a hover-lot, and Viridian was asking where we were planning to go next, but it seemed we stopped planning. It seemed that no one was truly on the same page. How could we be? I was forcing a bowl of rice and beans down my throat, and no one knew that it was more painful than the burning heat on my cheeks. I felt nauseated, as though I would erupt into oblivion if I consumed even a bite more. Hunger was but a hindrance of my past, a rouge phrase abandoning me in the hoax of its absence.

I placed the bowl in my lap.

"Can we go to Varna?" My mother looked back at me from the driver's seat. She glanced down at the map resting on her legs. "You said we would discuss it." A pause.

"That's on the coast." She was staring at the map. "We have no reason to go that far."

"I had a research project about it in Grade 9. It's absolutely beautiful. If I could go anywhere in the world it would be there."

"Right now, we're just trying to get to Israel."

"Right, so we can get off the planet and never come back and never be able to see the things we've always wanted to see." She thought about it for a moment. "Merû, I am begging you. Just one night. We're never going to be back in Europe ever again."

"What if we run out of time . . ." My father mumbled it from the passenger seat for only his ears, but we all heard it anyway. No one replied.

"We can't stay for long," my mother continued.

"I know that." She stared at me in the rearview for a moment. And in an instant, she was finishing the last of her meal and placing the map in the center divider between her and my father. "To Varna." I smiled. Somehow it felt real.

Even now, while writing this, I don't understand how it was. How I was able to find the strength to smile.

My mother clicked the car into gear, and we were pulling onto the road beside us.

A vibration sounded from my pocket.

➤ From "Unknown,"11:34

"Don't stay in Varna for too long."

My eyes narrowed in on the message. Everything came into focus again, just for a moment. Elijah. The river. The constant messages. Darbii, my note in Wëvii Soddom's pocket. And for just a moment, I feared how much he knew. If, one day, he would use his knowledge against me.

I mustered up the strength to submit a response.

➤ To "Unknown,"11:35

"What's considered too long?"

➤ From "Unknown,"11:35

"Sunrise tomorrow."

➤ To "Unknown,"11:35

"And what happens if we are there until then?"

I stared at my phone, anticipating a response. None came.

I leaned over to Sitka beside me.

"What time does the sunrise?"

He shrugged. "How would I know?"

"You know everything."

"No I don't."

I stared at him for a moment. Hesitated to speak again but I did anyway. "*Helii Cordell*?" His eyes shot over at me. I watched the scene of the Cordellia border roll again across the muscle of his mind. He said nothing.

I sighed. "Can you just check please?" He stared at me for a moment longer before he reached for his phone, swiping to a program and typing something into it.

"7:30," he said. His gaze locked with mine again. I knew he wanted to ask me why I had even asked him in the first place. What I knew that he didn't.

But I looked away, too fast for him to say a word. Again, I faced forward, the message settling into my mind. The weight of lies pressing against the glass of my conscience as though to shatter my morality that remained.

The gun dug deeper into my hip.

Its pressure seemed to shatter it on its own.

[27]

The Last Time

Silver and gold created a color of their own where the horizon met. Where the line was bruised and blurred and buried beneath the dormancy of day. The beaches bustled with fading commotion and yet bent beneath the drowned groans of those who had come before, those who would never come again.

We parked beside the sea. My parents grabbed a drink at a bar along the sand, and Viridian failed to sneak a sip, though it had been his intention. They walked like giddy children down the shore, and my brothers and I moved towards the sea and danced and laughed and splashed in the waves and felt the boiling water against our skin and yet, it didn't seem to burn. Perhaps we had simply chosen to not feel the burning. Salt soaked like a fresh fragrance against my tongue. Joy seemed again to be a safe companion.

I felt hungry for the first time in a day or two.

The last time I had been to the beach was last year, when my family had gone for a weekend to Saint-Nazaire in France. Where my grandparents owned a house right along the water and my brothers and I had spent all of Saturday playing in the waves. We left early the next morning because my mother had gotten into an argument with her parents. The car ride home had been quiet.

But today was different. It felt, for once, that everything could be okay. So I ignored the heat. Ignored the red sun and the light gray sky. Ignored the ever-impending fear that everything we were doing was all for nothing.

But soon the sun was setting, and I could only see the remembrance of its presence. Maybe finally it could be gone for good. The sky grew dark and dreary and dampened by the wet cast of the moon, rolling like a river down the sky. It stared at me. I smiled back.

The night became too dark to decipher through, and we were leaving the car parked by the sea and moving up the street to where a hotel lay ahead. I kept the notebook Darbii had given me clenched against my left palm.

We passed a woman on that street. The tight-fitting brown jeans she wore made her legs look longer than they truly were. On her torso rested a light green sweater, torn around the bottom, the threads unraveling. Her curly brown hair had been matted, covered by a cloth headband, the design on the fabric being of red and white tulips, tied off at the bottom of her head, the tail of it reaching down and sitting upon her right shoulder. And where her eyes were supposed to be white, they were red, accented by a tear on either cheek and the shaking of her thin lips. I kept my eyes down while passing her. I hated myself for doing it.

The hotel was hardly in operation. A single AI being was running the place whose programmer had not bothered to shut it down since the chaos arose. The walls had been covered in cobwebs along the entryway and I watched a rat run into a half open closet. We were given a room on the third floor with a large window overlooking the sea. I sat before it for a while, after bathing and being forced again to wear my old clothing, watching the last layers of light jumping across the sky and falling down into the waning waves. My bowl of rice and beans sat in my hands.

I remembered the warning from Elijah. Of how our stay had to be kept short.

I tried to push through the nausea that formed at the thought.

I swallowed my last bite; it had hurt.

At one point, my eyes dashed behind me. My parents sat on a beat up beige-colored couch, and Sitka was on the floor below them, eating from his own leftovers. A candle was lit upon the table before them. Viridian stood in the doorway of a closet across the room, looking through a stack of old board games. His gaze leveled out.

"Oh wow," he said, turning around. A smile was smitten across his cheeks. "Guys, do you remember this game?" He reached for the shelf, removing it from beneath a stack of other broken boxes. I followed him towards the coffee table, resting on the floor opposite my parents, gazing over the box he placed on the table. I stared for a moment, smiling when I realized what it was.

The Last Time. A game we often played as a family. It was simple—too simple even—but my mother had always appreciated the honesty of it all. Someone would pull a card, asking the question of when the last time had been in which someone performed a particular action. The one to draw the card would answer first, then the rest of the players went clockwise. Whoever did it the most recently received a point. Everyone got three "pass" cards.

"Can we play it?" Sitka asked. I glanced down at the time on my phone. It was already 20:47. We needed to leave early the next morning.

"Obviously!" my mother exclaimed. In an instant, she was reaching for the box and removing the cards. I tried to conceal a low sigh.

"I want to keep track of score." Viridian grabbed the scoreboard and the pen next to it. He wrote out all of our names in less than legible writing. Then, his eyes found my father. "Okay, Perû, you're first." My father looked up at him like a child. He grinned, grabbing the first card, his joy falling once he read it.

"I got the boring one."

"Just read it!" Viridian exclaimed, and my father forced a smile.

"When was the last time you went to the restroom?" He placed the card back on the table. "When we got here."

"Same," my mother said and then Sitka after her. There was a pause at Viridian's turn. He inhaled, held his breath. Smirked.

"Right now." Sitka burst out in laughter, and my mother and I rolled our eyes.

"Viridian!" she yelled.

"That's disgusting!" I exclaimed, and he was grinning in the same cocky way that he always did.

"I'm kidding. Take a joke, friends." He sighed, his eyebrows bending inward as stiff planks of wood. "It was when we got here."

"Me too," I said. "No points for that one since we all said the same thing." My mother went to draw the next card. Her eyes scanned over it resting soft in her palms. A smirk that slid up the sides of her cheeks and my heart began to race with it. Her eyes lifted.

"When was the last time you had a crush?" Her gaze shifted to my father. A smile grew red across her cheeks. "Twenty-two years ago when I met this man." She was grinning like a child, and for a moment, I wondered if I could see a glimpse of the teenager she had once told me about. The person she had been before she found her calling. When she had just met my father in a park in Paris. When he had moved there from Morocco to seek out the picturesque.

"Yeah, you're not winning this round. Sitka, your turn," Viridian said. There was a pause. Sitka frowned, his eyes focused on a spot on the floor, his hands rubbing against each other in his lap.

"Um . . ." He swallowed. We all stared at him.

Viridian just stared. "Sitka."

"I know, I . . . well." He sighed reluctantly. "Okay, well this is embarrassing."

A smile crept across my face. "Oh my gosh, you have to say it now." His eyes met mine for a moment, and I found a softness in his dark gaze that I hadn't seen before. My smile grew. His receded further.

"Well." He hesitated. A breath had been pulled in through his nose and I didn't think I saw him release it. "I . . . used to like Darbii." My jaw dropped.

"No. Way." I stared. Grinned. And suddenly, I burst out into laughter. My chest was aching in the matter of a moment as though a weight had been thrust atop it. Viridian followed suit, and Sitka was staring out the window behind me, licking his lips.

"You like my best friend?!" I said through my laughs. His laser eyes shot over at me.

"*Liked.* As in past tense."

"Darbii Elko," Viridian said. "It has a nice ring to it."

"Stop it."

"Guys, stop terrorizing your brother," my mother rested a hand on Sitka's shoulder. "That's very cute, sweetie."

Sitka groaned. He glared up at Viridian. "V, it's your turn."

"Oh, you just want the attention off of you."

"Correct." Viridian smiled and then he was pondering the question. His smile fell.

"The last crush I had was Clariia." Silence. No one wished to comment on what we all knew to be true. Clariia. The last girl he dated. How he broke her heart.

His gaze moved to me.

I shrugged. "I don't know, actually. I don't really have crushes."

My mother groaned. "Oh come on!"

"I'm being serious!"

"Aren't you supposed to be *my* daughter?"

"Oh my gosh. Perû, can you answer please so we can move on?" He chuckled.

"I have the same answer as your mother." My mother's eyes were still fixed wide on me.

"Eve, you *have* to have a crush." My jaw was clenched as I rolled my eyes.

"Fine. Johnny Cruz in Grade 2. How's that for you?"

"That cannot be the most recent crush you've had."

"It is."

"It's okay," Sitka began. "We'll get a secret out of her next question." They were looking at each other, smug smiles across both of their cheeks. My eyes jumped back and forth between them. They narrowed.

"Hang on, are you two teaming up against me?"

"Next question!" Sitka slapped his hand onto the pile, pulling the next card.

"You can't cheat in a game about honesty, guys."

Sitka ignored me. "When was the last time you drank alcohol?" He smiled. "Never."

My mother looked taken aback, "Never?"

"Nope."

"You guys are *not* my kids."

"Goody two shoes . . ." Viridian mumbled. My mother's eyes widened, a smile slicing the skin of her cheeks.

Her gaze met his. "Viridian?" They shared the same grin.

His right hand rubbed his opposite elbow. "Remember right before everything started when we were at Granmerû's house in Morocco? You know that liquor cabinet they have in the dining room?"

"You're not telling me you stole alcohol from my mother." My father sighed.

"Well I wouldn't say that—"

"Yemasii, we're raising our son to be a thief!"

"I'm not a thief!"

"The car?"

"Oh my—" Viridian slapped his face into his hands. "That was one time!"

"Oh yes because it's okay to steal a car once in your life." Viridian glared up at me.

"Okay, then what's your answer, Eve?" I stared at him. My smile quickly morphed into a frown that I used to cover my feeling of sheer terror. I remembered the night before. I remembered how out of character I had acted, how I regretted it all.

"I . . ." *I can't lie.* But I couldn't tell the truth either. "The same as you, Viridian." I forced a smile as I looked up at my parents. "He forced me to try a sip."

"I did not *force* you."

"You said you would tell Granmerû that *I* stole it if I didn't try it!"

Viridian shrugged. "Your life is boring, and I was trying to make it more interest–"

"My life is not boring—"

"—you literally just lay around—"

"—you're just cocky—"

"—and sleep and—"

"—and have . . . problems." Viridian stopped.

Tilted his head. "Problems?"

"Yes."

"What problems do I have?"

"Definitely not confidence . . ."

"Can I answer the question please?" My father was staring at us. Viridian and I blinked in unison. "I drank today. With your mother. So I want my point, please."

Viridian sighed, jotting a point down for both of my parents. My phantom vision saw his pen move beside my name. He reached for a card of his own.

"When was the last time you went on vacation?" He stared at the card for a moment, sliding it across his thumb. "Does this count?" No one replied.

"When we went to visit Granmerû and Granperû in Saint-Nazaire," I said with a forced smile. "Varna actually reminds me a lot of that."

My father nodded. "I was going to say the same thing."

"Me too," my mother said.

"Yeah." Sitka frowned.

"No points for that one." I reached for the next card in the stack. My eyes scanned the ebony letters across it. I froze fully and completely. A long moment passed before I was able to roll the words off my tongue. "When was the last time you told someone a big secret?" I continued to stare at the card, not fully processing my words until they escaped me. "Last night. I told Darbii a secret." I felt everyone's eyes stuck upon me; lasers, hoping to burn the skin right off my bones.

Silence remained moments longer. I couldn't move my head. It stayed stuck. Paralyzed.

"Never," My father continued. I couldn't look up at him. "I don't keep secrets." My gaze was still glued to the table when my mother answered.

"Um . . . I'm not sure." There was a long pause at Sitka's turn. Soon, he was slipping a "pass" card onto the table. My breath grew shaky. Viridian was quiet.

And then, it felt as though everything was shattering in the midst of silence. As though we were all stuck in space, our surroundings splitting apart but no one could hear. As though our bones were cracking in unison and yet we were all suffering separately.

"Let's . . . just go to the next question," Viridian said. "Perû?"

"You know, I actually think I'm going to go to bed," I stood as I spoke. I still couldn't seem to find the strength to make eye contact. "We need to leave before sunrise tomorrow."

"Why so early?" I could almost see my mother's eyes narrowing ever so slightly. My mouth opened, closed, and opened again.

"I read a weather report that it's supposed to be ugly after that. Not fun to drive in." *That was a lie.*

"What, rain? Is that even possible?"

"Yes." I looked up then. Everyone was watching me with a peculiar caution. Sitka's gaze was laced with an extreme suspicion. "I'll set the alarm. You guys don't have to do anything but get up." I tried to smile, but that too felt like a lie.

[28]

Falling . . .

What amount of foolishness did it cost one to remain somewhere, knowing they were in grave danger? How foolish had I truly been to sleep in that room that night? For I had felt the rotting of my bones. I had sensed the terror in my mind more greatly manifest through sensations rather than thoughts. And so I hardly slept, instead tossing and turning as the restless sea outside my window. As the flashes of color in the sky before the sunrise.

So when the alarm went off, I was already sitting up, my bones tender but muscles aflame. My knees were beneath my arms, and my phone was clenched in my left hand. The gun hadn't ever left my side. Sitka stirred first on the floor beside me. His eyes fluttered open, meeting my gaze, and I almost believed he could understand my thoughts.

The rest of the room began to stir. Viridian on the floor across the room, my mother on the couch and father below her. For they had neglected to sleep in the bedroom that night.

My phone buzzed a moment later. It felt louder than the quiet groans omitted around me.

> ➤ From "Unknown," 6:47
>
> "You need to be moving quickly. It's coming sooner than I had predicted."

It. I grew tense.

➤ To "Unknown," 6:47

"What is it? What am I running from?"

I stared at the message after sending it. My stomach began to ache. The gun seemed to dig into my side. I thought as though I could hear the sound of water in my ears, climbing up towards my skull. Thoughts had been pressed in by the weight of its rising and ceased to exist in an instant. And in a moment, every sensation from the days before was upon me again with greater pressure. Or perhaps they had never really left. Only hidden in a shadow of half-slept nights, lasting merely until the morning came. Until the dawn of reality arose.

A minute passed. Two. No response came.

➤ To "Unknown," 6:49

"Elijah?"

➤ From "Unknown," 6:49

"Just move quicker."

I scrambled out of bed. My feet slammed into the floor. Sitka sat up but not a single other soul moved.

"Let's get going, everyone," I said with such a lack of emotion that every eye in the room met me and questioned my motives. At least, I had thought they did.

I washed up in the bathroom—or made do with what I had. I had no clothes to change into and wore the same patched jeans and white T-shirt as I had for days. I went back to the living room. Everyone was sitting up. I remember saying something else to motivate their movements, and they all looked at me in that same strange way.

Minutes went by of me scrambling and them, less so.

"You guys are good if I take a shower, right?" Viridian asked at one point.

I had glared at him through my distress.

"No." He stared at me from across the living room. "No, we need to be leaving quickly. And I mean in the next couple of minutes." A frown formed across his face as he dropped the towel he had held in his hands.

"What are you so afraid is going to happen, anyway?"

I too wished I knew.

It took twenty minutes to get out of the hotel and onto the cobblestone street below. There, where the red sun was already beginning to bleach the once-black sky. I had a phone in one hand and Darbii's notebook in the other, and a gun on my side that I wished I could lose, but it seemed by then I was too afraid of what would happen without it.

I don't think I recognized that fear at the time.

We turned towards the sea. Down where the stolen car had still sat from the night before. The object in one of my hands vibrated.

➤ From "Unknown," 7:15

"Leave the car and go."

I swung my head up at my father. His back was towards me, further down the hill than I.

"Perû, leave the car," I hollered. Everyone's steps ceased, and there had been the most uncanny silence. Seconds multiplied before he turned to face me.

His face had been grave, his eyes beaten pinatas hanging from his stretched skin, nearly falling to the floor. "Aetheria, the sky is bright blue right now." It was red and gray, as it always was, but the sentiment still remained. "There is no sign of rain. We have time."

➤ From "Unknown," 7:15

"QUICKLY."

"No we don't. Leave the car, and let's go," For some reason, I was nearly screaming. I don't recall trying to do so. I guess it had just come out that way. My father's face was burning red by then. His nose was squeezed outward, his eyebrows pulled tightly across his face. Angry.

My father never got angry.

He stared at me. His gaze was intense, as though the blazing sun burned inside his very eyes. His hand lifted so slowly from his side, and soon it was beside his face, and he was shaking his finger at me as though I was a child and he was standing over me, looming like a shadow.

"I don't know what your deal is, Aetheria, but my daughter does not have the right to give me demands like I'm some . . . some dog!" I had felt as though I should have backed down. As though I should have cowered at his growing shadow. Yet, I shook my head, tears fighting to find their way to the corners of my eyes. I wished they would fight harder.

"Perû, *please* just listen to me."

"And what happens if I don't?"

➤ From "Unknown," 7:16

"Last chance to go."

"I don't know!" By then, I spoke purely from emotion, for what I had said was foolish, and those who are foolish are those who are emotional. So he stared at me ever so intently. His breathing grew to a low hum, and I tried to cry, but my eyes were paralyzed.

"Perû, I need you to trust me on this. I . . ." The phrase came to me. It seemed to work last time. "I have a gut feeling . . . a gut feeling that it's going to be worse than the reports read."

He shook his head. His forehead had been buried in his palms, and soon, words were rolling off his tongue.

"I'll grab the car and meet you at the top of the road." The muscles in my face twitched. I bit the chapped areas on my lips. My nails dug into the items in my palms, and I let them. And against all reason inside of me, I nodded, immediately hurrying up the hill in which we stood. Sitka was at my heel. My mother and Viridian had stood confused for a moment too long beside the hotel building.

"Guys, let's go!" I screamed. The hand that held my phone shook with terror. The other remained paralyzed. And somewhere in between, the rest of my body rested.

"What report are you reading?" Sitka mumbled to me. "I didn't see anything about a rainstorm." I shook my head. There was nothing more I could say, and so I did not speak.

And in it, it was as though fire was being fueled inside my bones. The more I let it turn me to ash, the quicker that next buzz came.

> ➤ From "Unknown," 7:17

"It's inevitable now. Stay calm."

I froze.

No.

My feet were planted into the pavement.

No. No, no, no.

"Eve?" Sitka's voice was muffled beside me. My ears rang, and my head pounded louder than a single sound around me.

Until the jet planes appeared.

Or at least the sound of them, but my eyes wouldn't dare to look up at the sky.

Then, I could see the helicopter in Munich. The memory met my mind with such gravity.

Instinct seemed to take control at that moment, and I was running up the hill, my phone meeting my back pocket, my notebook clenched under my arm. The thundering grew louder. My steps grew faster. All breath escaped me.

Moisture surrounded my feet.

It clawed into my black boots, and I looked down to stare at it. Paralysis struck me. I saw the river again. I saw the car sinking. I saw the terror in my father's eyes beside me, in Sitka's now. The moisture rose to my ankles. And once the word finally processed in my mind, I couldn't think of anything else: water.

I was being consumed by water once more.

My body tried to move forward. My mind kept me stuck. In a single moment of defiance of whatever amount of my peace remained, my gaze shifted to the sky. It was truly blue then. Unlike the red and gray I had become so accustomed to. Unlike the curse of the blazing red sun and the black hole. Unlike anything I had ever seen.

For the sky was growing closer towards me. It moved in rapid motions, in fits of clouds and shifting shades of blue and gray. As though a single wall of water. A wall of water . . .

Then it hit me. The momentary realization.

No.

And before I could understand the storm I saw, it came crashing down upon me. My feet swept off the ground. A wave consuming me.

And I was tumbling. Falling . . .

My eyes were glued shut. My body was a ball.

I was spinning. In circles . . .

The notebook slipped from my grasp.

My eyes shot open. The salt water stung them.

Scream. No. Don't.

Instinct fought logic.

Air. I need it. *Just a breath* . . .

Stop it. No. Persist.

My eyes . . . *the burning* . . .

Tears began to form. Air. *I need air.*

The surface. It was right there. Right above me, I could practically feel it.

Reach for it . . .

Something shoved me to the right. Pierced me. Debris. Metal. It ached.

Then, another wave. Then, I was falling again . . .

Faster that time.

Items pressed me on all sides. Pushing me, pulling me, slicing me, destroying me.

This is it. This is how Aetheria Elko dies.

All this fighting, all for nothing.

I am destined to die.

That wasn't true.

Oh, but it is.

Shut up. Stay awake.

No, I can't.

Please, just for a little while . . .

No.

Why?

Air.

And then.

Darkness.

[29]

Do You Trust Him?

I thought for a moment that I could see him after the darkness came. The silhouette of his body, the curves of his face. A smile stretching from one cheek to the other. Hair flopped across his forehead. What color was it? In my mind, I thought it was him. The one who tried to save me from this . . .

But he would have grabbed me if it was him. He would have pulled me to safety.

Pain.

Pain was what greeted me back into the land of the living. My body: throbbing. My eyes: stinging.

Air.

Air was what made me realize I was alive.

My eyes shot open. They had been fixed wide. I floated on a piece of wood, a door. Water surrounded me. A murky darkness that should have consumed me. Dead.

I should have been dead.

Suddenly, I was erupting into a chorus of coughs. Water shot out of my eyes. Spit shot out of my mouth. I was gagging. Harshly. I couldn't hear.

The water rocked back and forth around me, tossing around fallen debris and stolen souls. It encircled buildings with siding ripped off and windows shattered and roofing pulled to pieces. It formulated a reflection of such complete and utter destruction that I stared upon in undeniable terror.

For I was stuck in the middle of it.

And so was everyone else.

And then I was screaming. Hastily. Timorously. Pointlessly. I coughed through my meaningless noises. Sound slowly started to return to my ears and yet the waves muffled what I could hear of myself. Of my embarrassingly obnoxious groans. Those painful groans. I sounded as undignified as an animal.

I was an animal.

Nature had made me act as one.

I saw my mother in my mind. Her face whited out and eyes blank. Bare. Dead.

And then I was screaming louder, and my eyes were screaming with me, and I was coughing so uncontrollably that I was afraid I would fling my lungs out of my body.

"Merû!" I was crying. "Merû!" Not a single response came. People trudged through the water in roadways nearby, heads hung to the level of their necks. The brown and red liquid met their mid-thighs, their bodies soaked in sorrow. They ignored me.

"Perû! SITKA!" I coughed. Sucked in absent air. Coughed. "V!" I could feel nothing.

I brought us here. This is my fault.

Elijah, help me.

"MERÛ!"

My ears had fully unmuffled.

Screams echoed from all directions. Children cried. Mothers yelled. My heart raced. Pounded against the drums in my ears. Its pain sought to slaughter me.

"Merû!" I screamed again.

My head spun west. I searched faces. Searched for someone willing enough to help. A face I could recognize.

I have no one.

My family.

They're dead.

No. No, they couldn't be.

My eyes followed the jagged line of buildings, both standing and slaughtered. Everything was a mess.

Please. Someone.

Anyone.

Glass floated around my body that I could almost feel slicing my arms. There lay a porch at water level. A boy was stretched out upon it, his eyes closed shut. *He's dead.* No, he wasn't.

But then I recognized his black coils. I recognized the way they fell across his brown, bruised forehead, and I recognized the softness upon his cheeks that would come over him in the most desperate of times. *Sitka.*

Reason abandoned my mind, and I was slipping off the door, the water rising to my hips. The hands of the waves wrapped around me, stinging every cell of my skin. They stabbed something on my side. Burned it with a torch. I winced and scrambled through the destruction. Through the blurred mess. Through the pieces of debris decorating the current that yanked me backward. My brother grew closer with every few steps.

"SITKA!" my voice was shredding. His eyes were opening. Every fear of his death left me in an instant, and he stared at the water. I screamed his name again. He grew closer. And then his eyes were meeting mine, and his gaze was growing, and I could see the very skin upon his lips vibrating. I moved faster. With every intention inside my bones, I sought to meet him. My body ached harsher. Sitka sat up on his knees, watching feverishly as I approached him, as my eyes filled deeper with distress and my body burned beneath those waves. He was close.

So close.

The porch was in front of me, and then I reached for the railing at the staircase beside him leading up to where he rested. His arms reached towards me, and he was gripping my hands, and every bone and muscle was aching, and yet I couldn't feel anything at all. Then, he pulled me up towards himself, and I pushed against the current to reach for him. And then he had me completely, and he was pulling me on top of himself, and I was gripping onto his shoulders with such intensity. My feet emerged from the current. He pulled me to his right and buried himself into my embrace. He smelt of cedar wood and rosemary, of a scent so nostalgic, so sacred that it felt nearly unholy to take it in in such a setting.

"Eve," he mumbled.

"Why . . . are you always the first person I find . . . after . . . after these things . . ." I felt his chin trying to smile atop my shoulder. I held him for a long time. Held him as though he could slip from my grasp back into the waves. I couldn't lose him again.

I found the strength to release him. To flop down beside him, pain convulsing through my body. I winced. My eyes glued themselves shut. I took a long breath, ripping them back open.

"Are you . . . are you alright?" I mumbled. My eyes were focused on my soggy black boots. They dripped steadily onto the concrete below. Sitka was quiet for a moment too long, and when I found his gaze, he was already looking at me. He stared softly. His eyes were a deep red tone.

"I'm breathing," he said. My bones released some sort of sympathy for just a moment, and then I looked away. "Are you?"

Pain claimed my entire being. I couldn't quite tell where its origin lay. I pat down my body, feeling for abnormalities. A few slices on my hands, one above my left eyebrow, a gash where my gun lay, still present upon me. Not lost to the waves.

"I think so," I was able to say. My voice had wavered. Silence came in still, and I tried to think of something other than pain, but nothing met my mind. Then Sitka spoke.

"Everyone else . . ."

I nodded. "Yes." My mother's face flashed before my eyes. I shuddered.

"I mean . . . the chances of them?—"

"I don't really want to talk about it, Sitka." I stared at her eyes. Stared at the darkness in them. Stared at how pale her skin had become. Stared at her body buried six feet below water.

Sitka hesitated. "I know, but, I mean . . . we're both alright. That has to mean the chances are high, right?"

I sat in silence for a moment. "I . . . I guess so."

"Do you think they are?"

"I don't know, Sitka." Viridian lay beside her in my mind. Their bodies had been disfigured. I tried to forget them but their cold stares wouldn't forget me. "Let's just . . . for now . . . I just need to . . ." Rest. I needed to rest. My eyes closed for a moment. That was when I saw my father. I saw his soft face hardened as he walked towards the sea. And suddenly, something deep inside of my soul feared so glaringly for him. Sitka released a quick breath beside me. My eyes opened again. He was deep in thought, and I couldn't help but watch him out of the corner of my eye.

"Why wasn't a tsunami warning sent out?" I said nothing in reply. I couldn't even seem to breathe. His eyes found me suddenly.

I stared. "What."

"Perû—"

"I know."

"He was closer—"

"I know, Sitka."

The pain that is experienced when one fears a loved one to be gone is a pain that cannot be explained. And so I will not try to explain it.

"I lost my gun," Sitka mumbled a few moments later. My gaze shifted towards him again, and for once, I was really looking at him. The canopy above us shadowed his face, though I could still see the remains of tears on his cheeks. His eyes sagged, and his jawbone seemed to pierce his skin. His skull blared behind his flesh. Snot sat below his nose. His bones looked bare.

"Take mine," I said, reaching for it on my side. My fingers found my bloodied skin; pain shot through my side.

"No."

I froze. Looked up. Stared at him emphatically. "Please, I want you to have it." I took a long breath. Thought through my words carefully. "It would relieve me for you to have it."

"I said no." It was the least hesitant answer I had ever heard from his lips.

So I stared at the weapon in my hands—that which obtained the power to cause such pain. Pain similar to that of which I had sat in the midst. Of stolen souls beneath the waves. Of the echoes of crying children who couldn't begin to understand what had occurred. Of people who would never again see their mothers, grandmothers.

Their children.

So I stared at the weapon and in it, I felt just the slightest tinge of resentment towards my younger brother.

"Where did you get these, Sitka?" I spoke with such anger in which I hardly realized I had. The weapon stayed resting in my lap. Sitka stared down blankly. Moments passed. "Sitka, I need to know where you got these. After everything—"

"Corbyn gave them to me," he spoke before I could figure out how to finish my sentence. "He got them from his perû."

"That's as far as we got last time." His eyes stayed away from mine, focusing on a spot of destruction in one place or another. *I wish you could trust me.* I thought I said it out loud. "Why did he have them?" I watched the wheels turn in his brain. More effectively than mine ever could, and I wondered how they had ever become that way. But then I noticed something softening in his gaze. Perhaps the lowering of an eyebrow or lifting of a cheek.

Then, he sighed, and his hands met his temples to rub the words out of them.

"He was suspicious of the creation of Cordellia," he began, finally looking up at me. "He thought that we weren't taught the full truth of what happened 120 years ago. And that it might have a bigger impact on us now than we know." I was staring at him. He looked almost as though he was relieved to say it, as though he was trying to make sense of why he had said nothing before.

I repeated his words over again in my mind. I tried to make some sense of them. Something about his words awoke a curiosity in my mind that I never knew was there.

"And did you believe him?" I was asking. Sitka's lip twitched.

"I *did*."

"Do you still?" He didn't reply to that. I watched him. Blinked. "You don't have to keep secrets from me, Sitka."

"Neither do you." His eyes met mine again, and I found an unkempt stoicness across his cheeks. Then, he nodded. "I do believe him." There was silence as we stared. "How did you know the tsunami was coming?" My eyes fell to the brick balcony below me. I shook my head.

"That's the thing. I . . . I didn't." I swallowed harshly. It was then that I recognized he deserved to know. "Darbii's the only person I've ever told about this."

"I won't tell anyone else. You know that." My gaze found him again. A small smile replaced the seriousness in his gaze and then I was explaining it all to him. Everything about Elijah and about the car in Salzburg and how he had led me to Darbii that night in Belgrade.

"So . . ." Sitka began to say once I had finished. I stared at him softly.

"What."

"He's . . . tracking you?"

"What?"

"How does he know your location?"

"I don't . . . know." The question hadn't ever occurred to me. Yet, the second it met me, I felt my bones begin to shake. The weight of his words pounded upon my head, and it seemed for just a second as though I feared Elijah.

"Do you . . . trust him?" I hardly heard Sitka's words through my sudden panic. But then I was freezing. And I was staring at my lap, at the gun resting upon it.

Trust. I hardly seemed to understand its meaning any longer.

"He's saved my life multiple times. *Our* lives." Sitka stared at me as I said it. "But I don't know. I don't know if I can trust again after what Herr Krüger did to us."

"It seems weird that he would help you and not seem to want anything in return." And Herr Krüger *had* wanted something in return. If Elijah was anything like him, he would too.

"I don't know. Maybe he's just . . . good." It was easier to say than I had expected.

[30]

Paralyzed Tears

I hadn't realized how bad the cut was on my side. Not until I found the courage to lift my shirt, inspecting the four-inch wide slice above the holster on my hip, a thick, red liquid dripping down my skin, staining my white T-shirt.

I tried to look away. The cut had grabbed my eyes, anchoring them towards itself. And I was paralyzed. By fear or pain or some other sensation I couldn't quite identify.

There was a gasp beside me. My eyes found Sitka. His gaze was fixed wide on the gash.

"Why didn't you say anything about that?" He looked up at me, his eyes blaring red.

I looked back down at the cut. "I . . . I didn't know it was there." That was a lie. I had felt the pain. I had felt it stinging at the suffocation of salt water, ripping the raw skin off my bones. But I hadn't realized it was that bad.

"Eve, we really should do something about that." I couldn't find Sitka's gaze again.

"I know. Merû can . . ." I didn't finish my thought.

"We need to find them." My neck wouldn't bend back to look at my brother. Instead, it bent forward into a nod.

"I know."

"What if they . . ."

"Please don't say it. I can't think about it right now." I moved the gun from my legs to the left of me. Stared at the cut closer. Sitka grabbed the weapon. Both of our breaths became silent. Then, I was staring again at the mess before me. The water ruled as a river. I feared so deeply that it ruled over them too.

I fought a war with my emotions.

For once, I fought for tears to tear my face apart, but they remained hidden somewhere behind my eyes. With each step taken across the roofs of buildings, terror shot up through my bones. Pain accented unknown areas across my skin. The view that had once been beautiful now destroyed me.

There was a building across the street set upon its side. The red roofing had crumbled, crashing into the wavering water below. And upon the peeling siding, beside the windows smashed by the fists of the waves, read in French the word "orphanage."

I tried to cry. Nothing came.

There was a little girl standing on a balcony. Alone. Her sage-colored dress had been torn and stained with red around the top right shoulder. Her arms hung heavy at her sides, her short black hair was soaked and frizzy. She shrieked, her voice echoing through the air, followed by muffled sobs.

My eyes remained paralyzed.

I saw a pair of feet sticking up from underneath the water. The current moved downhill. A blue shoe was on one foot, and the other was bare. And then they disappeared, pulled under the water.

"Sitka, I can't do this." I stopped moving, staring up at my brother. He froze, hesitating a moment before turning to face me. Water was stained upon his cheeks. "I don't . . . I don't have the strength to see these things and . . ." My hand had already found my side. "The pain it . . . it's too much." He stared at me. His lips were quivering, and his eyes were bloodied.

"I need to find Merû." A chasm cracked within me.

"Sitka I . . ."

I spotted movement out of the corner of my eye. My gaze found the low roof of the building ahead. It had been covered in bodies laying out across the flat concrete. They reached for one another. Held each other, cried into each other's arms. Strangers became family in the face of disaster. Tears bled into each other, forming bonds deeper than blood.

And then my eyes found a woman. She had blonde curls upon her head, tied up into a bun, erupting across her almond forehead. She sat hunched over a man, holding his wrinkled palm in her hands, watching his eyes as he spoke.

A smile formed across my shaky lips.

"I have good news for you," I said. And suddenly, I was running faster than the pain in my side could handle, and I was reaching towards the edge of the roof. All of the hope that had left me at some point or another seemed to find me again, just for a moment, and it seemed as though I was screaming into an abyss.

But she heard me. And her eyes were shooting up towards me, and they were lifting and lowering at the same time, and tears seemed to be forming in the corners of them, and for a moment, I believed them to be my own. But I was still paralyzed.

So it was Sitka who spoke. I couldn't make out a word of what he said as I stared into her eyes of forests, unburnt by the rays of piercing sunlight. Then I caught a glimpse of movement to the left of me. Sitka moved towards the edge of the roof where a pile of wood lay, reaching down towards a long plank on top.

My eyes narrowed. "What are you doing?"

"We have to get down there somehow." He didn't look up at me but instead on what rested below us. My gaze fell down the side of the building, plummeting into the water below. It bent and pulled and crashed into itself. I imagined Sitka among the waves.

So I met my brother, gripping the other side of the plank and sliding it over the edge. My mother grabbed the other end, holding the base still with her palms. It had been slanted at a sharp angle.

I stared intensely. "Do you want to go first?" My back turned back to my brother, who simply stared. I sighed reluctantly.

I inched closer towards the edge of the roof. My vision caved in, my hands grew wet. I stared down at the raging waves, and for a moment, I believed I was falling.

I stood upon the board. It bent beneath my weight. And I scooted myself down.

But my mother caught me, as it seemed she always did. She held my shoulders and stared into my eyes with such solemn pride. She pulled me towards herself, and I fought to cry upon her shoulder, but my eye remained paralyzed. She gripped my back so, so hard, but I couldn't care to complain.

"Don't run away like that again," she spoke so firmly into my ear.

"Trust me, I don't plan to." Then she pulled away, holding me beneath her hands, inspecting me as though I was a ghost. As though if she let go, I would become one with the air.

"I can't believe you're alive," she said. The faintest smile grasped her lips, and her hand grasped my hair, pushing it behind my ear. I thought the tears would finally come. But they didn't. And then she pulled away from me, her hands back on the beam and my eyes began to scan the roof.

Bodies lay restlessly across it, tears soaking each petrified gaze. A woman held her two children to her chest, sobbing violently into them. An old man stared at a wound on his left arm, patting it with a piece of gauze, his eyes cowering at the sensation. A scream amplified the area. I couldn't seem to find its culprit. A girl who looked a little too much like Darbii sat in the corner of the roof, her legs pulled in towards her chest, her eyes staring blankly before her. Men bent along the edge of the roof, staring down towards the water, reaching for bodies below. A man with a long bandage across his arm.

Another with matted gray locks.

One with the same blond coils as my mother.

My eyes widened. "Viridian!" His head shot up from over the edge. His green gaze grazed the rooftop, reaching to where I stood. His body froze. His hands held themselves tightly at his side. His jaw dropped. His eyes opened as the dawn of day. I watched his lips mouth a curse word.

Then he was upon his feet, lunging towards me, and the space between us was killed in an instant. His arms were thrown around me, and he gripped me so tightly I felt as though I couldn't breathe. I shook at the speed of his breaths. His dirtied aroma met my nose, and soon, his strained mumbles met my ears.

"I thought you were dead."

"I thought you were too." The image of him beneath the waves pierced my mind, and I pulled away as though to make sure he was still there. For just a moment, I stared into his eyes and found such a deep, hidden affection that I hadn't ever seen before. Then, I ignored it. "Sitka's here too."

"What about Perû?"

I stared at him. Swallowed. "What?"

"He's not with you?" I stared at him as his grip around my shoulders tightened. My jaw lowered without my mind's command.

"No. He's . . . he's not with you?" Viridian shook his head slowly, pulling his lips tightly into his mouth. His eyes dashed to the right of me.

"Perû isn't with them," Viridian mumbled. My head turned to see my mother and Sitka behind me. Viridian raced towards my other brother and embraced him, though Sitka's gaze still shifted to panic. My mother's remained in rest.

"I know," she said. "I . . ." I could see her searching for a solution across the concrete roof below. And in her searching, some level of peace that had been so recklessly held together for so long fell apart, and I could see the panic that reigned so ruthlessly behind her eyes. Then, her gaze found Viridian. "I can send a team to go look for him . . . ? Or—"

"Merû, Eve needs your help," Sitka intervened, pulling away from Viridian. It took a moment for her gaze to shift to me and then to my hand gripping my side. I hadn't noticed it was there. Then, her eyes filled with terror.

Suddenly, she was beside me, lifting the bottom of my stained shirt and staring at the gash. Panic was bleached upon the whites of her eyes.

"How much blood have you lost?" I felt my bones tense at her question.

"I don't know." She stared at it for a moment longer, and I was suddenly remembering the gun. My eyes found Sitka behind her, his gaze meeting me. His hand touched it on his side.

"I need to stitch it." My eyes stumbled down towards my mother. She was still staring at the wound, her eyes taking inventory of its destruction. And then my mind was recognizing the meaning of her words. Then, everything inside of me shattered.

"No."

"Eve, it needs to be done."

"No. No, no, no. Merû, you know how I feel about this type of thing."

"You're going to bleed out if you don't let me take care of it!" I felt as though I would vomit. My head shook violently, and then I was sulking away from her, my hand instinctively reaching for the gash.

"You don't even have supplies."

"Yes I do." Her palm moved to her fanny pack upon her waist. I stared at it.

"No."

"Eve, this is not a request."

"Will it hurt?" Her gentle gaze greeted me once more. Then, it fell.

"I don't want to lie to you."

"How bad will it hurt?" She pulled in a breath, holding it in place. I didn't see her release it again until she spoke.

"I can get Viridian to sing a song to distract you."

"This isn't a joke, Merû. How bad will it hurt?" She only nodded. And then, I realized that I had no other choice. Not if I wished to continue crawling away from death's fingertips, the wish that seemed to be my casualty. "Just do it quickly. Please?"

She nodded again.

[31]

Gut Feeling

Viridian did sing a song. It seemed to pain me more than the procedure ever could. Every A was an A flat and every C a C sharp and soon my brain ached more than the needle in my side.

"Viridian you will kill me before this cut does."

"Eve, don't talk." My mother didn't looked up as she said it.

Viridian smiled. "It would be an honor, mademoiselle." He bowed dramatically, and I was trying to force myself to smile. Force myself to ignore the pain that burned more than the sun ever had. It felt as though my mother's hand was made of flames, reaching inside my cut, spinning it in circles. As if it was reaching for my lungs, removing all breath from within them. Everything turned to a blur around me, and soon the world felt as though it was going dark.

Maybe this would be how I died. From the hands of someone I loved.

It seemed as though it was the moment everything nearly went black that it was all over.

"Merû, what are we going to do about Perû?" It was the first thing Viridian said once my mother announced she was finished. She inspected my wound for a moment longer, finally pulling away, running her hand across my leg in comfort. And then I collapsed across the ground, every bone in my body aching, seeking to find the absent breath in my lungs.

"I don't *know*, Viridian," she said after a moment. My eyes were closed by then.

"We need to go search for him."

"I have people that need medical care. We are not going anywhere."

"Then I can go alone. Or with Sitka."

My eyes shot open. "No, please don't." I pushed myself up again, placing my bandaged arms beneath me for support. I easily ignored their pain. "We can't be separated again. I can't risk losing you." Viridian's gaze found mine. It had been hollowed, rid of the normal contentment it carried.

"Come with me and Sitka then." My mother shook her head at him.

"She needs to rest, Viridian. Are you out of your mind?"

"I'll be okay, Merû." I didn't believe my own words.

"Eve, you're as pale as a ghost right now. You need to rest."

"I need to find my father."

"No." She shook her head as she stood. "No one is going anywhere. No way. I will not allow it."

Viridian stared at her wide-eyed. "Merû—"

"*No*, Viridian. I cannot have you running around this city in search of someone you might not even find. Especially not while your sister is physically incapable of it. I will not risk losing a single one of you again." She took one more harsh look at me. "I'm sorry, Eve. I have others I must attend to." She rubbed my shoulder. And then she walked away, hastily approaching a man across the roof with a bloodied arm, leaving me to live with the weight of her words.

Someone you might not even find.

My eyes found Viridian. He was standing with his hands on his hips, his pointer fingers tapping his t-shirt, staring out across the horizon.

"You can't leave without me." His gaze found me. Stared. Nodded.

"I know." He swallowed, shaking his head. "But I can't just sit here while he could be out there . . ." He didn't finish his sentence. But I already knew what he meant.

"I know," I was able to say. He was watching me. His eyes were filled with such a fragmented image of unease that I wasn't sure I had ever seen before in my brother. I wondered if he was thinking what I was. Believing the same lie that I was: that we could leave that rooftop without my mother noticing.

"Viridian." It was all I could say. All I could do to get the point across to him. All I could do to hope he understood my thoughts.

I could tell that he did.

He moved his right hand to his chin, rubbing the bottom of it for a moment, shaking his head.

"Can you even walk?"

"I'll be fine. Worst case, you can carry me."

"I really don't think I can." I smiled. He didn't. We stared at each other for a moment.

"I vote yes." I almost forgot that Sitka was standing beside him. Our heads turned towards him.

I shrugged. "The smart sibling says yes."

"It seems like a sign." Viridian smirked. He looked over his shoulder, watching my mother as she cleaned the wounded arm of the man. "She's gonna be pissed."

I shook my head. "Not if we find him." Viridian stared a moment longer before shrugging softly. Then he was reached his hand out towards me, helping me to my feet. And before I knew it, we were moving across the concrete towards the back of that tormented area, and my brothers were helping me onto the roof of the building beside us. Then we were moving west again—inland—our eyes fixed on all that surrounded us.

I ignored the excruciating stinging in my side.

Then, we were out of my mother's view. Then, Viridian spoke.

"Okay . . . so, what are we looking for?"

"Perû." Viridian rolled his eyes at Sitka.

"Nice one, Sherlock."

"A search and rescue team might have information." My older brother's eyes met mine at the sound of my words. "Obviously keep our eyes peeled for him too, but—"

"Are there even search and rescue teams anymore? After . . . everything."

I shrugged. "I'd like to think that there are still good people trying to help one another." Viridian snickered at my remark.

"It would actually . . ." Sitka hesitated. "Be AI beings . . . coordinating search and rescue." Viridian rolled his eyes.

"Not the point, Sitka." We moved up a slanted roof in silence. I stared at my feet that moved onward without my mind's command, ignoring the fire burning in my side.

"By the way," Viridian began to say again. I looked up at him to see his fingers resting in his front jeans pockets, his eyes glued to me. "How did you know the tsunami was coming?" I stared at him. My eyes widened.

Could he tell?

He watched me for a moment. Watched the debate in my mind. The conflict brewing into complete disarray, hoping to send me into a spiral of rash speech. Because I had already told Sitka. So why couldn't I tell him too?

"Weather report." It slipped out of my mouth more than I told it to. He stared. Licked his bottom lip.

"You said it would rain."

I shrugged. "Heavy rain." He raised an eyebrow. I sighed, finally looking away. "I didn't want to scare you with the truth." And as I said it, I wondered if that was the same reason why Elijah hadn't told me what was going to happen.

That was when I wondered how he even knew in the first place.

"Also," Viridian began again, throwing his arms out to the side. His gaze shifted to Sitka. "Are there normally tsunamis in the Black Sea? Isn't that an *ocean* ocean thing?" Sitka watched my older brother for a moment.

"It's probably the effects of the black hole," he said. "Throwing of gravity, you know." There was silence for a moment as an idea caught me around the throat. I reached for my phone in my back pocket.

➤ To "Unknown," 8:29

"We're trying to find my perû. Know anything?"

Sitka watched me as I typed. Viridian was oblivious.

➤ From "Unknown," 8:30

"Continue west. When you notice the water become about thigh deep, you will

find a search and rescue team. Ask them about Ävon."

Seeing my father's name on my screen made me shudder. A name I felt I had responsibility for, a name that an unknown number somehow knew.

"I think we're headed in the right direction," I was able to say. I didn't look at either of my brothers, though I felt both of their eyes on me. "It's a gut feeling."

[32]

The Chaos Of Humanity

The water was calmer uphill. It rested in such stability that the world seemed as though it had never been shaken. As though neither the blaring sun nor the perilous throws of a storm could move it.

And yet, in its stillness, it unsettled me. Because it was all just a show. For the testaments to its pain remained upon my body. In the stitches across my side. In the cut through my eyebrow. Reminders that all I had been through might be for nothing.

The search and rescue team had been there as promised. They were swarmed by civilians with terror engraved in their eyes. The contrast was unnerving. The composer of the artificial versus the chaos of humanity. Viridian managed to find a way into a building beside them, leading us down a staircase and out onto the watered street below.

The officers were AI, as Sitka had predicted. Their bodies were coated in bright white plating, glowing in the reflection of the water. I couldn't ignore the genericness with which they spoke. Couldn't look away from their identical stances, poised and perfected as though to seem above the rest of us. Something about it deeply angered me.

We found one in the form of a middle-aged man standing in a corner beneath an overhang. It held a holographic tablet in its hand, its black eyes fixed upon it stoically.

"Sir," Viridian said as he approached it. Its eyes slowly lifted and met his gaze. Clicked into place. "Or . . . however I'm supposed to address you."

"Sir is just fine." It's tablet met its side. "What can I do for you today?"

Anger boiled my blood.

"We're trying to find our–"

"If you're curious about the whereabouts of a particular person, I apologize, but I am unable to be of assistance at the moment." Viridian stared at it. It stared back. I tried to decide whose gaze was colder. Viridian's eyes narrowed.

"What?"

"If you're curious about—"

"No, I heard you. What the hell do you mean you can't help us?" The AI being watched my brother. Its stoic tolerant seemed almost to shift to a glare.

"I. Cannot. Help you. Understand?" My heart began to race.

"I need to find my father, *sir*. Not sure if you noticed, but there was a tsunami," He motioned to the land around him. "We lost him, and I need to know where he is—"

"I am very sorry for your loss. Unfortunately—"

"No. Don't say that. Tell me where the hell he is. His name is Ävon Elko, about six foot two, dark-skinned, curly black hair, almost coily, but not quite—"

"I will say it one more time. I cannot help you. I apologize sincerely." My bones began to obliterate. I begged my eyes to rain, but nothing came. And in a moment's notice, a thought came to mind. A thought that had approached me before but with far less strength. For this time, it came to stay.

This was my fault. All of this.

"You apologize sincerely, huh?" Viridian was scowling so hard I wondered if it hurt. "Get a conscience first, and then try to tell me you apologize sincerely. Might work out better." The AI's gaze was back on its tablet, touching items on its holographic screen. It convinced even me that my brother had become invisible.

Viridian stared at it a moment longer. His face burned red with an undeniable anger. A swear word rolled off his tongue, and then he stepped away, pushing through Sitka and me. His shoulder against mine was cold in the growing heat of the day. And then he was before a bench across the street, sitting down bitterly, the water rising to the top of his legs. "This is *ridiculous*. They're AI beings and they can't find him? What a stupid lie." He buried his head into his hands, running his fingers through his hair, getting wrapped up in a curls. A groan emerged from his lips. A breath from mine. A sigh from Sitka's. "And as far as we know, he could be dead." I felt my heart stop. I didn't know whether it was capable of starting again. My lips sat slightly parted, and my eyebrows narrowed in, and for a moment, I believed I could feel moisture behind my eyes.

"Why would you say that?" There had been a long pause. Then, he looked up at me. No, glared up. Glared as though we weren't being pressed through the same pain. As though I was incapable of feeling what he felt. Of knowing what he knew. As though he was somehow more competent than I in some way or another.

And then, he rolled his eyes.

"Why would I say that? Because it's the truth, Eve." I shook my head. Hard. Fast.

"No . . . no. I don't know why you would say that." He stared at me. His eyebrows had been so close to his eyelids. I watched him open his mouth to speak, closing it a few seconds later.

My breath shook. "Me and Sitka could find you and Merû. It only makes sense that we can find him too."

His eyes narrowed in. "Do you hear yourself right now?" He stared at me. I was at a lack of a response. He began to wiggle his finger around at me. "You're doing the thing again. That you always do." There was a pause.

"What?"

He stood. "You're believing lies because it's the easier thing to do. That's what got us on this *adventure* anyway." I stared at him. My jaw was wide. Tense. And soon, my gaze was shifting to a scowl.

"You have got to be joking right now."

"I'm not."

"It was *your* idea to go looking for Perû. Gosh, it was your idea to go to the *Qadim*, Viridian! I just went along with it."

"It's different, Eve."

"What are you talking about? How is it different?"

"Because you actually believe it."

I stared at him. My jaw had been dropped. "Viridian, what are you *talking* about? Just because you're distressed doesn't mean you have to take it out on me!"

"Distressed? Wow, you sound like Merû now."

"Maybe that's not such a bad thing."

"Oh yeah?"

"Because Merû knows how to control her anger." He laughed at me. I remained staring at him with such anger. Then, the words came out. "And Merû knows that Perû is still alive."

"Did you even hear what she said before we left, Eve? Did you?"

"Stop it."

"Perû is *dead*."

"No he is not! Shut up!" A tear met my eyelid. The pain it formed had been a relief. For my legs had become weak. My face felt puffy from either terror or the growing heat. I couldn't look at Viridian for even a second longer. I couldn't stand to stare into his eyes of condemnation, for he had become a dictator, and I was beneath him.

But I knew he was wrong. Wrong about my father. For Elijah had known his name. Elijah had sent me here to show me he was alive.

So I spoke again when it would've been wiser to remain silent. "We will find my father, Viridian."

"You're right, we will." It was Sitka. His voice echoed from a distance. My body spun in its direction, and my eyes found him standing in the doorway of a building across the road, his eyes ridden with undisputable terror. Then, I heard a groan. It came from inside.

Perû.

Oh my gosh.

100 Ways To Describe Blood

I ran towards his voice.

No, it was more of a stumble. A careless hurtle towards a reality I had no comprehension of, one I felt as though I had no place in. An uneasy feeling met me in that reality, a thin thread waiting to be cut the moment I saw him. The second my eyes met his, understanding his agony.

And then, it was cut.

Cut at the sight of him laying out on a table that was missing one of four legs. His shirt soaking red,

rolling down his chest,

deliberate and dark,

seemingly grave.

"Perû!" I exclaimed. I rushed towards him. My eyes wouldn't leave it to rest. That stain upon his chest. Dark. Too dark. "Oh my gosh . . ."

"We're gonna fix this, okay?" Sitka stood to the right of me. Anxiously, confusedly. "We're gonna—"

"What do I do?!" Viridian's voice cracked to the left of me. I hesitated to find my words.

"We need to stop the bleeding."

"How?"

"I need a piece of material." No one replied. "Someone hand me something!" A moment later, Sitka's blue striped shirt sat in my palms, crumpled tightly into a ball. Perû groaned louder. *Calm down, calm down.*

"Calm down." Why did I say it out loud?

I moved the shirt towards the cut, pressing against it. A scream escaped my father. Then me. I pressed harder, he cried louder.

"I'm sorry." My lip quivered. "I'm so sorry." But then I felt something. Something on my hands. Warm. Thick.

His blood on my hands.

His blood on my hands.

"I can't do it." I pulled away quickly. Viridian took my place in an instant. "I'm so sorry, I can't—"

"Just be quiet" I hardly heard his words as my eyes fell to my hands. Red, shaking. *Red. No. No, this can't be.*

They shook more. Harder. Faster.

My eyes started to grow blurry. Tears.

"Someone needs to get Merû!" I hardly heard my older brother and hardly saw my younger one sprint out of the building. *My hands.*

There was a song I once used to love. It was called "100 Ways To Describe Blood."

But now that I saw it on my hands, I could only think of one.

Red.

"Eve, I need your help again!" I shook my head. My father groaned. "Eve!" My feet moved me towards my brother while my mind told me I could do nothing. "Just press down with me. You don't even have to look at it." I nodded. My hands collided with the shirt. Warmer. Wetter. I sobbed. "How long do I do this for?"

"Start with five minutes." My lip quivered. It was then that I knew why my mother made sure I had known this. "If it's not done yet, give it another five."

Five minutes passed. We checked. Still bleeding.

Another five. Then dry.

Sitka, still gone.

Perû was breathing steadier by then. Tears sat at the corners of his eyes, sealed shut.

"Just hang on until Merû gets here," Viridian mumbled. I heard a staggered laugh escape my father, his eyes opening and quickly looking at both of us.

"You're alive."

"You barely are," I glared at my brother.

"Merû's alright too," I continued, my father smiling.

"I know she is. She's a fighter." His eyes met mine, his smile quickly turning to a frown. "I should have listened to you, Aetheria."

"We're all alive, that's what matters."

"No. I should have listened to you." He coughed hard, closing his eyes for a moment. There was a pause until he met my gaze again. "I am so sorry." I shook my head.

"Please don't say that."

"Why not?"

"It will only make it harder for me."

One more tear found its way down my cheek. I believe that was the last time I ever cried.

My father shook his head. Continued to stare at me. "How did you . . . how did you know?"

I swallowed. "Know what?"

"About the tsunami. How did you know it was coming?"

I stared at my fingers. Watched them shake. "I don't know," I said. My teeth practically clattered. "A gut feeling, I suppose."

Sitka came through the door many moments later. He had been followed by my mother, tears stained on either of their faces. She hurried over to my father, mumbling something under her breath, immediately inspecting the laceration.

"The bleeding has stopped." She looked up at me, "Good job." I tried to smile. I couldn't. "I'll need to disinfect and stitch it."

"Whatever you have to do." She nodded at my father. Stared into his eyes for just a moment longer.

"I can't believe you're alive." And then she was looking up at me and all of my siblings individually. Her eyes stopped upon me. "The rest of you, however, are grounded."

"We weren't just going to let him *die*, Merû," I heard Viridian say. But my eyes were locked on my mother and hers on me. Then, I caught a glimpse of the terror in her gaze. Of the unfailing hope she once had, then beginning to fail.

And then a thought struck me like a bullet piercing through the once thickness of my skin. A thought I had found bits and pieces of before, but then it was all coming together into one complete idea:

If my mother was losing hope, was hope even real?

"What happened?" My father mumbled. Her gaze turned from me, and my eyes were focused on the floor.

"They went looking for you. Behind my back. Even after I told them not to." I stared at the water at my feet. It rested so still. The more I stared at it, the more I felt my mind begin to turn. My body grew dizzy.

And soon, my parents' conversation was fading behind me, and I was moving towards the door, though everything inside of me told me to stay inside. I emerged into the light of the sun, and it was shining down upon me, burning me. And my eyes were meeting the destruction before me. Everything broken.

And yet, I was still alive.

And my family was still alive.

And destruction swarmed around me, but I still stood. And none of it made sense. Why I had been there in that moment, living in the face of death. Why I stood so idle while chaos erupted in every direction, the chaos that seemed to follow me. The chaos I seemed to bring upon others whether I wished for it or not.

But who was I to believe I had such power?

And as I stared out across the commotion, at the burdened people swarming search and rescue teams. At those with tears drenching their eyes and those who no longer had life left in their bodies to cry. With those who wouldn't find their friends and those who had found them dead. Suddenly, I was remembering what I had always thought to be true, what Viridian had been trying to tell me all along, what Elijah had lied to me about.

I was destined to die.

Hope was only a delusion.

[34]

Hope Is Foolishness

Green things grow from flooded grounds. Surplus flourished when the Nile expanded its reach. Before the sun dried it up.

Something green poked out from beneath the muddy waters. A fragment of a forest. A fruitful land lost under travail. I reached for it in curiosity. The water along its surface melted into my palm, the velvety substance soaked to its very core. The blank pages had been mushy and bleeding off of my hands.

The notebook from Darbii. How it had found its way back to me, I could not understand.

We were relocated inland to a hotel where the sea hadn't flooded the streets. Where the sun sat still in the sky, its accomplice resting solemnly by its side. Where the world had been placid, acting as though it was at ease. As if I hadn't watched my father nearly die before my very eyes. In a moment, I was seeing it all again. His broken breath. His eyes rolling and bleeding. His skin in parallel.

It was something I hoped to never see again.

Sitka handed the gun back to me once we made it to the hotel. Once the two of us were alone. I was wise enough to know there was no use in arguing.

The buzzing of the television became the ambiance of my mind as I stared blankly at the floor in front of me. My lips were peeling, and my cheeks seemed almost sticky. My throat had been dried out once more by the unbroken beating of the sun. The skin around my nails had been bloodied, drying black. And I could feel my stomach ache, though nothing was inside to poison it.

And then there was my wound. The pain that might never cease.

There was a buzz in my pocket. I didn't move to check it, for every instinct that had once told me to no longer reigned. I could see the faces of strangers beneath waves, the faces of those he couldn't save. Why then, would he continue to save me?

My eyes found the television above as Sitka clicked through channels. He sat so lifelessly on the couch beside me. His head leaned against his hand upon the armrest, his other rested in his lap, ever so lightly holding the remote. His eyes had been tired but too unnerved to rest.

"How is the TV working?" I asked. My brother looked over at me, his eyes dried from emotion.

"What?"

"The TV. There are blackouts. Everywhere." I used my hands to talk. "We haven't looked at a TV in how long? Two months? Why is it working?"

He continued to stare at me. Looked back up at the cartoon on the screen for a moment and then returned to my weary eyes. "The solar flares are just . . . not as bad here yet, I guess."

"But there was a tsunami."

"From gravity." He was looking at his stringy hands by then. "Or the technology here is just more radiation-hardened. I don't know. They use that type of technology on vehicles but less so on . . . other things. So it's hard to know." He took a pause. "The transmissions probably aren't getting very far though."

I looked out the window beside me. Felt the weight of the world suffocate me once more. "Why is it . . . even worth . . ."

"Even worth broadcasting anything if it's not going anywhere?" He shrugged in response to his own words. That was when he landed on a news channel with a woman on the screen. She stood in front of a building near where Sitka had found our father.

"I'm here in Varna with a search and rescue team assisting in the process

of bringing those who are still alive to safety. The tsunami, given the name 'xaoc' by locals, was a relatively small tsunami due to the—"

"Small?!" I exclaimed. My hands slammed across my legs, and I was standing without my mind insisting I do so. "How was that small?! That tsunami could have killed me. It-it could have killed other people. It *did* kill other people. A lot of people. It almost killed my father—"

"Just because it was deadly doesn't mean it was large." My brother looked up at me through his red eyes. Not a single muscle in his body moved. I glared in reply. "The earthquake that caused it was probably smaller in relation to—"

"I know how tsunamis work." I plopped myself onto the floor. "I just . . ."

I didn't know what to say. What could even come close to measuring it all. So I didn't speak. Instead, I sat silently through the pain. Through the images, through the soreness, through the redness of my hands, all so evidently inescapable.

Yet, there I remained, trying to escape it. Trying to place a gun against my head and hoping that when I pulled the trigger, I wouldn't die. I was acting in ways of illogic and therefore in ways of foolishness.

It seemed Viridian was right about hope, that thing I relied so much on, only for it to continue to disappoint me. Hope was foolish. Maybe hope was simply telling yourself a lie long enough to get you through a tunnel only for the sun to burn you on the other side. Getting you through one test only to have another destroy you.

Hope was only real through faith, and faith had never been real.

"I don't care, Yemasii!" My father's shouts found my thoughts and shot them down in an instant. My eyes followed him as he entered the room, my mother close behind. Too close. "We need to keep moving. I cannot be the one who is responsible for my children losing the privilege of a future."

"Look at you, Ävon. You are *limping*."

"Well then, I will limp my way to Israel."

"No you won't." My father sat himself down beside Sitka, burying his head into his hands. He paused for a moment to collect himself. "You are just going to injure yourself more."

He sighed. "It is my *request* that we continue on."

"I understand that. But as your doctor, it is *my* request that you let yourself regain strength for a few days." He lifted his head from his palms, a look of anger or perhaps simply a hollow despair in his eyes. He lifted his hand to his shoulder, squeezing it into a fist and releasing it slowly.

"It will mean nothing for me to regain strength if it means that I die soon after because of it." There had been a moment of silence as my parents stared at each other as though trying to read the dark letters in the pupils of their eyes. "Time is not something I can willingly give up." There was another pause.

"Yeah," Sitka whispered the word to himself, but all of our gazes fell on him anyway. I couldn't seem to ignore the growing redness in the whites of his eyes. Maybe it was that moment when I saw the shift in my little brother. That his survival was no longer based on logic like it had once been. By then he was surviving purely off of hope. He was just as naive as I had always been.

I reached for my phone.

➤ From "Unknown," 19:07

"This is not a time to give up. Keep going. Even if it's just for the sake of your family."

For the sake of my family.

The phrase caught something in my throat.

I watched my mother's eyes shift to the bathroom doorway where Viridian then stood, with a towel around his waist and a toothbrush hanging out of his mouth.

"Gosh, Viridian, put some clothes on." I said.

He stared at me. "What, I'm supposed to put my wet clothes back on after showering?"

"They gave you fresh clothing."

"*I'm* not wearing that stuff."

I didn't wear it either. The fabric of the oversized pieces the rescue teams had given to us seemed as though it was from another century. It was heavy and sagging against the weight of the sun, and the seams had scratched every square inch of my being. So I still wore my white shirt, a blood patch pointing towards the stitches that lay beneath. The seams on my patched jeans seemed to come unraveled.

"Well then, do you have anything else to wear?" I asked. "Because please, I'm begging to know where you got them." He rolled his eyes, turning back towards the bathroom. Then, my mother spoke.

"Viridian." He turned around again. A pause. He raised an eyebrow. "How do you feel about continuing on to Israel?"

"That's the plan, isn't it?" He lifted his other eyebrow too. "Why, is there a reason we shouldn't?"

"Well I don't know how you're doing . . . with everything . . . and," her eyes found my father.

Viridian's gaze fell. "Oh." I could see his dreaded desire to be good and yet his pain in doing so. "I . . . I guess if . . . if . . ."

"I will be alright, Viridian. Don't worry about me." My father forced a smile. Silence swept the room, and soon, I watched it fall. He took a long breath. "Which leads to my next point."

Everyone looked towards him then. His eyes were heavy, moisture filling the base of them. His hands were clasped tightly in his lap, his knuckles becoming blue. His cheeks were pale, and lips tightly pressed upon one another. And soon, he spoke. "We need to discuss what to do if something like this were to happen again." Silence. Then Viridian.

"Like what?" No one spoke. The TV was off at that point. "Like . . . almost drowning a third time, or . . ."

"Like being separated." I sat up a bit straighter. My father took a breath. "This has happened twice now. It is very much a miracle that we have found each other both times. However, it would be foolish to think that there is not a chance of it happening again." Silence swept through the room as my father collected his thoughts. Swallowed. Spoke. "I want to make it clear that if I, for whatever reason, go missing again, and you cannot find me quickly, that you *must* continue on."

My mother's eyes widened. "Ävon—"

"I *refuse* to be the reason that the rest of you do not make it to the Qadim in time. I . . . I cannot. I cannot do that to the rest of you."

"Me neither," Every set of eyes shifted to set in upon me. Somehow, Viridian was the one who stared with the greatest disarray. His toothbrush was out of his mouth by then, his soggy shirt upon his body and his head shaking so slowly.

"Eve . . ."

My mother stood from where she then had sat next to my father. "No. This isn't okay. We stick together. That was the plan."

"That was never the plan," I said. "That was never discussed."

She stared at me. "Well it's being discussed now, and *that* is the plan."

"Merû . . ."

"Yemasii." My father's soft eyes found her. She stared back at him. Her gaze was wide and somehow narrow at the same time, and her hands cupped into fists at her side. And then her lips were being pulled into a straight line across her face, a thin thread so ready to snap.

"No!" she exclaimed. "*No*, this is not okay." For the first time in longer than I could ever seem to remember, I watched tears fill her eyes. My father looked as though his were close to doing the same.

"Yemasii, I need you to understand that this is not a request." She did nothing but stare with a quivering lip for a very long time.

"And what . . ." She swallowed. "What . . . does the-the other person do? Just . . ."

"They go onto the Qadim."

"Alone?" He simply nodded. "But . . . that's . . . that's not okay."

"And then the rest of us meet them there. We are all capable." I nodded. I don't know if anyone saw me.

After that, no one ever asked me if I wished to go on. Perhaps my acceptance of my father's idea seemed to say enough that I was in agreement with the plan. But I wasn't. Not for a moment. Only for the sake of my family.

[35]

Oatmeal

The river rested like a silk sheet across the mattress of the earth. It bent beneath the waving motion of the wind as though a hand was shaking out the seams. It bounced beneath the footprints of strangers it invited in as friends. It smiled at the laughter they carried, at the jokes in which the punchline went unnoticed.

A feverish breeze sliced along the rim of the fabricated waves, parching the land past it. Towering trees, blossoming, blooming, branching past the rollings of the river, rooted into coarse sand. It was enclosed into a ravine, holding us in the palm of its perishing hands.

Darbii stood beside me. Her hands rested upon her bare hips as she stared out across the river. Stared out across the teenagers plummeting in the waves: her other friends. I always thought she would one day leave me completely for them. She never did.

I simply sat on the sand. A book rested in my hands. The most apparent ease rested upon me. It bit into my bones and replaced them with steel, for my contentment had been impenetrable.

My friend looked down upon me. I couldn't quite hear what she said but her words had been kind and playful as they always had been. At some point, I had been convinced to follow her into the river against my better judgment. The water was cold upon my skin, for it hardly had the time to warm itself at such a time as early May.

There was a bulge over the horizon. It rested right where the river bent, seeming to slowly grow the longer I stared. I stopped as my feet waded deeper into the river and the shallows cupped around my ankles. I heard the voices around me beginning to fade. They rolled in and out of my mind.

And everything was freezing around me. The voices. The splashing. The wisping of the wind through the trees. Everything that once anchored me to reality was removed, and I was staring at the bulge as it continued to grow. As it inched its way toward me.

Until I could tell what it was.

But then it was too late. Then, the wave was right before me, and I was being pushed the wrong way down the stream, and it was consuming me.

And I couldn't breathe.

I was falling.

My eyes shot open, and my body shot up. I was gasping for air. Everything around me shook, and my eyes pressed into a blanket across my legs. My head burned, and my stomach ached, and fire erupted in my side. I could feel the weight of waves upon my face.

Everything slowly came back into focus. The walls around me reformed. The mattress beneath me consumed me again.

"Are you okay?" My gaze found my father on the couch above me. Viridian sat beside him. Their gazes were startlingly blank, their hands empty and dry. I forced a nod.

My eyes ran the length of the room. The mini kitchen in the corner, the bathroom beside it, the open door leading to the bedroom on the other side of the wall. "Where's Merû and Sitka?"

"Went to find food," Viridian replied monotone. He stared at a blank point on the wall.

"What time is it?"

He shrugged. "Six . . . something. Maybe seven."

"Why are you up?"

"Why are *you* up?" Then, he looked over at me, his eyes blaring. Our gazes met for just a moment and only then did I realize his implication. That none of us could sleep.

My head dug into my palms, abolishing the blurriness from my eyes. I forced my legs to stand and carry me across the room to the mini kitchen. I shuffled through the items on the counter; a few stale cereal bars, a jug of water, a leftover pot of cold coffee that my mother must have somehow figured out how to make earlier. My eyes found the open bag of grounds beside it. The hotel must have left it there for us.

I reached for a blue mug towards the back of the counter, placed it down in front of me, and poured some of the leftover coffee into it. My eyes searched the area for a microwave, finding one beneath the counter. I had no idea if it worked.

"I think she's still pissed at us." I heard Viridian's voice from behind me.

I placed the mug into the microwave. "Not if she went somewhere with Sitka."

"She *adores* Sitka, so . . ." I pressed the start button. Nothing happened. I stared at it for a moment, pressed a few more buttons as though they would somehow do something. They didn't.

"We all nearly died," I heard my father say. "It would be incredibly hard for her to remain angry with you."

I heard the growing intonation in Viridian's voice. "Right, but . . . we still shouldn't have put her through all of that. I don't know what the hell I was thinking."

"Language."

"Perû, you don't have to pretend to care just because she does."

"Neither do you." There was a pause as I reluctantly removed my cold coffee from the microwave, turning to face them. Viridian stared at my father, confounded.

"What?"

"You did what was right to your conscience, whether she agreed with you or not. If you wouldn't have come to find me, I would probably be dead right now." I walked over towards where they sat on the couch, standing at the other end of the coffee table. My mind searched for something to say in response.

"We're not talking about how you put me in danger?" I smirked.

Viridian didn't see it. "Eve, you *wanted* to come—"

"It was a joke. Viridian." I sat down on the floor. My father's hands sat wrapped into a ball in his lap, and Viridian stared at the floor. I forced the cold cup of coffee to my lips.

"If anyone's mad at anyone, then it is their job to get past it." My father's hands moved with his head as he spoke. "I am not willing to let any resentment stop us from continuing on." Neither I nor my brother responded. The coffee across my tongue tasted almost sour, as though it had gone bad months ago and no one cared enough to make any more.

My eyes soon found my brother in front of me. His green gaze jumped anxiously between two spots on the floor, his hands clasped into tight fists. And then his eyes found me. And we were staring at each other. I wondered if we had come to a mutual understanding in our gazes. If we both had come to believe that my father's faith in continuing on could be faulty.

There was a creak at the door.

My mother stepped through with a brown bag in her hands. Sitka was at her heel.

"Hey, you're back soon." My mother shook her head at my father.

"Hardly anything is open, of course. Oatmeal was the best we could find." She placed the bag down on the table. Her eyes found me. She hesitated to smile, and even then, it felt forced. "Good morning, how did you sleep?"

"Um . . . fine." That was a lie.

"Sitka's running out of money," she continued to say as she sat down between my father and Viridian, beginning to remove items from the bag. Individual bowls of oatmeal, loaves of bread, and dried fruits; I assumed snacks for later on. "We're going to have to start rationing. Or at least just being more careful about what we're spending money on."

"Is there enough for trains?" My mother looked up at my father.

"There are no trains going anywhere. Not in, out or through Bulgaria, that is. There might be in other countries but it seems for now like we're going to have to travel by foot." I expected Viridian to complain. He didn't.

My mother slipped a few European dollars across the table to each of us. "Everybody take some to hold onto just in case."

And then, everyone was devouring their oatmeal as though they hadn't eaten in days, and I was left sitting in silence, staring at my own bowl. Staring at its intimidating gaze up at me. It took a few minutes before my mother noticed.

"Are you going to eat?" I looked up at her.

Shook my head. "No I . . . I don't like eating in the mornings."

"When was the last time you ate?"

"Not that long ago." But then I thought about it. I had skipped dinner last night, and none of us ate breakfast or lunch yesterday. So it had to have been two nights ago. "Well I guess . . . I guess it was."

"Eat some oatmeal, please, Eve," she said. I continued to stare at the bowl as she and my father discussed something. I was sweating. I couldn't tell why.

Then I was standing, moving to the bathroom. My heart beat heavily against my ears. Everything inside of me was tense, and every breath I breathed I couldn't release.

Something was wrong with me.

Everything was wrong with me.

Nothing was wrong with me.

I locked the door behind me. Sat down on the toilet. My head was clasped in my hands, and I was trying to find breath inside my bones where there was none.

There were no trains anywhere. Sitka was running out of money. No one in my family fully trusted each other anymore, and I still had that gun on my side. Everything seemed to be falling apart, and we weren't even in Israel yet.

And then my phone was in my hands. I don't know how it got there.

➤ To "Unknown," 7:22

"I just need to admit this to someone other than myself. I am falling apart. I don't know what is happening or why. I don't want to go on to the Qadim, I know now it is a waste of energy, but I have to. There's no choice in that. I need to figure out how to pull myself together just for a little while longer for my family. I don't know what to do."

[36]

Evergreen

"After the sun slowly burns,
Before the earth fades,
Calm becomes rare,
Damaged days,
Evergreen.
In the smoke of night,
Heat of the tomorrow,
Grace grows finite,
Fields bare,
Evergreen."

I wondered if the evergreens were still green. If the deep, verdant colors they displayed had been a trick to the eyes of the animals on the tips of their branches. I wondered if the human gaze watched them for long enough, they would forget about it all. All that had become of the world sketched into the cave walls of the muscle in their mind, would disappear. As if a potion, a desired serum.

Because ignorance was bliss.

And bliss had been misplaced in a galaxy I had once belonged to. Upon a star I had once orbited until I lost my direction. Until my head had begun to spin the opposite way, colliding with the other planets around me. Until we drove ourselves down into the depths of the universe, and our seeming immortality became a curse. Because pain had become the only foe we knew.

It seemed as though I no longer made friends, only foes. That woman at the grocery store on our way out of Varna, whose crinkled, tin foil face flattened out at the sight of me. I'm still not quite sure why. That blank, dismayed expression set into permanence across my mother's cheeks, seeming to grow whenever she saw me. Though, perhaps that was merely my perception, I had been able to recognize.

And the heat, my supreme foe.

I once thought I would grow used to it by then. The peeling of my once beautiful skin. The sweat stuck like thick honey on my back and across my neck. I thought I would find a way to cope with it. But no ounce of water I could manage to uncover did even a dent in the armor of my foe.

I was being burnt to a crisp. Sometimes I wondered if it was safer to travel at night. But that was when the hunters were out.

There's no way we can survive this.

It seemed almost as though I had accepted the thought. At least, I didn't fight it as I once had.

It took six days to get to the city of Constantinople. Six days of endless questioning of who was worthy of our trust. For the despair in everyone's eyes looked too similar to malicion. I carried Darbii's notebook with me in the palm of my burning hand and I pretended the gun wasn't there on my side, but I was so undoubtedly aware of its potential necessity. My hope had grown to be only that which I could latch on to from my family, that which Elijah had somehow still instilled into me.

But then we made it; the crown jewel of the Neo-Italian Empire, once known as Istanbul, then returned to its prior name of Constantinople. We had studied its history back in Grade 11. How the Neo-Italian Empire had been weakened from war against Lebanon. How the Italian president at the time had decided it was his chance to recreate the Byzantine Empire. How he succeeded. But only by a fraction.

The modernized Italian embellishments had been clear beneath the light of the setting sun. The metal archways and Corinthian columns. In another life, it all might have been beautiful, with the colorful buildings and cobblestone streets, leading to the capitol building. The way the sea surrounded it all as if hoping to one day consume the land by its passionate, all consuming lust.

It was the first place we had been to in which the streets were completely empty. Stray cats lived on the steps of buildings with doors slanted on their sides and slashes driven through the wood. Ash had fallen over the city. It lay in the trees and in patches that reflected the footsteps of death. The shadow of his presence lay everywhere, in shattered glass windows, in the burning breeze, in the reflections of his face upon the alabaster stone buildings. In the all consuming darkness reflecting the red and gray sky. I had never known such a dreary place.

We found our way to the outskirts of the city. The buildings gradually grew more run down as the night approached us and soon, the moon greeted me, his grin a dying crescent. I tried to smile back at it. The muscles in my face seemed to have weakened.

There were buildings to one side of the road and a forest to the other. The trees covered the light of the moon, an eerie silence replacing its presence. The neighborhood had been rundown, a sure place to find an abandoned home, a place to rest for the night. Because hotels had become not only too costly but also too rare.

Our voices remained covered in silence as our footsteps echoed against the sides of buildings. The heaviness of darkness weighed upon us all. My mother's shoulders were raised high towards her head as they now always seemed to be. Viridian's hands were buried tightly into his pockets, his eyes dimmed in a way I had never known them to be. Sitka stood hunched at the neck, his eyes forever piercing the pavement. And then there was my father's limp that never seemed to subside. We all kept an uncomfortable distance from one another.

There was a voice heard over the silence. Breath caught in my chest. My eyes hurried in its direction, falling upon a figure on a street corner. There was a woman wrapped in robes upon a bench, holding a candle in her hand, one leg crossed over another. Her skin was just beginning to crinkle with age, her curly black hair sat still on her shoulders. She stared at us for a moment, a small smile beginning to form at the sight of my mother and Viridian.

"*Luut ba'jé xu?*" she asked again in Cordellian. My father responded in French, his voice deeper than normal.

"*Non, nous ne sommes pas perdus.*" *No, we are not lost.*

"*U'xu luut ba'jé mak.*" *You look lost.* She didn't abandon the Cordellian language for French as my father had. Instead, her smile shifted to a grin, my father reluctantly returning to his native tongue moments later.

"Who are you and what do you want?"

"I'm just trying to help, that is all."

"With what?"

"Well," she continued, looking down at her fingernails for a moment, then back up at us. "There have been many people wandering these parts lately, hoping to get to Israel—"

"Are you implying that—"

"No. Just curious, since most prefer to die at home rather than somewhere unknown. Unless they don't intend to die." She smiled again, this time softer. My heart pounded harder. She looked at my mother again, her gaze fixed on her green eyes. "Especially since I know Cordellia is a beautiful place."

"It's not as beautiful now," my mother intervened, the confidence in her tone something I couldn't understand. "So we chose to see the rest of the world instead with what time we have left." The woman stared at my mother. Her left eyebrow twitched just the slightest bit, and then she slowly nodded.

"Well, all this to say that I have a place for you all to stay if you are in need. I have been offering up my home to travelers for the past couple of weeks." My gaze shifted to my parents. The most evident unease pulsed through the blood in my veins. There was something about the darkness in her eyes. Something familiar and malicious. Something artificial. I thought of Salzburg in a single moment.

"I don't think this is a good idea . . ." I mumbled under my breath, my mother's eyes slowly falling towards me.

"Do you have any other ideas?"

"No."

"This is probably the best we're going to get for the night." I felt my stomach turn. My phone buzzed in my back pocket. Elijah. His messages had become sporadic by then, and I had never found the strength to respond, not after the paragraph I had sent so embarrassingly in Varna.

"We can find something better," I said. My body tensed more than what seemed possible. "I have a feeling."

"Eve . . ."

"And the last time I had a feeling and no one listened to me, we almost died." She stared at me for a moment. I watched her fidget with her fingers as though to wipe away layers of dust upon her nails. Then, she sighed.

"We'll be aware, okay? If anything seems off, we leave."

It was a decent compromise.

Silver Spoons Against Bowls

The smell of cooked vegetables and beef greeted us when we stepped through the front door. The walls were a pasty orange and seemed almost to cave in on themselves. Three wooden doors were placed around the space and a large cast iron pot sat in the far corner, steam rising from the top. The tiny room was crowded with strange abstract paintings along the walls and there were six chairs at her kitchen table as if she had been expecting we would come. She motioned for us to sit, making her way over to the stove and breathing in the fumes from the pot upon it.

"I have stew prepared for you," she began to prepare each of us bowls. "I know you must be terribly hungry. I ate earlier, so don't worry about leaving me any." I watched her closely as she began to hand out dishes, her movements fragmented, choppy, and yet still somehow steady. A small smile had been stuck upon her face, almost startling.

I slid Darbii's notebook under my leg, half sitting on it. The woman placed herself down across from my father at the end of the table and I stared at the bowl sitting in front of me.

"I'm actually not hungry right now." I slowly nudged the bowl back in her direction, not letting my eyes connect with hers. There had been a pause. Then, Sitka spoke.

"I'm not either. I'm sorry." The woman smiled. It seemed genuine.

"It's alright, dears. No need to apologize." My parents and Viridian reached for their silver spoons, beginning to eat the stew in silence. I swallowed as though I was eating too. Their eyes met mine and Sitka's from time to time as though to dissect the discomfort in our stares. As though our secrets laid behind our pupils to be discovered if they stared long enough and so I kept my eyes looking down.

"So where are you headed next?" My mother looked up at the woman out of the corner of her eye. Thought. Swallowed.

"Bulgaria," she said confidently. "There's a few villages there we've been hoping to visit."

"Ah yes," I watched her lean back in her chair, her arms crossed, the smile stained across her cheeks forever unwavering. "You know, I had a friend at one point that did some work in Bulgaria. Varna, I believe." There was a pause as we all hesitated to respond. "Some technological things. Very fascinating. Are any of you into science?"

My mother glanced over at Sitka, "My son is interested in the field."

The woman grinned. "Oh really! Isn't that darling! Science is our future." *There is no future.* "Oh, you would love my friend's work." Sitka nodded.

The woman's gaze shifted towards me. "What are you interested in, deary?" I stared at her for a moment, trying to decipher whether she was just trying to make conversation or get information.

"I dance . . . ballet."

"Oh ballet! How lovely!" I stared at her. Her smile was big. Too big. "Is there an academy you're hoping to go to?" My tongue slid across my bottom lip. My eyebrows narrowed, and my head leaned forward. I could feel my face beginning to boil.

"Why would you ask that?" The sounds of spoons against bowls ceased. I felt eyes upon me so ardently, and yet I was staring at the woman. Her eyes were curiously narrowed in towards her nose, yet mournful on the outer side. Her arms rested stiffly on the table for a moment.

"I beg your pardon?"

"You know we're all going to die. Why would you ask me about . . . about going to an academy? It's not going to happen anyway."

"I didn't mean to offend you, dear, I apologize." I stared at her for a long moment. Her eyes waned in upon me in the way of uncertainty and nearly to the point of suspicion. I wouldn't let my gaze move from her until she was shifting to speak to Viridian. Then, I looked at him too. He clenched his spoon the slightest bit too tightly and his nostrils had begun to flare in and out sporadically. His eyes shifted up to the woman and back down to his stew as she asked him about his life before the black hole. Asked him about basketball. Asked him about the league in Belgium he nearly made it to. He answered each question with a single word.

Many moments passed. The woman became less than enthralled with Viridian and began to speak with my father about his carpentry days. How he moved to Cordellia when he was young. He didn't tell her where from.

Then, silence became our ally.

"You know, I was actually told to keep an eye out for you guys." My head shot up at the woman, startled to see she was already looking at me.

"Oh yeah?" My mother shifted in her seat. "Told by who?"

"Oh, just a mutual friend. He said he ran into you in Serbia, and you'd probably need a place to stay in Constantinople." I stared at her for a moment. My jaw opened slightly as my father intervened.

"Are you talking about Wĕvii Soddom?"

"Yes, yes. Mr. Soddom. Wonderful man, isn't he?" My heart began to race. My eyes shot towards my father, his gaze already on me, his lips pulled in tightly to his mouth.

"Yes, he . . . yeah." I remembered my note in his back pocket. The hunters in Salzburg. Herr Krüger. All of the people that had betrayed us and hated us, and in an instant, I knew she was one of them.

"Is everything okay, dear?" she was talking to me then. My eyes shot up at her. For the first time, her smile seemed to falter just a bit. I didn't move.

"Um . . . yes, everything is fine. Perû, can I talk to you for a second?" My father nodded, beginning to stand along with me. I grabbed Darbii's notebook from beneath my leg. Clenched it tightly.

"Whatever you have to say to him, you can say here." She smiled again. "It's a safe place." There was a long lull for a moment.

"We'll be right back." My father reached for my arm. "Thank you for your kindness."

"No." Silence swept the circumference of the room. My eyes slowly lifted to the woman. All joy that was once plastered on her cheeks was then vanquished, a heavy stare replacing it, concentrated on my father. He returned the gaze.

"Excuse me?"

"You're not going anywhere." My bones stiffened more than they had been before. And then I was staring at the floor, waiting for my father to say something in reply. Nothing came to him.

"Perû . . ." I mumbled. But then I noticed the slow movement of her right hand, reaching underneath her shirt. I watched it tightly grip something there. Then, I realized what was happening.

No.

[38]

Shattering

The crack of the gun sounded before I had time to take it in. I didn't know where the bullet landed. All I knew was that I was heading towards the door. No, running. Sprinting. I pressed my feet into the wooden floors as though my life depended on it; because it seemed it did.

Shouts echoed around me. Arms pushed me. Feet slammed into the ground around me. I clutched Darbii's notebook in my arms. We were at the door, and there was another shot. I could feel the air as it brushed past my ear, connecting with the wall in front of me. And soon everything came into focus, and I was realizing what was happening.

She wanted us dead.

That was all there was to it.

I swung right, seeming to nearly thrust myself down the stairs and out into the burning night. The air was coarse through my aching lungs. It was sand running through rocks, slicing the sides of once smooth stone and I felt each breath a million times. We turned left down an alleyway. The stone walls were tight around our bodies and I had no choice but to lean against one, fighting to find air in the midst of its absence. My family crowded around me.

"What the hell just happened?!" Viridian exclaimed. He was hunched over on his knees, slapping them with his palms. My father's forehead was herded into the heel of his hands as if hoping to push away some thought that was forming frantically.

"That woman is crazy." He mumbled.

"All that because you two wanted to have a conversation without her present?" My mother's hands were against her temples, rubbing them as though to impose some amount of understanding into her mind.

"Next time I have a gut feeling about something, you guys listen." Everyone's eyes turned to me. "I've been right almost every time, and you guys still don't trust me." I sounded angry. I didn't mean to sound angry. I didn't even think I was angry.

Just, scared.

"Eve, it's not that we don't trust you," She began to say. My eye-roll came more as an instinct than a planned action.

There was an echo through the alleyway behind us. A voice, the woman's. She spoke again in a tongue I could not understand. There was a second voice. A third.

No.

Oh no.

There's more of them.

"Go, go, go." Viridian turned opposite of where we had come, sprinting down the alleyway. My feet hurried after him, and my head was spinning in the most confounding of circles, the heat pulling the very breath out of my lungs. We were turning the corner, rushing down the sidewalk, veering into a grocery store on the corner. The shelves were empty, littered with hollow cans across the floor and a few full ones hidden in the back of shelves. An AI being stood at the front register. It greeted us in a foreign tongue, and didn't seem to worry about the haste in which we shuffled towards the back of the store. And then we were kneeling beside a back shelf, an empty can rolling towards my toes.

My feet ached beneath my body's weight. I clenched Darbii's notebook tighter. Anger and desperation mended themselves into my very bones until I was fully against the ground, shaking under the fear of what possibly could be done. For we couldn't hide forever.

I closed my eyes. In a moment, images began to flash before my eyes.

No, please not right now.

The wave of the tsunami, its angry pull pushed me down into the earth. Breath escaped my lungs, tears becoming one with the waves.

No. Stop it.

The water of a river made its way up my throat. The thoughts of terror circled my brain, the cuts upon my arms ripping down to my bones.

Please don't do this right now.

The helicopter simmered upon the cobblestone courtyard of Munich. The Cordellian star burned my eyes, shock stirred in my stomach.

Wait.

My eyes opened. They dashed over to my mother beside me, my jaw clenched, my teeth becoming prison bars.

"Merû." She found me. Her eyebrows raised towards me and in her green eyes were a burning forest. "We're being hunted again." Again wasn't the right word if it had never stopped in the first place.

She stared. Blinked. Eyes narrowed. "What?"

"Remember in Munich? The helicopter?" I swallowed a lump in my throat. "The Cordellian star?" I tried to read the thoughts that jumped across her mind. Tried to pin a single one to my tongue so to speak for her.

Then, she shook her head. "No. That's ridiculous."

"Merû, hardly anyone knows Cordellian. It can't just be a coincidence that she knows it too." She stared at me for a moment. "Remember the hunters in Salzburg? They were the only others who spoke it. And Krüger? How suspicious he was of us? And we don't even know what he put in our arms. What if . . ." I remembered what Viridian had said beside the river in what felt like so long ago. How he had mentioned a tracker, and I had called it foolish.

And suddenly, I saw in my mother's gaze a deep understanding of my words and an even deeper fear. "That's impossible."

"You said yourself that it isn't." She stared. Stared so intently that her eyes seemed to burn my cheeks.

"Why would they do this? *Who* would do this?"

"I don't know. But it doesn't mean it's not happening." She watched me for a moment longer, and then her gaze shifted to the floor. Then I was thinking of Elijah. Wondering what he knew. Wondering if I should tell my mother about him. Wishing I knew what was stopping me from doing so.

She looked up at me again. "Do you have any ideas about what to do?"

"No."

"I . . . I don't either." She swallowed. "We can't sit here forever." My hand found its way to the gun upon my hip. I don't remember telling it to move there.

I felt my heart shatter inside of me.

No. I will not.

"Keep running." I stood off of impulse. Rushed back towards the front of the store and pushed through the front door. Hot air found its way up my nostrils. Heat clouded my vision. I no longer paid attention to my family around me. No longer noticed their feet at my heels.

Snap.

The echo of a gunshot shattered the air around me. Pain didn't seem to follow it. At least not my own.

"Eve!" Viridian screamed. I turned to face him. He stood behind me, his arms thrown out at his sides. "Where the hell are we going?"

"Just keep running!" I didn't know where I was headed. Somewhere. Anywhere.

My head ached.

My half-healed side cramped.

The wind sliding past my arms stung the cuts.

I just,

wanted to,

rest.

I turned back down the alleyway and around the corner. The forest lay to the left of me, the then vacant home of the woman to the right. And then there was a voice.

"*Héla, ba'jé.*" A woman, but not the same one as before. I spun to meet her down the road beside the alley, her dark skin nearly matching the color of the gun that sat in her hands,

pointed at me.

I heard the breaths of my family crowded around me. I felt their warmth against my skin. My hand slowly wrapped around the gun upon my hip. I heard the crack of hers. The scattering of my companions. The falling of the bark of the tree behind me.

You have to do it.

No I didn't.

There's no other way.

My pocket buzzed. Once. Twice. Darbii's notebook dropped to the ground next to me. My eyes could only look upon the weapon then in my own hands; heavy, terrifying. I didn't put it there. I couldn't have. This wasn't me. None of this.

And suddenly, my whole body shook, shattered.

Shattering as I watched the woman's body freeze, her eyes widening.

Shattering as I saw her fall towards the concrete, a puddle of red around her.

Shattered as I again saw the weapon of her demise held up in someone's hand.

My hand.

A gasp escaped me.

What have I done.

[39]

Periods.

I had always thought there was something so beautiful about periods. They brought an end to an idea. Closure to a way of thinking. They made the beginning more gripping by giving it an end.

And yet, periods terrified me. For once they were used, they could never be taken back. Once they were placed at the end of your words—of your actions—there they stayed.

I preferred to use commas, for then I was able to correct my mistakes before it was too late.

The first thing I saw was my mother. That look in her eye. Her dark gaze, her pale face, and her eyebrows raised high until they nearly met her hairline. But it was her eyes alone that haunted me.

For the eyes of one she had known all too well had been deceptive. The pacifistic ideology she had crafted into me had neglected to sustain growth. For the deepest desires of a person could never truly be discovered, not even by themselves.

That was why she stared at me. That was why her dropped jaw crushed me into the gravity of my deeds. That was why her gaze had been riddled with anger and fervor and fear. I couldn't think of the word for a moment. But then it appeared before me, clothed in scarlet robes.

Hate.

I stared a moment more. Stared at her red eyes. My gun fell to the concrete. It clattered.

What had I done?

I stumbled back,

fell back.

Back into the woods behind me. The branches sliced the cut above my eyebrow, the slashes on my arms.

I didn't feel anything.

Then I turned towards the woods. I raced through the trees, and they were pulling me into their embrace, and words of people I once had known encircled my brain. They grew in dissonance. In disaster, in despair, until a wave as great as a tsunami crashed them all upon me. Until every foreign language I had ever known escaped me, and only a familiar tongue remained.

"Xu je jekoh?"

"Ko ku je nu riit'h."

"Je kess pa korh?"

"Je, telt nu vut'h."

"Mulmii xu je."

"You're a monster."

And suddenly, I was on the ground, surrounded by dirt and fallen leaves, the trees overhead concealing the moon. I was suffocated by the heat. Burning to death as it seemed I was destined to. Stuck inside a cell of terror, of denial, until sleep consumed me. And even then, my dreams were a mirror of my reality, and no bullet I carried had the power to shatter that glass. No excuse I could conjure up could erase the smudges I had placed upon it. That red liquid shaped into the form of my hand, and all the lines and creases matched my own.

And then I saw my reflection in the shattered glass, my round and red cheeks meeting my chin. I saw my curls flopped and frizzed over my head as though seared at the tips. My ears that could only hear voices of condemnation. My nose that could only smell the burning of the morality within me. My lips that quivered and danced atop my teeth, but no words could find the strength to leave my lips. The bags under my eyes accented by the tears I couldn't bring myself to cry. Tears that I didn't deserve to cry, for no one wicked deserved to mourn.

The sun burned me awake the next morning. It whispered words in my ears of such slander so that I sat up instantly.

I don't quite know what I had felt when I first awoke. Simply the heat. Scorching my skin. Paralysis. The oddest sensation of a deep need for tears but none would come. But I remember that the faintest feeling of hope had fought to find me. The faintest idea that maybe I could find my way out of all of this.

And then, it ceased.

I sat up in the dirt. My arms were indented under the weight of the earth. Pressure pounded in upon my ears, and the light echo of the condescending voices met them soon after. I thought I could smell home for a moment in that burning forest. The smell of the apple tree out the kitchen window in bloom. My mother would pick a few just as they were ripening and make the most fantastic juice from them, and me and my brothers would await the day on which it would be sitting there on the table for breakfast. We would consume it to the point of stomach aches that would cease at the feeling of the spring sunlight upon our skin. For the world had been a medicine to us.

And then I thought of my mother. Thought of that look in her eye the night before. It was then I realized I might never see her again.

But it wasn't until I stood, until I was beginning to search my way through the woods that I realized she might prefer it that way.

I stopped.

I was surrounded. Engulfed by trees on all sides, the sunlight seeping in, rays of light highlighting a few still red leaves not yet coagulated. At another point in time, it might have been beautiful.

But it confined me. Trapped me in isolation, behind prison walls. And something inside of me told me I deserved it. For humanity was wicked, with all of its lies and schemes and turnings on one another, and I was one of them.

I walked a long time through those prison walls. The sunlight warmed my throat until the sensation of sandpaper stung my tongue. Not a single thought met me for a long while. Not until I found a clearing by midday, and, with it, such hesitancy to fall into it. To fall upon the concrete and lay there for just a moment. Just to let the heat strangle me.

That was when the thoughts came. The war. The push and pull between the desire to seek my family and the knowing that they were better off without me.

The knowing that I had told them to leave me if I would go missing. To go on without me.

It was then, that finally, all hope of seeing them again was gone.

Death Is Inevitable

What does a person do if they know they are going to die? Do they fight it? Spend everything they have on protecting themselves? Draining themselves out, draining the tears from their eyes, and multiplying the layers of blood on their hands. Or do they give in? Give in to the simplicity, the efficiency of death.

If I had been asked such a thing even a week ago, I might have said that I would fight. That it all seemed worth it. But since I had donated all my tears to the battle—since I had seen for myself just how thick that blood was on my hands—I had grown to think otherwise. Because what was the purpose of fighting what was inevitable?

I thought for a long while about returning home. Back to the cobblestone streets of Paris in the blazing summertime. Finding my way back to my bed and letting the comfort of familiarity consume me. So then, maybe, death would become less painful when it inevitably came.

I thought of the Qadim for a while as well. Thought of what it would be like if that thing in my arm could really get me onto it. If I really could have a future.

But reality struck me in a moment. Of how weak I had become. Of how my bones were rotting away and my skin was failing to protect my appendages. Of how foolish I would be to believe I could carry on either way effectively.

For then, I would wander the streets of Constantinople, hoping to find food, even if it be the scraps from the table of the kings of the land. I would wander alone until death found me, until I allowed him to take me to his abode. Until I decided that it would be easier that way.

I felt my phone buzz in my back pocket. It was one of many times that day, but the first time I had enough sense to acknowledge it. At first I feared Elijah's inevitable voice of condemnation, for I was so comically aware that he knew what I had done.

I turned a corner onto a wide cobblestone street. Clothing lines hung from windows, the once white garments then were now tarnished with ash. Red streetcars sat still with shattered windows and torn-up cushioned seats. Brick balconies chipped and fallen pieces lay out across the street below. Metal archways were dented and bent at the edges. Doors were broken open, and others stood shut. And through the mess and destruction, not a single human face did I see.

Everybody was gone. Accepting death as their fate or fighting for a life they couldn't ever truly obtain.

And then, the reality of what I had known all along appeared to me again. It shattered the silence in my mind, and there was nothing I could do to control it any longer:

there was no way I could survive this. None of this.

I was destined to death.

If only I had accepted it earlier, maybe then I would have been able to die happy. To force myself into a fake contentment that at least would graze the fingertips of satisfaction.

My steps faltered. In a moment, I was on the ground. Heat sunk into my cheeks. My lips were peeling ,and my throat was dry. My body leaned against a cobblestone wall, and for a second more, I wished I could cry.

I thought of my mother. Of her piercing green eyes, of her fervor and fire. Of her dedication to love, her hatred towards all things evil, her nearness and solace.

I thought of my father. Of his tender hands and tender heart and his eyes to see me thrive. To seek out nothing but the best in my character.

I thought of my brothers. Of Viridian's careless joy and careful dedication. Of Sitka's perfected speech, of his neverending concentration.

I would die without them ever knowing what happened to me.

And I hated it.

And for just a moment, I imagined the heat around me to be my blankets back home, holding me tenderly. I imagined my head against my pillow, with scraps of scribbled paper underneath, ideas left unfinished. I imagined the posters around my rooms of concerts I had seen and those I had wished to. Of thoughts and ideas of poets' past. I thought of the photos in my corner beside my desk, of Darbii and me over the years, photos from the ballet of the winter I had been the sugar plum fairy. Images of my brothers, of Sitka's wide grin as a child, of Viridian's smirk that never changed. Of my mother and father on their wedding day, with cake in their faces, the photograph faded and gray. And for a moment that seemed it would last a lifetime, I longed so deeply for home.

I felt my phone buzz in my pocket. It was a long, rolling sound, not the sporadic buzzes I had become accustomed to. It vibrated my burning bones, shaking the ash from between crevices, and soon everything came together in my mind, and I realized what it meant.

A phone call.

I reached into my pocket. I stared at "*Unknown*" printed so plainly across my screen. How such a word could evoke such extreme emotion in me, I could not understand.

I stared into the shape of the words. Stared until my fear of being undeserving was outweighed by my desire for answers. Until the burning breeze around me settled, and the world was so still that I could hear the faint whisper of my breaths.

I was terrified. And yet, I picked up the phone.

There was silence on the other line. Merely a distant humming, perhaps of a light or a receding tide. My lips quivered. My bones shook. My tongue tried to muster the strength to speak. And somehow, such a strength was found.

"Y-yes . . . ?" My voice quaked. The walls of buildings around me tumbled. The light hum remained. My eyes closed. They shook beneath my lids. My forehead followed as time passed and I felt my heart vibrate in my ears as though that was where it belonged.

Then, a voice came. "*This isn't how it ends.*"

A chill swept through my body. My mouth pinned itself to the pavement. His voice was deep, yet comforting. Smooth, yet sharpened. Thick with wonder yet laced lightly with realism. His words rang over again in my mind instinctively. They were beautiful, yet terrifying.

"Please." I was shoving vomit off of my tongue. "Please don't give me hope," I said it so faintly I almost believed he hadn't heard me. Not until he spoke again.

"*I'm not giving you anything. I am asking you not to abandon the one thing that will keep you alive.*" I shook my head. A long moment passed. The wind began to ripple the clothing lines above me.

"What . . . what do I do?"

"*Go on to Israel.*"

"I can't." There was silence for a moment. "I've lost . . . everything. It's all . . . it's all gone. My family, I . . . I am *weak*, Elijah."

"*I don't need your strength; I need your trust.*" I listened to his words. Considered them. Found something inside of me willing to take a deep breath and stare out across the street. "*I will guide you. There is not a single good reason why I would abandon you now.*" And for some reason, a fatal foolishness engraved into my very character believed his every word.

Part II

"The Guide"

[41]

Five Signs Of Idiocracy

"Dear Darbii.

I'm pretty sure that I'm an idiot. First of all, I thought it was a good idea to leave the comfort of my home for some country called Israel. And that's not even the worst part about it; it's the fact that it was Viridian's idea, and I was dumb enough to think it was a good one.

"Second, I started taking commands from some unknown number that's been messaging me. Which might not be idiotic, given he's actually been giving me good advice. But the very concept of it is . . . stupid.

"Third, I got us stuck in a tsunami. Yes. A literal tsunami. Just because I wanted to visit some stupid town on the Black Sea.

"Fourth, I shot a woman. Killed her. I stole a human life like it was my right. It's not . . . but that doesn't make me an idiot, that just makes me . . . wicked.

"And fifth, I'm stuck in Constantinople. By myself. Following messages and phone calls from said unknown number because he told me to have hope. That is the only reason." I stop talking, talking to no one. The world is still. Silent.

And then I scream. I tear my throat to shreds and pull my lips off of their dwelling around my mouth. The water before me drowns my cry. The wooden dock beneath me digs into my skin. The hot air stings every single inch of my being. My bones ache. My mind aches more. The sea in front of me tosses and turns and I stare at it as though we are friends rather than foes.

As though it has offered me peace.

But it has offered me nothing.

I am hopeless.

This is the very place where I promised you would find me, sitting on this dock in Neo-Italy, waiting for death to take me. It has been seven days of this madness. Seven days since I spoke to Elijah on that street corner, seven days of boiling and burning and somehow forgetting to care, for I have learned to hate myself. Seven days since I found myself back to that alleyway, picking up that velvet notebook off of the concrete, the pages bent and crinkled by water, but at least something to write on. Seven minutes since I finished recording all that has occurred, recorded for no one to read. Only for me to make some sense of it all. Before it all is over.

The notebook sits beside me on the dock. It sits with everything from this journey thus far, scribbled down inside, for what else can one do when they believe they are dying then write about it all? My phone rests beside it. I stare at them both in parallel. Demand my tears to pour down upon them, but seven days have passed, and not once could I find enough moisture within my bones to do such a thing. I am truly damaged.

I wish my body would decide to perish. So I no longer would have to hold onto these guilty hands and this twisted mind. So this impending shame, shifting to something so similar to hatred, would finally cease. So I wouldn't be haunted by it all anymore.

I remember the song Darbii and I had sung together all those nights ago when all of our cares had fled for just a moment. For some reason, I begin to mumble the words of the second verse to myself.

> "*I'll make no promises, won't make any excuses*
> *This was the tree where I had tied up all my nooses*
> *It's burned up now*
> *Can't even tell you how it got there.*

"The grass turned black so I looked to your smiling face and
Saw a faded picture of escaped brighter days and
It had been charming at first
Before I knew you were cursed."

My phone buzzes. I already stare down upon it as though I have expected it would come. Maybe I have. "*Unknown*" is stained across the screen as my only current sign of stability. I sigh. It scratches my throat. And then I answer.

There's a light hum on the other end. Elijah doesn't say anything until I mumble a quiet "Hi."

"*Day seven.*" I stare out at the ocean again. It seems to still the longer I stare. Undisturbed.

"I know," I say.

"*Are you ready to continue on?*"

"I still don't know where to start."

"*That wasn't my question.*" I try to breathe through the frayed skin of my nostrils. My gaze doesn't escape the sea. I wait for him to say something more. Moments pass before he does. "*Go again to the convenience store a few blocks down the way. Get yourself some food and water. Bring a bit to sustain you through the morning. Then, we'll continue on.*" Food. The thought of such a thing still makes me weary. Anger fumes around my mouth.

"With what money, Elijah? The money my mother gave me in Bulgaria is running dry. And to think it will sustain me all the way to Israel?"

"*It will.*"

"How can you be sure?" I wait for a reply. There is none. I shake my head and watch my feet dangle off the boating dock. Wondering once more how this all could be for nothing as it seems so clearly that it is. "I don't know . . ." There is silence on the other line. "I . . ."

"*I need you to keep going.*" I am blank-faced. "*For your family's sake.*"

For your family's sake.

My bones go stiff.

254 | Kassandra Grace

That is when I see them all again. I see Viridian's face on a night so long ago, when we had thought it would be best to leave. I see Sitka after the tsunami, his weary eyes fixed so curiously on me. I see my father's face after leaving Darbii, when he spoke of Mister Soddom's crookedness.

I see that look in my mother's eye. The night that woman died.

The thought comes to me again. Of why I have not found them. Perhaps it isn't that I had once told them to continue on, but rather they don't care to see me. Perhaps they hate me in the same way it seems I do myself.

But Elijah knows things that I don't. It is a reality I cannot ignore. Perhaps he knows more about them than I think I do.

So I hang up the phone. Stand up from the spot in which I have melted into the wooden deck. Immediately, my head spins beneath the weight of the sun, and I see nothing but darkness. But the moment passes. I look down at the velvet notebook beneath me. That thing that has consumed my entire past week with writing of days past that haunt my every moment. Memories of my best friend, who I will never again lay eyes on.

And then, I kick it into the water.

I turn around. Walk three blocks down the road to the convenience store on the corner of two once-busy streets, now still in the sunlight. The glowing sign is half burnt out, the front door shut tightly, just as it has been in previous days. I yank it open, stepping inside and taking a quick glance at the AI being at the register.

There are a few cans on the shelves, black and green beans and items with labels fully in an obscene language. I stare at them all. Try to muster the strength to reach for them yet again, and this time, maybe carry them into a new land. To ignore my impending pain and ever-increasing hatred. To push against these thoughts, against this demented voice in the back of my mind. To find Elijah's instead.

For your family.

I grab a few cans and the three bottles of water remaining, bringing them all to the register.

"*På, ko vut, plå ku je,*" I hardly realize the tongue in which I speak. Not until the AI being replies in French.

"*Je ne peux pas parler dans cette langue. S'il vous plaît, essayez encore.*" *I do not know this language.* Please, try again. I roll my eyes. The AI being scans the items, and I slip a few dollars onto the counter, less money for later on. It processes the payment. I leave the store, stepping out again into the burning sunlight. And then I'm sitting on a staircase, staring at the cans in my lap.

I have no choice but to face the thing that I fear the most.

I open a can of green beans. Force the substance down my throat and force my mind to ignore the sensation building in my throat. I stare at a red door across the road. Try to wonder who the last person was who used it.

It's the most I've eaten in over a week.

A cat appears a few steps down from me. Its orange coat shines against the burning sunlight. I stare at its figure for a moment, at its stomach that has shrunk away into a single fine line. Then, I call to it. The thing appears beside me and purrs beneath my palm, and I lay a few beans down on the pavement for it to eat. Then, I finish what remains in the can.

I am left sitting on this staircase, staring at the damaged buildings around me. At the stained fingertips of those who have lived such lovely lives in these parts.

Then, the war is beginning again in my mind. The deep, undying hatred towards all I have done—all I am. And yet, I desire so earnestly for the future to be real again. To find somewhere that can be home. But it seems I am unaware of what in my mind is real and what's a fantasy. What the difference is between a dream and a nightmare.

A text shows up across my phone screen.

➤ From "Unknown," 12:23

"Head left down this road until you're out of the city. I'll tell you where to go from there."

For the first time, I am fully realizing it. I am neglecting my denial and realizing what he has been trying to say to me all along.

He will lead me to Israel.

[42]

Favor In The Stars

A map without markings. That is what the world has become to me. Roads, rivers, the residue of earthquakes, and the flames of a broken and burning world. But it all is meaningless. Mere answers without first knowing the question. Chaos.

But chaos calms in the face of guidance in the midst of one who can lead. Even the innermost chaos is brought to rest through the faintest scent of hope. Hope brings both foolishness and contentment. And for my family's sake, I have decided to live with the first in longing for the second.

He leads me through unknown lands. He brings me to places where food is stored and reminds me to eat. He finds hidden places where rest is found. Hideouts he knows of with people generous enough to give without receiving. He is kind. I even begin to wonder if he understands me, even what I cannot understand about myself. Through it, I have somehow begun to trust him so effortlessly, so carelessly. To trust his words and memorize the sound of his voice without first seeking help from hesitation. Perhaps this is where the slight echo of a dying hope leads you: on into the face of naivete.

The Neo-Italian empire is in an uproar. Chaos on one corner and an uneasy silence on the next. Earthquakes happen every day, and somehow I only find their remains in rotting buildings and paralyzed faces. But above all else, it is humanity that hurts one another. I watch it as I walk through cities with people lying silently on street corners. They are passed by without a single glance. Bodies rest inside the ruins of buildings crumpled and demolished by the shaking of the earth, their limbs shrinking away to single strips of thread. The cries of children become a melody inside my mind, one I cannot escape. Not a single soul pays me mind and I come to wonder if I am invisible.

I begin to find myself immune to it all. I seem to have learned to balance hope with acceptance of the more likely outcome. And yet, it's an uneasy feeling, knowing I have become immune to such blaring terrors.

I find favor in the stars. In the glow that surrounds them. And yet, I find fear in the face of their ferocity. Perhaps even the most beautiful things can be broken.

Night turns to day, and day back to night. An endless cycle of only hoping the sun will continue to burn without my expense. Of placing my complete trust in Elijah, waiting for the moment when messages will finally cease, and I will truly be left with nothing.

But that day never comes. Not yet, at least.

There is a shop that he guides me to in a desert plain. I don't know how many days have passed. It sits on the outskirts of a small town, the metal worn by the weight of the sand brushing by. And on the side, in three languages, sits a sign reading: "*Nous donnons des provisions à tout le monde.*" *Supplies for everyone.* I find a smile beneath my hollow cheeks. It is like Elijah to bring me here.

I step inside. A cold gust of wind seems to push me further indoors, and the door shuts behind me. The room is small, the ceiling low, the popcorn-like walls covered with stocked shelves. Racks of canned beans and lamb and dried fruits. Long, colored bags of purple and green. Stretched black dresses that droop at the sleeves and gray T-shirts speckled with varying shades. I try to cry once more.

"*Bonjour.*" The corners of my mouth lift upwards at the stranger behind the counter. He sits with a book in his hands, his eyes dashing across words, clouded by concentration. He lifts his head, his eyebrows sliding up his skin at the sight of me. "*Est-ce que vous donnez encore des provisions?*"

"Of course, my dear." His French is broken. He stands, the stool he sits upon falling back behind him. My smile grows.

He is a short man, his body built wide. Over his stalky arms, he wears a long sweater resting midway down his fingertips. The glowing of his teeth is contagious. I haven't seen anything like it in ages. It is as if he has stared at the sun and seen the light rather than the darkness stuck behind it.

"What do you need?" My eyes jump between the shelves, meeting his bright face in between gazes.

"Whatever you can give to me." His grin grows. I didn't know it could grow any more than it already has. Soon, he is shuffling around the room, removing a green bag from the wall and beginning to stuff food inside. He makes his way to the far left wall, stopping in front of a rack of clothing.

"What size do you wear, dear?"

I tell him. He nods, beginning to shuffle through the stacks of cloth, stopping upon an item.

"How's a dress for you, dear?" My eyebrows lift at his remark.

"A dress?"

"It's the best for this type of heat."

I slowly begin to nod. "Yes . . . yes, that sounds good." I pause. "Thank you." He removes a black garment from the shelf, placing it into my open palms. I unravel it from its creases. The material is a lightweight silk that sits still inside my fingers. It is tight fitting along the arms, wrapping down to the hands, and beginning to trace the bottom of the first finger. The linen stretches up to the top of the neck, wrapping around it and then falling down to the ankle, where it splits into two. A shorter layer wraps beneath the longer one, resting just above the knee and hanging loosely. The whole dress seems to be one piece of black fabric wrapped around in different directions and sewn together at precise angles.

"It's . . . beautiful." I manage to mumble. The man is back at one of the shelves, ravenging through a basket.

"*Et pour ta visage belle.*" He approaches me again, handing me a piece of cloth. I stare at it for a moment, soon realizing its purpose. It's designed to rest upon the nose, falling down to the neck and wrap behind the ears. A face covering to protect from heat damage.

"*Merci, Monsieur.*" My eyes meet his peaceful gaze.

He leads me to a changing room where I try to pluck off the old garments that seem to have become sewn into my skin. To replace them with something new. If it wasn't for the way the world has become, it would almost feel poetic.

"It fits well, yes?" he asks me once I exit the room. I look down at the way the soft material wraps gently across my skin. Again, I wish to cry, but I can only shake.

"Yes," I say. My lip quivers. My eyes fall to the floor. "I wish I had money to pay you."

The man shakes his head. "If I wanted payment, I would have told you in the beginning, dear." My phone buzzes a moment later.

➤ From "Unknown," 9:45

"Time to get going. I need you in the next town by sundown."

"You should get going, then," the man says as I slip my phone into the pocket of my dress. I find his eyes, hoping for a moment to memorize the peace punctured so gently upon them.

"Thank you again, sir." I watch him for one more moment. Wish to thank him eagerly for all he has given me, but I can only seem to smile. Then, I turn towards the door.

"It's a pleasure," he says. The door closes.

Then I am back out into the blazing heat. The sun presses down upon my virgin garments. The man is right. They provide more protection than what I had once known. I take the cloth in my hands, pulling it across my face, taking in the sweet fragrance of lavender and honey. Already, it seems the heat has loosened its hold.

So I press on through the desert. My boots hold my feet from faltering, the ravenous sand rolling off of my garments. The lands are still around me. Silent, aside from the sound of the rumbling wind. I remain with my thoughts. Stuck in their endless cycle of hope and condemnation. Their perception of me—of my actions—changes from moment to moment. Spinning in circles between worth and worthlessness. Deserving and undeserving.

Elijah's hope seems to be the only thing that keeps me moving.

I sleep under the stars. Sleep under the glow of the moon, reflecting through my humbled eyes. My weary eyes and scorched cheeks. I sleep on top of a brick building on the outskirts of a nearly vacant town. Sleep atop years of history, pressing into my silk-lined spine. My body aching, mind racing.

I try to ignore the images as I fall into sleep. The flashing figures.

Tsunamis.

A woman colliding with concrete.

My gun in my hand.

My father, close to death.

His blood upon my palm.

I try to find Elijah's face in the storm.

[43]

Weakness

Too many days go by for me to count. Too many hours of walking. Passing through terrain stretching on for miles. Burning beneath this heat, forever embedding itself into the very soul I carry on feeble limbs. My two worlds of hope and realism merge together into one, and I can't tell if they've made an accord or have agreed to disagree.

All I know is I'm exhausted. Completely and utterly burnt out. I feel as though I am bending into the earth, as though my boots have become one with the ground beneath me. For the first time, it's not a lack of hope that keeps me from moving on. I've forced myself to rely on Elijah's. But instead, it's a lack of strength.

Suddenly, I am wishing I had strength, that thing that had been so present in me for so many years. In my practice of ballet where strength and delicacy would intertwine. But now, I am only delicate. And therefore, I am weak. Breakable.

There is a city Elijah brings me to in the middle of the Neo-Italian Empire. The streets are littered with the broken. Litter is everywhere. Ash climbs into pieces of garbage and lays upon the clothing of occasional figures in passing. The land is flooded with wealth and riches, with worth lost to this ruined world, for even shrines cannot live forever. In the center of the decayed driveways and crystalized cathedrals, a train station stands stagnant. Yet, I watch as movement blossoms from its base.

The trains are moving.

The trains are moving.

I rush inside. The air that meets me smells of molded leather and molasses. Steel arches stretch all around me, reaching towards the domed roof, rising like a rolling tide until I can see the sun and black hole through the ceiling.

I rush to an information desk. A woman stands on the other side, a dark crater covering the optimism in her gaze. She turns to me when I speak.

"*Bonjour, Madame. J'ai une question pour vous.*" The woman stares at me. Blinks.

Sighs. "*J'écoute.*"

"Do you have any trains going south? Or east?"

She raises an eyebrow. "You mean southeast?" I hold a breath in my throat. My body shakes. I pick at the skin around my fingernails. Swallow.

"Yes, that one."

She nods. "I can check." I watch her gaze shuffle through a file on her computer screen, her weary eyes scanning the words.

"There's one going to Kayseri." She finally says.

"Is that southeast?"

The woman glares. "That is what you asked for, is it not?" I try to glare back. It comes as a pout. My mind tries to find the words to throw back at her, but it falls short.

She looks back down at the computer screen. "It leaves in four days." I stare a moment longer. Her words find their way into my mind and spin for a long time. Spin until they plant themselves upon my tongue and burst out of my mouth.

"*Four days?* That's . . ." I'm staring at a wall now. All I can feel is my heart pounding against my ears, and I wait for them to erupt. They never do.

"Many of the rails have been severely damaged. And there's a limited number of trains and those to oversee their travels." I'm watching people bustle by. Moving in mobs through the booming station, the most alive I have seen a place in ages.

I shake my head. "Can't they just be programmed to their destinations? That's what was always done in the past."

"Who's going to program them?" My gaze is delivered back towards the woman. My lips are pulled into a straight line across my face, and I wonder for a moment if I can feel wetness forming in my eyes, but it never actually comes.

Four days.

I don't know how much time I have.

"There are really no other trains?"

"Not until next week. And you'd be heading northeast, if you know what that means." I'm shaking my head so hard it seems to make my skull cave in upon my brain. The woman is staring at her computer screen again. "The one to Kayseri leaves from Gate 42 at 7:15 on the 12th. You're welcome to stay at the station to wait. I know there aren't many places available anymore." I'm forcing a fictitious smile. Trying to find the ever-failing strength in my bones to bear more of the coursing heat. To forget about the trains and carry on walking.

Trying to convince myself that I'll survive if I do.

"*Eh bien, merci pour votre aide.*" She says nothing back. I expect at least a nod. Perhaps even a "*de rien*" if she's feeling generous. But instead she turns away, ignoring my gaze still strained towards her hollow figure.

It seems as though I'm seeing again what the black hole's darkness has done to humanity. How, when it is stared at for too long, it becomes manifest in the eyes of mankind.

I find a bench away from where she can see me. The metal beneath is tarnished and something sticky is plastered on my dress. I call Elijah.

"It's a four-day wait," I say. My bones are collapsing and mending themselves into the metal of the bench below. The very muscles inside of me fight a civil war.

Soon Elijah speaks. His tone is the most uneasy I've heard it before, and yet, it is still kilometers away from being unstable. "*Four days?*"

"Yes." A pause.

"*That's . . . that's a while.*" My eyes shudder. My gaze climbs up the walls of the encampment around me and soon I feel like an animal trapped inside this station. Forgetting for a moment that it is protection from that which lies outside.

"I can't walk any longer, Elijah. I'm too weak. I wouldn't be able to make it."

"*I know.*"

I suddenly think of the woman I killed. I think of how weak her body had become—how mine is shifting to become just like hers. I wonder if Elijah would be here on the phone with me if he knew. It is then that I decide he shall never find out.

The doors around me open and close, and gushes of air graze the burnt grass across my arms. It seems to grow warmer the longer it lingers.

"Will I run out of time if I wait? Will it be too late?" There's a long pause. Elijah's voice feels absent for far too long. Perhaps he's researching it for me. Maybe he's deciding whether or not it's worth it to lie.

But then he says a single word. "*No.*"

Then, I am left staring at the floor. Staring at my black boots that have become one with the concrete. Staring at the weary frowns across their laces.

"Okay . . ." I am able to spit off my tongue. "I'm . . . I'm going to wait then."

"*Good. That is wise.*"

[44]

People Watching

I search for sleep beneath this steel sky. Its absence comes to me as a taunt.

And so I people-watch as days pass. I watch as expressions vary and fear ferments into flames, burning the eyes of man. I watch green gazes turn gray and brown burn black. I watch steps stagger but never slow, and heads hung low as though not a single other soul matters. For they have all become selfish and I am just like the rest of them.

I wonder where everyone is going. If everyone is running as I am. If we all fear our dreams will never come to be. If that fatal hopefulness in our very human nature keeps us running until our bodies fail to give us strength. If we all fear that a day of weakness will come, but we won't accept it even when it arrives.

But perhaps there are those that aren't running at all. Rather, seeing the world before there is no longer a world left to be seen. And yet, I cannot help but wonder if our instinct for survival can truly allow us to accept death. Not completely.

I reside at Gate 42. The air smells of melted candle wax and rust, and I sit on the boiling concrete floor. It somehow manages to be more comfortable than the dented metal bench beside me. It is day three. I can feel my life slipping through my fingertips like running water that I pretend is ice. But even if it was, the sun would melt it anyway. I feel sick. My head is foggy and always aching, and the side of my stomach feels as though a rock is resting inside. I am dehydrated and underfed even though I have water and food. I am simply negligent.

And I wish I could leave. But my hands shake, and my knees are weak, and I can't seem to stand without stumbling back towards the concrete.

I am weak.

And I am so lonely. I often wonder if anyone can even see me. If Elijah is merely a psychotic hallucination. I think every day of my room back home. Of Darbii coming over after school, of us sitting on my bed and discussing things so simple that I cannot even remember now. I think of my ballet shoes being tossed beside my bed. Of lighting a candle to dispose of the stench. I think of endless writing, of endless music, of endless dreaming of what would be in years to come. But now I can hardly think of tomorrow.

I wonder if I will ever be able to sleep in peace again. For when my eyes shut, I see the face of a dead woman. And when I look at her for too long, I fear Elijah finding out. Finding out that I am a murderer.

"A Cordellian and an Italian." I hear a voice at the 23rd hour of the day. In the moments succeeding the hopeful threats of sleep. There's a man and a woman standing halfway across the platform beside a cement staircase. The woman's low tone catches my attention before it can fall. Her glass-like eyes stare at a transparent screen in her hands.

I find the man beside her. He is bundled up in a black down jacket, his gaze on a wall, his arms tied together as a bow across his chest. A puzzle is placed into position in his mind and he looks over at the woman.

"I'm sorry, did you say an Italian too?"

She glances up at him. Nods. "Male, age 18—"

"Since when are we after an Italian?" She looks back down. Points at her screen.

"It's on the list."

The man throws his hands out to the side of him. "I signed up for one Cordellian. One. This is more than what I'm willing to offer."

A Cordellian.

Me. They're looking for me.

"They don't care." The woman says. The man's head shakes ever so slightly, and I search for a glimmer of guilt in her gaze. They. It's the most I've ever known about who hunts me.

"Damn it . . ." The man trails off.

Or perhaps these hunters have nothing to do with my own. Maybe I am not the Cordellian they are after. But I remember the border, and I remember Sitka's secrets, and I realize in that moment the obscurity of a Cordellian away from home.

I force myself to stand.

My back aches as though my spine has been sanded down. I slip my arm inside the loop of my bag. Then I am turning from them towards the bathroom. Running with impaired speed. I can only hope that they think nothing of it.

Then I'm in the last stall, and my head is spinning so ineradicably, and I cannot help but think about anything but that one word.

Hunters.

I cannot seem to understand why humanity chooses to prey on one another when the sun is already the apex predator. When they have nothing left to gain from one another.

But perhaps their eagerness towards my death is their own type of kryptonite to death's certainty. Perhaps they have something promised to them.

➤ To "Unknown," 15:13

"Elijah, who are these people? Why do they want me dead?"

I watch my fingers vibrate upon my screen.

I carry fear like a friend.

➤ From "Unknown," 15:14

"What makes you think that I know?"

➤ To "Unknown," 15:14

"You know about everything."

There's a moment of stillness before his reply. Then I am reading his words, wondering whether they are a blessing or a curse.

➤ From "Unknown," 15:15

"They work for a name that I cannot put into text. They follow you because they fear me."

[45]

Another Type Of Gun

The train comes the next day. I hear it roaring down a dark alley before it meets my concrete chamber. I am eagerly aboard in an instant, heading southeast and finding peace in the silence of the seats around me.

The passing of time becomes something I can no longer understand once I board a second train to the Mediterranean. Elijah leaves me with a single message when I arrive, standing on the creaking wood of a boating dock where ruined ships sit with those still in use.

> From "Unknown," 9:45

"Find a ferry to Lebanon. Give them all the information they ask for, nothing more, nothing less."

Nothing more, nothing less.

The phrase sticks to me like glue.

The port stretches down the coast as far as I can make out through the thickness of the smoke wrapped in the reflection of the red sun. I have grown so undoubtedly used to the stuffy feeling of my nose, the pounding headache never ceasing. It all almost becomes a comfort with the consistency it brings.

There is a long dock across the way from me. It leads out to large ships rising and falling in the shifting tides. I wonder how the sea isn't more jagged with the pulling of the black hole above. Its stillness is eerie.

A solar-powered sign sits at the front of the dock, the name of a location resting upon it in a language I cannot read. I approach the sign. The words sting like blisters across my eyes, and in my dreariness, I seem to believe that the longer I stare, the clearer they will become. But they never do.

A presence appears behind me. It's lingering is followed by a man's voice, the sound of silk sheets against the wind. I turn towards him. He holds the height of a skyscraper, his skin like tan bark, his black hair creating a ridge along the top of his forehead. A slight smile spreads across his wide stretched cheeks, and I begin to speak.

"*Pá yådii siyeh?*" I watch his smile falter ever so slightly, but enough for me to notice. And in a moment between longing and fear, I recognize the un-settled look that clouds his marshy eyes. Because it was Cordellian in which I had spoken.

"*Qu'est que ça veut dire?*" I repeat again. I hope for amnesia to cloud his mind, for the language of my plagued race to remain a mystery to him. He slowly reaches into his pocket, retrieving a translator device for himself and handing the other to me. I place it in my ear.

"Repeat that again, ma'am."

I swallow harshly. "What does this sign say?"

"Italy," He hesitates for a moment. "Where are you headed, ma'am?"

"To Lebanon." Nothing more, nothing less.

"Hm. What for?"

A moment of hesitancy. "I was on holiday, and I'm returning home."

"Where is home?"

"Israel."

He looks skeptical. "You're Israeli?"

"Yes, sir." There is a pause as he stares at me, inspecting my features. "By nationality alone. I'm Moroccan ethically." I say it quickly. Before I have time to fear that it is too much.

He slowly nods, his gaze shifting to the docks behind me. "The ferry to Lebanon is three ports down," he begins. "I will, however, have to see some identification to get you aboard." My heart seems to scatter into bits.

"Identification?"

"Is that a problem?" He looks genuinely concerned. My mind finds its way to the chip Herr Krüger had placed in my arm all those days ago. To the uncertainty in what really lies there. I think about the hunters—about their association with him. Then, I think of Elijah—how these hunters fear him.

He wouldn't have led me here if I couldn't make it through.

"No, not at all," I force myself to say. My voice cracks. "Just . . . what for?"

"Have you not heard about the travel bans to Lebanon and Israel?"

I shake my head. "I've been a bit out of the loop, if I'm being honest. It's hard to know what's going on with—"

"The lack of communication and transmissions. I understand." He nods soothingly. And soon, he is starting forward towards the other docks, motioning for me to follow.

"Well, for a recap," he begins, a half-hearted grin plastered across his cheeks. "Only citizens of the country are being allowed in. Unfortunately, there are . . . consequences . . . if others are let in."

"Consequences for who?" He stops at a dock, turning towards me. His eyebrows lift ever so slightly, and yet they tell me everything I need to know.

"For those who sent them." A pause. He reaches behind himself, retrieving a large metal object, obtaining the same configuration as a gun.

I look at it. Process it. My heart seems to stop in my chest.

I see the woman fall again.

I see the blood on the blacktop.

I hear the voices of condemnation in my head.

What am I doing here?

He shouldn't be helping me.

I am guilty.

"Hence why we need to use this." He moves closer to me, and I flinch. The cool metal resets against my left arm where the identification chip had been placed. He presses a few numbers across the keypad, a beeping sound emerging.

And in a moment, I am shaking, longing for home. Longing to be out of this mess for good, fearing that my doom has finally arrived. That this gun will sentence me to death by the hands of humanity rather than the sun.

But Elijah wouldn't let that happen to me.

"Well, it looks like you were telling the truth." My eyes jump up towards the man. He is grinning so genuinely and I am wondering if he can see the surprise plastered in my eyes. "Welcome aboard, Miss Elkolai."

He leads me onto the ship. The deck is filled with a slim sleet of water below my boots, and I wonder if there is a hole somewhere aboard. If I will face death once more in the face of drowning and this third time will be a charm.

"There are sleeping quarters below if you're interested. No guaranteeing we'll remember to wake you though." He stops at the front of the ship, looking out across the waves that rock slowly back and forth. "And . . . we know it's hot here but, uh . . . no jumping in." I don't know what he means by that. Maybe he sees the misery on my face. Maybe the mask I wear is more see-through than I realize.

"Thank you for all your help."

The man shrugs. "Just doing my job, Miss Elkolai."

"And what was your name?"

"Roberto Parosso." He smiles. I wish I could still find comfort in a stranger's smile. But too many of them have turned out deceitful.

[46]

Man Made

I sit on a burning steel bench overlooking the sea. My eyes fight to sink into sleep, hypnotized by the rolling waves, by an endless vastness, stranding me so strangely in disorientation. Terrorizing me with a taunting vertigo. Stuck inside the understanding of how incredibly alone I am on this foreign vessel. Aware of the possibilities of what could happen upon such a ship, about how no one would know.

Yet, knowing so soundly that Elijah would not allow such things to happen.

Forms of water had once been my escape. Spending weekends in Nice throughout my childhood, playing in the salty waves. Showering to escape my brothers, to escape my mother when she insisted on game night. But perhaps now I have escaped too far. I have seen the arrogant agony its wet hand can create, and I dread it with all the life left in my bones. I have let it steal my contentment, eradicate my peace and now, it has become a prison. A beautiful, deceptive prison.

Much time passes before I am able to recognize that it is not merely the memories of such waters that so greatly trouble me. That these very waters in themselves upon which I travel are frightening. Unnerving and perhaps to the point of disingenuine. For I soon find myself thinking of the black hole, that thing I try so desperately to ignore. I find myself remembering Sitka first talking about it all when it first began. How the waters of the sea would never again be still, for the new gravitational pull would not allow for such a thing.

Yet, I stare upon still waters. For a long time, I wonder how such a thing could be.

I don't see Robertoo for the rest of the ride. I wonder if he is on board. I ask myself why I care, but perhaps it's simply the thought of having one aware of my existence that comes as a comfort.

Though I know I already do.

"I'm literally in the middle of the ocean, Elijah. How are you calling me right now?" I hear him laugh on the other end of the phone. The vibrations of his voice are the only thing capable of my honest comfort.

"*So I'm guessing you made it.*"

"Yes I did."

"*How are you doing?*" There's something about the way he asks the question. Something that almost says to me that I should be alright, though I feel every organ in my body continuing to fail. My voice shakes at my reply.

"I'm . . . I'm fine . . . thank you."

"*Are you sure?*" I want to tell him about it all. About the chaos boiling and brewing into something so all consuming. I long to tell him about the woman, about what my hands have done to her. I fear if I speak of it, I will no longer be able to push through its pain. Even more so, I fear then, he will realize I am not truly worth whatever he thinks I am worth.

So I keep my mouth shut. I keep the chaos cooped up in my mind, locked inside a chest, sealed shut with a lock in the shape of a raging fire burning my insides alive.

"Yes I'm . . . I'm alright." There is silence on the other end. I stare out across the waves. They rock and spin so softly, and for a moment, I wish I could throw myself in and lose sight of the ship slinking on forward. But that moment passes. And then, I hear his voice in my ear once more.

"*I hope you are being honest. Because there is information that I would like to give you.*" My head shoots away from the waves. A coursing pain pounds against my face. I recall the fear I once so fervently had of what he knows. Of what priceless things he has kept hidden from me.

"Information? Is-is it bad?"

He hesitates. "*It's the truth.*" I look down at my feet. Stare at the water surrounding my toes. Feel my heart beating so boldly in my chest, and wonder if I will even be able to hear his words through the sound. I release a staggered breath of air.

"Yes, please, I would like to know."

There is silence on the other end for what seems like a millennia. The tossing of the waves and the pounding of my heart catch a common rhythm. Then, his voice breaks it.

"*There is no easy way to tell you this.*" He pauses, and I want to say something, but I don't. "*I had suspicions, but I just learned for sure, given why I have waited to tell you. What happened in Varna . . . it was man-made.*"

My eyes remain on my feet. On the water. I see it rise to my legs and to my chest, and I am being swallowed by a wave. My eyes lose their sight, and my lungs have lost their breath, and all of my sanity is being stolen from me. Stolen by the severity of his speech.

"Man . . . man-made?" I repeat back to him.

"Yes."

"You're telling me that the tsunami was *man-made*?" I take a breath. My lips are slightly parted, and my eyebrows are tilted inward, and I'm looking around as though someone nearby would understand the perplexity behind my stare, but no one is near enough to notice. "By . . . by who?"

I wait for him to answer. He doesn't. Then I answer myself. "By the people that are after me? Is that who?"

"*It seems so, yes.*" I'm shaking my head so quickly that I believe for a moment that every thought will fly out and I will be left as just skin and bones and worth not even my mind, for it has become empty.

"Why? Who are they?" I pause. "And *how*?"

"*Implanted uranium into the sea floor, utilizing the effects of nuclear energy.*" I stare back out at the sea. Try to find what questions to ask and wonder if I even really want to know the answers. "*I apologize. I know this is a lot to take in, but I felt it to be wrong not to tell you."*

My eyes move quickly across the area around me. "I don't . . . I . . ." I swallow. Center my thoughts. Then, I speak. "Why?" I can't seem to breathe. "Why would people do such a thing? To harm one another? When we're all going to die anyway? What is the purpose?"

There is a long pause before Elijah speaks. *"There is more I could tell you, but I cannot do that right now."*

"Why not?"

"Because." I can hear him take a deep breath. *"Because one of these days, I will show it to you instead."*

I cannot seem to understand what he means, and so I don't try to.

"How do you know about all of this, Elijah?"

"I will show you that as well." I want to say something more. To argue with him. But he speaks again before I can. *"These are not things that I can just simply tell you."*

So, instead, I think of everyone. My parents, my brothers. I think of my father, of his blood-stained upon my hands. I think of us all locked up inside a hotel room, trying to make do with our silence. They all should know. They need to know.

Somehow, words roll off my tongue. "Elijah . . ."

"Yes?" I struggle to forge sentences. To unravel this thread tied into a knot inside my mind.

"Will . . ." I release a short breath. "Will I ever see my family again?" I can almost see him on the other end, his eyes jumping around, his lips pulled in tight. And then . . .

a slow nod.

"I believe you will."

"But you're not sure." A pause. He releases a breath.

"If it all goes how it's supposed to, and so far it has, I am very confident that you will."

"Will I ever meet you?" He releases a short breath that nearly sounds like a laugh.

"*We'll see.*"

"Is there a chance?"

"*Yes, there is.*" I am startled by his lack of hesitancy. I swallow. Then I force the question off of my lips that I truly care to know.

"Will you tell me the rest of everything if that time comes?"

"*I promise.*" It wasn't even a promise that I had asked for. But somehow, he had given me more than I desired. "*Let me know if anything happens, alright?*"

"Thank you, Elijah." I can see him smiling, releasing the phone from his ear, and selecting the end call button. Silence surrounds me again. I have never liked the silence.

The Lebanese port is run down, the dock creaking when I step across it. The wooden beams look burnt, charred around the edges, and I half expect them to break under the weight of my steps.

I approach a man at the end of the dock, tall and muscular, his black hair flopped over his forehead. Roberto slips a translator in his ear as I arrive, handing the other half to me.

"I didn't know you were aboard," I say. He shrugs, slipping his hands into the pockets of his trousers.

"I was manning the engine, making sure nothing malfunctioned." His smile softens. "Take care of yourself, Miss Elkolai. Don't want you getting hurt on your way back home." I feel a sudden softness to the reception of his kindness.

"Thank you, sir." It is strange to me, seeing one remain so optimistic in the face of death. I have seen a few acts in parallel in the past. The woman in Hungary, the man at the supply stand in the Neo-Italian Empire. Every time, their eyes remain as a precious photograph in my mind. And then I try to erase the thought that has evolved. To forget that Roberto will be left here to die while I am on a ship off the planet. Though his kindness deserves saving more than my bloodied hands.

I hear a chant echoing from the street ahead. Shouts in tones that nearly harmonize but instead fall flat. I turn my head towards the shrieks, my eyes settling upon a large cluster of people a couple hundred feet ahead, signs swaying in the air in a language I cannot understand.

"Ah. It looks like you came just in time for the anti-fire rally," I raise my eyebrows at Robert. "You know, 'put out the fires! Before it's too late'" He says that last part mockingly.

I try to nod. "Yes, well, I suppose we all need something to put our hope in."

He smiles. "You're a wise one, Sarai. I wish you the best on your travels back home and . . . into the stars, perhaps?" His words take a moment to process in my mind.

The Qadim. That thing I have been chasing after for so long. For some reason, I wonder how he is so clearly aware of my destination. But then I recall the part I'm playing. How right now, I am Israeli. How this is all just a show. I fear that in it, I will lose my true identity.

I hand the translator piece back to him, waving goodbye and turning to approach the crowd. To journey on into an unpromised peace upon painted skies.

That's the thing about peace these days; even when it's there, it isn't ever truly real. It seems real for a ceasing moment, only for more conflict to arise, more chaos to conspire against mankind. And then the reality of death becomes real once more.

But peace is manmade, as all evil things seem to be. And though the sky is dark, it is the darkness in man's eye that truly kills. It seems we are our real enemies.

[47]

A Few Things About Anger

There had been a day many years ago when Viridian and I were returning home from school. We saw two women standing quietly on a street corner with signs in their hands. Their faces were crumpled and unraveled again, their clothing wrinkled and eyes sagging. I was sure I had seen them before, working at a supply stand. But back then, they smiled, and when we had seen them then, they appeared practically in pain.

I was too young to read their signs. I insisted my brother read them to me. The first said, "Don't believe all that they tell you." The second read, "Trust your gut feeling before they take that from you too." I asked my brother what they meant. He didn't have an answer. I never saw those women again.

I don't understand these signs either. The Arabic language is wrapped across cardboard like ribbons on a gift I can never open. A taunt.

I understand the shouts more than the lettering. I understand the people's anger; I feel it running along the rims of my veins.

There are a few things I know for sure. First, that anger is an unavoidable characteristic of humanity, as much as fires are inevitable in the summertime. Second, to avoid it is to enact a greater sense of said anger. Third, that the only way to eradicate it is to express it as earnestly as required for extinction. And finally, when fueled by peers, the embers of anger erupt into a fire.

And I see fire before me. I see walls burning inside of a castle, and I see myself running to a balcony. I see my hands, desperate to climb.

280

And then I see the only thing capable of extinguishing flames. Water.

I am being dragged into a river. The particles of water take the form of bodies, wrapping around me, and in an instant, breath becomes my enemy. The warmth from these bodies, the undeniable heat created through their push, practically presses me into the pavement.

I think I see our car at the bottom of the river. Its blue paint job being ripped to shreds, its wheels trying to turn backward against the current. And me, psychotically breaking open the window. I feel my arms burning as hands shove them on all sides.

I look away from the river. I look up to the sky. There, I see the wall of water above me crashing down on me.

Burning.

Salty.

My eyes: stinging.

My breath: ceasing.

Death inching its way closer to me.

Pain. And terror.

And suddenly I am reliving it all again as I am pushed deeper into the crowd, swallowed whole, stolen as one of their own. I am suffocated again as I had been all those days ago. My ears are muffled at the sounds of their shouts, like the roaring of the weight of a thousand waves. My side aches against the slashing of a hand. Someone is pushing into me where my cut is struggling to heal.

Then I see it all. All that Elijah had spoken to me on that ferry, now alive before me. I see the tsunami, and yet I still see the bodies. Because the tsunami is man-made. Because we hurt each other more than nature can, before nature can.

Every single sense in my body is elevated. Every single fear I've developed is revisited. Every memory I've become accustomed to knowing is meeting me again, but this time, they are tainted darker into something so dreadful that I didn't know they were capable of becoming.

Because these are not just people. They are a tsunami, and I am caught in the middle of them.

I feel for my phone in my back pocket, my hand sliding past where my gun once sat.

I hear the crack again.

I see the woman fall. *Stop it,*

stop it.

Hatred spreads through my bones for no one other than myself.

I pull up the text thread with Elijah, quickly typing and retyping a message through my blurred lens. My fingers shake. My eyes fight to find tears. It isn't a surprise when nothing comes.

> ➤ To "Unknown," 15:30
>
> "Elijah, I don't know what is happening to me."

> ➤ To "Unknown," 15:30
>
> "What do I do?"

> ➤ From "Unknown," 15:30
>
> "Stay with the crowd, slowly make your way to the right. When you see a market, go to it. Breathe."

Breathe.

I search for any shape of silence inside of me. I look away from the chaos, from the panic, from my memory. I fight to ignore the pounding of my chest. The shaking of my legs. The faint whisper of tears wishing to come, but fearing their appearance upon my broken face. I try to find his face, the face I had seen in the tsunami once the darkness had taken me. I search for his smile. It's right . . .

there.

Elijah.

My eyes skip to the market on my right. It arrives rapidly as we march. I match the steps beside me. Match them until it grows close. Closer. Too close.

I shuffle through the crowd. Elbows slam into me, shove me, my side aches. A woman next to me stares. She shouts something at me that I can't understand. Then she stares. Raises an eyebrow.

"I'm sorry, I don't speak Arabic." I can't tell what language it is in which I say it. I pull away from her, staring at the market just across the road. Just out of reach.

Until.

I pull my body out of the crowd. I stumble so stupidly over my own feet, colliding with the cobblestone sidewalk below. My head spins, my breaths stagger, but never still. People step all around me as though I am invisible. Maybe I am invisible.

But then a man approaches me. A look of worry is plastered plainly across his cheeks and he extends his arm out to me. He says something and pulls me to my feet.

"*Je-je ne parle p-pas arabe. Je s-suis désolé,*" I am able to spit out. He holds my forearms so softly, his delicate gaze resting upon my watered eyes.

"Oh dear," He begins, a soft smile spreading across his cheeks. "Is there something I can help you with? Do you need medical care?"

I shake my head. "No I'm . . . I'm alright."

"You look famished. I have food at my stand."

"Thank you but-but I . . . don't have money." He chuckles softly.

"I'm not going to make you pay, dear. You've had a rough day." I am still searching for breath when he releases my arms, showing me over to his stand across the way. "Besides, money isn't getting anyone anywhere anymore. Not under these conditions. The ones who still seek it out are the ignorant and the greedy." He motions for me to sit on the wooden seat beside him, handing me a bottle of brandy and two pieces of naan bread.

"You let me know if you need anything else, alright?" he says. It is then that I finally take a good look up at him. I am startled by the familiarity of his appearance. For he looks so much like my father, the softness of his eyes, the way his cheeks round right at the bone. His unprecedented kindness towards a stranger.

"Thank you," I finally manage to say through the cracking of my voice and the cracking of my lips that try to spread to a smile. He pats me on the shoulder, standing and turning to approach the front of his stand.

Maybe humanity isn't wholly evil. Only me.

White Mulberry

I think of my father for a while after that. I think of his smile, of his soft yet firm hands. I do all I can not to think of what he must now think of me. Of how I will never know if my suspicions are correct.

"*Are you safe?*" Elijah calls a few moments later. I can't remember another time when he had been the first to speak. It has always been me to start the conversation, trusting he would reply. He always did.

"Yes," I mumble. I look up at the man behind the stand, explaining something with his hands to the customers before him. "There's a man here who took care of me . . . and . . ." I don't have anything else to say. He must figure so.

"*Good,*" he says. I sit with him on the other line for a long moment. Peace stretches into a colorful array across the burning membrane of my mind. Bright red dims to violet. Orange lightens to yellow, and for a moment, I am staring at a portrait of a creation harboring vast capabilities. For a moment, I believe this faint whistle of peace to be genuine. But the moment passes quickly.

Then I speak. I don't quite know why.

"Can I ask you something, Elijah?"

He hesitates, and yet his reply is less than agitated. "*I suppose so.*"

"Why do you care so much about . . . about whether or not I'm alright?" Silence remains on the other end. I revisit the sound of my words in my mind. They are weak and foolish, and yet I am bound so closely to them.

"*Why wouldn't I?*"

"I don't know, I just . . . I don't know." Then, the real question arrives before me. It approaches Elijah before I have the chance to greet it. "What am I worth to you?"

A long, long pause.

"*What are you worth to anyone?*" Nothing, is what I want to say, but I don't. Instead, I stare at my feet until I fear that I will see water rising upon them. Until I recall my desperation.

"So what now?"

"*Wander the market, grab some food.*"

". . . And then?"

". . . *And then it will become obvious.*"

I stare out across the market. Stare at faces covered in darkness. "What will?"

I hear him laugh on the other end. "*Okay, your question time is up for the day.*"

I hesitate. "My . . . question time . . . is up?"

"*Yes.*"

"Do I have a daily question limit?"

"*It's five, and I'm being generous because now you're at six.*"

I giggle. "Elijah."

"*No, I just have some things I must attend to. Let me know if you need anything.*"

So I wander the market alone. The smells of spices and forgotten fragrances insert themselves into my presence, and I am wondering how such things still exist. It is a place Viridian would have loved. A place unlike anything we have ever known, something new. When life had been normal, he was always seeking out the new.

I approach a stand covered in vibrant fruits. They stare back upon me with eyes of stardust, and I cannot seem to comprehend their reality, for canned and dried instead have become habitual. Even that has become rare.

My fingers slide across the rows of color, my eyes widening in awestruck wonder. They are the very definition of beauty, laid out precisely in silver storage bins. They stack upon each other like bricks under a building as a foundation for a way of living. A way in which I have forgotten.

"*Monsieur*?" A man stands beside me. He speaks in a language I can comprehend, his tongue like honey with turmeric to add edge. There is a subtle hint of something familiar about his voice that I cannot seem to discover in the midst of my disorientation. My gaze stays stuck upon my hands. They shift the slightest bit to the deepest shade of red. "What's this?"

"White mulberry." My eyes unwillingly fall to the man inside the booth. I watch as his gaze gradually grows harsh, his focus fixed firmly on the French-speaking man.

"Ah, white mulberry," The French man says. "Never heard of it." The merchant stares for a moment, perplexed.

"You're not from around here, are you?"

"Nah." My gaze falls to the brown and muscled hand of the man beside me, rolling the white fruit around in it as if hypnotized by its ambiguity. "I'll tell you a secret though, if you want." I watch his fingers fully wrap around the mulberry. He holds it tightly in his palm. My eyebrows narrow ever so slightly.

"Sure."

He whispers his next words. "I'm Cordellian." My gaze slingshots up towards him. My eyes pierce every aspect of his appearance. He is tall, thin, and muscular. His short, blond curls are familiar, forming a boxed shape around his browned face. His mouth stretches wide across his thin cheeks, his nose plump at the tip and green eyes like waxing moons.

Not a single thought comes to mind. Not a single concept that I can digest and spit out at him. Only his name; his name is what holds my tongue hostage.

"Viridian?" His eyes quickly leap down towards mine. Perplexity spreads across the horizon of his face. I watch a gear click into place in his mind.

Then, his jaw unravels like a ribbon from where it once sat. His eyes grow twice in size.

There is not a single thing subtle about his shock. "Holy *shit!*"

I stare at him. My lip shakes. My head rocks to and fro. "You're—oh my gosh—"

"How-how did you—"

"You're alive."

"*You're* alive."

There is a moment in most lives when a person recognizes just how much someone else means to them. When all of the comparison falls away. All of the disputes, the annoyances. Every single issue built up over a multitude of years is gone in a single instant, and you are simply seeing the other person for who they are. I think this is that moment for me.

Then he grabs me. He pulls me into his arms and holds onto me as though I will slip through his fingertips. I feel the mulberry pressed against my back, still wrapped up in his left hand. And I want so earnestly to cry into his heavy arms. I want to apologize for all that I've done to him. I want to release every single thing I have ever told myself over these weeks into the weight of his body. But I am paralyzed by his embrace. By the presentness of such a reality.

I can't even seem to wonder how he doesn't hate me.

Not when I am so joyously trapped in his arms.

Then I feel his body shaking, and for a moment, I believe he is crying. I believe to hear the echo of tears like oil pouring down his cheeks, sticking to his charred pores, shining in the light of the sun. Pouring like rain against my living room window at home when the two of us used to watch it for hours, hypnotized by its wonder. Hypnotized by the life it brought to the land, by how still the world would be when it was over.

But perhaps the stillness hadn't been found in the rain. Perhaps it was found in his presence.

"I thought I lost you," he chokes. I clench him a little tighter. Hold him for just a little longer. And soon, I find that I am smiling. Smiling in a way of such authenticity that has been lost for so long.

I can't remember the last time I have felt such simple joy.

"I am so sorry, V." He pulls away from me when I speak. Stares into my eyes and I back into his and notice the base of them coated in rain. "If I hurt you . . . by what happened, I . . . I am so sorry."

He watched me for a moment longer. Then, he shakes his head.

"I'm the one who *left* you," he mumbles. I see the words come as much as a surprise to him as they do to me. "Please believe me that I never wanted to. You're my little sister. I . . ."

"I'm sorry," I say again. I don't quite know why.

"I had faith in you. That you would find us. I . . ." He continues to ramble, I wonder if I see his own version of guilt laced inside the ponds of his eyes. "But I . . . I really do wish we wouldn't have left you. It was . . . it was stupid." For just a moment more, I am trying to comprehend the sentiment that is wrapped up so effortlessly in his green gaze. Trying to understand his hands' harsh grasp upon my biceps as though to make my existence real before him. To confirm to his imagination that I am not a ghost. That I acquire substance and thought.

I find a smug smile creeping up my cheek. "So you don't think I'm a complete idiot."

He grins. "Now, I didn't say that, did I," He laughs. Somehow, I find that I am laughing too. Laughing through such a burnt and broken reality and yet a somehow perfect moment. I can't understand how the two can possibly coincide.

It is then that the man behind the fruit stand clears his throat. Viridian looks to him and quickly back to me.

"We should get going." He turns before I have time to reply. His hand is placed on my back, moving me along with him.

"Where are the others?"

"Outside of town. They sent me to get food."

"Why you?" He shrugs. We walk a few feet away from the stand before

I speak again. "By the way, what are you thinking telling people that you're Cordellian?"

He grins. Shrugs once more. "Eh, just having some fun. He's not going to tell anyone."

"How do you know?"

A pause. "I . . . don't." Viridian's speed grows steadily. Soon, I am tripping over our steps, and then I am gazing up at him. His cheeks look just the slightest bit pale, his lips pulled just a bit too tight across his face. My eyes soon fall towards his left hand, slipping something ever so slowly into his jean pocket. My eyebrows lift.

"Did you put the berry back?" We turn a corner. He pulls in a breath and doesn't release it.

"Nope."

"Viridian—"

Shouts erupt behind us in a single moment. Viridian whistles a little tune.

"We need to go."

[49]

Settling In

I hear a crack echo through the air. I hear it the moment we begin to run.

It is then that I see the woman inside my mind. I see her hit the concrete again. I see an image of her blood running across the pavement and up my body, staining my hands red. I look down at them. Wonder for a moment if it's real.

"Hey!" Viridian is still holding my arm. "Dodging bullets! We haven't done this one yet!" I force my eyes to look up at him. I expect him to be grinning, but instead, his face is covered in the most plain expression of anger. As though this isn't his fault.

And yet, I try to laugh. "The funny part about that statement is that it's actually false!" I still stare at him. Watch the wheels turn in his brain. Watch them remember that night. That awful night. Then it all clicks into place.

He laughs. "Well, I guess we can mark it off the bucket list twice then!"

We are out of the market. I am thrown into the crowd of people still marching for a holy water to extinguish flames. Water that they will never find. Something on my side begins to ache. It is the moment before the shouts overtake me that I remember my wound.

The language around me presses a dent into my skull.

Then, I am being completely consumed again by the man-made tsunami. Signs fly above my head. The repetition of rhythmic words encircles me. My hand latches onto my side. My ears fight to block out the screaming around me with something else screaming in my mind. With some level of insanity

291

that has fought to consume me ever since I stole that woman's life. An insanity that is on the verge of taking me.

Until I look up at Viridian. He won't let me go. He holds onto this self-obsessed murderer that he can still somehow find care for. I hear him struggling to copy the shouts of the people around us. And suddenly I feel angry. Angry that he's put me here. But maybe it's only because it feels nice to be angry at someone other than myself for once.

"Viridian," I am soon able to spit out. His eyes shoot down towards me. Look me over.

"We're blending in."

"No," I feel my anger grow while my breathing recedes. "My . . . my side." He stares for a moment. His green eyes squint. Then, they shift to where my hand is pressed against my wound. Then, he realizes. I see it in the way his eyes lift so dramatically upon his face.

"I forgot about that." He looks out across the storm surrounding us. Then, back down upon me. "Do you need to get out of the crowd?" I nod. "Shit . . ."

He grabs me tighter. I didn't know such a thing was possible. Then he shuffles through the bodies, and they are pushing into me. The aching grows. I feel as though I shrink in stature, and I wonder if I am invisible.

For just a moment, every single fear I have ever had impedes upon me. I fear this pain is finally taking me. I fear that not a single human would know, that not one would care to know. I fear the gunshots behind us once more; I fear them stealing the life of my brother. I fear everything of the small bits and pieces of my life I still have left, gone.

The pain grows. My breathing ceases.

I see darkness for just a moment and wonder if Elijah's face will appear before me like it had in the tsunami.

Then, we are emerging from within the crowd the moment before I fall apart. Viridian's grip around my arm loosens as he pulls me down an alleyway and onto the next road over. Our steps slow. We stop next to a building, cracked along the edges, clear evidence of an earthquake.

"I think we lost them," he mumbles. My back is against a steel wall, and I am searching the red sky for air to fill my lungs. Viridian's gaze is on me. I can feel him inspecting my face, burning and disfigured by fears forever turning me to ash. He watches me for a long while as my anger towards him slowly seems to fizzle away.

After all of these days, there is one thing I still can't seem to understand: how I can possibly fall apart so quickly. And even more so, how it takes so long to put myself back together.

"Eve," my brother finally says. I look up from the concrete to him. Stare into his eyes that contain such concern. An emotion so complex that I've never seen so earnestly thrust upon him. He searches his knowledge for words that might help. "Just . . . breathe."

I nod.

"What happened to you while we were separated?" he asks. My eyes shift across the road. There is an elderly man walking down the sidewalk, his head arched forward at the neck, his eyes paralyzed in apathy. I wonder how such indifference had first appeared before him.

"Nothing," I finally say. My eyes shift back over to Viridian. He stares at me. His eyebrow lifts ever so slightly, and yet, not quite how it used to. "It's just everything that happened before. I guess it . . . it settled in."

Never in the past could I make Viridian understand me. Never would he even come close to trying to make something of my emotion hidden beneath poetic prose. Instead, he mocked what he couldn't understand. But there is something about this moment. Something that leads me to believe that maybe, just maybe, he is beginning to see something in my mind that just faintly resembles his own.

"I can't believe you're alive," he mumbles. I force my gaze to find him again. To find his eyes fallen towards the cobblestone on the ground. Then they lift towards me. "How did you get here anyway?"

I look away. Shrug. "I just kept on the path."

"What, like you memorized the map?"

"Something like that."

He shakes his head. "No seriously. How did you get here?" I'm looking at my hands now. At the skin peeling around my fingernails. I stare at the effects of the scorching sun upon me, and I wonder why I am still alive to see it.

And for some reason, this moment feels significant. It is as though if I don't tell him about Elijah now, that I never will.

My choice is made quickly.

"I don't . . . really know." It's true. I don't know how Elijah got me here. I don't know how I was able to obey him so effortlessly.

I don't know how or why I am still alive.

"I um . . ." I look back across the street where the old man had walked. He is gone now. "I followed the street signs. Looked at maps in train stations."

"How the hell did you keep yourself alive?"

I smile a bit. "There are a lot more generous people in this world than you would imagine."

That, too, is true.

We begin to move forward again, turning a corner and starting up a steep side street. My eyes are fixed on my feet as though they will cause me to tumble into the cracks of the earth.

"We tried to find you," Viridian begins. "Searched for almost a whole week. We knew you had told us back in Varna to keep moving if something like this happened, but of course no one wanted to. It was Sitka who was insistent we keep going, believe it or not. He said you'd find your way to us." He shakes his head. "I don't know how in the hell that kid does it, but he's always right."

He's quiet for a moment. Somehow, I am smiling. Smiling, because the only thing I can think of is Sitka's shared confidence in Elijah.

"Merû was the most hesitant to leave you." My gaze finds my brother's face.

"Merû?"

He smiles uncomfortably. "You seem surprised."

"No I just . . . I thought she . . ." He raises an eyebrow. "I thought she wouldn't want to see me again."

"What? Why?" I watch his gaze as it shifts. Shifts through scenes of everything we've been through together. The river, the tsunami. Then, it finds that night. The night when that woman's body came crashing down and everything with it. His head turns down. "Oh."

Our footsteps leave lingering silence. Soon we are approaching the outskirts of the city and entering the barren land beyond.

"We're right out here," Viridian says. He points to an ancient watch tower atop a hill. It is carved in senile stone, uneven, and gives the illusion that it's tipping. Falling ever so slowly so that the world might end before its life is fully lived. I see my own reflection in the sunlight cast upon it.

So I stare for a moment longer. I try to imagine where my family lies inside. What they are doing to waste their time.

Viridian is looking at me. "You okay?"

I wish I could speak in the absence of lies. "Yes."

[50]

The Grandest Of Fears

Viridian leads me up a spiral staircase to the top of the tower. The stones around me seem to crack beneath the bouncing of my eyes. Sweat seeps into the crevices of my hands, running like oil across the base of my palms.

I do all in my effort not to replay my mother's expression that night. But I can't resist such a poisonous temptation. So I watch her jaw drop. I watch her hand cover her lips like a door blocking me out. I watch myself run away from the scene, and I think of running once more.

I nearly crash into my brother at the top of the stairs. But instead, I stagger into his arms, and he turns to grip them beneath the strength of his fingers. He stares at me so strangely. His eyes narrow in upon me, and I am watching and waiting for him to say something of substance.

"Eve, what's going on?" My vision is clouded. My nose is full of smoke. I search for air once more, but none is found in a burning arena. "All of this, it's . . ." He searches for words. "Please just talk to me."

"Have they talked at all about that night?" My words come as a surprise to both of us. Viridian is staring into my eyes, his gaze shifting down to his palms that grasp my forearms. Something. There is something happening in his mind. Something more than what I normally watch happen. But I watch, and I watch him think through his words so carefully. I fear the trouble that will come with them once they erupt. And then he releases his grip upon me, slowly shaking his head.

"No," He stares at the floor for a moment, formulating his next thought.

Then, he shrugs. "Well, not recently."

"What did they say?"

"Eve, it's really not that big of a deal—"

"What did they *say*?" There's a pause. An undesirable silence grows as the algae across these stone walls. He licks his lips, his hands shifting to his jean pockets.

"They were more just worried about you," he begins. "How you were doing. Merû . . . asked at one point where you got the gun. I made Sitka admit to giving them to us."

"Did she make you give yours up?" Viridian reaches for his right side, removing the weapon from where it sits. We both stare at it. My mind makes him out to position it towards me. For it to fire and for me to die before I can even smell the smoke.

Insead he puts it back in the holster. "Nope."

I shake my head. "I don't understand. Merû's the biggest pacifist I've ever known. Everything she ever taught us was about how to avoid violence at all costs, and I . . ." And then I remember that moment from earlier. That moment in which I spoke to Viridian and it seemed for just an instant as though he understood me. And for a moment more, I believe that he will seek to understand me once again.

So I let the words roll off my tongue, hoping he won't look upon them lightly. "I broke her trust."

There is silence. A silence so severed by discomfort that it reminds me so deeply of the silence I had once known back home, back when the chaos was just beginning. He looks at me. I watch him decide how to receive my words. To seek my comfort or roll his eyes because it comes more naturally.

"You did what you had to do. You didn't break anything." I stare at him. I think my jaw sits slightly more open than it had before. "I promise you, Eve, Merû would have done the same thing to protect her family if she had been able to." He is staring at me dead in the eye. "I don't think you understand that she hasn't stopped crying about you being gone for days."

298 | Kassandra Grace

Astoundment forces my face to remain still. "Really?" He nods.

"I promise you that you have nothing to fear." He smiles just the slightest bit. "And you know that I've never been that good at lying."

And then he is turning away from me, setting his gaze to the wooden door set before him. He tugs at it with such authority that I wish I could grab just a fiber of it.

But I'm still standing in belittlement, seeming to shrink beneath the incoming light. I am a tulip, wilting beneath the summer sun. I am melting into the earth, and I am forfeiting my worth. But her voice is water as it seeps through from above. It is a river running towards me, and I cannot seem to decide whether it is feeding or drowning me.

"Oh my *goodness*, Viridian, you cannot do that. I thought we lost you too."

He shakes his head. "Everything's *fine*, Merû, I just went to the market."

"For what?" He begins to step through the doorway, glancing backward at me. I am frozen in time. Every fear I have ever acquired catapults down upon me until my vision is too blurred to see what lies ahead.

"I wanted food."

"We *have* food."

"I wanted better food."

"You, my son, are ungrateful."

Viridian groans. Looks backward at me one more time. He makes an agitated face in my direction where his eyes grow just a bit too large, and his mouth pulls just a bit too tight across his cheeks. "Okay, you know what, Merû? You're going to be glad I went, alright?"

"Am I? And why is that, Viridian Elko?" He looks back at me for the last time. All I can make out in his expression is just the slightest hint of sympathy.

"Because I . . . I brought . . . *something* back." It takes all of my remaining strength to follow him through the doorway. All of the breath I can conjure up to keep my eyes open. To turn the corner and see her standing before me.

To stare upon her blonde curls, her ragged clothing, her green eyes fixed on me, growing. Widening to match the size of the sun. Her jaw drops, shaking. Trembling to match the sea floor before the wave. Then she speaks, but only in a whisper.

"Oh my gosh." She approaches me, and I am paralyzed, and I am lost beneath disbelief, consuming me like a sea. I am abducted by the staggering scene of such a moment finally becoming real. That smile on her face just as I had remembered it to be. Those tears in her eyes, ponds of relief. Then she is standing right before me, staring at me. Her head shakes so, so slowly.

"Merû," I mumble. Everything inside of me bursts open. And she is hugging me, and I am holding onto her so tight.

And her tears are meeting my shoulder.

And her breath is meeting my ear.

And suddenly, I don't feel like a monster.

Suddenly, I feel alive.

I really do think that I will cry this time. Because, for once, every fear dissipates. Every lie is dissolved into thin air. All of my longing is met by fulfillment. And for just a moment, the sun is only a star with just a bit too much passion, and the black hole is simply a lover who has loved a bit too deeply.

She pulls away. Her eyes lock with mine. "Baby, I need you to know something." A lump is forming in my throat. The moments she spends in hesitation feel like an eternity as I tremble beneath her gripping hands. "I didn't want to leave you. I never ever ever wanted to leave you. But . . . but what you said in Varna. When you told us to keep going . . . I had to respect you, and I had to trust you. I had faith you would find us. I really did. I know you, I know how determined you are, and—" She hesitates for a moment, "—I just had this gut feeling that you would find your way back to us." She chuckles. I smile. My very bones shake beneath me.

Shake, just as that woman's had. Blood spreads to my hands once more. Then, words spread to my mouth.

"I'm so sorry, Merû," It is all I am able to get out. She tilts her head ever so slightly.

"What do you mean?"

"That-that night . . ." I mumble. "When I . . . when I shot her." Her gaze softens, her smile twisting to a frown as she pulls me back into her arms.

"Oh, baby."

"You looked horrified."

"No, no, no—"

"And I've hated myself for it ever since. I never ever wanted to betray you or lose your trust or—"

"No. Eve, please no."

"You hate violence, and you . . . you—"

She pulls away again. "Baby, I would have done the same thing if I had been able." I stare at her. Stare into the conviction in her eyes. A pillar falls upon me. I shake my head ever so slowly.

"But . . . you always said violence was never the answer. That there would always be another solution." Not a single thing about her expression shifts. Except, she lifts her finger, placing it against my chest, right where my heart rests so wearily.

"If someone was trying to hurt my family, and I had no other choice, I would have done exactly what you did." And then she says it. Those words I fear so much, the ones I believed for endless weeks that I would never hear again. "I love you so much, Aetheria."

Time stops. Our eyes link together until they are fully synced and I am trying to fathom the falsity of my fears.

She loves me. My mother still loves me.

"I-I love you too." And something inside of me shatters. Some personified fear that I cannot quite identify. One that had spread across my entire consciousness until it had become the very person I am. Gone in an instant.

My mother still loves me.

My mother still loves me.

A second set of arms wraps around me. I recognize my father's hold in an instant, his smell of wood and vanilla encircling my nose.

"It's my little girl!" He exclaims. I didn't know my heart could feel so soft towards him.

"I missed you, Perû." Relief laughs its way off his lips. His hold upon me is warm. Tight and comfortable, even protective, maybe. For the first time, I bring myself to wonder what shame my family might have felt for leaving me.

It feels like forever before I pull away from him, my gaze shifting to Sitka a few feet from me. He smiles, and I shake. Then, I practically run to him, throwing my arms around his shoulders and burying my head into his black curls. I feel the vibrations of his laughs beneath me, and I can't help but reciprocate them. And then our laughing subsides. Then, I only remember how much I had missed his warm touch.

"You knew Elijah would take care of me," I murmur more as a statement than a question. His head rocks underneath me.

"Yeah."

"I got a bunch of cool stuff from the market." I pull away from Sitka. Our bodies both turn towards the sound of Viridian's voice. He nears a table in the middle of the room, reaching into the deep pockets of his jeans and removing items onto it: pieces of naan bread, slices of cheese, and the mulberry that had been in his hand when I first saw him.

My mother shakes her head. "Please don't tell me you stole all of that."

He glares at her. "I don't steal things."

"You stole a car . . ." I mumble. His gaze quickly jumps to me and back to my mother.

"I used Sitka's money." She stares for a moment, Viridian's blank expression soon changing to an unconvincing grin. Then she sighs, shoeing him away to inspect the foods thrown out across the table.

"You do realize I'm out of money, right?" Sitka whispers once Viridian arrives where we stand.

I roll my eyes. "He stole it."

Viridian's jaw drops. "Look at you! Back and already ratting me out again."

"I could have told Merû, but did I?" He stares. "No. I did not. So a 'thank you' would be nice."

"You do not deserve my thanks."

"Not to mention they also have a different currency here," Sitka continues. "So even if you were to use my money, it wouldn't . . . work."

"That—" Viridian holds up a finger, slowly lowering it as he thinks "—is definitely a valid point, yes." A flickering light behind Sitka catches my attention. My brothers' voices are drowned out as I inch towards the cracked glass window. My gaze fixes upon a hill in the distance. It reaches towards the sun, slowly beginning to settle into the land, the ground before it covered in darkness. But above the hill sits an orange light, dancing against the darkening sky.

"Is that . . . fire on the mountain?" I point, turning to face my brothers. They exchanged a glance. Sitka inhales a breath without releasing it.

"There was a protest in town. Did you see it?"

"Yes, of course I did." He stays staring at me as though his point is obvious. Then it hits me. "Is that . . . ?"

"The fire is growing closer to the city, yes." I stare.

Roll my eyes. "We really can't get away from anything, can we."

"It seems to be something that we're really, really good at," Viridian adds, and I turn back to the window. The fire seems to grow by the second. I hope it to be just a trick of my eye.

Then my phone buzzes.

➤ From "Unknown," 16:46

"It shouldn't be a problem right now. Keep an eye on it though. I will as well."

That is enough for me.

Nothing Is What It Seems

So then, what now is factual? It seems everything I have managed to swindle my brain into believing has ended up being false. My family doesn't hate me. In fact, they've hardly mentioned what I have done. Yet I have spent endless days obsessing over it all, telling myself that death was destined to find me because of the way I had broken them. But the only thing I had done to break them was run away. And even then, they knew I would return.

I had led myself on.

On into insanity.

Because nothing is what it seems, not anymore. Or perhaps it never has been.

I think of the tsunami again. I think of what Elijah had told me on that ferry. For a while, I try to craft a way to tell my family the truth. Eventually, I decide it is best to leave it be. At least until we are aboard the Qadim.

We spend the evening catching up, and I, catching myself before I reveal too much about him who has kept me alive. I notice Sitka's eyes on me often when I speak. Each time, I wonder how he is interpreting my words. If he reads into them in the way that I wish for him to.

The night draws to a dim. Fire dances on the mountains that I desperately seek to ignore. It is then that my mother calls us all together. She sits atop the table in the center of the room. Her hands are tucked behind herself, and her eyes stare down upon the floor in seeming absence of thought, and yet, I can't help but wonder if it is rather that her mind is crowded with too much thought to process. She reaches for the frail map behind her, her gaze following the lines and staring at her scribbled notes along the sides.

"With rest, it's about a six-day walk to Jerusalem . . . or a six-hour car ride," Her eyes travel to my older brother, raising an eyebrow. "Just in case you find a vehicle."

Viridian stares at her. Swallows. "It was *one* time."

"Oh, so we're going pretend like you didn't steal things today?"

"It was necessary!"

"Oh, necessary my a—"

"A six-day walk!" I practically yell. They both look up at me. Stare for a long moment, and I stare back. My mother nods, looking back down at her map. She looks at it for a long moment, and I stare at her forehead as though her thoughts will be printed out across it. She doesn't look back up when she speaks.

"We'd arrive . . . June 25th."

A pause. A long pause. I take a breath. "My birthday." Everyone's gaze is already upon me. My eyes find the floor. "I'll be . . . eighteen." I nod once. No thoughts meet my mind.

They say that adulthood approaches us sooner than we know to realize. But I feel as though it has been expedited for me. For I have hardly realized that it is only six days away.

Viridian frowns. "I didn't get you a gift." My frail eyes find my mother once more. I notice the way she looks at me. Her ever-present concern, leaking acid across her cheeks, burning them red.

"Are you alright arriving there on your birthday?"

I show just the faintest reflection of a smile. "Yes. Are you kidding? It would be a great birthday gift." I mumble my next words so that only I can hear them, "being allowed to live again."

There is a loft overhead. It's filled with old velvet pillows and wool blankets covered in layers of dust. We claim areas inside the space and claim blankets to wrap around our bodies solely out of comfort. For there is no need for warmth in this tower.

My mind races as I lay still. I can feel it moving, but I can't find my thoughts. So I count the pounding beats of my heart, losing attention somewhere around 30. My eyes find a blank spot on the ceiling, searching for just a spark of light in the complete darkness.

I thought this would all be gone now. That these sleepless nights would become but a memory. I thought that after that moment with my mother, after seeing her loving eyes upon me again, that I might be able to get past all of this.

But I still see the woman fall to the pavement. I still watch the wave crashing all around me. I still see fire crawling up walls, and even when I seem to remove the images from my brain, the pain still remains. It lingers like a bad perfume, clogging up my whole canal so that all I can smell is its effects. And even if I try to erase it, to replace it, it still seems to crawl back to me.

It lingers like the tension at the climax of a good movie. One that follows you to your dreams. That chases you into your nightmares, and you try to run away but can't seem to move your feet.

I remember having sleepovers with Darbii and never seeing her sleep. For once, I might understand why.

So I try to listen to the breathing of my family around me. I try to duplicate them as my own.

In, out.

My mimicking seems to stagger.

In, out.

There's a short moment when reality feels rather like a simulation. A moment where I can feel my body, and yet my mind seems unattached from it.

I close my eyes. My mind is too fatigued to fabricate images. So I watch figments of light lurch their way across an abyss, and I wonder if I stare long enough, if I will become one of them.

Then, there's a voice.

My eyes shoot open. I sit up. The sparks of light slip out from the abyss and fall to the room below the bunk.

"Viridian," It's my mother's voice. Her shadow dances against the light of a single candle. "You realize what we might have to do."

"If what?" He sounds almost dazed. As if the effects of sleep have stolen his sanity. As though nightmares have implanted themselves into his mind.

A pause.

"If the people allowing us onto the ship recognize that we're Cordellian. Me and you." I'm listening closer now. Listening as silence stretches the circumference of the room. And then . . .

"Yeah." His voice is low, uncomfortably calm. Or perhaps that is fear that I hear.

"I just want you to prepare for that to be a possibility." No response is spoken.

Yet, my head is loud. Voices shout in all directions. Different interpretations of her disconcerting words. Different languages blend together into one mess. I try to breathe as the questions formulate.

"*Qu'est-ce qu'elle veut dire?*"

"*Yur på plå'a û'sfél, korh?*"

"*Elle ne veut pas faire . . .*"

I topple back down to where I lay before. Perhaps the pressure of the voices place me here. Perhaps I am too weak to handle them alone.

So I try to close my eyes, but the words keep rolling over again in my mind. They are ships being toppled against raging waves. Constant, never-ending. She can't be saying whatever I think that she's saying.

For nothing is what it seems.

[52]

Improv Act

The Lebanese sky is cherry and pewter the next morning. It is ever so deeply saturated in smoke, glazed by the gaze of the spiraling sun. It is a dessert, a delicacy, crushed by the hand of a careless child with burning eyes. Destroyed by his lack of understanding. Obliterated by his gaze set so steadily on stagnant things that neglect the beauty of longevity.

We follow the coastline. Follow past the ruins of a world gone to waste. Buildings are cracked, and some buried wholly beneath dirt. The waves have grown just a bit grander today, and I wonder why they didn't look this way when I was upon them. I feel eyes watching me. I neglect to care. Locals see us and stare as it seems they do everywhere. The pain in my side is manageable but ever so present. My legs become weary fast. The world seems warmer today.

We stop along the edge of a market. It's just a few towns down from where we had been the night before. There is a woman there with sheets of linen lining the walls of her stand, a futile attempt to escape from the sun. My mother manages to swindle two pieces from her, leaving gaping holes in what had once been her jesting protection.

"Here." she turns to face Viridian once we have stepped out again into the boiling air. His left eyebrow is already raised. "Put this over your head."

He looks genuinely appalled. "What? Why would I do that?"

"Because our hair gives us away." She seems to submit a cryptic code to his mind through her stare. "Remember?"

307

"But my hair is my best feature."

"I disagree." His gaze glides towards mine. I stare. Shrug. "What? I think you have better features."

"Are you complimenting me or messing with me right now?"

I smirk. "I like your nose."

"Okay, you're definitely messing with me."

We move on. Viridian falls into line with me as the rest fall ahead of us. I look out upon the horizon, at heat waves wrapping themselves around the base of stone buildings. At people standing beneath overhangs that seem to tip toward them, at others passed out in the dirt. The world seems to rise and fall, and my head seems to rock with it, and for a moment, I have the strangest sensation that I am falling. It seems as though I speak only to ignore it.

"I do like your nose, though." Viridian's head slowly lifts, his gaze meeting mine. I am somehow surprised to see a smirk swept across his cheeks.

"Oh yeah?"

"Yes," I try not to smile too big. "I like the way it rounds at the bottom. Nice and smooth."

"You're strange, do you know this?"

"I honestly think that's how you got all the girls. With that *round* nose of yours." He's staring blank-faced now.

"You done yet?"

"Nope." There is something about my intonation that sends us both into a fit of laughter. My mouth remembers the feeling fondly. My eyes squeeze together as though to squeeze out my ever-haunting memories. But there is something about laughter. Something about everything good in a world that is dying. Because even in its beauty and in its carelessness, it seems to bring me back to reality. For in a moment, I am controlled by the lightness of my head once more. My feet stagger just the slightest, and I adjust them before he has the time to notice.

It is not the physical pain that lasts a lifetime but rather that of the mind. For even when I recover from my weariness, I recall all that haunts me. The wave, it washes over me. The river, it surrounds me. The woman, she finds the floor once more.

Then, I remember last night.

Then, I think of the words of my mother in the glow of candlelight.

I look back up at Viridian, searching his burning green gaze for any sign of distress. Any fear my mother might have left him with. I search in the way his eyes drop along the bottom of the shadowy places formed from his lids. I search in the way his skin has begun to sag along the sides of his face, as though years have been stolen from him in a matter of days. I search in every irregularity I can see since the days this has all come to be, and I am realizing that there are many.

It is then that I somehow find a desperate urge to understand him. It sweeps over every thought of my conscious mind, and so I speak before really knowing why.

"Have you ever . . ." I'm not looking at him any longer, yet I'm not quite sure where to place my eyes. "Have you ever thought about what would happen if we weren't able to make it on the Qadim?" I watch him out of the corner of my eye. Something about his complexion shifts. His gaze tightens ever so slightly, yet remains fixed on his feet. His lips are pulled in tightly into his mouth as though to hold back the thoughts that seek to escape. It is then that he shakes his head.

"No, not really." That has to be a lie.

I turn my head a bit towards him to watch him a bit closer. "Really?"

"I don't know why I would." He shrugs. "I don't think it's really helpful."

"But what if we get there and the Qadim is already gone? We don't have any way of knowing the departure time or whether—"

"I know," he says it quickly as though to silence me. To exterminate me before I speak something into existence As though he's fearful of what could slip off of his lips.

I look away from him by then. "I guess I just . . . try to prepare for the worst, you know? Just in case it gets to that point."

310 | Kassandra Grace

"But then you're just surviving. Then what's the point of any of this?" It's the most profound thing I think I have ever heard him say. I cannot find a single thought to meet it other than that single idea that has consumed my waking days. That thought that has become less of a concrete idea but instead wrapped itself into every single thing that I do. That anxious, undying belief that I am destined to die. That it is a part of my very uncontrollable fate.

It is then that I think of Elijah.

For just a moment, I am staring through a window. I am watching him, and his back is turned towards me. My brother stands beside him. I am a foolish onlooker staring into it all, simply wishing I had the key to open the door. To stand inside the room they so happily stand inside. But I am stuck outdoors and I'm the one who put myself here.

It seems my brother and I have traded places since this all began. That the hope I once belonged to, he has now taken reign over. And as for me, I no longer know where I reign. Perhaps I don't.

"I don't understand you, V." He looks down at me. He jests without shifting his deadpan expression.

"We speak the same two languages."

I roll my eyes. "That's not what I mean."

"Well you're gonna have to be more specific than that." I sigh, pressing my face into my palms as though it will remove the thoughts from my mind and onto my lips.

"I don't understand how you started all of this being so sure we were going to die, and now you won't even consider it. How does that happen?"

He shrugs. "I don't know."

"You don't know?"

"Nope." He's being serious. I stare at him as he stares at his feet. He glances up for a moment, our gazes meeting and his quickly retreating. "My opinion of all of this has shifted over time, as I am sure it has for you too. That's just how it goes. So I just roll with it, I guess."

"You roll with it?"

"Yes."

"You don't . . ." I'm trying to formulate a question, but no words come to mind. Then, he looks down at me. Stares at me so sternly. I don't think I've ever seen him so serious before.

"I don't, what? Overthink it all?" He shakes his head, a light laugh limping off his lips. He looks off into the distance, where the heat wave rests. "No, I uh . . . I do a bit of that, actually, Eve. Believe it or not."

For the first time, maybe ever, it seems that I see myself in his olive eyes. I see the game that it seems we all play. The fighting. The turmoil. I see it all springing back and forth across his mind, and I see a show. A line of dancers following a routine that they don't really know. I see it all; the improv act we all put on. But one day, inevitably, we will all fall short.

"Viridian, put the headwrap on!" I look forward. My mother is facing us, glaring at my brother.

Viridian groans. "I am old enough to make my own decisions, you know that, right?"

"You weren't in Serbia." I think of that red car racing down the highway. I think of the vehicle flying on behind us. Viridian stares at her. His eyebrows narrow in. Then he throws his arms out to the side of himself.

"That doesn't even have anything to *do* with this!" She turns away from him.

"I am not *asking*, Viridian!" There's a long pause. He groans again, throwing the white linen over his head. He janks it around his curls, pulling it tightly behind his neck, his ears sticking out from beneath. He looks just the slightest bit like a monkey.

I conceal a laugh. "You look ridiculous."

"Shut up."

[53]

Exploitation

12 hours. 12 hours and 46 minutes. 12 hours and 46 minutes before I feel as though a fire is burning the skin off of my feet. Until the flames meet my lungs, and every breath I breathe takes away another useless cell of my being. 12 hours until we arrive in a small coastal town where the sky is darkened by both the night and a penetrating layer of smoke. We are getting closer to the fire.

We stopped for the restroom a few hours ago. I hid out back to call Elijah. It had been a short conversation. I thanked him for all he had done. Told him where we were as though he, for some reason, didn't already know. He seemed glad that I had checked in with him, glad to hear my voice. He left me with a comment that had struck me. A prompting to contact him once we had made it to the Qadim. That he had something to reveal to me then.

Then, 12 hours and 46 minutes pass. We find a small shack along the outskirts of a town, the wooden siding ancient and peeling, the door sitting sideways on its frame. There are three rooms inside; a kitchen with a steadily dripping faucet and two bedrooms, both with creaky beds and one with a large mirror on the far wall. The shack seems to have been there for centuries, since before Cordellia was founded, in the days when technology was a choice, not a necessity. It's strange how, in the growth of our desperation, so also grows the decaying of our abodes.

I wonder when this place had lost its habitation. If humans decided they deserved something better than what it had to offer or if death decided it was bored of waiting on them. And if the latter had been the case, I wonder why no one claimed residence again. Perhaps rumors were spread about those who used to live here, about their ghosts that now make their dwelling. Perhaps the myths made men laugh, and children toss and turn in their sleep. Maybe the stories were passed down for generations until they were stolen by time.

Or maybe it was nothing like that at all. Maybe the shack's loss of possession was more recent. Perhaps the sun drove its occupants out and scarred it to seem older than it truly is. Perhaps its age is but an illusion.

I feel every single inch of my body the moment we step inside. I feel my feet ache as though they will split into pieces. I feel some phantom knife slice my side on and on until it is bloody and dripping down my whole body. I feel my head spin as though every single remaining thought will fly out. And maybe, along the way, my pessimism will cease to remain. But in the blurriness of my thoughts, I continue to see the woman fall. I believe for a moment that I will fall forward upon myself the same way she had. But I would be selfish to do such a thing. To compare my momentary pain to hers eternal.

Then, I am able to move towards one of the bedrooms. I rock side to side with each step, and I can't quite tell if I'm running or falling behind my feet. The pounding in my mind tears me apart, and I feel nearly as though I can hear voices screaming. They feel as though they are ripping away every remaining known truth of the universe that I have held onto. I wonder again if I am slipping into insanity. I wonder why Elijah would care to take me this far. Why such a person would care to save me. Then, the insanity slips away and the thoughtlessness that comes with fatigue abducts my mind. Not a single other question meets me. Nothing, aside from this undying longing to rest. A desire to slip away into delirium, into an overwhelmingly consuming sleep I haven't set my eyes on in weeks.

But then I see it; my reflection in the mirror.

I haven't seen it in so long.

I haven't thought to look.

I see through the cracks of the glass, through the smudges and the dirt on my face. I see my hair in a bun, curls falling in every direction, frizz sticking through the bumps across my head. It seems to be darker now, a deeper brown, nearly ebony, as if aged by pessimism, eclipsed by hollowed thoughts and drowned dreams. My skin is darker too, sagging, reaching down into a grave to which I have told it it belongs. It is blistered, red with acne and the taunting threats of the sun.

There is a scar above my left eye, the residue of a disaster I had once faced that feels like a lifetime ago and yet haunts me as though it never truly left. It is perpendicular to my eyebrow, reaching towards the corner of my matted brow hairs, red and brown and bruised. My eyelashes sag, untouched by makeup or moisturizer or anything that could show signs of beauty. My brown eyes are dark, both emotionless and yet injected with every emotion I have ever known. Curious and yet desperate for stability. I wear no smile across my lips, no joy across my lightly freckled cheeks, no wonder at the peak of my chin where the bones collide. Where my face comes together to create a miserable masterpiece. Where my neck soon approaches, turning away at the sight of me.

It finds my shoulders sagging under the weight of the obsidian dress that I wear. There is a tear along the right collarbone where wind rolls in and out, a hot, aching air I have learned to anticipate, and yet, it still tears me apart. The dress wraps around my torso, reaching down towards my knees, the bottom layer gripping me with such severity. Layers stack atop it, blowing with the ever-so-gentle draught pulling through the still room. Each piece seems unique, each with their own life, their own story. But now they all seem the same under the dim light of the candle in the room, highlighting my sweat-soaked hands. My torn-up hands, bruised and blistered, covered in blood that I will never be able to erase.

And then there are my boots. Once deeply black, now with dirt creeping up on each side and reaching into every crack and crevice. They were once my favorite accessory, but now they only seem to be a burden. They have carried me far and yet on into the very face of death. They have brought me through waters and across lands in which I do not belong, through the glares of strangers and soft gazes of my family. But now, they have caused my feet to be torn apart as it seems I deserve, for I have exploited their kindness.

And as I watch myself in the mirror, staring at a person I once knew, it seems as though I too have exploited myself.

Exploited my thoughts.

My existence.

My power.

I almost think I can see a younger version of myself before the exploitation had come to pass. Before the chaos had arisen. In my now matted bun, I see one slicked back in perfect, pointless symmetry, accented by the leotard across my torso.

I see my pointe shoes upon my feet.

The ones I had let burn inside castle walls.

And as I search for the memories of them, it seems I have burned those too.

And then I see it; a smile across my face. My cheeks lifted high, my eyes bright. Untouched by the world, my innocence not yet stolen. My thoughts not yet rewired, chaos not yet a constant.

And then suddenly.

The glass shatters.

[54]

It Doesn't Burn The Way You Expect

I can't hear.

My ears are muffled. They are being ripped apart, torn to pieces, obliterated into oblivion. My body is vibrating as though tiny needles are puncturing through every square inch of my skin. My eyes are glued shut. I know I am on the ground, and I know that I am surrounded by shards of glass. Pieces pierce through my skin, and yet I can hardly feel them. But I am unaware of what else surrounds me. What terrors will appear before my eyes once I allow them to open.

My ears slowly begin to ring, like a camera coming back into focus. Stinging.

Stinging so badly.

The more they focus, the sooner I hear the cracking. Crackling, spreading.

Fire.

My eyes shoot open.

Flames surround me, dancing around me in circles just beyond my scarred skin. They are plastered like paint along the walls, like oak planks along the floor. That is when I think of Salzburg. When what once was a distant memory becomes alive before me once more. When I can't help but wonder if the hunters are after us again.

"Eve!" a voice through the crackling. My mother. "EVE!" she calls again. My gaze falls upon her silhouette in the doorway, blood dripping from her temple. I seem to have sewn my jaw into the floor.

"Are you alright?" She approaches me, stepping around the flames. I nod. "Baby, we need to go." I nod again.

I try to get to my feet, stumbling to the left into the bed behind me. My mother reaches for my arms. She presses a piece of glass into my skin. Pain shoots through my body. I scream.

"Oh my, I'm so sorry." I fall to the doorway. My head throws itself up and down and fumbles for stability, but I can hardly see a thing as I run through the kitchen and out into the burning evening air. The sky is filled with layers of smoke, stronger than it has ever been before, accented by flashes of light. The strangest sounds of roaring ripples through the night.

A moment goes by, and then it hits me.

The fire has arrived at our doorstep.

Or perhaps we have arrived at its.

"Is everyone here?" my father's voice calls. I hadn't realized that he is standing beside me. My mother nods in reply. "Where are we going?"

"I don't care. We just need to get out of here. We're in a fire zone." A blast sounds beside me. My body spins towards the sound, and I gawk at the shack, for it is now wrapped in electrical currents. They burn a boiling, bright white, wavering in and out and up and down and multiplying by the very moment. There is a crackling that emerges from the light. The sound strengthens until it is all I can hear. The light crawls anxiously up the sides of the shack, dancing across the siding and the rotting shingles. And in a single moment, the sound goes silent, the shack disappears, smoke emerges where it had before been. I gasp.

"Holy *shit!*" Viridian screams. I am shocked to hear my mother say nothing in reply.

Yet my eyes are wider than what seems possible. "I've never seen that before."

"It's an antimatter blast." Sitka hesitates. "They're illegal in Cordellia."

"I thought everything was legal in Cordellia." He stares at me for a long moment, his expression changing in the very slightest as if assessing my ignorance.

"Everything is *illegal* in Cordellia." Another boom sounds in the distance. I jump. Someone grabs my wrist, and I am being pulled towards the city. My feet fall behind me, and my mind spins inside of me, and soon, steel walls consume me. My father releases his grip on my wrist.

"Since when?!" I continue on.

"Since always!" Sitka screams from in front of me.

We are deep into the city. My eyes stay fixed on Cordell in my mind, upon his face I once believed I knew so well. For the first time, I am fearing what hides behind his brown eyes. What forests he had burnt down to create such a shade.

We round a corner. Fire rolls down the road we had once been upon. It moves with such hurried precision it hardly looks real. Our backs rest against a steel wall and the only sound that I hear are our breaths.

I look at Sitka. "I don't understand," I begin. He glances over at me. "I thought matter couldn't be created or destroyed."

"It can't," Sitka says. "The gun converts solid matter into gas, hence the smoke."

The smoke. The smoke that has consumed my nose for ever on stretching days. It smells just a bit different now.

"Are you saying," I look back up the hill. Something catches in my throat, "Someone is *starting* these fires? With these weapons?"

I hear a crackle beside me. My neck whips around and starlight dances up and down the building beside us. I stare at it, my eyes widening in the most apparent terror.

"Go," Sitka whispers. And then we are sprinting down the road, spinning back down into the alley. It is then that I begin to feel my side ache once again. When it's pain overtakes every other sensation in my body fighting for attention.

It's not until we meet the waterline that everything is flooding back over me. That my head is ripping itself to shreds. That my feet are shaking and breaking atop cobblestone. That my lungs are moments away from erupting, and I am seconds away from losing control of everything.

I need only to rest.

I see the tsunami. I feel the debris shove into my side. In a moment, I am hunched over my scar.

"Merû," I call through the cracks in my throat. Swallow. "I can't go any further." She looks at me. I watch her stare into my eyes, and in her own, I watch something shatter inside.

"Baby, we can't stop right now. I'm so sorry—"

"Get on my back." An invisible string pulls my pupils towards Viridian. He stands beside me. His eyebrows are pulled into a straight line across his face, decimating any doubt I have about his seriousness.

I shake my head. "I'm going to slow you down."

"Get the hell on my back." He stops beside me, lowering his body to my level. I stare at him for a long moment. But the pain I own overtakes my arguments, and soon I am jumping upon him, and he is cradling my legs beneath his arms.

He grunts. "Did you gain weight?"

"Pure muscle." I hear him snicker.

He is running again, following my family down another alleyway. Sitka's eyes continually look back at me. I meet his gaze, and he stares for a long moment. I squint. He mouths something towards me. I squint again. He mouths it once more.

Then, I understand him. "Elijah."

I move my hands from Viridian's neck. Grab my phone from the built-in pocket on the bottom layer of my dress.

"Wow, wow, wow, what the hell are you doing?!" Viridian practically yells. "You're going to fall off!"

"Give me a second!" There's a message sitting on my screen from earlier. When Elijah had warned of the coming fire, and I had somehow missed it. I stumble to our thread, swiping my fingers across my keypad.

> ➤ To "Unknown," 19:17
>
> "Where do we go?"

> ➤ From "Unknown," 19:17
>
> "Get out of this town. The fire will stay here for now. Keep south. You'll be safe
> in the next town over."

I slide my phone back into my pocket. My eyes find my mother running ahead. I stare at her feet, at the way they zig-zag with each step. Something in my heart breaks for her.

"Merû, we need to go to the next town over. The fire won't travel there." I see her shake her head.

"We need to get out of Lebanon! The fire is spreading rapidly."

"And it won't spread into the next town over!"

"At this rate it will!" I shake my head. I beg her in my mind to listen to me.

"It's a gut feeling, Merû." She continues on quietly. "Can you just listen to me? Please?"

I think of Constantinople. How I said we shouldn't stay with that woman. How my mother had ignored me. I wish there was some type of technology that could transfer memories between minds. Maybe then she would listen to me then. But she does anyway.

"Fine!" She shouts. Soon, the town grows as a distant tombstone behind us as the night grows darker and the sounds of chaos fainter.

[55]

Out To Get Us

I think there is a moment for many when they begin to question what has always been known to them, those beliefs which are engraved so firmly into their minds. When those things that have always been known as truth, begin to smell just the faintest bit like a lie.

I think that moment is now, laying on the concrete floor of an abandoned warehouse in the next town over. I watch the sun approach the red morning sky out the window before me. I stare at photographs in my mind of images circling without any sign of an end. Of these memories that follow me into my sleep and so I don't sleep, even when it becomes the single most thing that I am desperate for. Instead, I see walls of water, walls of waves. But now there is something new; walls of fire. Lurching, dancing, running down roads without an end in sight. I stare so sternly upon the sparks of starlight encircling buildings and obliterating them and I wonder how such a thing had ever come to be—how I had never known of it.

That is when I look upon a portrait of Cordell in my mind. I watch his smirk fall to a frown and I watch him hold one of those obscure weapons. I watch him throw it in the fire.

Something causes me to question it all. Everything I have ever known to be real, everything I have ever experienced. I think of home, of every memory of such a place and soon, they all grow to lose their heavenly taint. I think of the tsunami, of how Elijah had called it man made and I think of the people following us into foreign lands, realizing so clearly that they must have something to do with all of this. That there is some incomprehensible reason that they are after us, so clearly wanting us dead, so clearly fearful of something we could do that even I am unaware of. Then I think of Elijah, wondering so earnestly how he knows the things that he does; why it matters to him to aid me. Soon I am met by utter absurdity, wondering if the sun is even truly burning me.

I hear someone stir beside me. I remain still. My knees are pulled into my chest, and my arms are wrapped firmly around them. My body is warm, but for once, it doesn't feel from the sun. Instead, it is as though every single thought inside of me is burning my insides alive, and my skin is merely having to pay for it. Yet, I stare at the sky. I watch tulips dance through the heavens, exploding into strips of color, peeling out across the black that was there before, pushing it down into the earth. It's ironic how something so beautiful can cause so much pain.

"Why are you always the first one awake?" Viridian's voice is groggy beside me. I feel his eyes on me, and yet I continue to stare outside.

I shrug. "I tried to sleep. It didn't work." I don't plan to say anything else for a moment until more manages to slip off my tongue. "It kinda gets to the point where I don't really see the point in trying anymore . . . especially if I don't sleep well anyway." There's a pause. I watch him through my peripheral vision, sitting up, his legs sprawled out in opposite directions, his eyes focused on the same sky as me.

"You said the same thing the night we decided to leave." I look over at him then. "Well, something similar at least." He meets my gaze. "You don't remember that?"

I watch him closely. "I do."

"It feels like so long ago."

"Yes. Yes it does." Our eyes shift back out towards the sunrise. The bright red is beginning to settle in, and then the black hole comes into view. My eyes don't falter from the window as I speak. "Do you regret the decision we made that night?" Silence.

"I don't know." Our gazes find each other once more, and I seem to find an unforeseen softness in his gaze. "Do you?"

"I think a part of me does," I shrug. "But . . . this feels so cliché . . ." For a moment, I consider saying nothing more. But I notice the way in which he looks upon me, and I believe for just a moment that he truly cares to hear my mind. So I continue on. "I . . . I know things happen for a reason." I'm looking out the window again, feeling his gaze still on me. "And if we had stayed, I wouldn't have had any hope for a future. At least now I have . . . something." I'm not even lying when I say it. For somewhere along the way since I found my family, some amount of hope has been restored. Perhaps even something beyond just what Elijah has given me. I'm not quite sure how.

Viridian takes a short breath. "Even if it's false hope?" My gaze shoots back over towards him. I am finding something so peculiar in his eyes. There's a substance-like fear that lingers there, holding onto the darker green around his pupils.

Then I realize that this is what he wished he could have said to me in that market yesterday. When I had asked him if he doubted our faith in the Qadim. That his idea of doing something more than simply surviving was a fake philosophy he had forced himself to say, perhaps even to try to believe. But he didn't mean it. Not really.

He had lied to me. A lie to fabricate some feeling of false peace. But whether it was for his sake or mine, I do not know.

"What's it with your whole gut feeling thing?" His question catches me off guard.

"What?"

"You were able to get Merû to stop here by saying you had a 'gut feeling.' What's that all about?" I feel my breath cease. Heat flushes my cheeks. "Not to mention they're always weirdly accurate. Except for Salzburg," he mumbles that last part. I stare. Search my thoughts. Search for a reason why I can't tell him about Elijah.

But I fall short. Yet, I speak in opposition to my convictions.

"You just underestimate your little sister's smarts." I smirk.

"No seriously." He stares at me for a moment. Nothing about his expression shifts. "It's, like, something with your phone. Which doesn't even make sense 'cause I can't get anything to work on mine."

There is one single moment of hesitation. One single moment when I truly consider telling him about all of it. But the moment passes swiftly, and soon, I choose once more to remain in my own lies.

"It's this . . . disaster tracker app I got when everything was first beginning. It still works for some reason."

He stares for a moment, slowly beginning to nod. "You're telling the truth?"

"Yes." I choke on the word.

"You sure?"

"Why would I lie to you?"

It's a genuine question.

We leave an hour later. The town is silent, the streets speckled lightly with people who have not yet run from the fire. I watch them each closely, hoping to find secrets plastered in their paralyzed faces. I find nothing. But every single thought and question still circles my mind, so I pull Sitka behind everyone on our way out of town.

"Tell me about Cordellia," it's the first thing I say to him. His head slowly lifts up towards me, and I watch his eyes trace the lines on my face for some sign of my jesting.

He stares so firmly at me. "What about it?"

"Something is very wrong with it."

"Well, it's a good thing we left then."

I roll my eyes. "Oh my gosh, you are just like Viridian." He looks at me just the slightest bit confused.

". . . Am I?"

"Sitka." He continues to stare at me for a long moment. His entire world seems to fold and unravel in his mind, and I watch as the faintest sign of fear creeps up the sides of his cheeks. It is then that I wonder how long he has waited for one of us to ask him this question.

"What do you want to know?" he finally asks.

"Everything."

"Where do you want me to start?"

"Anywhere."

He releases a quick sigh. "Okay. So, I need to know what you already know so that I know where to start."

"Well," I think for a long moment. "Not really anything." He stares at me. Blinks once. "I just . . . Well, you said that those weapons last night are illegal in Cordellia." He nods. "I guess . . . I had always thought that everyone just tended to be a pacifist. And that was why we didn't have weapons. But it . . . actually doesn't make sense for everyone to think the exact same thing."

"Yeah, well . . . they have a way of manipulating thoughts."

My head reaches outward towards him. "They . . . they what? Who are *they*?"

"Well, there is some level of government. It's just unclear how much."

"There *is*?"

"Yes. Remember the announcement from the cabinet? Right before we left?" Our eyes are locked upon each other in the same earnest way, and something is settling into my brain. "It's likely all AI, but we're not positive. They would've needed to be programmed at some point in time, but it is also possible that they've developed on their own past their initial programming, like . . ." He smiles just the slightest bit. "You know that really old movie *The Matrix*?"

I grin. "Yes, I introduced you to it, dork."

He smiles. Looks down. "Well, it's like that. But at the same time, their current level of advancement is . . . somewhat recent, so the programming needed to also have been done somewhat recently. Of course every country has its own version of AI, but . . . there are a lot of components. I won't go into all of it." He looks over at me. I am staring at him closely. "We have ways of tracking many of them, though. It's how I knew about the glitch at the border."

I think of Mister Soddom. I think of the note in his back pocket all those days ago. I don't know if I have ever truly realized it, but it is becoming inescapably clear to me now. He has an enormous role in all of this. Then, I wonder how much Darbii knows, if anything.

"What if . . ." My finger and thumb grasp my chin in the most cartoonish manner. "What if there are . . . actual people still involved like . . . like now. Like today. Who would those people be?"

"No idea."

"Because how would they even recruit for something like this?"

He shrugs. "Generational ties . . . ? Someone being a part of the bloodline from the beginning of everything? I have no idea. That exact question is one of the reasons we think it's just AI."

"Who is 'we?'" I watch him look away from me. His face seems melancholy and yet somehow deeply alive. I cannot quite understand how the two can meet and merge into a single thing.

He sighs so severely. Then he speaks. "There's an organization made up of people who believe that something is wrong with the country. Corbyn's dad is involved with them. That's . . . how he got the guns. We supply resources to one another from out of the country."

"Corbyn's dad." He nods. Then I am thinking all the way back to that helicopter in Germany, onto the hunters in Austria, and those in Neo-Italy. The question simply slips off my lips. "So, the AI, or the 'government,' or whatever . . . do you think there might be any reason that they would be . . . out to get us?"

"*Bow chicka bow, bow bow bow bow . . . out to get us.*" I look up. Viridian is moving backward towards us and dancing through each step. "*Bow chicka bow, bow bow bow bow . . . out to get us.*" He stops. Stares at Sitka and I. We stare back. His eyes fall very closely on me, and soon they narrow. "Do you not remember that song? From Grade 7? I think."

My eyebrows raise just the slightest bit. "No, no, I do. I just don't particularly like it."

"Don't *like* it? That's one of the best songs of all time!" I stare at him. My lips mold just the slightest into a smile.

"Mm. Who's the artist?"

"I don't know."

"Full Nap." He stares at me. "Remember that really awful band?"

"*Awful?* I say, if I am able to remember all of the words after this many years, they clearly did something right."

The three of us all begin to laugh. Something about our tones complement each other. I haven't laughed so easily in longer than I can recall. It is then that I realize that some amount of hope truly has been restored to me. Something more than just what Elijah gave to me.

[56]

The Land Of Salvation

The rest of the day doesn't take much ground in my memories. We stop in-land for the night at a small agricultural town on the road to Israel. I realize then that we will be in the land of our salvation the next day. I imagine what the Qadim will look like, if it will measure up to all I've dreamed it to be. Yet, I realize that I've never truly tried to imagine it. I'm not quite sure why.

The sky is dark when we leave the next morning. Overcome entirely by smoke, the sun a bloody red, the hole by its side appearing ever the more somber. It looks larger now. Perhaps it isn't. It seems my world has become distorted, that the lines between factuality and falsehood have intertwined. Even more so, it seems I have forgotten every way I have ever known to decipher between the two.

I think of Cordellia for a long while. I think of all I once thought it was, all that it truly is. It's a good distraction, really, to look disparagingly upon a country that is no longer my problem.

The border is flooded with bodies. With minds that have all been disfigured into a herd of madness. Eyes that have been swallowed up into pools of utter darkness. Waters of such franticness as the tormenting waves of the sea. Pupils float as vessels upon their swells, and tears taste the sandiness of their cheeks. For humanity and nature, they're very much parallel. Beautiful, but all of their beauty forgotten in the midst of chaos.

Then, there is the wall. It sits between us all and salvation. Electricity dances up and down its steel pillars, stretching towards the sky. Stretching with such grandeur that it nearly blocks some of the smoke. Again, I think of Cordellia, but not out of distraction, but rather out of juxtaposition.

Then, I seek to look upon those who stand at the base, where the wall becomes simply one thick plank of concrete. Those in dark uniforms, with guns placed on their hips and some on their backs and a completely other type of weapon in their right hand. I watch them place it upon a woman's arm. Hold it there for a moment. Then, they let her through.

A man appears next. They scan his arm, then send him away.

My eyes find Viridian. His skin looks pale against the smoke. My father and Sitka's hands are both grasped tightly in front of their bodies. Their knuckles are white and blue. Sitka coughs into his shirt. My mother stands beside me. Her shoulders are pulled uncomfortably close to her neck, and I catch her gaze for just a second. I am startled to see her instantly look away.

I feel something sink in my stomach. I wonder for a moment if I will throw up, throw up food that I haven't even eaten. For we are all thinking the same thought. It is clear in the bloodied daylight.

"Hey." My father's arms wrap around our shoulders. He pulls us all into a cluster, into walls blocking the traveling of sound. Then, he looks us each in the eye, staring at my mother for a moment longer than the rest of us. "We have identification. Okay?"

She simply stares back at him. But it is Viridian who speaks.

"Will it work?"

A long pause. "It has to."

"And what if . . ." Viridian doesn't finish his question, and no one answers. Then we break away. My hands burry into the pockets of my dress. My body burns stiff, and I am staring at the long line in front of us. I think of messaging Elijah. There is only one question I can think to ask him.

➤ To "Unknown," 12:40

"Will it work?"

He responds immediately.

> ➤ From "Unknown," 12:40
>
> "The ferry."

It takes me a long while to recognize what he is saying:

It already has worked.

We stand in line for hours. It feels suffocating. The sounds of wailing, the sounds of laughter. The contradiction of the two. And in the midst of the various outbursts of emotion—my paralysis. My blurry eyes. My memories, slicing through the remaining sanity of my mind. Yet, there is the faintest scent of hope. I try to hold hands with it. To feel it's every crevice. But I can only find the tip of its finger.

I wonder if Darbii is among these crowds. Standing here with her father or rather alone, pushing on to the Qadim. Suddenly I feel guilty for how little I have thought of her.

The sky lightens and darkens just the slightest bit, and then we are at the front of the line. A woman stands behind a table, brown circles under her dark eyes, indignation settled in across her flattened cheeks. There's an outdated computer system before her and a keypad on the wall behind her, lined with blazing buttons. Beside it is a steel gate, with an inch of separation between it and the rest of the wall above. I stare through the gap for just a glimpse into the other side. For anticipation of what might lie in the land of salvation.

There's a translation device on the face of the woman. Tubes rest inside both of her ears and stretch down to her mouth, placing a black circle across her lips. Any language in which we speak is translated into her own inside her ears, and the words she speaks in her tongue are released from her lips in every known language of the world. Gibberish, it would seem, and yet it is designed for our ears to pick up only our native tongue.

The woman glances quickly upward. She doesn't meet a single face before her eyes fall back towards her screen.

"How many?" she says it more as a statement than a question.

I see the tensity in my mother's stance. "Five."

"I'll need to check one of your identification."

The statement cycles again through my mind until I land upon a single word in the center of the phrase.

One.

She just needs one.

"Do mine." I approach her before she has time to react. She swings the identification reader up towards my arm without looking in my direction. As though this very process has become pure muscle memory. My mother stares at her for a moment.

"You don't need all of us?"

The woman practically groans. She doesn't look up at my mother when she speaks. "Ma'am, I have been doing this all day, *every day* for the past five weeks. I am sick and tired of it. If an outside comes through, typically they have no form of identification. So yes. One of you will do just fine if it gets my job done quicker." There is a beep on the reader. The device is removed from my arm in an instant and I watch her look down upon it. "You are . . . ?" She finally looks up at me.

"Sarai Elkolai."

"Birthday?"

"June 25th, 2128."

"Place of residence?"

"44 Shawq Drive." The woman's gaze shifts to my mother.

"See? Not an outsider." She turns from us immediately. My hands leak acid into my dress. I watch her body move so suddenly towards the keypad on the concrete wall. My heart starts to race from some all-consuming level of excitement rather than the better-known fear. And in a single instant, the gate is dissolving behind her. "Welcome home, Elkolais." Her gaze shifts to me. "And, Happy Birthday, Sarai." I grin.

I am the first to step through. To enter into the land of salvation.

The world seems brighter, and the sky seems nearly blue. The smoke is soft against my nose and just the faintest bit reminiscent of the mustiness of my room after returning home. The earth is soft beneath my feet, and for a moment, the heat feels like a friend. For I quickly recognize that I will soon be long gone from it.

[57]

Out Of Character

June 21st. Four days until my 18th birthday. Four days until I lay my eyes upon the Qadim. How ironic that the most important day of my youth has managed to align with that of my current circumstances.

I hope for it to come sooner. That the mystery of the anomaly would no longer be hidden from me. That the earth and the sun and the moon would all line up at the perfect angle, and a shadow would be cast across the earth. And in that shadow, I could find a peaceful silence, lasting long enough for my mind to still, for my aching bones to loosen. For I to no longer grip the wrist of hope so tightly but that she would reach for my hand instead. For it all to finally make sense.

Yet, at the same time, I hope for it all to be slowed. I wish to look upon the earth again for the beauty it contains, not the pain it disperses. I want to see the sunrise and not just think of what it has done to me. I want to see rivers roll and not simply fear drowning in them. I want to see a stranger's smile and not fear what hides behind their crystal teeth. I want to believe in something again, something good.

I want to believe there is good.

The Israeli people seem good. I find favor in their smiles and hospitality in their hands. They seem to understand our pain, and so they take us in as one of their own. As a project unto them, to make us feel welcome in a land in which they believe is our own. It feels strange that people of such kindness would be so restrictive in driving only their own population out of misery.

But perhaps they only see us like family because they believe we are.

June 21st; the smoke begins to lighten, the heat remains the same, the trail we take along the river gives my feet an ache.

June 22nd; there is a boat across the river, five spots just for us, a free market on the other side, and a three-story hotel.

June 23rd; a rumble awakes us that morning, a party below our window, we smile through the crowds, something for once feeling normal.

June 24th; normality ceases now. We are close to Jerusalem, taken in by an old woman, fed well, and given a room.

June 25th; I'm not sure what happens here. I'm still stuck up a line.

We lie upon a roof the night before my birthday, the roof of an old woman. We stare at the stars blanketing the sky. Crowning it in the dignity it seems to lose during the day.

My family lies beside me. Silently, yet I know they are awake. With their minds as loose as mine has always been, dropping screws and wheels across the floor, scrabbling to put them back into place. Except, I have already accepted that I can't fix it all.

So I stare at the sky blankly, the silence of the small village below me irresistible to enjoy. The moon overhead, impossible to look away from. For tonight is the last time my childish eyes will stare upon it. Perhaps it will be the last time I find comfort in it before my grown gaze tells me that finding comfort in such a thing is naive. That I am naive. Maybe I am. Maybe I am okay with it for just one more night.

I find my phone in my dress pocket. Place it into my warm palms. Type a quick message on it to Elijah and wonder if he is still awake.

> To "Unknown," 22:33

"I just wanted to say thank you. Thank you so incredibly much. For everything. No words in all the earth can truly tell how much it all means to me. I am alive and it is only because of you."

I read the message a few times over. Then, I send it. A smile stretches my cheeks, and for just the splitting of time between two moments, I feel an overwhelming wave of peace. It leaves quickly, yet I anticipate a day in which I will find it again.

A message appears beneath my own.

➤ From "Unknown," 22:33

"It's a privilege. Check-in with me before boarding tomorrow, alright?"

➤ To "Unknown," 22:33

"Of course I will."

"Eve." There's a whisper beside me. It's Viridian's voice. I place my phone down slowly as though it will make him fail to question me. It seems it does.

"Yes?" A longer pause. "What's wrong?"

"Nothing, actually . . . shockingly," He is quiet for a long moment, and I, too, fail to speak. "It's just . . . wild, you know. That we're going to be up *there* tomorrow." He points towards the stars, his finger landing upon one I had noticed moments earlier. It is grander than the rest, its color a muted red, its glow rising and falling. I feel my cheeks fumble towards a smile.

"I didn't think you looked at the stars."

"I don't. Well, I didn't. Not until . . ." He stops speaking. His mouth is still open slightly. Then he closes it.

I look at him closer. "Not until what?"

"No, never mind."

"What were you going to say, V?"

"I don't want to say it now. I was . . ." We're both sitting up now, and he is using his hands to talk. "I was going to try to say something out of my comfort zone, and I decided that my comfort zone is a totally wonderful place to be."

A pause. I find myself giggling. "Well, based on everything we have been through, saying something . . . *new* is probably the least of things to get you out of your comfort zone."

He sighs. I watch him look away. Then, he speaks slowly. "What I was going to say, was. Not until our star decided it wanted to crush us, so I chose to look to others instead."

My smile grows even more. "You know, that's the most poetic thing I've ever heard you say."

"That's why I wasn't going to say it."

"I'm very impressed."

He finally finds the strength to meet my eyes once more. I am shocked to see him smiling in the most simplest of manners. As though smiling has become just that once more; simple. Then, there is a stillness that comes over us, one I can't quite explain. "I have something for you," he finally says. I watch his fingers reach for his pocket.

My eyebrows narrow just the slightest bit. "You what?"

"I knew your birthday was coming up, and I thought you should still get a gift, even if the world is kinda . . . ending. I mean, you're turning eighteen. So." He removes an item from his pocket, placing it into my open palms. My eyes widen in wonder. It's a necklace with twelve green beads dispersed evenly across a short chain the color of rusted bronze. "I know green is your favorite color." It's an ugly green, the color of mucus, light and yellow, outlined by the strangest of blues that seems almost black. It's held together by a metal clamp in the back, matching the shade of the beads.

Unfortunately, it's quite literally hideous.

"Where did you get it?" My eyes jump up at him.

He's watching me for signs of approval. "A market on the way from Lebanon."

"You stole it?" He stares at me for a moment longer. Then, his gaze falls to the floor. My heart catapults down with it.

"Viridian I—" I am stunned. Flabbergasted. Enticed by such niceties and completely unaware of what to say. Shocked by his sudden shift of character, and yet, I cannot help but wonder if this is simply who he really is. If he, for some reason, felt as though he couldn't ever show it.

So I say the only thing that I can think of to say.

"Thank you, V. I um . . ." I look up at him. Smile so softly. "Thank you."

He nods. "You're welcome." Then, he lays back down. His palms are pressed against the back of his neck, and his eyes meet the moon once more before closing. I continue to stare at him. To watch his chest lift up and down. To wonder what thoughts wander the paths inside his mind. For perhaps they are different than I have thought this whole time.

Eighteen

I awake a year older. I don't feel older. I feel just as foolish as I was the day before. Both as hopeful and hopeless as I've always been.

But the excitement that comes with birthdays still seems to follow me. My mother is sure to embarrass me by singing the birthday song every few seconds, just as she would back home. My father stands beside me with an eager grin painted across his cheeks, just as he once had always looked. My brothers use the day as an excuse to channel their anxiety into excitement. And I forget for a moment what it feels like to have my mind focused purely on the chaos.

That is until I see it: Jerusalem.

The city of gold, the city of desolate, the city of history and modernization. The holy city, the faithful city, the city of truth, the city of God. With all of its names, it stands before me, staring eye-to-eye with me. It stretches as far as my gaze can reach, from north to south, east to west, metal built into each ancient structure. Voices arise from it, cries and screams and laughter. A city of peace, a city of disorder.

Beautiful; terrifying.

I stare upon it in the most utter optimism. Stare at a long shadow cast down upon its narrow streets. My eyes travel the length of it, my jaw sewn into the fabric of my dress. I am here. I am alive. Jerusalem is an arm's length away from me. I can touch the metal of the structure before me, and place my hand around the knob of its door. Awe is an understatement for the complexity of emotion I feel.

And then my gaze falls to it, that in which has cast the shadow. That which I have come here to find.

I think it is simply a skyscraper at first, built by the same hands as those who have built the rest of the city. But this is built by scientists, by geniuses, by names in generations that have been lost to history. By engineers, by carpenters, by the best of humanity. This will be my salvation.

And I am staring at it.

And I am alive.

The Qadim.

And soon, a shout for joy like I have never before experienced escapes my tongue, and I am laughing and screaming and squealing all at the same time. All my dignity is stolen by contentment, and I don't care. My family surrounds me, and we laugh together, and we hug, and for a moment, it seems as though I have forgotten about it all. Forgotten about the flood after the storm, about the car in the river, the bullet in the woman's body, the blood pouring down my father. For just a moment, none of it matters. Because I am here, staring at my salvation, and I am no longer afraid. For a moment, I am free.

We roam the city, just for a little while. We pass through markets, our ears filled with voices of a tongue we do not know, a tongue that is so beautiful simply because it is the tongue of salvation. The tongue of freedom. The tongue that reminds me that I am here and I am alive and everything I did was for a reason.

We pass through the old temple courts, where money changers buy and sell goods. We wedge through the crowds of people, all shifting in our same direction. The further we go, the louder voices grow, the more urgent their tones become. The more hasten their expressions shift to be.

Soon we are out of the city. The bustling does not end. It follows us around a large metal building, to a plain of brown grass, to a ship that sits atop it, that skyscraper.

The Qadim.

I stare upon it in the most genuine form of wonder. It is built from a solid dark silver, shining in the light of the sun. The glare is blinding, and yet I stare anyway. The structure is tall. So, so tall. Hundreds of meters high, reaching beyond my comprehension, blocking my sight of the red and black circles in the sky. It is wide, stretching on until I can hardly see the end. I can hardly understand how such a thing can fly. Its beauty is amnesia, and I am gladly taking it. Gladly looking upon its kilometer-long stretch towards the sun, towards its rounded ridge at the top. At the crystalized windows scattered like hidden jewels along segments.

I've never seen something so beautiful. Something so overwhelming.

We push through the crowd, through their screeches and shouts, towards the front where guards stand, and I cannot help but recognize the weapons they carry. In between them stand men and women in uniforms, identification readers in their hands, allowing crowds through and sending individuals back.

Soon we are before one of them; a woman with large, brown curls, a translator piece upon her like that we had seen at the border. She stares at us for a moment, beginning to speak.

"How many of you?"

My father answers, "Five."

"Hurry up please, we don't have much time."

My father steps forward first, answering the identification questions. He is pushed through to the other side. My heart releases a beat of tension. 1/5.

Sitka is next, answering hastily, then being pushed through. 2/5.

Are we really doing this?

I am up next.

"Name?"

"Sarai Elkolai."

"Birthdate?"

"June 25th, 2128." She doesn't acknowledge that it's today.

"Place of residence?"

"44 Shawq Drive."

"You may continue on." 3/5. *Oh my gosh.*

It's actually working.

Viridian comes after me. The woman places the reader up to his arm. It beeps.

It beeps faster than it had for me.

It beeps longer than it had for me.

The woman looks up at my brother. She hadn't done that for me. She looks back down at her reader. Back up at my brother.

"You're Cordellian," her words are sharp. Sharper than the shattered glass on my arms from our car window. Sharper than the piece of scrap metal in my side after the tsunami. They pierce my body, draining the very life out of my veins, the very breath from my lungs. And all I can think of is one word.

No.

I watch my brother's eyes widen. Larger than I have seen them ever before. I can almost feel the exploding of his chest, the shattering of his mind. His lip quivers. Faster. Soon, he is speaking.

"Excuse me?" She looks at my mother now too. Her gaze is stuck on her blonde curls. *No.*

"You're both Cordellian." The woman's eyes dart around us all. *No.* "You're all together?"

That's when I see my mother. When I see her eyes, her wet eyes, her drooped lips, her hand wrapped around my brother's wrist as if to tell him something. *No.*

He hesitates. So, so long. He hesitates so long that the veins in his neck seem as though they are about to pop, his blood exploding onto me. *No.*

"No," He finally says. There are tears in his green eyes. "These-these are family friends of ours . . . they-they said they would try to get us through." *No. What. No.* The woman turns to us.

"You are a disgrace to your country." Then, she begins to push them away, back where they have come from. My mother, my brother.

My mother,

my brother.

No. NO.

"NO!" I feel my lungs shatter. "No! Let them through! What are you do-ing?!" *My mother, my brother. Oh my gosh. What have I done?* "LET THEM THROUGH!" I scream. Louder. NO. "I NEED THEM!" Someone's hands are on my wrists. Strong. I pull away. They pull me back. I kick them. They kick me back. "STOP IT! LET THEM THROUGH YOU IDIOT!" And then I'm on my knees in the burnt grass.

And I am staring at my brother being pushed backward. Shoved through the crowd. Tripping, stumbling, falling. He hits the ground, lurching for-ward. Someone is kicking him, and I am screaming.

"DON'T YOU TOUCH HIM! LEAVE HIM ALONE!"

And then I see my mother. She is staring at me. Staring at me as they push her away. She is smiling, water coating the skin upon her cheeks. And through the blurriness of my eyes, I see what she is saying to me; "I love you."

"NO! STOP!" Someone kicks me again. Breath ceases from my lungs, and I am choking through my screams, and my eyes are trying to find my mother in the crowd again, but she is gone. And I try to speak, but I can hardly hear my own words.

"Don't leave me, Merû." My very bones collapse atop each other. "Please, Merû. Please don't do this." *Just hear me, Merû. Please. Merû, please.*

My head hits the dirt. Dust flies into my nose, and I cough. Someone is yanking me to my feet again and facing me toward the Qadim. We are mov-ing. On towards a salvation I no longer desire. *Please,*

   Merû,

But then I hear a sound. A rumbling from what seems as though it is emerging from underground. My bones rumble. My lips shake. I look at my feet; they are planted still into the ground. I look back up at the Qadim. Stare at the thrusters below the ship boiling with an orange rage.

My screaming ceases in an instant.

I stare.

Stare as it slowly begins to lift into the air.

And I am not on it. My mother, my father, my brothers.

They're not on it.

And I am on the ground.

And it is leaving.

And I am on the ground.

Screams come from all directions and I stare. It moves up into the atmosphere. Chaotically. Cyclonically. The thrusters throw me back towards the earth. My back collides with the grass, and I choke on my ceased breath. I gasp. I cough. Harder. The rumbling grows. The screams multiply. Louder. Too loud. My ears shriek to be rescued. My bones cry to be on that ship.

But then I watch closer.

The Qadim begins to shake as it shrinks into the sky. It shakes violently. The thrusters seem to enlarge. Orange fades into red. Bright. Brilliant. Brutal. I can't process what I am seeing.

Can't process it when it blows.

[59]

Fire

Fire. There is fire in the sky. Embers raining down on me.

ROYGBIV

Red; the boiling of the flame.

    Orange; the sun grinning, laughing.

        Yellow; the embers raining down on me.

            Green; who are you? Where have you gone?

        Blue; my tormented tears–they never do come.

    Indigo; my blood—why does it still flow?

Violet; the static in my mind.

    Brown; the grass stabbing my back.

Gray; the suffocating smoke.

        Black; the hole that will forever be my doom.

[61]

Could

Could a critter creak under cracked concrete?
    Could their songs be heard beneath a bellowed blow?
    When the enemy from above disturbs it's daydream,
    Could it learn to cope with its croaked throat?

[62]

➢ To "Unknown"

"Tell me why I ever trusted you. Tell me why I ever believed you to be good. For you kept me alive, only to see me suffer greater. Left me with a promise of hope, only to cause it to shatter. You molded me into a plate of glass, colliding with the cold, dust covered floor. I was truly foolish to trust you. Foolish to put my hope in a stranger. Into one who refused to ever show his face. For how could I know one to be good if I knew not who that one was, not really. Perhaps it was even you who put that ball of darkness in the sky. Perhaps it was you that wished desolate upon humanity. For who else would have such power of manipulation?"

Death Is Inevitable: Part Two

And so that's it. That's the end. What more is there to say?

This is how I die. Drowning among the shattered pieces of all of my remaining optimism. Suffocating under the weight pressed down upon me until I am simply a part of the earth. Until I am doomed to burn right along with it. I am trapped in a nightmare, begging myself to wake. To escape this all-consuming darkness, to run from the figures that follow me, yet I cannot seem to move my feet. But I know there is no waking. No second chance. No life to escape to after this one has escaped me.

This is the end.

Sprawled out across burnt grass. Paralyzed stiff.

This is the end.

Eyes staring in awe. Scratch that. Terror. Complete and absolute.

This is the end.

And now I hate myself for ever being hopeful, for hope has turned out to be foolish, just as I had once thought it to be. I hate myself for despising humanity, for they are just as miserable as me. I hate myself for hoping that there might still be good in the sun, for all he desires is to burn me.

I hate myself for my faith. For my stupid, stupid faith, I placed in an unknown number. In a distant voice without a face. For believing without a cause for belief. Such a thing is simply childish, to trust in something only because it feels good to trust.

And where will I go now? Return back to the home I have come from, to a place in which I no longer love? Will I crawl back into the walls of my room to rot away into oblivion until I am snatched away by the sun's furious hand? Or will I die along the way, trapped inside a land I have never known? Dying behind these metal bars I have built in my mind. Built so firmly so that I will never escape.

Because death is inevitable.

Death is my destiny. Death is my fate, that thing so greatly beyond my control. For I am not in ownership of my own life. No, it seems that fate is unavoidable in the ever-present flow of time, and I am simply bound to it as we all are. If only I had known to accept it sooner. To give into my thoughts, for the subconscious is always truthful. Forever all-knowing.

Maybe then I would not be stranded here. Maybe then I would not be paralyzed on burning shards of grass. Maybe then I would not be shattered by the shouts that erupt around me. Maybe then I would be able to push these tears out from my eyes instead of them being stuck inside my head, trapped with the rest of my body.

Maybe then I wouldn't hate Elijah the way I do now.

There is a hand on my back. I barely feel it through the numbness of this skin that no longer feels like my own. Through the shallowness of my mind that has dried to a desert until I am nothing. I am simply outside of it all. Outside of reality, watching a movie of my surroundings. Of the swarms of people pushing past the barrier between the concrete and the grass. Of the shouts, the horrendous cries escaping from mouths, sounds that emerge more animal than human.

For we are animals. We are worthless. All fighting to survive, but our lives are nothing but dust that will dissolve back into the earth from which it came.

There is a voice in my ear. Muffled. I try to make out the phrase that is said. It is repeated. Once, then twice, then on and on, and I can't seem to count the amount of times I hear it.

"Eve. Eve." My name. "Eve." My mother's voice.

"Merû." And suddenly the paralyzation ceases, and I am falling back into her arms, and she is hugging me, and I am trying to cry, but nothing comes. I feel my insides both relax and rip apart, and I am trying to pick up the pieces of my identity that are shattering around me. The pieces are slicing my fingers as I reach for them, but I no longer know pain.

"Baby, we need to go," her voice remains but an echo.

My lip quivers. "What?"

"The Qadim. It's falling. We need to go." I want to laugh. So, so bad. I want to laugh at my mother. Laugh at her desperation. At her fight for survival when death is all we will ever know.

"I . . ." I don't know what I mean to say to her.

"Eve, we need to go *now.*"

"I got her." It's my father's voice. He appears before me, seemingly out of thin air, kneeling down and scooping me up from the earth. He begins to run. Run towards the city. I see my brothers in my peripheral vision: running. My eyes are focused over my father's shoulder, stuck upon the fire,

fire in the sky,

falling towards the earth.

And in a moment, the most striking sense of the deepest desperation stretches down my throat and slices through my body, and I am helpless and hopeless and hardened all at the same time, and I just want my eyes to shut, but they won't leave the fire alone. Burning. Boiling. Climbing the length of the sky and planting into the ground. A single drop of water lands on my neck. My father's tear.

A metal structure blocks my view, and we are in the city, and the shouts around me only seem to echo. And in the chaos of the people around me, I only feel alone.

I am sure now that I prefer the shouts over the silence. For the silence only allows the shouts in my head to grow louder. For the inevitable insanity to consume me. The shouts of reality, those I can tolerate. But the ones in my mind. Those tear me apart.

We are in a cave on the eastern side of Jerusalem. The stone walls trap in the heat of the day. No one speaks a word. No one has a word to speak. For what can be said to another who knows death as a friend? What can I say when I know I could have said something sooner to stop all of this? To end the ruthless reign of this hope?

Of this foolishness.

"I knew this would happen," my words are raspy. They burn my throat. But I don't think that I care any longer. No one responds for a long moment. For a while, I wonder if they've even heard me.

Finally, my father speaks. "What?"

I stare at my feet. Stare at my boots that have become a curse. Try to remember what they once looked like before they became a burden. I look at my hands. My hands that could have prevented all of this had I been honest. Had I allowed my subconscious to have a home upon my lips. Had I recognized my enormity, my chosen obliviousness.

But I did not. And now we have paid for it and they deserve to know.

"This whole time," I begin. I clear my voice through a crack. "Before we even left home, I . . . I had this thought. This knowing that we weren't going to make it. That we were . . . destined to die. And I knew it was true the whole time, and I tried to ignore it, and I tried to be hopeful that we had a shot at this. But in the back of my mind, I knew we never did. It wasn't even a fear, I . . . I truly *knew* it." Then, there is only silence. Everyone watches me with calloused eyes. I stare at my hands and imagine my words falling to them. I try to read between the lines of what I have written. "And now we're here," I continue, "stuck in a random, burning cave in Israel with no way home . . . and I know that if I would have said something sooner, we wouldn't be here right now." I release a sigh. It is long and heavy, and it hurts my chest. My eyes have never felt more dry.

"I've had the same thought." My gaze finds Viridian. He sits in the corner, leaning against a wall, tears staining his somber eyes.

"Same." It's my other brother. His head is buried in his hands.

My eyebrows narrow. "Did we *all* think this?" My parents nod. "Then it's all our faults, I guess. I'd rather not blame myself for yet another thing." I kick a rock beneath my foot. It hits Viridian in the leg.

He looks up at me. "That hurt." We simply stare at one another. And suddenly, he is jumping to his feet, kicking a rock of his own. "What the *hell* are we doing here? Sitting in a cave, waiting to die?" He throws his arms out to the side, flinging his eyes towards my mother. "I mean *seriously*. Why? Why do we think that *this* is the answer?"

"Because there's nothing else to *do*, Viridian!" My mother's voice is the same pitch as sirens. "You know that!"

"What if there is? There has to be."

"There isn't! I didn't want to be the one to admit it, but I am. So unless you know of some other country somewhere with a way off of this planet, then I am sorry, but we have no options."

"I'm sorry? That's it?" They stare at each other for a long moment, and I almost wish I could hear their thoughts. But I'm left with only a distant echo. And in it, all meaning is lost.

All I know is that if my mother is saying it's over, then it's over. And with that, any last remaining optimism inside of me is crushed.

There is a buzz in my pocket.

➤ From "Unknown," 14:14

"I never intended for you to get onto that ship."

Part III

"The Revelation"

[64]

Audacious

It seems as though a bullet slices through my skin.

Which doesn't really make sense. Because bullets don't slice; knives do. Bullets piece. But maybe that's just it; the message doesn't make sense. And I am staring upon it with such distraught, with such hollow eyes and a hollowed face caving in upon the weighty words as an avalanche.

Yet it is just like a bullet, for it pierces my dusty eyes. It kills every single thought that erupts and dissolves in my mind in a single moment until all I am thinking of is the only word I know of in which to describe Elijah.

Audacious.

Completely and disdainfully audacious to send me such a thing at such a time as this. I cannot help but reply.

> To "Unknown," 14:15

"So then what did you intend? For us to all just die here?"

> From "Unknown," 14:15

"Not in the slightest."

I stare at the message.

It is so simple. So frightening.

> To "Unknown," 14:16

"I don't understand you, Elijah.

> ➤ From "Unknown," 14:16
>
> "There's another cave next door."

I stare blankly. The skin of my fingers begins to rattle above my bones.

> ➤ To "Unknown," 14:16
>
> "So what?"

But I know what he means. I think. That something lingers there. Something to aid the absurdity of his words.

There's no reply.

> ➤ To "Unknown," 14:17
>
> "Elijah."

I sigh. Then I force my legs to straighten out and hoist up my worthless figure. My hand traces the stone wall and grabs hold of it for a long moment while the world goes black. Then it subsides.

"I'm going outside," I mumble, turning towards the cave mouth. "I need air. It's freaking stuffy in here." Then I stumble into the sunlight from which I have hidden, and its hollowed gaze is painless to my numb mind. I listen to the silence of the world around me. Try to imagine what it would sound like if the birds still sang. There's the glow of fire on a far-off plain. I wonder if that will be the one to consume me.

The other cave is quite a few meters away. It's hidden by a looming tree rid of leaves, the bark charred and peeling and scattered upon the amber grass below. The cave mouth's edges are jagged, carved away so carelessly by time, soon to be its killer. I stare for what feels to be centuries, slipping from my fingertips. Years that I cannot possess. Hesitancy clouds my steps. But soon, I am swept with the understanding that there is not a single thing now that I have to lose.

So I enter the mouth of the cave. A warm line of light shoots through the ceiling. It settles down upon a second spotlight emerging from the back wall. And in between the two pillars of brilliance stands the silhouette of a being, the silhouette of a man. His sandalwood hands are tied like ribbons behind his back. His head is fixed towards the second window of light.

And I feel my heart drop,

break,

shatter into a million pieces as I stare. Shake. He wears cloth pants of charcoal, blowing in the soft current encircling the cavern. A long black shirt wraps around his arms and runs towards his fingertips. The rim reaches towards his light copper neck, and ebon curls explode across his skull. He stands in such stillness I almost wonder if he is even breathing.

But then he turns ever so slowly. The light from above shines across his stoic face, and suddenly, I realize that I have seen him before. That I have seen his eyes in the face of a storm. I recognize the soft way in which his cheeks round and are painted so gently with evolving shades of red. I recognize the width of his bottom lip, the strength of his jawbone, and the stumble painted above it. I know his eyes, so somber yet so strong, like pools of coffee, as piercing as the end of a wooden spear. His eyebrows are thick and settled in with such magnitude above his curving lashes. I try to guess his age for a moment. Thirty-five, maybe forty.

Then everything I know to be true is coming together into one person. My jaw shatters and rolls across the cave stones, and I blink ever so quickly.

"You're . . ." I fight through my cessation of breath. Fight to force the words off of my lips. "You're Elijah," I say.

He smiles with such gentleness. "I am."

My lip quivers. My hands bury themselves inside my pockets, and my left wraps around my phone. The world seems to spin and jump and dance and erupt, and yet I am staring at him as though he has power over all of it.

"I-I thought I wouldn't ever meet you."

His expression doesn't seem to change in the slightest. "That's not what I told you." I shake my head. Once. A moment passes. His gaze finds the hole in the stone wall behind him. "I didn't intend for you to be on that ship."

And in a single moment, all of the wonder I feel vanishes and I realize that I'm staring at the man who gave me hope where there was none. In only a moment, I remember how much I hate him.

"You told me that," I say. He stares for a moment longer while my eyes trace the length of his profile as though something more will be found along its edges. "You know it . . . it would have been easier for me if you had just . . . let me die instead of letting me come this far. You know, because I'm going to die now anyway." I grind my teeth against each other. My gaze stumbles to my feet and the pebbled ground beneath, and I feel Elijah's eyes find me. I look up, almost appalled to see a smile set across his cheeks. My eyebrows furrow. "What? You think it's funny?"

"You're not going to die," he says it so softly I almost don't laugh at his words. But I do. I laugh at him like a hopeless idiot, and he stares at me, void of expression.

"Elijah, my only way off of this planet is destroyed. I don't know if you saw that explosion in the sky—"

"I saw."

I nod once. Quickly. "You saw. Okay. So then what are you proposing I do because I see no other solution."

"I have a way out," He speaks with such confidence I hardly realize the absurdity of what he says. "Not many know about it . . . not many would believe it."

"What is it?" His eyes stay focused on me. His tongue rolls across his lips as if carefully tasting his words before releasing them to me.

Then, he speaks. "You have to trust me."

"What, you're not going to *tell me*?"

"I can take you to it. I am more than willing to. However, I cannot yet reveal to you what it is. You have to trust me on that front."

"I have to trust you, huh?" I nod slowly. Of course I do. For he is unchanging in his ways, once more asking me to trust him without giving me a reason for trust. Yet, I cannot fail to remember what he has done for me. The ways in which he has been a guide to me, even among his lies in where he has been leading me.

But then I try to remember a time when he told me he was taking me to the Qadim. I can think of none. All he has promised is to keep me alive.

I am nodding ever so slowly. "You know, I'm sure my family would be more than happy to follow me and a random thirty-something-year-old-man into the unknown." But they already have, many times, whether or not they have realized it.

"I can't force you to do anything, Aetheria." I stand a bit taller. Never has he said my name.

Then the conviction comes upon me, and I cannot find a reasoned cause.

He is telling the truth. He knows a way out.

"Remember what I told you that day when you were waiting in a train station? All the way back in Neo-Italy. You asked me who these people are who are after you. And what was my answer? 'They follow you because they fear me.'" He takes a long breath. "What I am wanting to show you is what it is that they fear. It is something that holds unexplainable power. This of which I speak is better than anything the Qadim could have ever had to offer you."

I stare at him so firmly. So curiously. And suddenly, I am desperate to know what he knows.

"How long is the journey?"

He smiles ever so softly. "A day and a half by foot."

"We're going by foot?" He nods. "I . . . I guess I'll try to talk to my family about it."

"Would you like me to come?" I stare at him for a moment. For a reason I can't quite understand, I release a nod.

"Yes," I begin. "Please . . . please do."

The Disaster Tracker

The world meets us outside those hollow walls. Elijah stands to the left of me. We walk across the burning grass, and the sky zooms in and out upon us until my head becomes a carousel. I feel his steps on the ground beside me. I feel them as though they have always been there, and I suppose that they have. That his invisible figure has been holding onto my molten palm, placing water upon the flames. Injecting steroids into my shriveled bones. It is then that I am consumed by the most apparent dread. That I cannot help but wish I had said something to my family about him sooner.

There's something about dread. About that moment when a million little lies fly through your mind with the hope of pinning only one down. And in that cyclone, in that hurricane, in that all-consuming storm, the only thing that can be found is the truth.

That is what I find when I turn the corner into the cave. When I stare upon the eye of my mother before the storm comes. Then it does, when her gaze meets mine and then rushes on towards him, and her feet fly up from beneath her. Words scatter out of my mouth.

"Before you say anything." My eyes jump between each person before me. "This is Elijah."

He stands beside me. His shadow looms as a pillar of history lost to time. Its jarring cast lands upon Viridian, his green eyes blaring as a forest fire. My father stands beside my mother in a matter of a moment. Their faces are scratched and scarring into streaks of black, resembling the wrinkles of age.

And then there's Sitka. He hides his small smile behind confused eyes, and yet I cannot help but notice his subtle relief.

Perhaps it is his acceptance of Elijah's presence that leads me to continue on.

"I've been in contact with him for a while now." I wait for a reaction. All I see is my mother's eyebrows narrow ever so slightly towards me. "He's been giving me directions to Israel . . . keeping me away from danger. He's the reason I was able to find you all again after we were separated." I swallow. So, so harshly. "He's . . . the gut feeling." There is silence as I collect my thoughts. "He has a way off of the planet. Something . . . better than the Qadim. We must go with him."

"He's . . . the disaster tracker . . . ?" Viridian's staring at me. His voice is rough and irritated, like coarse grains of sand caught between layers of rock.

"Disaster tracker?" He and my mother stare at each other now. "What are you talking about?"

"She told me she had some disaster tracker app." Viridian's eyes venture back to me. "Was that . . . was that a lie?"

I stare at my brother. His lips slip down his face. His eyes shrink down into crescent moons, and his cheeks seem to sag beneath the weight of my lies, the same way my own mind has.

"Why didn't I know about this?" I can't even stand to look at my mother after her words. And so I look upon my father instead. His gaze is so firmly placed upon me and then, he speaks ever so slowly.

"After that tsunami, you told me you had a gut feeling. That was how you knew it was coming. I decided it would be better not to question you." There's a long pause. "Aetheria, did you lie to me?" I just stare at him. For what else can I do?

Then, he nods. "Why did you lie to me?"

"He saved your life, Perû."

"That wasn't my question."

My mouth opens just the slightest bit. "I didn't know how to tell you."

My gaze shifts to Sitka. He leans against a wall, his hands tucked into his lap, his head pressed against the stone. He stares at me through the bottom of his eyes. Stares with such fervor, with such fear, with such great questions that I only wish I could answer for him.

"I apologize for the distress I have caused you." Elijah steps forward into the cave until he is in front of me, and I am staring at the back of his head. "I never intended on such a thing. I have only come to aid. I know of a way to save you all, and if you are willing to trust me, then I am willing to take you to it." There's an eerie silence. Breath escapes me and is replaced by something so similar to poisonous gas.

"Eve, may I speak with you for a moment?" My eyes bounce up towards my mother. Then, she is beside me, her hand around my arm, pulling me outside.

The sun meets us. It scowls down upon me.

"I'm sorry, I'm not . . . I'm not understanding this." She stares at a point beyond my being, stumbling through her scattered words. I am looking at my feet, hugging my arms across my chest as though it will stop my heart from pounding. "Why didn't you tell me about this?"

"I didn't know how to."

"I thought we told each other everything." We do. Well, we used to. "Remember the helicopter in Munich? We talked to each other about that." But so much has happened since then. So much confusion, so much chaos.

"I know."

"And now you're expecting me to follow him to . . ." She pauses to think. "Gosh, I don't even know where it is that I'm supposed to be following him!"

"Merû, this man saved my life," I say it so firmly I almost question if it is I who says it. "When I was in Constantinople, I was convinced that I was going to die, and I thought that I deserved it. But Elijah called me, and he talked me through it, and he got me back on my feet and took me to you. Merû, I would have never seen you again if it wasn't for him. And maybe he's lying about a way off the planet and maybe he does have evil intentions, I have no idea.

But what I know is that he kept me alive, and we can either put some faith into the idea of him being good, or we can keep sitting in this cave until we die. Those are our only two options." She stares at me. She stares for so long until I feel as though my mind is about to shatter into pieces, and my legs will crumble beneath them.

Then she shakes her head. Slowly. "I just wish you would have told me earlier."

"I know. I wish I had too. I . . ." I swallow something growing in my throat. "I'm really good at hiding things when I fear . . . when I'm afraid of how they will make me look and . . . I don't know. I guess I feared this would make me look weak. And I couldn't do that to myself." Then her arms are around me. Breath returns to my lungs, and I am finding some amount of peace inside the darkness behind my eyes.

"No more secrets, okay?" I nod in reply, my chin pressing into her shoulder. "We need to tell each other everything from now on, or this isn't going to work." She pulls away from me. "Do we have a deal?"

"Does this mean we're going with Elijah?"

"Do we have a *deal*, Eve?" I feel a smile form across my face.

"Yes, we have a deal."

Her cheeks lift just the slightest bit. "I'll talk to your father about it, okay?"

"He's going to hate it."

"I know." She giggles. "I'm still in shock that we were able to get him out of the house." She places her hands on my shoulders. "You don't worry though, okay? I will make it work. I promise."

"Thank you." All I can do is smile and hope she realizes just how much that smile has cost me. The cave seems to darken by the time I return to it. Sitka sits to the right of me and Viridian, our backs pushed against the back of the wall. I can hear the distant mutterings of my parents outside. Elijah sits right at the door, ever so still, and I can hardly understand how.

"This is just . . . really weird," Sitka mumbles. I don't even look over at him.

"What is?"

He shrugs. "I guess I just imagined him to be older."

That is when I feel Viridian's eyes find me. They stare upon me for one, two, three seconds until words spiral off of his tongue. "I'm sorry, are you saying he knew?" I nod. "Since when?"

"The tsunami." There's a pause.

His gaze is stuck upon me. "So you told him but not me?"

Anger saturates my senses. "He knows how to keep his mouth shut."

"What is that supposed to mean?" I am looking at him now, tilting my head ever so slightly to the side, watching as he reads between the lines of my expression. "Because I said something about the disaster tracker just now? Is that what you mean?"

My gaze falters. "I just mean in general, Viridian. I can't trust you because you talk."

"And that warrants you lying to me instead?"

"I didn't—"

"Do you know how much easier it would be if you just told me the truth? Why wouldn't you have just told me the truth?"

"Because I knew you would say something!"

"You're right, I probably would have. Because I don't keep secrets that are that massive from my *family*."

"Viridian—"

"You just made your life harder by telling everybody something different." He is suddenly standing, throwing his arms out to the side of him. "I mean, why couldn't we know about Elijah? Why does it matter?"

"I don't know!"

"If he's leading you to lie, then why should we be following him?" He looks over at Elijah in the doorway. "No offense." Elijah's gaze lifts, and he politely shakes his head.

I roll my eyes. "I didn't *lie* to you I just—"

"You lied to me, Eve. You lied. I asked you a question, and you answered it with something that isn't true. That is a lie." He looks over at Sitka. "Right? That's a lie." Sitka shrugs. "Oh yeah, right. I shouldn't be asking you this. You keep secrets too—"

"Keep him out of it. Please?"

"Gosh, you two are the same. Of course you would defend him." Viridian stares at me, his eyes filled with the most apparent rage. My head tilts ever so softly to the side.

"Why are you so angry?"

He practically laughs. "Why am I angry? You *lied* to me, Eve. My own sister lied to me while we were this close to dying—"

"I know what I did, and I wish I hadn't."

"—and you didn't even *consider* telling me the truth."

I pause. "I considered it, but I thought it was a *stupid* idea—"

"Viridian." It's Sitka's voice. I look over at him and find the simplicity in his stare. "Just because she made a mistake doesn't make Elijah bad." They stare at each other for a long moment, and I wish I could see the words moving between the whites of their eyes.

There's movement at the doorway.

"Okay, are we ready?" It's the voice of my father. I look up at his eyes, dropped and scattered across the cave floor. It seems we are all falling apart. But I stand anyway. Viridian seems to release some amount of his anger. Sitka hides behind my shadow. And we're all approaching the mouth of the cave as though it will relieve all of our tension. But it doesn't. Viridian mumbles beside me.

"I still don't trust him."

I shake my head. "I do not care."

[66]

A Train In Motion

Moments have learned to pass me by like a train in motion. I try to peek through their windows, but it is all but a blur.

I seem to have forgotten that it's my birthday. The moments of this practically holy day have become blurred faces inside of those train cars. They are teal blue eyes, washed with a weathered sorrow so somber that one would think they live in the darkness of the night rather than the brightness of the day. They are red scarves across necks, blowing in a crisp and cool and bloodied breeze conceived by ash. They are blurred creases on aged cheeks, with lines meant to be read in between. But they are lines I cannot read.

Lines I cannot see.

Faces I cannot know.

But I know Elijah's face now. Perhaps that is enough. He takes us along for a couple minutes to a desert plain. He says he has food kept away there, buried into a chest in the ground, reserved especially for those "like us." I don't know who he thinks we are.

We sit in a circle on the sand. Cans of rice and beans and pickled greens sit in the center of us, but all I can pay attention to is Elijah sitting beside me. His peace intimidates my impressions of this hollow world.

"Are you from this area?" My father fights to make conversation once silence becomes an unbearable discomfort.

Elijah's cheeks rise as balloons into the air. "Jerusalem."

"Really." I can't tell whether it is said out of passion, precaution, or prejudice. Perhaps they are all the same. Perhaps my father owns none.

Elijah swallows a bite of beans. He nods slowly. "I was raised in the technological district." He places his can back on the grass to use his hands to speak, stretching them above his chest to visually narrate his speech. "My father was a brilliant scientist. I was always deeply inspired by him. Dreamed to be like him." There's a pause.

"So you're a scientist?"

"I am."

My mother finds Elijah's eyes. "Did you have any part in building the Qadim?"

He shakes his head. "I saw flaws in their ideas." I had seen flames in their ideas.

"So did we," Viridian speaks with an unprecedented confidence. He grins. Chuckles a bit. And once he notices that his eyes are the only ones filled with laughter, his gaze falls. The more the moments fly by, the more he seems to lack some form of necessary humankind fragility.

"Where did you learn French?" My mother speaks once more.

"I pursued science for a while in France," Elijah begins. "Naturally, I had to learn their language."

"Sitka likes science."

His excited eyes find my brother. "Do you?" Sitka nods. "What type of science are you interested in?"

Sitka hesitates. "AI development mostly . . . well other stuff too, but I find that the most interesting."

And when Elijah's smile seems like it cannot grow any larger, it still does. "You're absolutely right, it's very interesting." Sitka begins to smile. "I've spent time studying AI's attributes. It's fascinating. Their rates of advancement have become quite exponential in the past ten years, even more so than the early twenty-first century."

"Right, because that's when everything was first becoming a big deal."

"Absolutely." Elijah pauses for a moment. Thinks through something.

"You know, what I find the most interesting is their reaction to anakate. Have you heard of it?" Sitka practically doesn't blink. His hands are frozen midway into the air. His jaw lowers ever so slightly, and I'm searching his tongue for the words that he doesn't dare say.

"I . . . yes. I-I have."

"It's interesting, isn't it."

"It . . . it is. Yes," His eyes shift from confusion to amusement to just simply joy. "And the way it affects humans is . . . it's fascinating." He laughs. I forgot Sitka knew how to laugh. Elijah shares in his joy.

I notice Viridian then. I notice the way his eyes jump between Elijah and Sitka and the way his eyebrows are narrowed in upon both of them. I see that face he makes when he is deciding to say something that he probably shouldn't. But then, he says it anyway.

"You're probably an expert in all that tracking stuff too, huh?"

Silence. All eyes pierce Viridian with varied levels of passion. I come in first place. My stomach stirs in the silence that spreads. My fingers find each other and begin to pick away at the skin around my nails. My eyes find the food in front of me. It stares back at me. I swallow something beginning to grow in my throat.

"It's actually a really well-known technology," Sitka says. There is the slightest scent of agitation in his tone, but only enough for me alone to notice. My ears begin to ring. "Of course, so much is still being developed, but most of it is available to the general population."

My head thunders. Viridian looks from Sitka to Elijah. "Do you develop it?"

Elijah is unfazed by his questioning. "I have done some development, yes. Though, it's not particularly my main field of study." Something slithers beneath my skin.

"What's your main field of study, then?" My very bones are shaking.

"Neuro-tech."

Elijah's fingers touch mine. At first I think it is an accident, but then I look down and see his hand resting with such firmness upon my own. Viridian is rambling on about something. I'm not listening. I'm watching Elijah as he reaches for something with his other hand, placing it next to our fingers.

It's a green apple.

His hands retreat back into his lap. I look up at him as he says something to Viridian. He doesn't look at me, and yet I see a picture painted in his brown eyes, telling me clearly what I must do.

I hesitate. Steal a breath from the burning air around me. Soon, I wrap my hand around it, move it towards my mouth, and force a bite. I focus on the sweetness of the flavor. It tastes like a summer day spent in the once splendid sun. It tastes like autumn beneath bowing trees. I can almost see my mother out the kitchen window, dancing in a pile of leaves, taking a bite of a green apple. I try to remember the potential promise of seeing such a thing again.

Then, I take another bite.

[67]

Living Water

Viridian doesn't speak much after that. I watch him stray behind as we struggle through sand beside a deserted highway. His eyes are fixed towards the dimming sky in the most apparent and unnecessary pride. His cheeks are locked firmly across his skull, and his lips are pulled so tightly into his mouth that I wonder how such a stance can form any amount of comfort.

But it doesn't form comfort. It forms control. And it seems that control is all he really cares about. Yet, above all, he is angry. Angry with me. Angry that he thought he finally understood everything, only to realize it is not what it seems. Because I have lied to him, and I hate that I have.

I seem to cling to Sitka's side. We don't speak, but it is comfortable. We stare, and we watch my parents talk with Elijah for what feels like hours and listen to the way they laugh together. I smile out of what I can't tell is joy or restlessness.

But the sky stretches on into that deep purple that comes moments before the moon makes its appearance. I walk beside Elijah by then. I am attached to his peace. His breaths match the heat of the flames of this world, and somehow, it brings light to this very thing I have labeled to be so dark. Because his peace is a light. And I am a moth, so stuck upon it and yet so afraid that if I get too close, it will burn me. Afraid that his light is more similar to the ways of the sun than that of the moon.

So I walk beside him. I don't dare look at him, but I only take in the sweetness of his presence. I stare upon the moon that has begun to shrivel away into a single sliver, and I wonder what lies beneath its darkness.

"I have a lot of questions for you," the words simply stumble out from my tongue. I fidget with my fingers until the tips of them are bloodied. It is then that I look up at him and watch the way a smile climbs across his cheeks.

"I'm sure you do." His smile settles in. "There will be plenty of time to come for answers."

"Is there not time now?"

My gaze does not stumble away from him. His eyes reach towards the moon as mine always do, and his hands are tied behind his back so gently. He thinks through something with such caution, and I feel a sudden passion stir inside my bones. They rattle with such an undying desire to know what is simply common to his mind.

That is when he speaks. "There are things that I must show you. Things that are too complex to simply be stated in words, or else that is just what I would do. The world right now it's . . . it's tainted. It is on fire, both literally and metaphorically. Minds are burning, emotions are raging, but . . ." He turns his body towards me, bending just the slightest bit to my level and using his hands to speak. "To put out the flames, we need water. And this water is not one that can be simply spoken of, but rather, it must be put to action."

I stare at him for a long moment. In all my meaningless metaphors that I know all too well, I cannot begin to decipher whether or not he speaks literally.

But he speaks of water and so I think of the wave.

"Who built the tsunami, Elijah?" At that, he turns back towards the sky. I blink. Once. "You told me that it was man-made by the people that . . . that fear you." There is a pause.

"Do you understand why they fear me?" He looks down at the same time that I look up. Our eyes meet, and something crashes between them, and the faintest scent of something unearthly sweeps through my whole being. Then, my eyes are narrowing, less in confusion but more in curiosity.

"What do you mean?"

Elijah smiles. Then, his eyes find the moon once more. "This water that I speak of. It is the only thing that puts out the flames. The flames that they made."

My eyes narrow, "That they . . ."

"And this water it . . . it is like living water. The guidance I have given you all of these days, they are just sips of relief from the turmoil I am sure you are suffering. But this water . . . it sustains. It doesn't go away."

I take a breath and hold it for a moment too long. "Are you speaking in metaphors or literally?"

He still doesn't look at me. I watch something settle in his chest. "There will come a day when that which you do not see, you will see. When the little pieces that have been given to you will be multiplied. But for now, speaking of this water in ways that seem unclear is all I can give to you."

"Will you give me this water? Whatever it is."

He smiles. "Soon."

My hands find each other once more. My left hand yanks at my right pinky finger, and I find that some amount of stress sweeps over me in a moment.

"And what about . . ." I pause. "I have a friend. Darbii Soddom? Have you met her? Did you . . . find her yet?" He is looking down at me. "I don't know how you get in contact with people or . . . I just . . . I want to know that she is okay." He stares ahead, thinking for just a moment. Then his head moves back and forth ever so slowly.

"I do recall a Darbii Soddom, though that is no longer her name."

My head tilts to the right. "What? No longer her name? I don't . . ."

"She changed it."

"She changed her name? To what?"

"Sélah. Darbii Sélah." Her mother's name. The only person in her life who ever knew peace. "She wanted to break away from the label mankind had put on her."

"Her father . . ." He nods. Then it is all making sense.

"What happened?" I ask. Elijah continues to stare ahead. He rubs the hair on the bottom of his chin, moving a single piece around in a methodical circle.

"I don't know how much she wants me to tell you and what she would prefer to tell you herself. All I can say is, she's free."

Freedom. It is a phrase I can no longer seem to comprehend. And yet he speaks of it with such conviction, with such apparent understanding of bondage as though to make such freedom more legitimate. More real. I dream to wonder what he has seen to make him know such things.

"I . . . I can't believe she finally did it," I rub my temples as I speak. "I never liked her father. He was never really . . ."

"Fatherly."

I slowly nod. "Yes." Think. "Yes, that's the best way to describe it I think." My gaze slowly rises to Elijah. "Then you've talked to her before, yes?"

"I have."

"When I saw her in Serbia, she wasn't getting messages."

"I didn't send them until the day you left. I hoped seeing you would give her some time to think through the decision." There were so many decisions he could be referring to. But I don't ask which one he speaks of. For instead, I bury myself inside the comfort of maybe seeing her again. Of seeing stitches on the cracks she carved in her mind.

Then, I shake my head. "Sélah . . ."

"You could do the same, you know." My eyes jump up towards Elijah. He doesn't even look at me.

"What do you mean?"

"You go by Eve, correct?"

"Yes . . . ?"

"But your full name is Aetheria."

I stare. "What's your point?" There is a pause. Elijah is configuring his thoughts into words, and I am trying to see the full picture before he has every piece.

"The root of your name—the ether—is thought to be a place beyond the stars. A heavenly place. You were meant to be rather otherworldly. So why go by a different name?" I stare. Blink. I've never thought of my name with such complexity.

Yet I shrug it off. "Eve is a nickname, I guess. Shorter, easier to say."

"But is easier always better?"

A pause. I blink. "There's more you're trying to say. What are you saying?"

He looks down at me in such a manner of intentionality that I feel my steps begin to stumble. "There is more for you, Aetheria. Beyond the labels you have placed upon yourself."

We approach the ridge of a hill. It overlooks a small cabin on the other side of a valley and a small pond sitting stagnant beside it.

"We'll stay here for the night." Elijah turns around towards my family. "We shall continue on to our destination tomorrow."

"Wherever the hell that is . . ." My glare meets Viridian. Elijah is unfazed.

Little Girl

The cabin is snug in the quaintest of manners. It holds a warmth that can neither be described as painful nor pleasant. It is simply there. It holds me ever so softly as a willow tree embracing a withered soul. Large portions of food are preserved in a refrigerator-like case on the northern side of the room. Elijah feeds us a dinner of dreams. Thin bread with the softest flavor of butter and herbs. Hummus and brown olives. Salad with meatballs and a pastry with a taste that I have never before known. I force it all down my throat.

Viridian says he is going to bathe in the pond after dinner. Elijah tells him to stay indoors for precautions. That there is always a chance we have been followed. His words seem to stir up a deeper desire for disobedience in my brother, so he goes out anyway.

And when the night approaches and the rest of the cabin retires to bed, I stay seated at the table, staring at the closed front door. I stare at the secrets that hide behind it. I stare at my birthday, which has slipped away from me and kidnapped the last of my remaining purity. For it seems as though my childhood—that single thing that I have been able to sustain—had been ripped from the skin upon my fingers. And I have let it happen.

The thoughts keep me awake. The memories, the fears. Terror rips across my mind, and screams encircle every crack and crevice until I feel the insanity begin to consume me once more. Until I remember the sound of a gun cracking, and I am staring at the face of the woman. I try to apologize to her. She looks away. For a moment, I wish that bullet would pierce my skin. Then,

I think of Elijah. Of his purity in the presence of my insanity.

The front door opens.

Viridian steps through. He wears the same dirty clothes he has had on for weeks, even though Elijah told him there were clean ones in the armory. I wear a deep purple dress that smells of lavender and hugs my arms and my hips and hits the floor. The necklace he gave me rests in its pocket.

He stops in the doorway when he notices me. A towel rests in his right hand, ruffling the feathers of his head. He stares at me for just a moment. His eyes narrow in the strangest of manners, and then he steps through the doorway, passing the fabric into his other hand and fluffing the other side of his head.

"Do you ever sleep?" He sounds angry. I cannot decide whether or not it is genuine.

"Not really." He stares at me for a moment. His face is plain. Then, he sits down on the chair across from me. "We do seem to always meet like this, though," I continue on, testing the waters of his anger. "You know, kitchen table while everyone else is asleep."

"I'd like to be at my own kitchen table."

"I know." A pause. I stare at my palms pressed into each other. Try to drive out the screams with my words. "Do you think our house is still . . . *there?*"

"Like, still in one piece? Probably not." He leans forward on his forearm just the slightest bit. "Eve, I bet the moment the psychopaths found out we were gone, they raided the hell out of that house." There is no lie in his words, but I still tell myself that there is. It seems I've never been able to change that about myself.

"I mean . . . we took our valuables at least, right?"

"Oh you mean the stuff burnt up inside a castle? Or the car at the bottom of a river?"

My throat dries up in an instant. "I . . ." My eyes find my hands. My entire right hand is spotted with blood. I sigh. "You act as though I am not also upset by it." Viridian looks up at me, only a single muscle changing in his face.

"You were the one who got us in that water."

There is silence. A weight slams into my chest, and I look deeply into his gaze to find such burning anger. Such deathly venom spilling out from the pools around the base of his eyes. There is some darkness around the edges of his pupils, something so closely related to hatred that spills out across my skin and boils it into nothing.

My head leans the slightest bit forward. "Excuse me?"

His anger doesn't even begin to falter. "You were the one who brought us to Varna . . . you . . ."

My heart begins to race. My eyes begin to scatter in every way. "Viridian . . . why are you . . ."

"You were the one who lied to us . . ."

Something feels as though it is piercing through my skull. The screaming grows. My hands curl up into fists, and my nails dig into my palms. "I—"

"You were the one who *killed* someone."

The room goes silent. His eyebrow lifts in the same way it always does, except this time, it slings an arrow through my skin. I begin to bleed. Everywhere. A red substance tugs my very limbs down into the dust until I am paralyzed. I feel my body perish, and my mind explode, and my eyes are as shock-stricken as the last soldier on a battleground. And in a moment, I am nothing. Nothing but simply alone.

Then, fury consumes me. "What is *wrong* with you?"

"What is wrong with *you*, Eve?" He stands up. His towel falls to the floor, and I watch it rather than him. "You're so naïve, and yet you expect me to willingly follow this man who you think is so righteous?" He uses his fingers to make quotation marks.

I stand now too. "He has saved my life. Multiple times. He's saved your life too, whether you realize it or not."

"Only for us to die."

"He has a way off the planet."

He laughs. My hands grow purple beneath the pressing of my nails. "Yeah. Well. He probably lies too. Just like someone else I know."

My gaze meets him. My eyes narrow. "I am not him."

"Well thank goodness for that because we'd probably already be dead if you were." Silence stretches the length of the room. He doesn't even yell when he says it. Perhaps that is what makes me the most angry.

That is the first time in too many days to count that I feel as though I really could cry if I wanted to. But I don't. Instead, I simply shake my head.

"Why are you so . . . mean?"

"I'm not mean. Just realistic."

"You're so . . ." My voice is weak. My breath is short. My eyes skip between the floor and the table, but do not dare land upon him. "You're so stubborn, and you . . . you say awful things, and you don't even care, and I . . . "

I swallow. "I . . ." spit catches in my throat. "I—"

"You what? Spit it out, little girl."

Little girl. I see myself as a little girl once the screams go quiet for a moment. I am no more than seven. My cheeks are red with tears, and my hair is mangled and messy and decorated in pieces of dust. And my brother is yelling at me after the neighborhood basketball game. Screaming at me. Ensuring my guilt for our team's defeat. I remember the words he said to me, words we never said and still never say to each other: "I hate you."

And I never said it back. Instead, I gave into my weakness, as I always seem to do. But not this time. Not in this cabin, eleven years later. Not when such anger pulses so strongly through my veins as though they will erupt.

Then, the words finally come out of my mouth.

"I hate you."

There is silence. Viridian stares at me. His eternal smugness begins to slip from his cheeks. His eyes become hollow and hardened at the same time as he stares. Stares until my bones begin to rot within me, but what is rot if not a sign of survival?

"You mean it?" he finally asks.

"I can write it out for you if you want."

And then he is nodding. Slowly. Deliberately. His body begins to turn towards the door, towards the light of the moon peering into the cabin. It stares at me. I stare back. Normally I would smile at it, but I don't.

"I left my gun outside." Viridian doesn't look back when he says it. Doesn't look back before he steps out into the unknown, and I am left standing frozen. My insides burn and explode and disintegrate all at the same time, and I am searching for the tears I neglected moments earlier, but I cannot find them.

Then, I truly realize what I have said to him. What I have said to my brother.

I feel a piece of me split into two. Split like a rocket descending from the clouds. Split like a head across concrete. And I am panicking, and my body is shaking beneath the weight of the strongest of winds. The world becomes blurred under this lens of insanity in which I own so honestly. Then, the voices come. *You made him leave,* they say. But he'll be back.

But I am walking in circles.

Pacing.

What am I doing? Why won't I rest? It doesn't matter that he left. He will be back soon enough just for the two of us to be okay again because that is what always happens. We get angry, and we apologize, and the void between us grows smaller with time. We always figure it out. Every time. This is no different.

Except for I feel that it is. For this time comes with a sickly, otherworldly paralysis lacing itself into the microfibers of my bones. Tying zip ties upon places that are quite alright on their own until they're just the slightest bit too tight. This time, I feel bile building in my throat. I feel my muscles turn to stone. I feel insects crawling up and down my appendages, and I wonder how to itch them all away. For something isn't right.

I stop pacing. I stop in front of the door from which he left. It lays open. Burning air seeps through into the room and lands upon my skin, eating away at it. I watch for him. Watch for him like a little girl watching for him on his way home from school, and soon, I am willing myself to leave. To find him before something worse does.

But then my gaze falls upon him in the distance. He stands upon a sand hill beside the pond. He is merely a silhouette against the black of the sky, and soon I find a second figure behind him, a few meters away. I stare at it for a long moment. Stare at such bleakness embedded into a single being and my eyes narrow in upon it as though to make sense of where it has come from. That is when I remember Elijah's warning: to stay inside in case we have been followed.

My heart jumps and my eyes jump with it back toward Viridian. I know how he stands. I know his posture, his tight fists and straight back with a slight hunch at his neck.

Maybe that is what makes it even more surprising when his posture falters. I notice that before I realize what I hear. The crack that whips through the air. The wind that pierces my ears. The same crack I had heard when my bullet hit that woman all those nights ago. That crack that had sent her tumbling to the ground.

Just like Viridian now.

[69]

Stubborn

What makes a person more righteous than another? What dreadful mystery of such a broken universe determines each of our inherited rations? Works and words and actions that are committed out of convincingly good intentions, it seems, are never enough. Because one day, the truth is always revealed. For in all the days of my youth, I have believed myself to be truly righteous, to be worthy of what goodness still belongs to the soil in which I stand. But adulthood has come upon me, and in the lines of its forceful hand, I have come to see that I am none of that at all. That I am unworthy of all that I have desired. All that I have ever dreamed of, it deserves be taken from me. For in all the ways that I have found myself fair, it is nothing but a shell. And once such a thing is cracked open, the pearl inside is black, plain, and wretched.

And so I stare. I stare for a long moment.

I stare until every single thought, every single memory, every screaming voice, every inherited sign of insanity wells up inside of this wretched soul,

and then? It erupts.

The most distasteful sound emerges from within my throat. A scream unfit for humanity. The scream of an animal in labor. Something dreadful is birthed inside of me. The most unspeakable sensation wraps itself through my veins and deposits poison upon my appendages.

What have I done?

Viridian.

The feeling stretches through my body. Through my muscles, through my

384 | Kassandra Grace

bones, through every single shattered piece of me until it meets my feet and tells them to run. And I am lunging towards my brother. The earth climbs up my legs, wraps itself around them, and suffocates them stiff until I am wading through vines. Until I am killing them as I kill all things. I see a second being in the distance, and for a moment, I wish I still had my gun.

Then I am beside my brother's shaking body. My knees bury themselves in the sand. The bullet hit just above his lungs. Something red pours down his T-shirt. Blood. No, I hate that word.

Because blood out of the body means something is not quite right. But he is okay. He has to be. Maybe his eyes roll backward in his head for a different reason. Maybe his groans have nothing to do with that scarlet liquid.

"Viridian," I spit his name out of my mouth. "You're okay, you're okay." I grab his hand. Squeeze it with all the energy left inside of me. To transfer it to him. Any of it. All of it. I don't want it anymore. "Please, just breathe, V. Breathe."

He coughs. The red liquid lurches out of his mouth.

Rolling down his lip,

touching the edge of his chin.

That's normal.

That has to be normal.

He's fine.

I see my father for a moment. I see his eyes in my brother. I had saved him when he was dying. I can save him too.

"I'm going to fix this, okay?" Viridian's eyes shut. His mouth is covered in red. My bones burn. "I'm going to . . . I'm . . . I . . . it's fine, it's okay, it's . . ."

Think.

I reach for the bottom of my dress. Press it against his wound as I had my father. My hands are coated in scarlet in the matter of a second. It runs down my forearms in the most erratic drops. And then his hand grabs my wrist. It shakes. I look up at his eyes to see them wide with terror. Something catches in my throat.

My hands release from his stomach. "Viridian, it's okay. It's fine, I promise. I'll fix this."

He moves his lips. I watch them. They tremble. His hand holds my wrist harder. It pins it down. I hear words fight to escape his mouth.

"Don't say anything. Just let me . . . let me . . ." I look away from his mouth. Reach back towards my dress. I press my hands into his body with all the strength I can find. He shakes. Convulses. I try to hold him still while everything inside of me shatters.

"Eve," he coughs as he says it. I look up at his mouth. More red. It is upon his neck now.

My gaze grows. "No, don't talk. Please."

"I'm . . . sorry . . ."

"NO, Viridian." His eyes close. "VIRIDIAN!"

Perhaps that is his last attempt at being stubborn. For as his name leaves my mouth, so does the shaking of his hand upon me. Then, everything is still.

I have always thought that I would be the first of my siblings to die. Sitka is too cautious, too logical. Viridian, too stubborn to let death take him. But me? I am careless. Careless with my actions, with my movements, with my words when I get angry. But that's what I got wrong.

My carelessness wouldn't lead to my demise; it would lead to his.

So I stare at him.

Stare at his eyes like sage paint, dripping down a wall. Touching the floor so gently, so meticulously. As if the last of his strength had been found in that drop. In that single drop below his eye. Wet. Idle. Slowly drying into the brown pores of his cheek.

A single tear.

I stare at his skin as it droops. I stare at his cheeks that fall towards his lips. I stare at his neck, dripping with red. I try to find life in his still eyes. Try to find breath inside his hollowed features, chiseled away by the same force that carves away life from lungs.

And I stare at him. No longer am I able to feel the bones beneath my skin or hear the screams inside my head. Instead, there is only silence. A silence more paralyzing than any I have ever known. A silence more patronizing than any word he has ever spoken to me.

I am frozen in time. I am frozen through the screams that begin to surround me. Frozen through the force of my mother reaching for his body. I fall backward into the sand, but I don't seem to notice. And I am frozen through my father above me, staring past me. Frozen through his gasps.

And I am watching a movie. I have paused it at an ugly frame and I am searching for the remote to move on. But it is gone, and I am out of control.

It is cold inside this frame. Yet I feel as though I am burning.

My eyes are burning. For I ask for water to extinguish the flames, but nothing ever comes. And yet they blur out of something so close to confusion. But this feeling is deeper. Wider. This feeling is a canyon that I have fallen inside and I am lost, looking up at the sky. Perplexed, for there is no way I am truly here. I can no longer make out what I am staring at through the blurred lens I have crafted. My bones are being broken beneath my skin, and I am torn to bits, but I am idle. There is not a thought in my mind aside from this pain. Aside from this torture. Aside from the picture of his eyes dripping blood.

My head finally turns. It turns to my father, now sitting beside me. And through the blurring of my own lens, I see that of his own. I see thick brown paint dripping down from his eyes, delicately and deliberately and dreadfully, all at the same time. Then he is looking at me. His lips are shaking so, so quickly and he is reaching for me, and I for him, and his arms are tight around me. His body shakes my bones, but I don't feel as though I move at all.

I see Sitka. He stands over me, steps towards me. His body is hunched, his eyes dripping like my father's. He holds a single dark object in his hand. Then he tosses it to the ground, and he throws his hands over his head. My eyes fall upon it.

"It was his gun," Sitka's voice shakes. I stare at the object. And then he is saying what he really means. "The gun I gave him." He shakes his head. Fast. He digs his palms into his eyes as a hand of darkness wraps around him. "I got up when I heard the arguing and . . . and saw it happen out the window . . ." He collapses into the grass. "So I went after her and grabbed the gun, and shot her back."

"Who did this to him?" My father's voice is angry. More angry than it has ever been.

"Some crazy woman."

"No." My gaze finds Elijah. He stands to the left of us, his hands behind his back in the most solemn of manners, and I stare upon the water in his eyes. I cannot decide whether it is beautiful or pitiful how Elijah mourns my brother the same as us all. When he had been given no reason to mourn.

Then, he speaks again, "It was AI."

Sitka stares at him. Agitation grows inside his eyes. "No. That was a woman. Clear as day. International law says that AI beings must have some distinguishing factor so it is not perceived as human."

Elijah nods mournfully. "They've been going against that law for a while now." Sitka stares at him for a long moment. Something shifts at the bottom of his lip.

Then, my brother looks down at the sand, "They can get away with a lot that way, I guess."

A picture comes together in my mind. A portrait with the parts I have seen before and the pieces I am noticing now hidden beneath layers of paint. Words begin to come from my mouth ever so quietly.

"It's from Cordellia. The AI."

"They've been after us, haven't they?" I don't look at Sitka when he speaks.

"Yes," Elijah's eyes look upon my older brother's body. I look with him. I wish I didn't. "They didn't want anyone leaving Cordellia. They didn't want you to board the Qadim. But now that it's gone, they just didn't want you to find me." I try to shake my head, but it doesn't move. For I knew it all along.

I knew from the day when I saw that stupid helicopter burning in that town square. I knew that my country is evil, and I knew that I am just like it. For we have killed my brother together.

And I am staring at the gun in front of me, taking it into my burning palm and throwing it into the pond. Something like acid rises up in my throat, and I try to hold it down, but I spit a bit up into my lap. More comes, and it sinks into the sand. No one notices.

"Who is doing this to us? To him?" I am able to make out the words of my father. The silence that passes between the two men is loud. Then, Elijah sighs.

"Your government," he says.

70

Numb

I have a dream that night. Viridian is standing in front of me, and I have a gun in my hands. My grip upon it is strong. And then I am shooting him in the chest. Again and again and again until he is just a pile of red and brown. I feel no remorse.

I awake beside the pond. Awake to the sand, gouging like needles through my singed skin. Awake to my hair in my mouth and roused upon my head and covered in blonde grains. Awake to those who had before been around me; gone. My senses are instead met with the rising sun on the back of my head. I can hardly feel it.

The sky is bright in a way that is almost poetic. For it seems nearly joyous, marked by slits of sunshine resting as water across the rocks of a stream. The red is as pastels: light, and simple, and good, childlike, and innocent. Rolling and spiraling as though touched by the very hands of Van Gogh. But insanity led to his demise, and insanity is what I see. An insanity concealed by beauty, for the beautiful are the ones who hide their pain the greatest.

I've always found it odd in literature that when the morning after something detrimental arises, the protagonist seems to forget, even just for a moment. But I don't forget. Not in the slightest. I stare at the red of the sky as though it is my brother's blood. Scathed, scattered, and all-consuming unto death. I feel almost as though my own flow is right there beside his, for I myself feel dead. As though the same creature that hunted him is out to get me.

But it doesn't attack. Or perhaps I don't feel the pain of its attack.

I am numb.

Stuck inside skin that doesn't feel like my own. Trying to shed tears that I don't believe I will ever truly know. My heart throbs heavily, and yet I only hear its echoes.

I sit with my knees pulled into my chest. My arms are wrapped around my legs. I try to feel the purple fabric, but I feel nothing and I catch a glimpse of the bottom of my dress, which is stained red. I look at it for a long while. And then I stare up at the water. It is still. So still. It seems we are very alike.

There is silence. Silence around me and somehow still within me. But that within me is haunting, and it is terrifying, but I cannot be afraid of it, for I am only paralyzed. Not a bird sings a hollow song, nor does the wind meet the sand and throw it up into the air. Not a single thing finds me but my own sweat seeping into my skin and clinging onto it like a heavy cream. And I wonder if anything is even real. If the sun is even burning, if the black hole is truly all-consuming. If my brother is really dead. For all I know for sure is that I am alone.

There is a presence beside me. A still being sits down to my right. I see his figure out of the corner of my eye. The way he rests with his legs pushed out before him. With his hands tucked behind him, with his eyes fixed ahead of him. Staring so peacefully at the pond. Elijah's presence is comforting.

I search for words to say to him. I try to find something to make up for the silence, but nothing comes. My heart pounds inside my ears, but I hardly hear it.

"You don't need to say anything to me." My eyes dart up at him. He looks out at the pond, the water reflecting in his eyes. He breathes with such unvaried amity. I try to follow along. My gaze falters to the pond. I stare for a long while, yet I don't see the water at all. I see him. Watch him fall in the distance. Watch the blood roll

        down

           his lips.

I see his body beside me that night on the rooftop in Israel. He stares up at the stars. His arms are tucked behind his head, and a smile is spread across his lips. His eyes are glowing, dancing in a dauntless delight. Intertwined so familiarly with contentment. His lips are parted ever so slightly, words waiting upon his tongue, soon pushed forth. But I can't hear what he says.

So I simply stare at him. Stare at him for all he was, not merely what I had made him out to be. I stare at him so gently, lost inside the forest of his eyes.

"It was my fault he left," my voice trembles. I feel Elijah's eyes upon me. His deep, brown eyes,

so still.

"We got in a fight," I continue. "I told him I hated him. He looked at me like I had just . . . I don't even know. Like I said something so terribly awful, which I suppose I did. We never say . . . or . . . or said those words to each other. We just didn't." I see my brother's face once more. I see the way his eternal smugness had begun to slip from his cheeks at the sound of my voice. At the way his eyes had become hollow and hardened at the same time.

I shake my head so sporadically. "Did he die believing that I hated him?"

I look up at Elijah. My eyes are weak, and my gaze is unruly. There's a pause for a long while, and I almost think he won't reply. But then he shrugs ever so softly.

"We've all said things we didn't mean." Elijah folds his hands around his knees now, just in the way in which I sit. "But you went after him." He looks at me. "Your actions showed what your words are incapable of showing. And who was the last face he saw before he died?"

I look down. "Mine."

He nods. "And I'm sure you weren't mad at him by then." It takes me a long moment before I finally shake my head. "He knew you loved him, Aetheria. I am sure of it." I stare at my hands. They smell the faintest bit of blood, his blood. The blood of the woman in Constantinople. Red and tarnished and unveiled. Layers building and building until I am nothing but the wounds of everyone around me. For it seems my true intentions have emerged in these moments in which I am given a choice between selfishness and humility. Each time, I have failed.

"Why would you save me?" I ask it the moment I feel such self-hatred stir my bones. "I asked you this before and you didn't give me an answer. But now you've seen me. And now you've seen what I am capable of doing, and it isn't good things."

Elijah continues to stare at the pond. "Is it the healthy that needs a doctor? Or is it the sick?" There is a pause. He looks down at me once I have considered his question for a few moments too long. "I don't need your righteousness to see your worth. Your brother, you don't need his goodness to grieve him. Because he was not always good to you. You grieve because he has value simply because he was alive."

I look away from him. I look to the sky. The deep red is fading the slightest bit into pink. I wonder if it will be cooler today, but I know never such a thing will come to be.

"Are your people more worthy? More righteous?" I am staring at a cloud when I ask it. Its shape ever so faintly resembles that of the Qadim.

"What measures righteousness? Deeds? I think we are all equal in deeds."

I dig my nails into my palms. I cannot feel the pain. "Why wouldn't you save them instead?"

I see Elijah shake his head out of the corner of my eye. "I am not here just for my people. I am here for every person, every family, every language. My people, yes, they are easier to reach because they are closer. But they have the same problem as everyone else."

I look down to the sand. My head shakes. Because he does not understand. For the first time, I am so deeply desiring to make him. So that he will leave me here to rot.

I hardly think before I let the words leave my mouth.

"He's not the first person I've killed." I feel his eyes fall down towards me. I stare at the sand. A light breeze rises up, and the grains graze my skin. I look up at him. He doesn't even seem the slightest bit concerned. "Do you know about it?"

"Constantinople?"

A vine climbs up my legs. It grabs my heart and squeezes it. It grabs my hands and balls them into fists. It reaches for my lungs and holds and releases them in the most inconsistent of manners. Then, my hands slam into the sand. Grains fall into my fingernails, and my face is scrunched into a ball. I practically begin to yell.

"Then why are you still helping me? When you know about what I've done, why . . ."

My words cease. Then Elijah shakes his head. "Aetheria I . . . I . . ."

My eyes shoot up at him. I have never seen him at a loss for words. But I stare at him, and I watch him fumble through thoughts, and I wonder if this is him finally giving up on me. "What?" It is all I know to say.

"The being you shot that was . . . that was AI."

We stare at each other. We stare for a long while. I cannot tell if I feel every single organ inside of my body erupting or if I am making something up through the numbness.

"You can't tell me that." I grab handfuls of sand. I hold them tightly. Stare down at my fists. "I have hated myself for that for so long, and you . . . you . . ."

"I am so sorry," he says.

I glare up at him. Such anger clouds my senses. "She bled."

"Faux blood. To create just the effect that it did."

I laugh. I don't know why I laugh because it's not funny at all. It's just cruel. "And this is my government at work?" Elijah nods. "Then he truly died for nothing. I got angry with him for saying something about killing her. But that wasn't even true." I drop the sand. Throw my head into my hands. "I just wish. That I could hug him. One more time." Then I dig my nails into my face. "And swear to never be so stupid with my words again."

And then I stand. I walk back towards the cabin, and the weight of my dress drags against the sand. I look down upon it. Stare upon the blood stain at the base where I had tried to save him. The most angered screech escapes my lips until I am reaching towards the bottom of the fabric and tearing a line clean up the middle of it. I tear off the whole bottom of it so that what remains sits jagged at my knees. The stained strip drops into the sand. I walk away.

71

Ash In Black Curls

So that searing thing called anger roars through my bones. It seeps into every single part of me until I am drowning. Until I am forcing breath into my waterlogged lungs, and then I emerge through the door of the cabin. For a single moment, everything ceases inside of me at the sight of her.

My mother.

She sits at the table in the center of the living space. Her head is buried in the palms of her hands. Her elbows gouge the table. The very essence of pain known at some point by every man encircles her, and my very bones shake as I stare upon such despair. Her eyes lift towards me, drenched in the most terrorizing tears.

"Merû," I push the word off of my lips. She stares at me through her shattered gaze. And then she motions towards me, and I run after her, sitting down on her lap like I had done when I was a child. When I would hurt my knee and she would hold me while mending my skin. She would kiss me ever so softly in that same spot just left of my ear and below my cheekbone. It seemed to leave a stain, a dent. A sign of such love without condition.

I place a kiss of my own in that same spot, below her cheekbone, left of her ear, and she cries. Mourns so anxiously, so bitterly, with such amplitude until even my thoughts become silent in the face of her cries. Until even my anger vanishes, and all I know is the sound of her despair. And I feel an aching so strong that it's almost as though I don't feel anything at all. My very soul is shoved into the dust of the earth. Buried beneath a grave, and I am shoveling myself in.

My mother goes quiet for a moment. I feel the silence stretch through my veins. I wait for her to speak. "I couldn't save him."

There has been a chasm growing inside of me. I have watched it expand ever so slowly ever since the day we first learned of the black hole. But her words. They crack it wide open until there is nothing I can do but fall in.

"Where are Perû and Sitka?" My voice is fragile. The air grows sour. My arms weigh too many pounds. We breathe out of sync.

"Out back." She motions ever so softly behind her. "We're planning to . . . cremate him." She swallows. "They're preparing the fire." Cremate him. Burn him alive, for he cannot truly be dead. Because I wouldn't let such a thing happen. I would save him as he would save me. I would draw out the blood from my veins if it went instead to him. And if a dagger was being launched in his way, I would throw myself between them. For love is often ignored until it is lost.

Moments pass. I smell smoke from inside the cabin. A fire burns outside that I suppose I started, for I was blind to the dagger when it came. Or perhaps I was foolish enough to believe it wouldn't truly slice. But it did.

It seems as though I am the monster that little children fear is lurking in their closets. I, who keep them up at night, dreading what lives in their dreams. Except I am not tall and hairy like they think. In fact, I look just like them. Because all I really ever have been is a child, dragged along into a world of disaster, too naïve to understand why I should fight for my innocence. And through this ignorance, this foolishness, I have grown to become the monster I have once feared. The one who preys upon adults and children alike. She who ushers in pain from the power of her fingers and that from her lips.

And the worst part is, I cannot understand how I have arrived here. How I have become the very thing I have hated. For what is worse than not knowing someone else's intentions? I'll tell you:

Not knowing your own.

"There is an old Chinese saying," I begin to murmur. "It's something along the lines of those with white hair should not have to deliver off those with black hair." I swallow. Fire pulses upon my face. "I am . . . so sorry . . . that I have caused such a thing to be your fate."

Her arms wrap firmly around me. Her head rests on my shoulder. I feel it rock to and fro. "This is not your fault, my child."

I stare at the door. I watch him leave again, but this time, he hesitates a moment longer. I still cannot seem to stop him. "He . . . he went outside," I begin to say. "Because of me. Because I told him I hated him and I didn't. I didn't hate him. I lied to him, and it led to his death." I swallow. "I lie more than I would like. And every time, it harms someone."

My mother sighs. "All I wish from you is that you wouldn't blame it on yourself any longer."

And we are silent again, just for a little while. I sit myself down in the seat beside her and stare at the cracks in the wood before us. Until a creak sounds in front of me, and my eyes are on the door, following three men stepping through with faces of melted iron. With drips that slip into the floor. My father is last to enter. Ash sits in all of their black curls. It is collected the greatest upon Elijah's head. A black box sits in his palms, and he places it down on the table in front of us. That is when the chaos arrives.

My mother begins to wail once more. My father buries his head into his hands, and the softest of cries escape him. Sitka sits on the floor with his head planted into his knees, and Elijah stands in the corner, his back leaned against a wall. A single tear rolls down his face, and nothing but the sour taste of desperation encircles the space.

I stare upon the box. My eyes narrow in upon it until everything around me ceases and all I can feel is anger. A new kind of anger. All I know is the way fire burns inside of me, and in a single moment, all of my self-deprecation ceases, and I become so aware of what this means. That I must search to no end for some way to redeem him. That if Elijah knows of a way to destroy Cordellia, I need to be the one to carry it out.

"So what now?" All I can do is stare at the box at the table. To imagine the ash that lies inside and imagine my country turning into such a thing. For it to burn down. "We are all in a shack in the middle of nowhere . . ." My body is shaking. "And we might have a chance to make it out of this alive, but I don't . . . I . . . he should be here. To come with us . . . he should've . . ."

Silence stretches the circumference of the cabin, and I fail to make eye contact with anyone but my brother. Him and his ashes. In the moment of silence, I hear my father's voice.

"We need to keep going." More silence.

"We can get there by tonight." My eyes find Elijah. His gaze lifts from the floor. "Though we'd need to leave soon, and I do not want to pressure you into anything."

"Well we can't stay here," my mother's voice is muffled inside her hands. They slide up her face and to her forehead and press back her curls until she is staring at the table again. "We would be stupid to stay here."

Silence. I take a breath. Then I slap the table.

"Then let's go." I stand suddenly. Look around at each person in the room. All eyes press in upon me, but not a soul moves. "Now. We . . . we need to go now. We can't keep sitting around."

My left hand slips into the pocket of my purple dress. It latches around a chain. I hold it gently. Feel each bead upon it. The necklace Viridian had given me. I had forgotten I had placed it inside this dress.

But I take it now. Take it into my hands and tie it around my neck.

72

Home

I have come to realize that I no longer miss home. I miss comfortability. I miss the smell of my mother's perfume. I miss watching the leaves falling outside of our window each autumn. I miss the sound of my family around our table for dinner, laughing with all that is inside of us. I miss the taste of homemade chai. I miss the feeling of my bedsheets. I miss the smell of candles burning in my bedroom. I miss all that has ever been known to me as comfortability.

Because this world has become so incredibly uncomfortable. One of the only things keeping me at ease had been the voice of my brother. But now all is silent. The walk through the rest of the desert is silent. The sand hears the weight of our footsteps but doesn't dare reply. The red sky sees our hollow eyes and fears to turn them against itself. And with each step, my anger settles in so fully. But I find the strangest thing occurring. For where the anger had once been fueled against myself, it is now against my home, against Cordellia. And it burns ever so brightly.

No one speaks to one another while the sun works its way across the sky and the moon arises. No one speaks for hours. The night grows heavy, and bones grow weary, and my mind is screaming, but it sounds different this time. I can't quite describe how.

Then we stop. Elijah stands on the ridge of a hill, frozen as a pillar of salt and we are lined up behind him. He turns ever so slowly towards us. We stare so solemnly upon him. A smile is tucked into the lines of his face.

"We're here," he says. No one moves.

"Where are we?" my father asks. Elijah looks back out at that which rests before him.

"The Dead Sea." Silence. A wind picks up and pushes through us. My hair brushes across my face. "I'll take one at a time."

"To what?"

Elijah's head swings back over his shoulder. "To the answer." His eyes meet mine. Everyone else follows. My mother holds my older brother's ashes. Her eyes remain drenched in tears. My father's gaze is feeble and seems to fall into the sand. Sitka stares at me with the faintest glimpse of hope in his eyes, and so I look back up at Elijah.

"You guys go first," my mouth is dry when I speak. "Please." A pause. Elijah's eyes find my mother, and then she follows him. They disappear behind the ridge. I sit down upon a stone. The three of us who remain don't share a word.

Many minutes pass. I stare at the moon. It stares back. This time, it doesn't condemn.

Elijah arrives back without my mother. He motions for my father to follow him. He does.

Then it is simply Sitka and I. Me and my brother. The world is still. The air is silent. The patches of weeds move just the faintest bit against the wind. Sitka sits down beside me, running the sand through his fingers. His eyes raise up to the sky until I am sure that we are staring at the same constellation.

"Viridian liked to look at the stars," I swallow through my words. Sitka's gaze slowly shifts to me. I study the scarcity of his smile.

"Are we talking about the same Viridian?"

I am able to release a laugh. "Yes." My eyes move to the moon again. "He told me about it the night before my birthday. We stared at the stars on the roof of that old woman's home in Israel. It was like when we were little, when you were a baby, and we would sneak onto the roof and stare at the stars. He

taught me about the constellations, but I always cared more about the moon."
I shake my head. "I thought he stopped looking at the stars as he got older.
But I guess that's something that no one can truly quit." There's a moment of
silence. I can hear the rippling of water below.

"He had more of a heart than he gave off."

I nod. "Yes." My left hand wraps tightly around my necklace.

We sit for a long while as night waits its turn to shift again into day. Soon
enough, Sitka speaks. "What do you think is down there?"

I shrug. My eyes find him. "Are you afraid?"

"Hardly."

"But a little bit."

"Of course, a little bit." He laughs. "I'm not a robot."

I wrap my arm around my brother and pull him in towards me. He leans
his head into my shoulder. And for just a while, I am holding him. Holding
him so that he won't slip away from me. Then Elijah appears above us. Sitka
stands and follows him.

Then, I am alone. But I do not feel lonely. For I am only aware of my anger. I wonder if I will ever reap anything else than this feeling, but for now, I
don't seem to care.

Elijah appears for the final time. Our eyes meet. Energy pulses through
my bones. Then, he nods. So I stand and follow him down to the water.

I stand on the edge of the sea. I stare at the black water reaching for my
bare feet. Elijah stands beside me. I listen to his breathing. Wait for my mind
to create words to say unto him.

"I'm sorry," the phrase limps off my tongue. "For getting angry with you
beside the pond." I look down at the purple fabric upon me. "And for ripping
your dress."

He looks over at me. A smile rests on his cheeks. "I wasn't going to wear
it anyway." I giggle. He does too.

"I was just confused . . . I still am. And I was angry." My hands press into
each other. They squeeze one another, and my teeth press into each other.

Then, I sigh. "I think I've been too hard on myself. When I saw my mother mourn for him, I hated myself for what I had done. But when I saw his ashes . . . I knew there was no way I had done . . . *that*."

Elijah nods. I look up at the moon, where his eyes already rest. I wait for him to speak, but he doesn't, and so I continue on.

"This whole time . . . I have put so much pressure on myself to do everything right. But this whole time, I . . . I've only been a child. And I've been thrown into this awful world that I don't understand, and I act as though I have chosen to be ignorant when really . . . there are things that are genuinely a mystery to me." I swallow. "You know, it is so easy for me to tell myself that I am a terrible person, but . . . but I'm deciding not to anymore."

"Good." He looks down at me. I find his eyes. There is kindness inside of them. "That is good."

The water rocks back and forth. I see the river in it; I see our car sinking. I see the tsunami building and crashing and ripping me apart. I see my father bleeding out on that table. I see the last time I ever cried. I see my gun pierce an AI, and I watch it crash into the ground. I see the Qadim erupt and I see my brother tumble into the sand.

And I see Cordellia. I see my home up in flames, and I see myself standing beside it. And I am not afraid, but there is a smile upon my face, ever so faintly.

"Somehow . . . I don't know how, but somehow." I shake my head slowly as I speak. "Even if it's on my way off this planet . . ." My head turns to Elijah. "These beings that have done this to him. I want to destroy them."

Elijah stares at me. He stares at me for a long while, but my eyes do not fall away from him. Then he nods. Once. A smile slides up his face.

"Well, let's get you to a place where you can do that."

I nod. Then I turn back to the water and watch it wave. "What do you want me to do?"

"This is going to seem strange," Elijah begins. He wrings out his hands between each other. "I need you to turn your back towards the sea and let gravity pull you in." Silence stretches between us. I repeat his words over again in my head. Once. Twice. A third time. Then, my head shakes.

"I'm sorry, what now?"

He shifts his stance. "I know it sounds strange—"

"You want me to fall backward into the water . . . ?"

"Yes." I look at him now. Stare. Sense all of the muscles in my face lift and squeeze together at the same time. My hands crumple into fists.

"Elijah, you need to explain this to me."

Then he says the most frightening of phrases. He says it while looking me dead in the eye as though he knows so deeply inside his soul what such words mean to me. His gaze grows. His lips part ever so slightly. Then, he speaks. "Do you trust me?"

I stare. Stare at him. Stare at his lips as they roll off of them. Stare at the softness of his cheeks painted lightly red at the tips. And suddenly, I am nodding. Somehow, I mean it.

"Yes," I say.

A single second passes. Then, I am moving towards the water. I wade into the soft rocking of the waves. Liquid rises to my knees. It is warm but not quite hot. My dress forms a purple circle around the water. Then my back is turning, and I am facing Elijah. He smiles at me so delicately. Smiles like a father staring at his child. Smiles like a friend holding all of my fragile thoughts so gently. So I smile back at him.

"I'll be right here when you wake up," he says. I nod and stare for a moment longer. And then I am leaning backward. Watching his words dance across my mind as my eyes fall to the sky. Watching the essence of a promise collide with my mind,

right when I collide with the water,

and it consumes me,

wrapping its arms around my eyes and my body. Clenching me like a lover. Suffocating me like a foe. For the water has always been both to me. And I am sinking. Slipping away into a chasm. A canyon deeper than what eyes know to see. I am being wrapped up in ropes and pinned to the ground. I am being burned alive. And then searing fear shines lasers upon my bones. Panic grabs me and snags strands of my hair.

Then, I see the tsunami crash down upon me. Feel the shards of glass slice my arms as I punch through a window. And it is all too much in a matter of a moment.

I try to move. But I cannot.

I try to scream. But nothing comes.

My bones are tied to a chair. My arms are held hostage. My legs are victims to this idleness and I am looking at all of my limbs and shaking them with my mind. They fail to give a reply. Paranoia consumes me. Terror of Elijah's villainy.

He's trying to kill me.

Elijah is good.

He wants me dead.

Then I see the moon above me. It is still. It vibrates the slightest bit under the waving of the water. Its shade is deeper beneath the darkness of the sea. It seems to fade the longer I look at it. It fades ever so slowly. I stare. Harder. I stare. Longer. Tension releases from my bones, and I stare.

And it fades.

And I stare.

Falling . . .

Fading . . .

Black.

The Vision

I see the face of my father. Darkness surrounds him. He is illuminated by a single light. The moon. It sits there above him, brighter than I have ever seen it before. He searches for something in the darkness. His skin is pulled firmly across his face. His eyes search frantically. *Perû.* I call to him in my mind. *Perû.* My mouth won't open. My lips won't speak.

His eyes fall upon me. Emotion ceases from his face. He stares at me. Stares at me so plainly, and I try to narrow my eyes, but my face won't move.

"Who is she?" he speaks now. I continue to stare.

Another figure appears to the left of him. His hands are tied behind his back, and a soft smile is painted upon his lips. Elijah. He looks at me too. Stares. They are talking about me.

"Where did she come from?" my father continues on.

Perû, it's me. Your daughter. You know me.

Elijah takes one good look at me. Nods.

"This is one of the ones emerging from the chaos," Elijah replies. He turns towards my father, watching his eyes as he speaks to him. "She is being cleansed now. She is before me, and I will protect her. She won't be hungry or thirsty any longer. The sun's heat will no longer burn her. I will guide her to water, and I will wipe the tears from her eyes."

They watch me for a long moment. Their smiles grow across their faces.

And soon they are gone,

darkness taking their place.

405

Cold

I burst through the water. Snap through the ropes. Break through the glass that has molded around my body and suffocated me. My knees gouge the sand. My eyes burn with unquenchable flames. My hands dig into grains, and I feel them slip beneath my grasp. I am coughing and choking and expelling every ounce of breath from within my lungs. My eyes are stuck shut. The image is stuck in my mind.

My father. Elijah.

Hands are held upon my shoulders. They press me into the earth. My eyes launch up towards Elijah, and I find his hazel gaze stamped in on me.

"What was that?" I choke. Stare at the sand laced in my hands. Chills leap up my bones, and for a moment, my skin aches for warmth. For the cold has consumed me. Cold.

I am cold.

How.

How am I cold.

Elijah begins to speak, "That water. It was designed for—"

"No. That vision. What was that?" He takes a look at me. Smiles. And then he pulls away and approaches the sea. I follow his body and his hands as they rotate around the water as though something dwells inside.

"Yes, having visions is a common side effect," he says.

"Side effect for what? What did you do to me?" I turn my torso towards him now. His hands brush over the surface of the waves. And then, they clench something. He stares at his palm for a moment too long. Then, he returns to me.

"See this?" He holds an object up in his hand, the size of a grain of rice. "This was inside of you." *Herr Krüger.*

I sigh, "I know. We um . . . we paid this man in Germany to give us identification to . . . to board the Qadim." Elijah shakes his head. Then he reveals an object in his other hand.

"That's this one." I stare at him. Stare at his hands. My eyes jump from one to the other. From his brown fingers so tightly holding two separate objects. Two. Two chips. One in his left hand, one in his right. My eyes begin to flutter. My jaw rolls into the sand.

"I'm sorry, what?" His eyes lift to the sky across the sea, and my body spins to meet it. There, I find the sun melting into the clouds. I watch the world on the eve of morning. I stare upon the cast of crimson and chrome across the darkness.

But the longer I look, the greater I notice something so apparently different. So inexplicably strange. For a moment, I wonder if I have just gone plain mad. For the black hole. It isn't there.

"This chip was connected to the visual cortex of your brain." Elijah sits beside me. My wide eyes jump at him. He places the chip into my left palm, and I stare at the daunting thing. It looks similar to a tree, with a wide black surface leading up to a mess of wires all crumbled into a ball. "It has been there since birth. Its implementation is required by international law, not voted on by the people but implemented by members of the state in all European countries. It has the ability to manipulate what is seen by the eye and mimics sensations in the nervous system, such as extreme heat. I found a way to extract it from brains by embedding this water with nanoparticles made to eradicate anything of its sort." There is a long pause. I stare at the object.

My eyes jump up to Elijah. "What are you saying to me?" But I know what he is saying. "Are you saying that everything that happened to me was . . . was *fake?*" He stares for a moment, adjusting his posture so his knees are pulled up to his chest.

"Most of it was not. Most of it was real, just inaccurately represented." My body shakes. My hands begin to sweat into the wet fabric of my dress. He continues on, "However, the black hole is a hoax. This is true."

Heat courses through my veins, "No," I stand in an instant. "No, what do you mean? It was right . . . right . . . there." I point at the sky. Point at where such darkness no longer rests.

Elijah stands slowly, "But it isn't there now, is it?" I stare into his eyes. Stare at the words that are wedged inside his pupils and try to read them. Stare as though it will hold back the waves, hold back all of the memories from exploding across my mind, but they do anyway. Then, the screaming begins. The insanity ignites inside of me, and my eyes look back at the sun in all of its solitude.

"W-why . . ." I choke on words that never fully come.

"Aetheria, do you recall when you had first asked me who I was? What my response had been back to you?" I think. Think back through every idea, every thought, every fear that has consumed me all of these days until I find myself upon a train car, staring in terror at Elijah's words on my screen.

"Yes," Something forms in my throat. "You . . . you said to me that . . . that I believed I was destined to die. And I did. I did believe that."

He nods. "This device. It cannot plant thoughts into your mind. It cannot change your beliefs, but it has the ability to mimic the nerve patterns of someone who believes a certain principle in order to hope that you come to believe it too." He inhales. Holds his breath until he continues on, "That is what this belief was. Once the black hole appeared, this chip mimicked the nerve patterns of one who believed they were destined to die in order to cause less people to fight for survival. And you, being Cordellian, have had sensations planted into your body for as long as you have been living in order to maintain control. Such as pacifism."

"This is a Cordellian invention," I say it as a statement. He nods in agreement. "But it affected everyone?"

"All of Europe."

I shake my head. "Then . . . then was I ever actually going to die?"

"Oh yes. You were being burned alive, Aetheria, from the inside out. That chip was on its way to killing you."

It is as though something rolls through my bones. As though water drip, drip, drips down my spine and to my feet, and then it freezes. Because for a moment, I cannot seem to move. I cannot seem to think. I cannot seem to do anything but stare at Elijah and clench this chip inside my fist with such ferocity that I hardly feel as though I am holding it.

Then, I shake my head ever so slowly, "Who would be so wicked to do this?"

Elijah nods. Then, he motions for me to sit back beside him in the sand. I hesitate. Then I follow.

"It was put in place by Apgar Cordell at the founding of the nation," he says. I simply stare at the object inside my palm. "He was bought out by his desire for power, but he recognized that facism, communism, all these means of control are unable to be maintained for long periods of time. That the people always find a way to rise up. So what better way to make people cooperate than to make them believe that they are truly the ones in power?"

And we were the ones in power in Cordellia. We most truly believed that we were. For no one had been so plainly above us, and AI beings had been there simply to aid us. But everyone agreed on everything, and so nothing was questioned. That. That was control.

"Who runs it now?" I look up at Elijah. "Cordell is dead. That was over 100 years ago."

Elijah looks out across the water. "We call them The Big Seven."

"The Big Seven?"

He nods. "They control different parts of the operation. Which ultimately led to The Chaos Order." I hear the sovereignty in which he says the phrase. I hear the undertone of anger behind such ambiguous words. And so I ask my question quietly as though it will make it mean less.

"What is that?"

That is when Elijah sighs and shakes his head ever so slightly. His hands run against his temples and through his hair, and I stare at him in intrigue. "There may not be a man in history more corrupted by power than Apgar Cordell. I will never truly understand his motives, but . . ." He looks up at the sky. Stares at the sun for just a moment. "He created The Chaos Order in the initial design of these chips. It was only a matter of time until ninety-three percent of the population was under their influence. Then, The Big Seven would initiate The Order. That is, when the black hole would appear, and that world would slowly burn, or so it would appear. So that the continent would be consumed by fear, because it is fear that controls the mind of man."

I lean back the slightest bit. Stare uncertainly upon the water, "And the other seven percent?"

"Those . . ." He swallows, "Those are then left for The Seven to have dominion."

A tidal wave crushes down upon me. Breath runs away and I stare at the waves, watching them shake. Staring at the night, watching it fade into morning. My stomach aches. My throat grows dry and heavy, and my left hand finds my right and begins to pick at the skin around my nails.

"This is . . . this is really bad. Elijah, this is . . ." My eyes jump at him. "Can you even solve this big of a problem?"

I am shocked to watch his lips change to a grin. "They cannot track the chips, Aetheria. Only I can. Their way of finding runaways is by word of mouth alone."

"Then you already won. You can free everyone, right?"

"I suppose so." His fist is against his mouth, and I watch his mind tinker with something. Then it resolves. Then he looks back down at me. "This is where I ask you questions." A lump forms in my throat. I swallow. "Aetheria, when you left Herr Krüger that day in Germany, did you tell him where you were headed next?"

I search my mind for the memory. Find it. Look upon it closely, "Yes I

... I guess we did." And then I look upon where we traveled next. Salzburg. I gasp.

The hunters. Our car colliding with the river.

"And Wèvii Soddom," Elijah continues. "Did you tell him you were headed to Varna?"

"Yes," I freeze. "The tsunami." Elijah nods in the most solemn of manners. My chest shatters. "Oh my gosh, that town was destroyed because . . . because . . ."

"Because you were not meant to find me. Because *anybody* finding out the truth is bad for The Big Seven. But a Cordellian, who has been programmed for years, coming to realize all that they have been programmed to believe? That is lethal."

I nod ever so slowly. My gaze slowly lifts to him. "Do they know who you are, Elijah?"

He breaths in, holds his breath, failing to release it until he speaks.

"I do not know. As far as I am aware, all they know is that something is wrong. That there is a mole in the system, and they cannot finish The Order until it is found. And me, I am not finished with my own mission until all are set free."

75

Figments Of Light

He leads me down the beach. Down the sand to where my family stands, huddled around a wooden bench. My mother sits with her forehead in her palms and with tears streaming down her cheeks. My father rubs the back of her head. Sitka stands still.

Every eye meets mine in a matter of a moment. Their gazes soften, their distress weakens, and their lips shape the slightest bit into smiles. And for a moment, I expect to see Viridian. For a moment, I believe that he never truly died, that such a thing, too, was a lie. But the world is silent once I come upon them, and that tells me enough.

Instead, the black box sits beside my mother on the bench. I take a long look at it. Then, my body goes numb.

And then, the living finds me. They throw their arms around me, and their tears chemically react with the dryness of my cheeks. My eyes remain wide open, staring at the shoulder of my younger brother before me, and the numbness subsides. Then, my whole body aches, but at least I know the aching is real.

And once my parents pull away, Sitka remains, just for a moment. He holds me so tight, and I let him do so, and I sink into his embrace, for it is the only thing I know to do with such affection. His teardrop hits my neck. It is cold against my skin.

"Do you believe it?" he mumbles into the fabric of my shoulder. I stare at the sand behind him. I watch the wind pick up grains and throw them away, and I feel it brush past my bare legs. Small bumps grow upon my skin.

"I don't see a black hole," is all I can say in reply. I feel him nod beneath me. Then, he pulls away.

Elijah stands behind us. His hands are cupped in front of his torso. His eyes are solemn but soft. His cheeks lift and paint themselves the shade of cherries. Then he releases a breath. I do too.

"There is a boat down the way," he speaks ever so softly. "It will take us across the sea."

"What is over there?" my father's voice is tainted by tears.

Elijah's eyes lift into the slightest of smiles. "Everything." His arm stretches out towards the waves. "Everything that is left to be explained."

The boat is inside a wooden shed. Elijah pulls it out by the bow, and my father is there for his aid. The metal rests the slightest bit in the sea when we board. Then, he pushes us out.

We pass slowly through the water. Elijah sits with an ore upon the bow and rolls the silk-lined waves against us. They encircle and dance around our movement to the sound of an unsung song. Sparks of light jump up and down upon the tips of the sea, and I see vibrations roll down toward the bottom of the pool. It is the most beautiful of displays.

And I look upon the sun. I watch the world on the eve of morning, on the eve of something new. Something before unseen. A revelation irrevocable once it has come. And here, it has come. Day meets the sky in rolling colors. Clouds are painted pink and white. The air tastes of candy, and the wind rolls past me as the rolling of thunder. The world is quiet. No one speaks. My mind is still for just a little while.

Sitka sits beside me. Time slips by, and soon he slides himself towards me, and I am holding him with both arms. His body presses into my side, and his head rests upon my shoulder, and I rub the black curls upon his head. For a long while, I simply cradle him, cradle him like a child. Cradle him as though he will slip away, and I suppose I fear he will. I feel his breathing. I feel it rise up and down, and I try to follow along. I feel his heart beating on my chest, and I hope for it to never stop. I close my eyes. I hold onto the warmth of his body in the cool of the morning. I hold onto his head as though it is my lifeline.

I see darkness beneath my sealed eyes. I see lights dancing around and shooting into oblivion, and I see figments of color erupting into nothingness. And I see Viridian. I see the green of his eyes glowing, and I stare upon them for just a little while, if only to make them real. Then, anger consumes me and I see Cordellia in my mind. I watch fire fall upon it.

My eyes open. Look out across the water, then down to my brother. His lips are pulled into his mouth, and his eyes are sealed shut.

"Are you okay?" the whisper rolls off my lips just loud enough for Sitka to hear. There is quiet for a moment.

His head leans up to look at me. "Yes. Are you?"

I nod in reply. Light continues to leap across the tops of the waves. I wonder for a moment if it is from the technology embedded into them.

"Are you scared?" I ask. There is a pause. Then he speaks.

"Of what?"

I shrug. "I don't know. I just feel like I should be scared." His chest rises up and down. Up and down.

"Are you?" he asks.

I shake my head. "No. Not right now. Just angry." The shore rolls closer. A small village sits on the coast, and beyond it lie mountains, the lowest of mountains. The clouds roll away to reveal a blue sky. I had forgotten how such a thing looked. How beautiful the world is when it is truthful.

"I am," Sitka mumbles. I look down at him. His eyes lift towards me. "I am scared." I think about asking more, but I don't. "I don't want to be. I don't really even know why I am. I just . . ." He pauses. Looks down upon his knees, "It's the unknown, I guess."

I nod. "It will become known. In time."

"Yeah."

The breeze picks up ever so lightly. It carries grains of sand and splashes of water upon my face. I try to feel it, but I cannot quite tell if I do. Then, I shake my head ever so slowly.

"We're going to destroy them, Sitka. The Big Seven. We're going to destroy them for what they did to him."

The boat washes up upon the shore beside an abandoned shopping mall. My father gives me a hand off the vessel, and I help anchor it to shore. Elijah leads us through a maze of buildings, and I am staring upon them as though they will topple over. He leads us across an abandoned highway, and on the other side, we are met by a stone wall and a silver door. Windows line the sandstone, and I look them up and down as though I will find a way to peer in. I don't. And so I approach the door on Elijah's heels. It is small. Too small for the extravagance I expect on the other side. He places his hand on the metal. It glows blue around his fingers. He turns back to look towards us, and all he does is smile.

76

Tawila

We step inside.

The air is crisp when it meets us. It smells of frankincense and cinnamon and swirls around my nostrils as though a wisp of smoke. My eyes open wide and stretch out towards the high stretched stone walls far off with the most exquisite of carvings. They swoop in patterns like that of Van Gough, like flowers on stems, like the stars of the Milky Way. There is a staircase to my left. It is carved from the same orange stone, rolling up into the unknown above. The space is wide in each direction, beyond what I can see. People of every ethnicity wander around the area in the most apparent amity. They sit upon sage-colored cushioned benches around stone pillars. They laugh and smile, and for a moment, I feel the deepest nostalgia at such a sight.

There are metal tables around the area. They are painted the same shade of green as the benches, and people eat off of trays of food. Trays so colorful, so whimsical, so bright that they have not been seen since before The Chaos Order arrived.

"There's so many people," I mumble. Elijah stands beside me. He looks down at my eyes.

"And there are more to come."

He leads us into the crowd. Faces grin and wave at Elijah as he passes. He says hello to them each by name. There are people of all ages. Women with gray locks pinned upon their heads and walkers locked in their hands. Young men with that unfazed, unaltered innocent gleam in their crystal eyes. Children stand with their mothers, playing with their hands and sitting out upon the cobblestone flooring, tracing the lines.

Every now and then, someone will catch my eye. Someone will look so closely upon my torn purple dress. Stare a bit too closely at my matted hair as though they have seen it before. I watch their gazes shift. They grow and shrink at the sight of me, and my palms begin to water into one another. I look down at my boots.

"What is this place?" my mother asks Elijah.

"Tawila." He looks back at her. His expression is calm. "This is where I was planted in order to exterminate the evil we are seeing. Everything that I do—that we do—it comes from here."

There is a doorway on the right. Elijah points towards it with his palm facing up. "That is the cafeteria. Everyone living at Tawila who is capable has a facility job. Some choose to be chefs. We grow all of our own food in a room downstairs. The Big Seven released toxins into the air in order to make it difficult to grow vegetation in a traditional outdoor manner. So our farmers do everything below ground."

He leads us past the cafeteria towards the end of the communal space right before the stone wall. There is a second doorway on the right. Elijah stops before it.

"This is what I want to show you," he says.

He leads us inside a room full of screens. Pictures float across each of them, passport photos of different people. Control tables sit beneath each of the screens, and office chairs rest below them. There are a few people in the room reading bullet points of writing beside photos. There is a large screen in the center of the room. Three people rotate between it; a blond man in his mid-twenties, a long black-haired woman in her forties, and a curly-haired blond boy.

"Who are these people?" I ask. Elijah turns to face us.

"These are the ones we are currently working to bring here. We call this place the mission room. I identify people in need, create a file on them and send it down to this room. From there, we come here to identify who is in need and then go out and find them."

My mother tilts his head in the slightest bit. "You mean, you're not the only one who brings people here?"

Elijah shakes his head. "I most certainly am not. Everyone in this facility who feels fit to do so is sent out to retrieve runaways. In most cases, they use instant transportation devices." He looks over at me now. "The reason I neglected to take such an action with you is because runaway Cordellians are followed very closely. Whenever an instant transportation device is used, there is a flash in the electrical currents, which are able to be tracked by The Big Seven. If I had transported to you, it would have put you all in grave danger, as well as everything happening at Tawila."

I look down at my feet. I stare at my laces for a moment and lace together his words in my mind. Numbness sweeps over my being.

"The people at the top of the retrieval list are on this larger screen." He points towards the blond boy whose face is there now. I look up to find Elijah already looking at me. "You were on that screen for a long time. Which is why you are getting stares."

My eyes narrow. "What? I was?"

Elijah nods. "The ones on this screen are typically the ones I am personally on mission to retrieve. The most unique of cases."

"So you . . ." My mother's eyes jump back and forth around her head. I look over at her. My eyes find the black box in her hands. Something catches in my throat. Energy jumps back and forth across my head. My hands turn to fists at my side, "You run . . . all of this? How did you . . . how did you even know about The Chaos Order? I . . ."

Elijah smiles. I stare into his eyes for a moment. I watch him retrace days gone by, and for a moment, I am desperate to know his past life. "There was a man," he begins. "He worked very closely with Cordell just before the time of his rebellion against the French state. He was fearful of what Cordell would do with these chips and inserted a tracking protocol in them that only he had access to. That Cordell could not undo, or else it would void every other feature of the chip. He created it as a power source, almost. It's difficult to explain." Elijah takes a breath. Something shoots around in his mind. I watch his eyes closely. "This man knew my kin very well. Confided in them. He passed the tracking protocol onto them when he passed away, and it was soon given to me when the time came."

"You've known about this your whole life," I say as a statement.

Elijah nods. "And I have spent my whole life working to figure out how to extract these devices from everyone under their influence."

There is quiet for just a moment. A million thoughts fight to free themselves into my mind, and yet I hold them hostage inside a cage of my undying confusion. Of my paralysis. For no one can truly be this evil. I cannot bring myself to believe such a thing. And yet, I have seen it all play out plainly before me.

Denial is a confusing thing. It is a parasite. It creeps inside a person when they are made vulnerable, when they are near to collapse. And when strength is regained, it eats away at it. It feeds off of insanity. Feeds off of that which cannot be understood by the knowledge planted and grown in our minds. And soon, there is no way to fight it off.

So I stand in denial for a moment. I stare at the screens and watch them jump between the faces of people in captivity. My eyes fall to the box my brother rests inside; the cage. And anger crawls up my bones. Because he deserves to be here. But I see him fall upon the sand once more. I see blood on his lips. I hear his final words to me: "I'm sorry."

Then, the screaming fills my mind once more. Every single ounce of strength inside of me fights it off, for maybe it will bring him back to life, and so I ignore the impending pain that it will not. Elijah pulls up a graphic on the large screen. On one side, there is a chart of the chip, with words written around it in a foreign text. On the other sits an image of a human brain, the chip resting in the very back of it. He begins to speak about the chip. I can hardly hear him.

"The chip is implanted into the visual cortex, creating the manipulation of what is seen. However these blue wires across the front of the chip—" his points back to the first diagram "—connect to nerve endings in order to formulate false sensations throughout the body."

And then, I am tuning him out almost entirely.

"Originally designed as an anecdote to severe mental health . . ." *My brother.* ". . . designed to make the world appear brighter to shift negative thought . . ." *He's alive. He has to be alive.* ". . . designed to imitate sensations in the nervous system associated with specific emotions . . ." *I kept him alive. I wouldn't let him die.* "An anarchist country such as Cordellia would copy the nervous patterns of a very peaceful individual . . ."

Cordellia.

My eyes find Elijah. He is looking at the screen, pointing at something. "Naturally, people react differently to these nerve patterns than others, leading some to be more pacifist than others." Elijah glances over at Sitka. "Leading some to ask questions that others would never ask."

My eyes shoot over at my brother. He is standing so still. Staring so closely at Elijah. Then Sitka's eyes shift to me, and I am staring into the brown inside of them. The strength and the fragility that has evolved over time. There is a silent conversation between the two of us. A conversation where I ask him what he knows. Where he says he will tell me later.

Something catches my eye beyond him.

There is a collection of smaller screens in the corner behind his body, and a face stares up at me. A face I know. A girl. She is no more than ten. Her black hair is tucked behind her ears, and her blue eyes pierce something still alive in my soul.

"Who is that?" I blurt out. I continue to stare at her when Elijah answers.

"Those screens host images of individuals we have identified that are not under the influence of these devices. There are fewer of them because they are harder to identify, given they cannot be tracked."

"No. That girl. I saw that girl." I run over to the screen. "She was in Hungary. I saw her." I sit down at the chair in front of it. Use the controller to select her image. Then, a long bullet-point list of information appears before my eyes:

NAME: Elizabeth Juga

AGE: 9

LOCATION: Budapest, Hungary

L'ARBRE STATUS: N/A

"What is 'l'arbre'?" I look back at Elijah.

"That is what Cordell named the chips."

I nod. Continue to stare at her face. There is silence in the room. Her eyes stare at me with such despair. With an endless longing for removal from those streets of Hungary. My heart pumps in every inch of my body. My eyes hope to fill with the same tears I once cried for her, but they never do. Such passion overtakes me that seems so closely related to anger. It is remarkable how often the two coincide.

"I want her." I look behind me. My father's eyebrows are tilted ever so much inward. Sitka holds his hands in his pockets, his eyes dancing around between me and the screens. Compassion is flooded through my mother's eyes. And then I see Elijah. He stands just a bit taller. He looks at me with just the slightest bit more pride. Then, I see him smile.

"I want to save her," I say.

[77]

Anikate

Her face remains locked in my eyes. Elijah leads us across the hall to another room. But I don't see my surroundings; I only see her, just for a moment. Then my gaze falls upon the archway. It is carved from the finest tangerine stone, rolling and swooping up to the ceiling and opening into a sanctuary. I step inside and stare at the room, filled to the brim with books. They are planted upon marble shelves, resting open on tables, sitting beside cushioned reading corners.

A softness comes over my mind. A gentleness I have lost in substituting anger. My eyes gleam upon the sight of such lovely things, and soon, my hands fall from where they have become fists.

"You all are welcome in this room at any time," he says. His hands extend outward to model the majesty of such a space. "When I can, I try to collect any books that I am able to get my hands on. Especially those that have been banned in Cordellia. Maintaining knowledge is important so that it is not lost to time or to modern ideas as it so easily can be."

I step out further into the room. My hand finds a shelf, and my fingertips run over the spines of novels. My heart races with the greatest joy I have experienced in ages, so much that it nearly feels selfish. My hand wraps around a larger work, and I remove it from where it rests upon stone. It is a novel I had loved once, long ago. A story of a different planet, a different time. Of a girl fighting the evil powers that lie there, so far into the future. I tuck the book under my arm.

Sitka stands a bit down the way. He is hunched over a textbook open upon a wooden stand. I approach him. His fingers rest upon a page with the most exquisite flower. The red is so bright that I almost feel as though it is truly before me. The petals roll around the center in the most unique of patterns, in the way that waves roll around a vessel. The beauty of such a thing hypnotizes me as beauty often does.

"What is that?" I mumble.

Sitka doesn't move in the slightest. "A rose."

"Where are they from?"

He looks up at me at that. "Everywhere. They used to be in Cordellia. But they evolved to . . . to produce this poison on their thorns. Anikate, they call it. It is able to deactivate AI beings and is also incredibly deadly for humans. So they eradicated it and never spoke of it again."

"How do you know this?"

His eyes look back down at the book, "Because I was poisoned by it once."

My heart lurches forward. "What?"

The room is simply still for a moment. I hear the faint whispers of my parents and Elijah across the way. Sitka continues to stare at the image. To find strength upon the page to say more. Then, he speaks.

"Remember when I ended up in the hospital a year or so ago?" I nod. "My hand got cut on an anikate-infused blade. It was Corbyn's. I got really sick. Almost died. He refused to tell me anything for the longest time until I forced him to. That was when I learned about everything."

"How much did you know?" I let the words slide off my tongue so delicately, so deliberately. His hands sit restfully in his pockets, his brown eyes fixed on the book before us.

"About this?" He extends his hands outward. I nod. "Nothing."

"What did you know?" His stance shifts, his left leg turning towards the stand, his lips sliding up the side of his cheek.

"Really, just everything I told you. I knew that something was off about Cordellia, especially with their AI." He looks at me now. "And that I needed to be prepared for something to happen. Never did I think it would be . . . this." His voice lowers on that last word. I almost wonder if he is upset with himself that he was unable to unravel it on his own. "I mean, there were qualities of the black hole that didn't make sense, but that doesn't mean . . ." He sighs. "That didn't make me . . . not believe it."

I look down at my feet. Stare at the thin gray carpet that rests beneath them. Something aches inside of me, but I can't quite tell what.

"I knew there was some newer technology that we weren't told about," he continues on. "Anti-matter blasts, mind reading . . . possibly immortality."

"Immortality?" I look up at him.

He nods. "There was talk that it had been around for a while but kept a secret."

"Do you believe it?"

"At this rate, yeah. It's probably true. My history teacher last year, Mr. Klerii?"

"Yes, I had him too."

"Right, do you remember that he was able to stay alive for . . . honestly way too long because of this . . . I don't know, this metal plate on his chest?" I think about the man. I see the plate in my mind. And then I nod. "So it really would only make sense that there is technology to eliminate death altogether."

"I suppose so." I don't really mean it when it leaves my lips.

We leave the library a few moments later. Elijah leads us back down to the old shopping mall and inside one of the buildings. People walk around through indoor walkways carved of stone. A few stare at me. I tell myself not to mind. Elijah shows us to an old store that has been converted into an apartment. The living area is encircled with that same orange stone. A red couch rests in the corner, and a kitchen lies across the wall. Behind it is a large bed with maroon sheets. A grand window looks out upon the sea. I stare at the residue of the rising sun.

"If you choose to stay at Tawila, this is where you will be staying," Elijah says.

"Where else would we go . . ." my father mumbles.

There are two doors behind the red bed; a bedroom and a bathroom. I spot a stone staircase leading to a loft. It runs alongside the bed, and in a moment, I am enslaved to curiosity. I stumble towards it. There is a wooden railing to the left of me, lining the area. The bed beside it is large and covered in navy sheets. The brown desk in the corner is stacked with paper and pens, and a few books on the shelf beside it. I release my lips from where they are pulled tightly into my mouth. My left hand places the book in my palm on the bed.

There is a closet in the corner. I approach and open it. There is a large row of clothing lined up by color. Dresses and jeans and T-shirts, all my size. My eyes grow weak. My jaw slips down my face and into the cement floor.

There is movement behind. I turn to see Elijah standing with his hands held behind his back, and I stare at his solemn face. My body is full of the truest anger and yet the most genuine humility. I nod my head slowly as I stare at him.

"You knew I was coming," I say. "You never doubted it for a second."

He simply nods in reply.

[78]

The Girl By The Water

I stand by the sea. For it is the only place I can feel something other than rage. My hair is washed out and rested stoically upon my head. A white dress holds my body. It lays just off the shoulders and swoops down to my bare feet. The fabric blows against the wind, and I close my eyes. I feel the sand launch itself across my cheeks. I feel the water set ablaze upon my forehead.

I remember the song Darbii and I had sung together that night on the roof in Serbia. The lyrics of the bridge arrive in my mind, and so I mumble them to myself:

"But it was you, it was you all along
In joys of summer, you were the greatest con
It was you, it was you all along
Daylight came, but your smile, it had gone."

And I try to cry. For the first time in so long, I very truly try. I squeeze my face together and squeeze out whatever moisture rests behind my eyes, but nothing comes. So my hands grow to fists at my side, and my eyes shoot open. A scream rolls off my lips, for an undying wrath boils inside my bloodstream.

And then I wrap my hand around the necklace upon my neck. I hold it as though I am holding the hand of the one who gave it to me. Clench it the way I should have clenched him that night.

426

I close my eyes once more. Search for the rain behind them a second time, but I only see him. His green eyes and his blond curls, and I see him smile at me. I try to smile back, but I cannot. For he will never know what I know. Never see the world as I see it. Never understand that this was all just a hoax, and he died stuck inside of it. I see him bleed again. I see the red on his lips, and this time, I wipe it away and replace it with a smile. The smile fades fast.

A presence emerges beside me. I expect it to be him, but I open my eyes, and it is not. A chill rushes through my bones. Elijah stands with his hands behind his back as he always does. His curls roll against the wind. His eyes meet the sea, and mine follow him. He breathes in and out. I match the manner of his breaths. My anger slowly subsides.

Then his hand motions out to me. I look down to see an apple resting in his palm. My gaze meets his eyes, and I smile at him. He smiles back. I take the apple and take a bite.

"Is there any way," I shake my head slowly as I speak. "Is there really any way I can ever repay you?" The breeze brushes past his hair. He takes a breath.

"I don't need you to repay me."

I look back out at the water. Look out at the sky. I take another bite of the apple and force myself to swallow it. Silence reigns as a friend.

"I really do want to destroy them."

"I know," he mumbles.

"He should've been able to see this. That the world is okay . . . he . . ." I shake my head. Look down at my bare feet. Feel the sand beneath them. "His favorite season was winter." I smile. "He liked to be cold. Winter will be back soon. And he won't be here."

"I put four beds in that house for your family," he says with a crack in his voice. He says nothing else. My eyes shut to scare away the insanity from creeping in. It doesn't come this time.

So I lift my head, and my gaze scans the beach. A girl sits down along the water, the waves washing over her feet. I stare at her and wonder about the familiarity in her posture.

I look up at Elijah. "Who is that?"

He follows my gaze down to her. Smiles, "Why don't you go see?"

So I approach the girl by the water. She sits with such peace, staring out across the mild waves. And once she hears my footsteps, her neck springs up towards me.

That is when my heart freezes. Drops. Shatters at the sight of her, and I am staring. Staring at her brown locks combed out so daintily. At her green eyes, bright like that of the splendid sun. Stare at the spot below them where bags once were, ironed out into an unwrinkled cream blouse, reaching down towards her mouth and lifting at the corners of her lips.

I stand shaking. Trying to decipher through dreams and reality. But I forgot how to dream a long while ago.

"Oh my gosh . . ." The phrase frantically leaves my lips. For, in a moment, Darbii is standing, and I am racing towards her, and my arms are around her, and she is gripping me so firmly. For a moment, I am overwhelmed with the most astounding feeling of relief.

"You're alive," I mumble. She pulls away.

"*You're* alive." She stares. Her jaw is glued to the ground. "Happy eighteenth birthday!"

Then, we both erupt into laughter, for solace feels nice when it rolls off the tongue.

"I can't believe you're here," is all I can manage to say to make up for my loss of words. "And . . . and your father."

"I left him," she says it so confidently I hardly believe the phrase is from her tongue.

"I heard."

"Elijah?"

"Yes."

She laughs softly. "Of course."

"What . . . um . . . how did you . . . decide to—" Something strikes her. She reaches into the large pocket of her jeans, removing a folded piece of paper. She places it in my palm.

"This will tell you probably too much information, but . . . it's everything I feel you deserve to know." I stare at its creases. At the lines that stare back at me with such urgency.

A smile creeps across my lips. "You wrote me a letter?"

"Yeah." She stares at the sand. "I mean . . . you said you wrote me letters, so it would only be a cool friend move of me to—"

"You're writing again?"

She looks up at me. Her tongue rolls over her bottom lip. "I guess so."

"You loved to write."

"I do love to write." And I've always loved to read her stories. "Read it later though, preferably when I'm not around."

I laugh. "Yes ma'am."

Silence sweeps through like a warm breeze. We stare out across the water again, light rising from the mountains beyond the other shore. It lands in soft raindrops upon the sea, bending and bouncing reflections of a brighter world.

"How do you feel about it?" Darbii mumbles ever so quietly. There's only one thing she can be talking about, and so I don't ask for more of an explanation.

"I don't." She looks up at me.

Her eyes narrow, "Do you believe it?"

"Of course I believe it. I just . . ." I shake my head, "It's a lot. And there's a lot I am already processing and . . . it's all coming at the same time, and so I just don't . . . *feel* it."

"What else is there? Just . . . the journey here?"

I close my eyes. In the darkness I see a green gaze. My hand wraps my necklace. Soon I find the strength to say that which my mind cannot comprehend, "I lost Viridian."

She looks over at me. I don't look back, "You . . . you lost him? What do you mean . . ." She must catch a glimmer of grief in my eyes because suddenly her own shift to sorrow. To a deep, heavy hollowness that I cannot fully render to be real across her cheeks. "Eve . . ."

It's all she says.

All she says before her pupils become pools filled with such fervor and fear and, above all, anguish. I cannot tell whether she is falling into my arms or I into hers, but I know she holds me so so tightly, nearly to the point of discomfort. I still cannot seem to cry.

Somehow, we end up on the ground, her arms wrapped tightly around me and I staring out in front of us at the mountains.

I feel her eyes glaze over me, "You look . . . traumatized."

"I watched it happen. Even convinced myself it was my fault."

"It wasn't."

"I know." Silence is preserved in the small amount of space between us. Then, she speaks.

"I used to have a fat crush on him, you know."

I try to smile. "And I had to hear about it for two months straight, in case you don't recall."

"No I do." She grins.

I begin to laugh, "Hey, at least you're moderately self-aware."

"You know what, it entertained you. If anything, you should be telling me thank you."

A grin remains on my cheeks. "I will do no such thing."

"You, my friend, are very stubborn."

"Yes, I am," I look at the sun above me. "Stubborn enough not to stop until they pay for what they did to him."

We are staring at the sea again, and I cannot help but see how bright her eyes are in the light that reflects off it. There is something about her. Something so drastically different that I cannot seem to wrap my finger around. A replenished innocence perhaps, unwaved by the world. It is a beauty that cannot quite be put into words because words were not created for it.

She releases me from her arm. "So you're going to do it."

"Of course I am." My hands gouge the sand. "These people are being lied to in the same way I have been. I can't . . . I can't just watch it happen and do nothing."

Darbii nods. "I think I will do it too. In time."

Still

My feet rest firm in the sand, ever so still. My eyes look out across the water. At what I have known and all that I will forever fail to know.

I wonder if death isn't all that it seems. That when one awakes from their eternal slumber, they see the world for all it is. All that the living are unable to see. That every question we have asked without answers has become common knowledge in their mind. And I wonder if the world seems bright. If it is joyous in all the ways we have learned to ignore, or if it is dreary in all the pain we have never known.

I wonder what Viridian sees. If he watches me now, standing upon the sea. If he has learned to miss me, for I wish I could have sooner.

Sitka stands beside me. A single tear sits in his left eye, so so still. For a moment, I think I can see my reflection in it. I think I can see us all, Viridian, Sitka, and I, back in the days when we would run through the streets of Paris simply because we could. When the sun shined, and we loved its light, and the wind would brush past our excited minds. When dusk would approach, and we would watch the stars together, laugh together. When nothing in the world could possibly go wrong.

Sitka's gaze falls on me now. His eyes are filled with the most apparent sorrow. I try to smile, but I cannot bring myself to do so.

"You're not crying," he says.

I shake my head and look out across the water. "I haven't cried in a long time."

"Why not?"

Lights dance across the waves, as I think they'll never fail to do. I stare at them. Watch such beauty evolve before me, and yet, it cannot seem to quite fill my mind with wonder.

"I'm fearful," I begin to say. "Almost all the time now. But I never . . . I never feel the fear anymore. It's just there."

He doesn't say anything to that. Instead, we stare at the same spot on the waves. The same water rolling in and out, and for once, I am glad that we can see the world in the same way. A smile grows on my lips. It is more out of sorrow than delight.

"I love you," I say to him. He smiles up at me. Looks me right in the eye when he replies.

"I love you too."

And then I pull him into my arms, and I hold him there for a while as my eyes shift to my parents and Elijah beside them. I watch my mother's hands carefully open the black box. She stares in upon what lay inside, ashes, gray and dreary. I watch a tear fall from her eye. It melts into his remains.

Then, she kneels in the sand, placing the lid on the ground beside her. She steals a breath from the frigid air. Then she places her hand into the box, taking a handful of the ashes and looking down upon them for a moment in her grasp. Her body melts in upon itself.

"May you be able to see what we have the pleasure to see," she speaks through her tears. Her hand gently touches the water. The ashes move through the ripples, rolling out into the sea. I watch them wade away, wade into a new reality.

And then I approach my mother. I approach the box beside her, and I stare at the gray inside of it. My soul aches so heavily that I can hardly feel it doing so, and so I simply hold the necklace upon my neck. I hold it until I can make myself believe that he is here. For he would never truly leave me. Because in all of the hate we ever showed towards each other, it was never really real. And then I reach for my own handful of ashes. I feel them in my palm, feel my body go numb. Feel such paralysis in their presence that even anger has left me to be. And for a while, I simply stare at my hands. And once I decide that I still cannot cry, I place them into the waves. My head lifts to watch them follow the path of that which came before, deep into the sea.

My father sits in the sand to the left of me. His hand extends outward into the water, and I watch the ashes roll. And once they shrink away, his arm wraps around me and I let it. His hand holds me so tight, and I close my eyes, for perhaps then I could feel affection. He places a kiss upon my head. My lips drop to a frown that shatters everything else inside of me. For he could say a million words to tell me he loves me, but his conscious silence is enough.

So I sit there for a while. Sit there with my family around me. With their hands wrapped around me. I sit there as we stare at my brother coming back to life. I feel Elijah's presence behind me, a certain warmth that cannot quite be brought into words, but rather painted so beautifully in the skies. For the world has become a mere reflection of his light, of his all-consuming peace, of his joyous sustainability. I feel him behind me and so my hand reaches back towards him, resting upon his brown boot.

And I look upon the sky. I look at the sun in the sky, its glow warm and poised into a precious perfection. It is still. We are still.

I am still.

[80]

Dear Eve

I lie beneath the navy sheets. My eyes are weary, and my bones are weak, and yet I fear for the moment when I find sleep. I fear for the nightmares that never fail to arrive. I fear I will see his green eyes. That I will see them shut. That I will never fail to see him die over and over again every night.

Darbii's letter sits in my hands. I stare at it folded before me. Moments pass. Then, I unravel it.

Dear Eve,

There's too much I haven't told you, not when you've always told me everything. Not when you deserve to know it all. I've realized that so much of me has fallen apart. And I used to ignore it and keep pushing on, and whenever something felt wrong, I blamed it on myself.

But I found the note you meant to give me when you left Cordellia. The one you told me about in Serbia. It was with my father. That's when I began to think that something was wrong. Then, when Elijah messaged me that same day, it all made sense. I think that was the first time I realized that maybe this pain wasn't all imposed by me. That maybe my father had something to do with it.

I wasn't honest with you when I told you he was good to me, though you probably figured that out anyway. He was never good to me. He yelled at me, and, on occasion, would do worse that, for my own sake, I'd rather not speak of just yet. But it only happened after my mother died. It really did make him spiral, partially because I remained, and I was not her. He was a good man before that. I guess changing my last name to hers is almost a remembrance of how he used to be because I dare to dream that there might still be a part of him that remains like that.

I don't know when he got into all this Big Seven nonsense. I've always wondered if we were related to a revolutionary who fought with Cordell with the same name of Soddom, but I'd like to not think this insanity is a part of my bloodline. I fear that I am again simply lying to myself.

So I guess that's why this all happened. She died, and I was broken, and then he broke me more. But the one who really destroyed me was myself. I told myself that he hated me, so I thought I needed another guy to love me; they never did. I hated the way that he treated me, so I tried to numb myself to it; the alcohol only lasted so long. I was forcing myself into a spiral, and I truly believed it was just what everyone else does too, until I saw that it never happened to you. That made me wonder.

Honestly, it's been your presence more than your words that have captivated me, though I appreciate both. Your genuine ability to love. Your dedication towards ballet. Who you've always been as a person is so consistent, and that's what always helped me. Your failure to abandon me was a dream I couldn't believe I was having. I really am forever in debt to you.

So yeah. I left my father. I yelled at him the same way he always yelled at me, and he seemed so dazed he didn't fully realize I was leaving. Maybe I wasn't clear that's what was happening. Either way, he definitely knows by now. My only fear that remains is that his loyalty to Cordell's ideas will lead him back to me. And I never want to see him again.

From there, Elijah led me to Jerusalem. He brought me to places with supplies and supported me emotionally. I didn't realize I could trust someone other than you again until I met him. And once I made it to Jerusalem, he told me to leave. I forced myself to trust him as much as it pained me. Then, he led me here. I think I like it here. It's peaceful.

Looking back on the part of the journey with my father, I don't think we were ever really headed to the Qadim. I think he lied to me for my compliancy. He was after something more wicked, and his possession of your note worries me that it had something to do with you. It hurts because I want so badly to love him and to be loved by him, but I truly do not think there is any way that will ever be possible.

So, I'll stick with you and Elijah. You both have been more like family than he ever could be.

All my love,

Darbii

Epilogue

We stand beside a rushing river. It wanders and rolls beneath the most extravagant of bridges. Lights line the bottom of cobblestone and reflect off of the water. Lanterns are hoisted upon poles along the railings. Sculptures of lions sit alongside the lights, and I stare at one for a moment. A drop of sweat rolls down my forehead.

"Gosh, it's so hot out," I mumble. I look over at my mother.

She raises an eyebrow. "Hot? My love, nothing is considered hot anymore." I giggle. We move up the road. The cobblestone slides beneath my brown boots, and my hands slip into the pockets of my green shorts. The July sky peers down upon my bare shoulders, turning them red, but at least the red is real. The street is lined with the most beautiful of buildings, with gold embellishments and sophisticated carvings. I stare upon them in wonder as I wish I could have when I once traveled here.

"I like how you decided to invite me along on the most difficult mission possible." My gaze shoots up at my mother.

My eyes narrow. "Most difficult? How is this the most difficult?"

"We can't track her. She's unchipped."

"We have eyes."

"This is a large city."

"We have feet." There is a long pause. My mother laughs.

The streets are more bare than they had been last time we were here. People sit in corners and wander alone beneath figments of affliction. Budapest has begun to shrink away into how Cordellia once was when we had left all those days ago. Various buildings are burnt down. Fecal matter is scattered across the ground. The world takes on the strangest of smells. Soon, we emerge into the square in which we had once seen her, beside the train station. There is no one in sight.

"She has to be around here somewhere," I say.

"I hope she is. I'm roasting."

I smirk up at my mother. "Aha." We giggle together.

Then, we scout the area. My eyes scan the overhangs and window. The busyness begins to pick up around a curve. And then my eyes fall upon someone with the most piercing blue eyes. With black hair tucked behind a purple robe. My lips lift up on my face. My hand reaches for my pocket. I place a translation device over my mouth and across my ears and run to the young girl. Her eyes find mine immediately. I stop a few feet away from her as Elijah told us to do.

"It's warm today, isn't it?" I speak in French, but the words emerge in Hungarian. She stares at me. "But not as warm as they all think it is."

Her eyes narrow. "Who are you?" I hear her words in my own tongue.

"My name is Aetheria Elko, and you are Elizabeth Juga. I am here with my mother, and we are here to tell you that you are right. The black hole is not real. The people here are deceived."

She stares at me. She stares at me for a long time, and I feel my heart pound in my ears.

"How do you . . ." She begins. "How do you know?"

"Because I once believed the lie too." She simply looks at me. "Do you have family here?"

"No they . . . they . . . they're gone."

I nod. "Come with me and my mother. We will show you everything, I promise you." Elizabeth's eyes jump between me and my mother. Over and over and over again, and I let them do so without saying a word. Soon enough, she stands. I take her hand and lead her west where the sun is sweeping into sunset. Down the hill where we can deliver her to Tawila without a single soul in sight.

Acknowledgments

Firstly, greatest thanks to everyone who ever showed interest in this story. Whether a friend or family member, or just a stranger in passing. The people who asked me questions, who joyfully listened to my answers. The ones who used the exclamation of, "oh my gosh, you're writing a book?!" Well, here it finally is. Thank you for sticking by for the two and a half years that it took for this process to come to fruition. I pray that you were touched by every single word as I was when writing it.

To my mother, my greatest fan. The first ever person to read this story all the way through and to deal with my questions every other page of what she was thinking about the plot. Thank you for investing in me, cheering me on, by shocking me when saying you were amazed by the story, because you never do lie about those things. I love you so very much.

To my father, for always being so proud of me. For taking my drawings from when I was a toddler and writing words on them to turn them into books. Thank you for such lovely cover art. For sitting with me while you were attempting to learn photoshop again, and while I was being a grumpy teenager during the entirety of the process. You are truly so patient.

To my wonderful editor, Elena. For investing in such a long story. For giving me new things to think about in editing, and for asking questions I wouldn't think to ask. For making me chop out all of those uses of, "and for a moment," because you are very correct, those got so annoying. And finally, for sobbing with me through THE scene.

To my lovely friend, Katie Barry. For all of our early Wednesday mornings together at Peets, me with my iced oat milk latte, and you with your matcha, discussing the plot of this story as it was just developing. For being my physics major friend who aided me in the development of the science part of it all, whether I chose to listen to your input or not. Oh, and for just so happening to have the same birthday as Eve. How peculiar.

To my best friend, Sydney Pfefferkorn. You don't know it, but you inspired the plot twist :)

To Zach Venzor, for all of your wonderful long comments while reading this story. For making me think outside the box. For inspiring the idea of Sitka converting a normal record player into a crank player. That is still so sick.

To Marvel Studios' "Loki," episode three, for inspiring this whole thing. For constructing that question in my mind of, "what would you do if you knew you were going to die?" I had no idea where that question would lead when I wrote it down in my notes app all those days ago.

And above all else, to My King. The One who has always been so near to me. Who came to my aid in the midst of all of the anxiety I once felt, and carried me out of it. For giving Yourself on a cross and rising again on the third day so that I am able to know You and be known by You. There is no greater gift, and no greater joy in my life than to look upon Your face. To tell Your story over and over again in a million different ways. Thank you for sending me. This is most truly all for You.

"For 'everyone who calls on the name of the Lord will be saved.' How then will they call on him in whom they have not believed? And how are they to believe in him whom they have never heard? And how are they to hear without someone preaching? And how are they to preach unless they are sent?"

Romans 10:13-15

Printed in the USA
CPSIA information can be obtained
at www.ICGtesting.com
LVHW05075829052
781182LV00001B/32